CW00740872

Falkirk

Casey Morales

WWW.AUTHORCASEYMORALES.COM

Copyright ©2023 by 3Aussies Press.

All rights reserved.

No portion of this book may be reproduced in any form without written permission from the publisher or author, except as permitted by U.S. copyright law.

Before you begin . .

.

Thank you for joining me on this journey. To express my thanks, I would like to give you a free eBook copy of My Accidental First Date. This is a light-hearted contemporary mm romance, the beginning of one man's quest for love.

Click here to tell me where to send it.

A note from your author

M y dear readers,

As you have no doubt discovered, this series is quite the leap from our normal contemporary MM romance novels. I'm not entirely sure why, but I felt compelled to create something new and different, something unique within our genre, while preserving the toe-curling, heartwarming romance we all crave.

As our beloved heroes move forward in their tale, World War II no longer lingers in the distance. Europe's Conflict—as Americans bent on avoiding entry into the war referred to it—becomes deeply personal to Will and Thomas. It's time for them to do their part.

To respect history and those who shaped it, I do not shy from this story's backdrop. Nations fell. Lives were lost. Atrocities occurred. This was life, and while this book is not about war or battles, I did try to accurately represent the setting in which our characters must operate.

Many of the missions, locations, and people in this book were real. I took some liberties to make them fit the story, but also chose to honor them with notes of their true events in the back. Unless you're into spoilers, don't read the Appendix until you're done!

Will and Thomas are now secret agents working for their respective government agencies. They head into the unknown and do exciting, dangerous things. But this is still MM romance. I want to curl your toes and make you sigh. There is so much love (and yes, spice) between these two. I think you'll enjoy the romance that continues between them in this novel.

Thank you for going on this journey with me. My words are meaningless without readers to enjoy them. I truly appreciate you.

Casey

Chapter One

Vogt

SS-Sturmbannführer Jÿrgen Vogt stormed into the Becker Chemical Company, slamming wooden doors against metal frames as though they had personally offended the Reich.

An ambitious major climbing the ranks of the infamous Nazi secret service, Vogt had long since lost his regard for anyone, German citizen or otherwise, who could not further his career in service to the Führer. The petite, middle-aged woman who shrieked and nearly leapt to her feet upon his entry was little more than a blur in his vision as he strode past.

"Sir, please. May I help you, sir?" she asked, darting around her desk in a race to beat him to the door that led to the company leaders' offices.

He halted, squared to tower over her, and offered a crisp salute: "Heil Hitler."

She shrank back, but echoed his words.

"Good," he said after a moment of uncomfortable scrutiny. "Where may I find Herr Becker?"

His words formed a question, but his tone demanded submission.

The woman backed toward her desk, feeling with her hands behind her. "Herr Becker? He is here, I believe. Let me phone him—"

"No. His call dragged me out here, to the middle of nowhere, away from vital business of the state." His gaze was almost as cold as his sneer as he peered around the small reception area. "I will go to him. Where is his office?"

"Sir, please, let me—"

He closed the gap between them, causing the woman to bend awkwardly over her desk to avoid his touch.

"Where. Is. His. Office?"

"At the end of the hallway, through those doors." She pointed a shaky finger toward a set of double doors beside her desk.

"Good. *Danke.*"

He glanced toward the door where his driver, Unteroffizier Uwe König, stood. "See that we are not disturbed."

Neither the sergeant, nor the secretary, missed his implication.

Vogt eyed the woman one last time, nodded curtly, then disappeared through the double doors. He passed two closed doors on his right and one on his left before reaching another set of double doors at the end of the short hallway. Without breaking stride, he gripped both handles and flung the doors open.

A balding man in a light gray suit dropped his pen on a stack of papers and rose slowly, as though the action required every ounce of strength his legs possessed. Neither his expression nor his movement betrayed the sudden jolt in his heart rate or the flood of heat that traveled up his neck.

"Sturmbannführer, welcome. Please, come in," the man said. "Would you like some tea?"

Vogt's eyes never left the man's as he strode across the office to stand at the edge of the desk, where he snapped to attention and offered another salute. "Heil Hitler."

"Yes, yes. Heil Hitler," the man said, raising a weathered palm. "Now, sit. You may not need refreshment, but I am old, and a visit from the SS makes one's mouth dry, you know."

Vogt scowled. "I have no time for pleasantries. Why am I here, Herr Becker?"

The old man's mouth twitched. Everyone knew better than to disrespect a Nazi officer, but they also understood these men respected only strength, only force. One needed to tread carefully when handling an adder. "Because we have discovered something to help our Führer, why else?"

Vogt cocked his head and waited for Becker to continue.

"Now, would you like tea, Sturmbannführer?" Becker asked with a smirk that belied his trembling hand. He stepped to a side table and poured steaming liquid into two delicate cups, then dropped a cube of sugar in each. "Cream?"

"No, thank you," Vogt said.

"Please sit, Sturmbannführer. Our conversation may take a moment, and I know you have been on that motorbike for some time this morning."

Vogt's legs and rear ached from the rough ride in the sideboard. Reluctantly, he nodded, sat in the well-padded chair opposite Becker's desk, then accepted the cup and saucer from his host. The steam that curled into his nostrils smelled wonderfully bitter.

"I assume you know of our weevil problem?" Becker said as he settled back into his chair.

Vogt's cup clanked against his saucer as he glared up.

"Terrible creatures. They burrow and nibble and, well, they reproduce faster than any vermin in the fatherland," Becker continued without acknowledging Vogt's irritation. "You see, my company, along with a few others, was tasked by the government to find a solution to this problem. It appears the little devils are causing issues across our farmland, even destroying many crops in Poland and other places that now feed our troops. Isn't it interesting how something so small can gum up the gears of our great machine?"

"Quite," Vogt muttered.

"What is also *quite* interesting, Sturmbannführer Vogt, is what scientists discover along the path to an objective; what they *accidentally* uncover."

Vogt leaned forward and set his tea on the desk. "Go on."

Becker's lip curled slightly. "My chemists tested many solutions. Finding a way to kill the long-nosed beetles was never an issue. It was finding a substance that killed them without rendering the crops inedible that was the challenge. What good would our farmlands be if they were freed of pests, but the food that grew could not be used?"

"So, you found a solution?"

"Oh, no." Becker shook his head and sat back. "The weevils continue to confound our people."

The skin around Vogt's eyes began to twitch. "Then what, Herr Becker, have you found that is worth my time?"

"This is worth *all* our time, Sturmbannführer." Becker said. "If we cannot feed our people and our troops, the liberation of Europe will fail. Is that important enough to you, Sturmbannführer?"

Becker adjusted his spectacles and drew a deep breath before continuing. "My scientists have tried many combinations, aiming for a mixture to eradicate the beetles without damaging the crops. This is quite complicated. Most ingredients we employ remain on the leaf of a plant for a very long time, or seep into the soil where the roots become tainted or poisoned. Some only dissipate when washed away. A few, we have found, do terrible things to one's lungs when water is added, so the washing away becomes ... how shall I say it? Problematic."

Vogt scowled. "Is there a point to all this or do you just enjoy talking about poisons? Have you found a solution?"

Becker tossed his spectacles onto his desk with a clatter, his lips pursed. "We have not solved the riddle for the weevil problem, but I believe we have found a solution to one of our Führer's much larger issues."

Vogt tensed at the invocation of Hitler.

"By combining phosphorus with cyanide, we have created a new substance that is quite effective at exterminating, shall I say, much larger pests, and quite quickly. It is, perhaps, the most efficacious substance I have ever seen for such tasks. Perhaps more impressive, however, is how quickly it then degrades. In only weeks, perhaps months, no trace remains."

Becker paused, then lifted his spectacles and began cleaning them with a cloth. "Would this not help our Führer in freeing England of those pesky British?"

Vogt sat back.

Neither man spoke as Becker continued diligently scrubbing and avoiding the SS officer's stare.

"Have you tested this new substance outside of a laboratory?" Vogt finally asked.

Becker spread the cloth onto his desk, smoothing its edges, then folded his glasses and set them in the exact center, adjusting them a few times to ensure they were precisely positioned.

The tapping of Vogt's boot against the hardwood floor and the whirring of the ceiling fan were the only sounds in the office.

"Of course, Sturmbannführer Vogt. We are scientists. We test everything many times before bringing it to anyone's attention. There is a farm not too many kilometers away where we perform most of our experiments. It is positively riddled with weevils. Or, it *was*. We will need a new location for future tests."

"Who knows of this?"

Becker thought a moment. "The scientists, perhaps one or two of our staff ... oh, there is one person still living on the farm. She knows of this experiment, but not the details of the substance."

Vogt eyed the man, then nodded once and stood. "You will take me there."

"Now?" Becker stared up, his eyes widened. "I have many—"

"Yes, now, and tell no one our destination. If this is as you say, the Führer will want to know of it immediately."

"The Führer? He would personally—" Becker rose, suddenly unsteady, then grabbed his spectacles, his palm smearing new oil across the lenses. "Well, yes, alright. Of course, we will do all we can for the Führer. Of course."

Vogt ordered König to drive Becker's Mercedes-Benz. Becker protested, but Vogt ignored him and climbed into the back seat. A little over an hour later, the car coated in dust from the rough rural road, they stopped before a mid-sized home with white-painted wooden sides and a brown shingled rooftop. A wide porch encircled the house, and intricately decorative carvings adorned the deck's railing and eaves. Several chimneys rose above, but only one billowed a thin gray plume that smeared across the crystal sky.

Vogt exited the car and strode around the house, with Becker shuffling to keep up.

A wide field spread beyond the horizon. The nearest section, which stretched many hectares, consisted of perfectly ordered rows. Barrels where potatoes had been harvested stood every fifty yards or so. Beyond the rows of dirt, tall stalks of golden wheat shimmered with the ever-present breeze.

Several areas within the potato field had been sectioned off with orange tape. Scattered between the cordoned sections were bodies. Dozens of them.

Vogt halted; Becker almost collided with his shoulder. The men could not see the faces of the dead from where they stood, but the body language was plain: some with frozen hands held to their throats, others with arms outstretched, reaching for help that never came.

From the bodies' haphazard positioning, it was clear the poison had stilled them before they could flee more than a few steps.

Vogt stared a moment. "You had best explain this, Herr Becker. Start from the beginning."

Becker's eyes remained fixed on the distant field of wheat as he spoke. "As I told you before, we were testing combinations of chemicals to alleviate the weevil infestation. We found substances that killed the vermin above ground, but could not penetrate their tunnels, so most escaped. We tried tainting foods they enjoy, but they smelled the chemicals and avoided the poisoned bait. We needed something stronger, something that could kill them before they could escape below ground, perhaps something that could travel down into their holes."

Becker turned to meet Vogt's gaze.

"The poison we discovered works when breathed into the lungs. We ... we did not know this until ... we spread the poison in a wide pattern across the potato field marked by the orange tape." He pointed to several of the marked sections. "Workers continued harvesting in between, but ..."

"But what, Herr Becker?"

"It did not take long, perhaps thirty minutes, maybe an hour for the last. The breeze, you see ... it carries ... Sturmbannführer, it was terrible. There were so many bodies." Becker pinched the bridge of his nose and breathed deeply several times. "I have seen death. We try to exterminate animals, for God's sake, but this ... there must have been fifty or more workers. And the family, the farmer and his wife ... two of their children ..."

Vogt waited as Becker steadied himself, the wheat once again capturing the man's attention.

"One daughter survived. She was in the house when all this happened. Her name is Marta. She is seventeen, and is now alone on this farm."

The whistle of wind tickling stalks sounded in the distance.

"When was this? I do not understand why we were not notified. Why are the bodies still strewn about?" Vogt asked, his tone clipped.

"Only yesterday. I sent word as soon as I returned to my office. The bodies ..." Becker's voice caught as he gestured across the field. "We are still unsure how long it takes for the gas to dissipate. I could not risk—"

"Was this your first test with this new compound?"

"Yes."

"So, you have not perfected a delivery mechanism?"

"We would need tests with the compound before advancing to delivery. There is much we still do not understand; long-term effects on crops, for example. We believe this will dissipate within weeks, but as you said, this is our first experiment outside of the lab."

Vogt stared across at the bodies, his face an emotionless mask of calculation. He spoke, more to himself than to Becker, "I will send for SS men with protective gear to clear this field today. Word of this cannot spread."

Becker's quiet voice asked, "Sturmbannführer, do you not wish to speak with the daughter? Surely, the Führer would wish to compensate her ... and the workers' families ... at least recognize—"

"What did the workers know of this test?" Vogt's voice sliced through Becker's compassion.

"Why ... nothing, Sturmbannführer, beyond a poison for vermin. We have tested many compounds on this farm over the past year. They did not appear to give this much notice until—"

"The daughter?"

Becker cocked his head. "I believe she knows nothing, but her father—"

"Take me to her."

All resistance in Becker's voice withered under the iron fist of Vogt's gaze. "Yes, Sturmbannführer."

As they approached the front door of the house, a blonde girl with lightly freckled cheeks stepped onto the porch. Her light blue dress hung loosely on her waifish frame. Strands of disheveled hair blew across her red-ringed eyes.

"You are Marta?" Vogt asked.

The girl nodded.

Vogt reached to his holster, removed his pistol, and shot Marta in the forehead.

"Sturmbannführer! Why did you—?" Becker raced to kneel by the dead girl's side. "She is a child!"

"The state comes before any of us, Herr Becker. She died a hero of the Reich." Vogt re-holstered his weapon and strode back in the direction of the car. He barked over his shoulder, "Come, now, Herr Becker. We must return to your office immediately."

"Yes, Sturmbannführer," Becker said, struggling to his feet.

———◆○◆———

The silence in the car was broken only by the growling of the Mercedes engine and occasional thud of stones kicked up by their passage. Becker stared out the window. Vogt made notes in a small pad he kept in his breast pocket.

"When we arrive at your office, you will gather your scientists and anyone else who knows of this substance, along with all of the notes and research. This program is now under the guidance of the SS."

"Yes, Sturmbannführer," Becker muttered at the window.

"Everything will be moved to a classified facility." He tapped his pen against his pad a few times. "I will require one of your offices where I may not be overheard for the rest of the day. Is that a problem?"

"No, Sturmbannführer."

Vogt scribbled again, then paused. "What is this called?"

"I'm sorry. What?" Becker asked, finally turning to look at him.

"What is this substance called? Have you given it a name?"

"At first, the scientists called it *tabun*. That was before we added the last of the ingredients, making it even more potent. Yesterday, as we started the first experiment, they decided to name the new compound after themselves: Herrs Gerhard

Schrader, Otto Ambros, Gerhard Ritter, and Hans-Jürgen von der Linde."

Vogt scrunched his brows.

"We call it sarin."

Chapter Two

Will

WAVES AND NTS ENJOY PICNIC

Approximately one hundred twenty-five officers from Communications School and one hundred WAVE officers from Radcliffe enjoyed a picnic last Sunday afternoon in front of Briggs Hall. Music from recordings was audible throughout the grounds by means of a public address system, where three softball games with mixed teams were in progress, while at the other end of the grounds on a badminton court, the shuttlecock (bird) was taking a terrific beating from the rackets of both men and women. The tennis courts and the Ping-Pong tables on the porch of Briggs Hall were used continuously.

ENTERTAINMENT

Depicting a story of a counterfeiting gang who are operating against this government, I Escaped from the Gestapo *is good enough to hold your attention and to make you cheer when the FBI takes a hand in disposing of the band of saboteurs.*

The co-feature is False Faces *starring Rex Williams and Veda Aun Berg.*

MIDSHIPMEN

Praise the Lord, and pass me my commission ... Just a few more hours of nervous prostration, men, and we'll all be free ... in one way or another. The day of judgment has [arrived] (yeah man) ...

The major—code-named Manakin—held a folder across the metal teacher's desk.

"Go on, son, take it. You'll be better briefed next week, but that should get you started."

I half-stood and leaned forward to retrieve the folder. Manakin sat back and watched as I opened the file. There was one sheet of paper containing only a handful of neatly typed words.

EMU—MISSION BRIEF—CLASSIFIED

Report to 107 Loeb House, 0800, Tuesday, June 1, 1943.

Brief will last approximately one hour.

Transport to Logan Airport at unspecified.

Transport via Air Technical Services Command to unspecified at unspecified.

I looked up to find an annoying smile on Manakin's face.

"That's it?" I held up the paper. "You could've just told me to meet you Tuesday at Loeb."

"I just did." He motioned to the paper and nodded. "Welcome to the OSS. Try not to share everything you know."

I ignored his taunt. "Why are we meeting at Loeb? That's President Conant's building. Everything so far has been in Andover."

He shrugged. "Maybe Conant wants to offer President Roosevelt's personal thanks for your service. He's pretty tight with FDR."

"Very funny," I said, resisting an eye roll. "I don't know why I asked. You're not great at sharing."

His fucking grin widened. "Don't pack anything. Your dorm will be cleared and your personal items stored. Our people already have outfits specific to your destination and mission prepared. We can't lose you because you forgot to leave your American razor or English language book behind."

He stood and extended a hand. When I took it, his grip was a vice and his eyes bored into mine.

"You are about to do very important work, Will. You will never know how many lives depend on your success, and you will likely never hear the words 'thank you' from the lips of a government official, but what you will do matters to this nation in ways ... I hope, one day, a time will come when I might tell you just how special your work truly was to America. For now, the thanks of this grateful man will have to do."

I barely knew what to say.

My mission, my future, had never been more vague, and yet, for some reason, I believed him. What I was about to do *was* important.

I was important.

I squeezed his hand and held his gaze. "Thank you, sir."

I walked into my dorm room to find it eerily quiet. Following commencement, Arty had left for a week with his family, leaving Thomas and me with a few days to be alone. Only a few days into our private vacation, we had desecrated Arty's bed coverings in more ways than I'd known possible. I wasn't entirely sure why we were both so determined to spend our naked time on his bunk, but it had become our favorite place to do naughty things to one another.

When I went to toss the useless mission folder onto my desk, a folded paper with my name scrawled across it stared up.

W,

Out for a run. Back after my meeting.

Should we do something later, like leave the room?

T

I could see his smart-ass smirk as I read.

He'd been the primary reason we hadn't left the room for nearly three days. Every time I'd suggested dinner or a stroll—or a shower, for heaven's sake—he'd clawed me back on top of him and refused to let go.

Not that I was complaining.

Still, our time at Harvard was nearly at an end. In normal times, adulthood would quickly steal the last vestige of youth from any newly graduated alum, but these were far from normal times. The world was at war. The Nazis controlled most of Europe, the Japanese had consumed half of China, and the Brits had nearly been bombed into the last century.

If there was ever a time to relish our last moments as carefree college men, this was it. I decided to resist any seductive charms he might employ until we'd at least had a proper dinner in a restaurant and taken a long walk.

At least dinner. An evening stroll might stretch my resistance too far. Thomas had become a most wonderful addiction.

I tossed the note onto the desk and changed into shorts and a T-shirt. The week between terms was one of the few times Harvard let her hair down. Thomas often joked that we needed to don a tie just to walk across the yard. I'd tossed mine aside and was determined to not wear one until it was absolutely necessary.

Sneakers laced, I set off to find lunch and enjoy a late spring day.

I treated myself to a heavy bowl of pasta at a nearby Italian restaurant, then wandered aimlessly around Cambridge. I wasn't sure why I started walking, but something deep inside called for me to visit the shops and stores of Harvard's village one last time. I'd taken them for granted for four years, barely noticing most of them as Arty, Janie, and I blundered down the sidewalk. Half the time, Janie had Arty and me so drunk I was incapable of appreciating a bookshop or candy maker.

Now, I wanted to drink them in, to savor ancient pages and let delicious sweets dissolve so slowly they'd imprint on my mind as much as my tongue. I wanted to see and touch—and remember—all of it. Maybe I hadn't fully recognized it over the years, but this place was special. Being here was special.

It struck me then how we rarely recognized that something was truly extraordinary until we were about to leave it.

That made me think of Arty and Janie. God, Arty made me smile.

He'd become my best friend and brother the moment I'd set foot on campus. I'd often marveled at his remarkable intelligence, but laughed at his utter lack of awareness in a social setting. One glance from a girl sent the poor boy into a tailspin, and that was a sight to behold. A flustered Arty might be the funniest thing ever.

Somehow, Elizabeth had seen past his awkwardness. She was a stunning creature who could've graced any Hollywood screen or printed page. How our Arty had captured her eye was a wonder, but she'd seen the massive brain on his spindly body and understood just how unique he was, how brilliantly special, how kind and considerate and deeply loyal. She had recognized the innate goodness that was Arthur Wendel Ableman. Despite all the odds, she'd fallen in love with him, and he was hopelessly smitten.

He proposed the night of commencement, and they set a date for the ceremony in the fall.

He'd been so nervous that night, I worried he might throw up rather than pop the question. And yet, he managed it beautifully, if in a most Arty-esque way, dropping to one knee in the middle of the chemistry department's most well-equipped laboratory. He claimed the backdrop of fizzing beakers was romantic, like tiny scientific symphonies.

Mystically, Elizabeth agreed. They really were an oddly matched set.

It pained my heart to know I would miss their wedding.

Janie had lost her way throughout most of our senior year, bedding any boy with bulging arms and a willing smile. She was half-drunk more days than not, and God only knows how she didn't end up pregnant.

Then, by some quirk of fate, she, too, got engaged.

Her mood swung from despondent to elated, but her drinking never slowed. There were days she would show up in her finest dress, face painted to perfection yet reeking of liquor. There was no amount of makeup or fashion camouflage that could hide her drunken stupor. If any of us broached the subject, she either laughed us off with a wave of her hand, or became irate and stormed away.

When her engagement evaporated with the melting of winter's snow, her effervescent smile dissipated once more.

Walls rose between her and Arty and me, and I felt my parents' loss all over again. Janie's friendship, her kinship, had helped bind my wounds in those dark days. I'd been new to Harvard, new to being on my own, and searching for my footing as a burgeoning adult when my world had lurched beneath me. Nothing felt stable. Nothing felt real. I was walking in a waking nightmare whose only desire was to darken my heart.

Janie took my hand and led me back into the light. She helped pull me from those depths.

Seeing her adrift, and the vacant, hollow look in her eyes, was like ripping a piece of my soul and tossing it aside. She spent more hours angry than smiling, mad at the world for a rainy morning, or at the dining room for cold coffee, or at everyone who ever lived for some other offense that threatened to destroy her entire existence.

Looking back, it was all a cover for something deeper.

Sure, she was hurt over the loss of her fiancé, but I had never been convinced about that match. She'd rarely spoken about him, beyond his generosity and the size of her diamond, and she'd never dared allowed us to meet the man. That was, perhaps, the oddest part. The three of us had shared everything. We *always* shared everything. It made no sense ... until I stepped back and watched the pieces fit into place.

She was hurting and didn't know how to express it. She was terrified, but fear was not something a Harvard woman spoke openly about during wartime. It wasn't acceptable. Speaking against the war was even less so; still, I lost count of the number of times she'd railed against America sending *her* boys to die. She'd screamed at the top of her lungs, drawing the eye of every soldier, sailor, teacher, and student milling about the yard.

I'd never been one for grand metaphors, but in a strange way, I supposed she was the voice of many who simply wanted to breathe following the depths of the Depression, only to be thrust headlong into a conflict that risked far more than any job or market could claim. They were tired, frustrated, and angry at a world that continued to spin out of control.

At no point had I realized her fears were far closer to home—for Arty, Thomas, and me, and for the possibility we might, in the end, leave her alone.

I wasn't sure what had woken her up. I was just thankful her eyes finally opened.

Thomas and I had been back from Camp X for a week when she'd shown up on our dorm's steps. She'd refused to enter, sending some random guy up to retrieve us. I don't even think she knew who he was. She'd just flagged a stranger and begged his assistance. When we opened the door, her tear-streaked face and wind-strewn hair shattered any wall that had existed. She fell into my arms and wept, right there on the steps.

"Please don't leave me, Will. Please. I'll do anything. Just don't go," she begged.

My heart wrenched with every word.

There was nothing I could say, so I held her close and stroked her hair as she cried.

In the short time that followed, she'd returned to the old Janie we'd known and loved. Well, almost. Her smile brightened, though it never reached her eyes quite like before. I supposed we were all losing a piece of ourselves to this war, each in our own way, and we'd yet to even join the fray.

Then there was Thomas.

I couldn't think about our group of friends, our little family, without his playful smirk infecting my every thought. That man had become the best part of me, and I couldn't imagine a life without him in it. I didn't *want* to imagine that life.

Battling society's morals and norms was challenging enough. Now, we had to face the possibility—no, the likelihood—that our respective assignments would send us worlds apart with little hope of reuniting anytime soon—if ever. It wasn't that long ago that the idea of being near Thomas had sent my skin crawling and heart racing. Now, the thought of being apart nearly stole my breath.

I hated how the world saw us, what they thought of two men who sought the simple comfort of a loving embrace. While they slept secure with their lover's arms cradling them close, our eyes never stilled as we sought anyone who might see, then denounce, then condemn. They enjoyed a lifetime of carefree love and laughter, while our fleeting moments of companionship were often tinged with fear and dread.

What did it matter to anyone else if we cared for each other? What did our passion change for their families, their lives, their futures? It changed nothing for them, but their hatred or loathing—their contempt—changed *everything* for us.

Thomas shrugged it off, said it was just how things were.

It made me so angry.

The war changed everything too. A few evil men, fueled by hatred and hunger for power, had irrevocably altered the course of history for everyone on the planet. There was no resisting their pull. Their insidious scheme was a vortex of lies and loathing that devoured anyone with even the slightest difference to their own perceived perfection.

People gave them the ability to reshape the world for the rest of us. People gave them that power.

How had so many given over so much to so few?

The world was burning, and nothing made sense, beyond the fact that we had to do something. It might cost us everything, but we had to help.

I checked my watch and knew Thomas was likely meeting with the major, or whoever the Office of Naval Intelligence's equivalent was, at that exact moment, receiving his orders for life post-Harvard. My own cryptic orders laughed at me from my desk, and I wondered if his would be as ridiculously vague as mine had been.

Then my smile faded. We would be parted soon, and might never see one another again.

The war suddenly felt very real.

"You're not going to fucking believe it." The door flew open, slamming into the wall, and Thomas barged in, waving a piece of paper in the air. "I got my orders, for what they're fucking worth."

He usually reserved cursing for the basketball court. This was going to be good.

"Language, good sir. This is a respectable establishment," I teased.

"Watch your own fucking language," he snarled, wadding his orders into a ball and hurling them at my chest. I ducked, but his aim had been true.

I feigned injury. "Ow! You wound me."

He kicked the door and it slammed shut, then he bolted across the room and grabbed me roughly by the shoulders. "I'm going to wound you in more ways than one if you keep that up."

My dick sprang to attention faster than a private being greeted by his sergeant. Why was fake anger so erotic?

He felt me stir beneath his weight and grinned.

"So, how was your day, dear?" I singsonged, desperate to ignore my growing problem.

He pushed back off me and paced across the room.

"My orders weren't orders at all. Here"—he motioned for the ball of paper that had fallen to the floor—"toss that back." He snatched it out of the air and smoothed the page. "Let me read them to you."

"Hey, stop." I sat up. "Are you allowed—"

His eyes practically rolled out of their sockets.

"I quote: *Report to 107 Loeb House, 0800, Tuesday, June 1, 1943. Brief will last approximately one hour. Transport to Logan Airport at unspecified. Transport via Air Technical Services Command to unspecified at unspecified.*"

I shot out of my chair.

"What?" he gaped as I turned and grabbed my own orders from the desk behind me.

"Our orders are the same. Not just the time—every word. Thomas, every word was exactly the same. Look." I held my paper out.

He hesitated only for a second before taking the page from my hand.

"Emu?" Frustration vanished, replaced by his goddamned smirk. "Your code name is Emu? Seriously?"

"Shh," I hissed, as if someone might overhear us in my dorm room. "You can't know that."

He began laughing and fell onto the bed. "Emu. My man is a fucking Aussie bird of ... not prey, definitely not prey. What the hell does an emu do anyway?"

My fists flew defiantly to my hips, all on their own. I didn't remember doing it.

He laughed harder.

"Fuck you. What's your code name, then?"

"Condor."

I stared as his snicker subsided. "Seriously? You get something fierce, and I'm basically the stupid cousin of an ostrich?"

His laughter returned, this time with tears and a side of snorts.

"I hate you. You know that, right?"

His hand shot out and, before I knew it, I was on top of him on the bed with his lips making fart noises into my neck and his fingers digging mercilessly into my sides.

I tried not to laugh. I really wanted to resist.

"Fuck, I hate you!" preceded my own fit.

"I love you too, Will Shaw."

The tickling ceased as his lips found mine, and I lost myself in the passion of the man I cherished more than life.

———— ◆◇◆ ————

"What do you think it means?" I asked into his chest. My head was nuzzled beneath his chin in my favorite place on the planet.

"What?"

"That our orders are the same, that we're both meeting at Loeb at exactly the same time. I mean, you're ONI and I'm ... well, I'm another agency."

I felt him grin, the fucker.

"You can say OSS. I already know, remember?"

"Yeah, I guess."

"The brief will probably be broken into parts. The first will cover transport, logistics, equipment, that sort of thing. Then they'll probably break us out into teams, where we'll learn about our specific missions. I wouldn't read too much into it, other than that someone is having fun teasing us a little."

A heartbeat passed.

"Thomas, I'm scared."

His arms folded around me and held me close. I felt his lips press into my scalp and linger.

"Me too."

Chapter Three

Thomas

WHAT CAN I DO TODAY FOR UNCLE SAM?

Write a letter to a soldier, or sailor, or Marine, or WAAC, or WAVE. In fact, write a letter every day. This is what Lieutenant Anthony Alex, of Lowell, with a piece of Jap shell in his back, says: "Give a man a letter, and you can send him on a thirty-mile hike through the hot jungle without a murmur."

BUY WAR BONDS AND STAMPS

As a kid, I hated mornings. The sun's angry glare disturbed my blissful slumber. How rude.

The navy abused me of the notion that slumber was anything but a necessary exercise that should be limited to only the minimum required amount.

Even ruder.

And yet, waking before that lazy orb in the sky became my reality meant an eight o'clock meeting felt more like a lunchtime affair than a first-of-the-day activity.

Will, however, had yet to learn the navy's lesson.

"What are you so happy about?" he grumbled as we walked across the yard.

I grinned, earning an even deeper scowl. He'd woken late, hadn't showered, and his hair was still mussed in the most unruly and adorable way.

"We're finally learning what the future holds. I'm nervous but excited too. The waiting and not knowing has been killing me."

"Yeah, me too." He nodded. "Although, I'm not sure how excited I am. Abject terror may be winning the emotional battle at the moment. They are sending us into a war, Thomas, an actual war."

If he hadn't been talking about shipping across the world where bullets and bombs filled the skies more than birds, I would've smiled and made a joke. His somber tone stole my mirth.

"War. God, how did we get here?" I muttered, more to myself than to him.

"Small men with huge power."

I grunted. "That's the truth."

We climbed the short stairs to stand beneath the portico of Loeb House, her white door the portal to our life beyond Harvard. We stood there, staring, neither of us reaching for the doorknob, as if refusing to enter might somehow delay our fate.

"You okay?" I whispered.

He looked up. His eyes were hollow caverns of themselves. Without a word, he nodded.

Loeb was the president's house. It was among the sacred places on Harvard's campus. Rich wooden floors and furniture whose cushions had comforted the rears of presidents and kings greeted us. Electricity had been commonplace on campus for years, but unlit candles in gleaming brass holders and oil-fueled lamps still adorned the walls. I supposed they were more homage to the past than utilitarian lighting.

A primly dressed woman sitting behind a small colonial desk quickly dispensed with my tour of the home's foyer. Her tight gray bun crowned her snowy head, bobbing slightly as her crisp movements bounded between stacks of paper and inch-thick folders.

She glanced up, her lips twitching in annoyance. "What room?"

"One-oh-seven," I said.

One frosty brow raised. "You go first." She pointed to Will, then turned and pointed to a door set in the wall beneath a staircase at the back of the room. "Tell the Marine there is another waiting up here."

"Marine?" Will asked, alarm creeping into his voice.

"You"—she pointed at my chest, then stabbed her finger at one of several chairs lined against the far wall—"sit there."

Will and I shared a nervous glance.

"It is almost oh-eight-hundred hours," she said.

Will shrugged, then made his way to the door as I took my assigned seat.

A few moments later, the door beneath the staircase opened, and a young man in the sharp blue dress uniform of a US Marine appeared. It always amazed me how Marines kept their pearly belt and brass buckle so spotless and gleaming. This one even wore his white gloves.

"Next," he called, as if dozens waited rather than one.

For some reason, I raised my hand like I was being called on by a professor.

The Marine's lips quirked.

We descended a dozen narrow stairs that allowed only one of us at a time. The ceiling stood well above my head, yet I felt the need to duck within the tight confines of the passage. He trailed behind, and, as silly as it sounds, a sense of imprisonment threatened to overwhelm me.

A few paces from the bottom step, another Marine sat at another colonial desk. Unlike the gray bun's workspace, there were no papers on his desk, only a black, leather-bound book the size of his palm. A rifle rested in the corner behind his chair.

The seated Marine glared a moment, allowing his partner to retrieve a rifle that was leaning against the wall and take his place blocking access to a plain wooden door.

"Code name," the seated Marine said.

No one had ever asked for that before. I'd been told to guard it, to never share it with anyone. Was this a test? Was I supposed to refuse?

I'd apparently hesitated too long. The door guard's hands tightened around his rifle.

"Code name," the seated man repeated.

"Condor," I said, hoping my choice to reveal a secret was correct.

The seated man opened his little book, scrolled through the pages with a white-gloved finger, then glanced back up and nodded. The door guard shifted, pressing his back against the wall to allow access to the door. "Through there, sir."

I gave each of them a last glance, then grabbed the handle and stepped through.

Loeb House wasn't a small building, but the eternal hallway I entered spoke of an underground structure far more extensive than the president's home above. Doors on either side appeared every twenty paces, each labeled with a stylized font one might expect from a signature on the Declaration of Independence.

Halfway to the end, I found 107 on the right.

This was it.

I was about to learn where Uncle Sam was sending me. Will would end up in Europe. The only foreign language he knew was German. They wouldn't waste a resource sending him somewhere he couldn't blend in. I hoped he would go to England to help bolster their homeland efforts but knew that was unlikely. He hadn't been training to help our allies in their own territory. He would be sent behind enemy lines. God, I hoped they send him to Norway, or Switzerland. The Swiss were still neutral, though riddled with diplomats and spies. That would be the safest place for him. He could blend in well there, posing as a German businessman.

This was what we'd trained for, but my stomach still churned at the idea of Will being thrust into harm's way.

I didn't care as much about where I would be assigned. I would do my duty and come home. Europe or the Russian front made the most sense, especially given my language skills, but I knew the Japanese invasion of China had drawn the attention of American intelligence agencies. Few knew about the thousands of men and women streaming into that country to assist the resistance, but I had seen hints of our efforts. However unlikely, it was possible I would be shipped east rather than west.

For the second time that morning, I stood before a door and tried to remember to breathe.

I opened the door to find Will, one of our army classmates, and a woman I didn't recognize sitting around a conference table. Unlike the furniture that greeted us in the lobby of the mansion, these tables and chairs looked to have seen better days. Large maps of Europe lined the walls, some containing push pins, while others were littered with colorful ink and neatly scrawled notes. The place smelled of ancient paper and cigarette smoke. I wouldn't expect an underground room to have any windows, but the absence of other doors made it feel even smaller and more confining. Unsure what to do, I sat beside the woman, opposite Will.

No one spoke.

I guessed we were each too lost in our own thoughts, our own possible futures, to engage. I certainly was, and the creases around Will's eyes told me more than any words could. Will stared at my hand for a long moment before I realized I'd been twisting my ring so quickly an angry line was forming on my finger. I did that a lot, twisting the ring, normally to remember my friend Baker, whom we'd already lost in this damned war.

Today, as I looked down at my reddened skin, I turned the signet for the same reason the girl refused to make anything more than fleeting eye contact, or why the army guy's leg kept bouncing beneath the table. Time could beset a person in the best of circumstances, but today, our shoulders were laden with the weight of our entire futures in this single moment.

This was the moment we'd learn our fate, and it was clear each of us held terror in our heart.

I started to say something—I wasn't sure what—when the door creaked open and a thin man with thinning black hair wearing thin spectacles strode in. It was like watching a pencil wearing copper wire walking on toothpicks.

"Emu," he said, his deep voice in dissonance with his waifish appearance.

"Manakin," Will replied.

Now my eyes widened. Will already knew this man.

Manakin walked around the table and dropped a folder before the chair at its head, then looked to each of us in turn. "Egret, Sparrow, Condor. Welcome to the Birdhouse."

I shot Will a glance. He shrugged, as if pleased he finally knew something I didn't, then turned to face our host.

"Each of you has completed your training—some with the OSS, others with our friends in the ONI, or others in the alphabet soup community. You bring unique skills and talents to the table, which is why we believe you will make a strong team."

He paused long enough for Will's head to snap back toward me and for him to mouth the word "team," his brows practically forming a question mark with how hard they quirked.

"Yes, Emu, a team," Manakin continued. Will slowly released my gaze. "Sparrow is the best radioman—I suppose that should be radio*woman*—we have. Before any of you ask, women began training with the OSS a long time ago. They're some of our best agents, and I expect each of you to respect Sparrow as you would any other team member."

He eyed each of us, then nodded to Sparrow, who had her eyes lowered. "Sparrow, that will probably mean they will dish out a great deal of shit. I hope you like it."

His self-satisfied chuckle was met with dumbfounded stares and uncomfortable silence.

He cleared his throat. "Egret is a demolition expert. He will handle all of your munitions and explosives. I would prefer if the rest of you kept your fingers intact. Agents without digits are hard to hide."

Again, his humor fell flat. Egret's shoes scraping against the floor as he repositioned himself was as close to laughter as Manakin would get.

"Sour lot," he said, scowling. "Condor is the team lead. He has the strongest German language skills, and is well-versed in strategic military planning. Emu is here for his pretty face."

Will coughed out a laugh and had to cover his mouth to contain himself.

Manakin beamed at finally landing a joke. "I only jest a little. Emu's skill rests with his ability to gain trust, his sense of empathy, and his natural awareness of his surroundings. He will help recruit assets and manage them. He will also play point on keeping up with local attitudes and enemy propaganda. Think of him as your eyes and ears within the community; although, that is the responsibility of each member of the team as well. To survive, you must never close your eyes."

To survive.

Any humor he'd infused whooshed out of the room with that statement. Tension lined each face as we examined our new partners.

"Questions so far?"

We stared at each other, then shifted back to Manakin.

"Good," he said, finally taking a seat and opening his folder. "Time for your mission."

Chapter Four

Will

E very bird in the cage leaned forward with elbows pressed into the hardwood and seats tilting off the floor. The agencies had trained and teased us long enough. It was finally time to glimpse into our future.

"I'm sorry to tell you, but your mission is a bit vague," Manakin said.

The imaginary puppeteer tugging our strings released the tension, and each of us slumped back in our seats. Thomas's chair actually thunked as its rear legs returned to the floor.

Manakin read the room and held up both palms. "Don't be frustrated. This is just how things work sometimes."

He unfolded a large map and slid it to the middle of the table, then pulled at the end of his pen, extending it into a pointer, aiming it at each location as he spoke.

"From here, you will be transported to Canada, then London. The Brits will transport you to a small airfield in the countryside a hundred kilometers outside of Hexham. From there, the SOE will handle your insertion into France. Understand, the Brits are transport only. They are not read into this mission. They may ask, and yes, they are our allies, but you must reveal *nothing*. Understood?"

He eyed each of us, waiting for our nod of assent, then let his pointer hover over a large blank section of the map within the borders of France, halfway between Paris and Nancy.

"If things go well, you will be greeted by a host and taken immediately to a safe house. Your first objective is to travel from your landing point toward Paris, gathering intelligence on Nazi troop movements and strength along the way. Any information you collect will be valuable, including local attitudes, resistance activities, rumors, and the like.

"You will not enter Paris. Your primary objective lies in the small town of Crécy-la-Chapelle, about fifty kilometers from the heart of Paris."

Manakin removed several photos from his folder and tossed them on top of the map. One displayed a picturesque town with ancient buildings, lazy rivers, and a sprawling emerald landscape. The second showed a four-story building whose back wall abutted a river. The watery motion of a paddlewheel blurred part of the image. The third photo was of four Nazi trucks parked outside the front of the building. Uniformed men hauled crates, each stamped with Hitler's pet arachnid in angry black. The frame captured at least a dozen guards with ready rifles surrounding the trucks, with many more likely taking up positions the camera could not capture.

"These images were taken by one of our local assets. We believe the Nazis are working on some kind of new weapon, using the cover of a small French town to camouflage their activity. Our assets within the Nazi High Command have long described how Hitler harbors extreme paranoia and assumes Allied spies track everything inside Germany's borders. The theory that his people are conducting research outside their borders aligns with this intelligence."

"Do we?" Egret asked.

Manakin raised a brow. "Do we what?"

"Track everything Hitler does inside Germany?"

Manakin's composure cracked as he laughed, an odd mixture of deep rumble and churlish giggle. "I could *never* answer that question, but think about it—how would that even be possible? It is a silly notion, don't you think?"

I got the impression Manakin knew a lot more than he was saying, that his laughter was genuine and the suggestion that our network blanketed Germany was ridiculous, but I was sure something in his eyes held secrets—so many secrets.

Manakin smoothed his features and resumed. "Your primary objective is to find out what is going on in that building. We need to know everything: who the researchers are, what they are working to develop, what material is in that building, their notes ... everything. Once you have secured the intelligence, you will destroy the building, its contents, and those working on the project. You will then return to your host at the landing point and await further instructions."

He glanced down at his folder, flipping through a few pages, then looked up. "Questions?"

The four of us stared blankly at the map and photos, then looked up and met each other's eyes. Curiosity and anxious tension had been replaced by something deeper: hesitant resolve. The set of Thomas's jaw told me he was bent on success, that he would do everything he could to see our team achieve its goals, but there was doubt there too. I could feel it wafting off him like a bitter breath.

None of us had been outside the comfort of our country, much less attempted subterfuge against a well-armed, highly secretive enemy intent on killing us in territory they controlled. But I would have worried about my teammates if their stomachs had *not* been doing the same gymnastics mine was performing in that moment. It was oddly reassuring to see those same fears reflected in their eyes.

Still, no one spoke, so Manakin barreled forward. I had hoped for some inspiring exultation to boost morale or rouse our patriotic passions. Wasn't that how Hollywood would have portrayed that moment?

Alas, there was no waving of the flag or lifting of the spirit.

"You will receive a more complete briefing on the ground situation from the SOE before leaving England, but I will reiterate what you learned at Camp X: transmit only what is essential, move immediately after transmitting, remember that you are only one wrong word or move from being captured, and trust no one."

As he was closing his folder, the rattling of the door shook us out of our collective "trust no one" fog. Manakin strode across the room, unlatched the door, and opened it.

When our latest arrival stepped into the room, Thomas and I shot to our feet, our mouths agape. I was too stunned to speak.

Thomas was not. "Arty?"

Chapter Five

Will

"Hi, guys." Arty did his half-wave thing, as though we were standing across a classroom and he wanted our attention. His smile was tentative, his hand a flurry.

Manakin, now standing behind him, cleared his throat.

"Uh, right," Arty said, peeking over his shoulder with an unspoken apology. "Condor, Emu, good to see you."

"Team, this is Stork."

I bit my tongue.

Thomas, never one to hold himself in reserve, nearly doubled over the table laughing. "Stork? Seriously, Manakin? You made Arty the baby-delivering bird?"

"That's just a fable, you know," Arty said, sending Thomas into another fit, this time joined by snickers from the rest of us.

Even Sparrow abandoned her shy flirtation with the tabletop to glance up with a grin. I couldn't help but think how appropriate her moniker was when I saw her head snap into each new position. Maybe Manakin was onto something.

Manakin stepped forward. "I think you lot will understand this lad's name, perhaps even appreciate it, when you see what he has for you. Follow us, please."

I gave Arty a curious brow, but he simply smiled and turned to follow our leader.

We strode to the end of the hall where yet another armed Marine stood watch. He snapped to attention when Manakin approached, then reached out a gloved hand and opened the door. Manakin never broke stride.

If the basement complex beneath the President's home had been a surprise, the football-field-sized room we now entered left us speechless. A dozen men and women, some students, others with a dusting of silver, scurried from one waist-high table to the next, tending beakers or machines of every size and shape. The sound of boiling ... something ... and the grinding of gears was punctuated by the occasional deafening pop of the firing of a weapon at the far end. The four of us nearly jumped out of our shoes the first time that sound echoed off the chamber walls. I squinted down the length of the place to find practice targets attached to at least a dozen feet of what looked like rolled rubber. Given the rest of the room, I was sure it was something more interesting and sophisticated.

Near the testing range, several cars bore Nazi flags, as though Hitler himself had come to call. One wall was covered with racks that held rifles, pistols, grenades, and every other sort of armament one might carry. I'd been in uniform for years, but I couldn't even identify some of them, they'd been so altered from their original state.

On some of the tables near us, strange rubber suits with gears and what looked like built-in gas masks sat. There was even a pair of rubber molds shaped like a man's feet large enough to slip over one's boots. I assumed they were meant to hide boot prints left in muddy ground, though the replacements were so large they might cause Germans to think massive gorillas had invaded their land.

I decided some of these inventions might best serve the cause by remaining in the lab.

"Welcome to the Nest," Manakin said. "Stork, would you like to give our friends the tour?"

Arty nodded and turned to face us. I was dumbstruck. We'd known Arty was doing some kind of scientific research at Loeb, which was pretty odd, but neither of us had any idea something this vast even existed on campus, much less that *our* Arty played more than a peripheral role in it.

Arty locked eyes with me for a second, then grinned and winked.

"Did you see that? The little shit actually winked?" I whispered to Thomas.

He chuckled a grunt, but seemed too overwhelmed to reply with words.

"The Nest is one of the primary product development sites in the United States for special OSS equipment," Arty began. "Our mission, if you'll allow me to steal your term of art, is to create tools to aid you in yours, to increase the probability of your success, and to help you exit a theater alive."

I couldn't decide which was more baffling: the enormity of the underground space beneath the campus we'd trod for years, the odd array of items and workers arrayed before us, or the unrecognizable man speaking with the confidence and authority of a seasoned officer. I knew that tone. I'd used it. How had *our* Arty—?

"Like your training program, we take the ordinary and make it extraordinary," he continued. "We aim for two objectives with each item we produce: obscurity and lethality. As you will see this morning, this is often accomplished through miniaturization."

He turned to the table an arm's length to his right and lifted an object, then held out his palm, displaying a metal cigarette lighter that looked like it had been run over by a train. Its metal was dented and dingy, and the only evidence of the maker's logo once pinned to the front were two bare holes that glared up like tiny eyes.

Arty gave us a moment to examine the lighter, then held it to his eye. "This is the most sophisticated field camera ever made. It contains enough film to take a dozen photos of nearly the same quality as many of the market's best lenses." He flipped the lid and spun the dial. A flame appeared. "Best of all, it is a lighter too."

Arty grinned and giggled as though he'd made a joke. In any other setting, it would've been cute in a *very* Arty way.

He clamped the lighter shut and laid it back on the table. "You will not travel with your gear. Clothing, toiletries, those sorts of things, will all be provided by the Brits. We can't risk you taking something with an American manufacturer's logo into enemy territory. Some of the items in this lab, however, will travel with you and become essential to your team's success."

He turned to the table and retrieved a large envelope, then removed a smaller packet and held it up for us to see. *Egret* was scrawled on the outside of the sealed packets.

"These are your new identity cards and other wallet items. The cover legends you developed during your training will now become your identities. Sparrow, due to your proficiency in the language, your identification is that of a French national. Everyone else is German."

Arty led us down the central aisle between the lengthy tables, stopping to retrieve and explain items that would be shipped with us on our journey. The variety of mundane items they'd transformed into clever tools was overwhelming:

A deck of German playing cards whose faces could peel back to reveal part of a map of France. When all fifty-two were laid side by side, the whole of the country was revealed.

A plain wristwatch whose winding mechanism, when pressed inward, ejected a metal coil to be used as a garrote.

A functioning fountain pen with a secret cap that twisted off to reveal a razor-sharp dagger the length of one's index finger.

Cuff links and coat buttons that hid tiny compasses to aid in navigating foreign terrain.

"Now we come to munitions," Arty said, stepping behind a table with larger items. "Please, don't touch anything on this table. We'd like to keep the lab intact."

His grin earned a smile from me, but the rest simply gawked at the tabletop.

"This," he said, raising a beat-up metal case. He removed the top to reveal four pencils one might find in any schoolroom. "Is a time-delay incendiary device. Each pencil will mark with lead if removed. However, when the third one is pressed down, a three-minute timer is activated. The explosive charge is far more powerful than you might expect from an item this small, as the case is packed with plastique, compliments of our British friends."

He returned the pencil case and lifted a water canteen. "This is an even more powerful explosive device. Two-thirds of the canteen is packed with 808, which would devastate much of this room. There is also a version of this device containing tiny balls for elimination of enemy personnel."

Arty's matter-of-fact description of man-killing devices made me shudder. I'd expect such talk from any of the military folk who'd instructed us, but Arty had always been so innocent, the purest among us. It made me proud to see his burgeoning confidence, but a part of me was sad at his loss of innocence.

Arty led us further down the table. "You were trained in the use of a mole." He pointed to several pieces laid out on a table, one of which was a light-sensing device designed to trigger the explosive charge when an unfortunate train with the device attached via magnet entered a darkened tunnel. "We now have many of these devices in-country."

His eyes landed on me again, and something in Arty's bearing shifted. "The British will brief you on a few other tools they've been preparing for your mission, but there is one final item to discuss." He took several small boxes from the table, checked their labels, then handed one to each of us. "These are personal to each of you; a replacement for something you already possess that must remain here. For example, Condor"—he turned to Thomas—"the ring you wear is clearly American. The one in your box is identical, except the face bears a German crest. The crest itself twists off, opening a chamber containing one cyanide pill."

His voice fell away, as did his gaze. When he spoke again, he was the tentative boy we'd known for years. "If you get captured … just … don't get captured, okay?"

Manakin stepped forward and clapped Arty on the shoulder. A darkness settled over his eyes, and the pleasant curl his lips maintained smoothed as he looked at our friend through his thick spectacles. It was one of the few overt acts of compassion I'd seen from the man. He'd attempted humor with us a few times, but even his brightest smile had failed to touch his eyes. I was starting to think he'd spent so much time sending men and women off to die that he'd lost a bit of his humanity. Would that happen to us? Had it already begun?

"You will receive more detail once you land in Britain. Report to the lobby of Loeb House in two days, on June third, at oh-nine-hundred hours. Stork and I will be here to see you off. You will be driven to the airfield, where your flight will depart promptly at ten-hundred hours. Leave everything except the clothing you will wear on the plane. Our people will handle storage until you return."

Our instructions complete, we were ushered out of the lab, up the stairs, and out of President Conant's home.

———◆○◆———

Arty promised to see us at dinner, then returned to the lab. Egret offered to walk with Sparrow as she began the eternal trek back to Radcliffe. Thomas and I headed across the yard toward my dorm.

Campus felt so empty the week after a commencement. The military students who remained, waiting for the summer term to begin, were a sparse few compared to Harvard's usual bustle. It felt a bit like a slumbering beast drawing a deep breath before rising to begin its daily stalk.

"France," Thomas whispered without turning his head. I wasn't sure if he was thinking aloud or talking to me.

A few strides later, he asked, "What do you think?"

"Well ... we're on the same team," I said. "All I could think about for the past term was how we'd be sent a world apart to God knows where. I wanted to believe we'd see each other again, but the more we trained, the more all this became real ... I don't know, Thomas. I think I was starting to lose hope we'd both ..."

Whatever I was trying to say stuck in my throat, and it took everything in me to hold back rebellious tears.

Thomas waited, walking in silence, as I gathered myself. "When I walked into that room, and Manakin said we were going to ... you know where ... together, I almost forgot to listen to the rest of what he was saying. All I could think was that we'd be together. Whatever happens, we'll either come home or we won't, but we'll do that together too."

Thomas still didn't say anything. His jaw ground as he swallowed his own thoughts. When he started to speak, his mouth clamped shut as quickly as it had opened.

I wanted to take his hand in that moment, to tell the world to fuck off and hold him, right there in the middle of Harvard Yard, but we weren't allowed such simple acts of compassion. Other people could comfort their lover, but our grief, our fear, our love, it all lived within the shadows.

It was a bitter twist of the knife that the rest of our lives were about to be cast into similar darkness.

"At least we'll be together," he said, summing up the only shard of light slicing through my gloom.

Two soldiers approached from the opposite direction, men we played basketball against a year before but hadn't seen since.

Their uniforms were sharp, and each of them bore a pack slung over their shoulder, as if they were taking their final steps out of their youth.

One of the men made eye contact with Thomas, then the pair did the last thing I expected: they halted mid-stride, dropped their packs, snapped to attention, and offered Thomas a crisp salute.

Thomas's eyes widened. He stopped walking and returned their respect.

"Heading out?" Thomas asked once their hands returned to their sides and their postures relaxed.

"Yes, sir. Time to join the fight."

Something crossed before Thomas's eyes, then he stepped forward and grabbed one of the men's hands, shaking it firmly, his other hand gripping the man's arm. "You come home, soldier, you hear me?"

Their eyes were unshakably locked, neither willing to release their gaze.

The soldier's lip quivered before he nodded once and croaked out, "Yes, sir. You too, sir."

Thomas released the man, then nodded toward the other. "You too. That's an order."

The second man smirked. "You're a squid, sir. You can't really give me an order, but I'll do my best to follow that one."

Thomas returned his smile, and clapped him on the shoulder like he'd done his friend. "Get the fuck out of here."

With a chuckle from one and a grimace from the other, the two grabbed their packs and marched away.

"Do you know them? I mean, outside of basketball?" I asked after the men were out of earshot.

Thomas shrugged. "They're headed to war. They're my brothers."

And that was really all that mattered, wasn't it?

A bond was a funny thing. I'd never worn a uniform, though I had, technically, enlisted in the army. I had glimpsed what it might be like throughout our training, but had yet to fully experience its imprint on my soul. In that brief interaction, I knew Thomas had.

"We need to study the maps of France. Most of our time was on Berlin and the areas surrounding it," he said, his subject change as subtle as a cabbie slamming on his breaks.

"Probably, yeah. That's a good idea."

"I don't even remember that town. What was its name?"

I lowered my voice to an urgent whisper. "Thomas, we should wait until we're in the room to discuss this."

The smirk I loved flashed across his lips, and his eyes burst to life. "Look at that. The rookie guiding the veteran."

I fake-stumbled so I could elbow him off the sidewalk into the grass.

"Hey! That's mutiny."

I laughed. "Only when you're actually in charge. Out here, you're just an anchor clanker talking about things best kept quiet."

"Anchor clanker?" He bumped my shoulder as he fell back in beside me. "You've been hanging around too many army guys."

I shrugged. "And you call yourself a veteran. I'm pretty sure this will be your first mi—*adventure* too."

I scolded myself for almost using the word "mission" in public. It wasn't exactly a giveaway for us being spies, but I didn't want to start relaxing my language right before we flew into danger.

He quirked a brow. "You sure about that?"

"What do you mean? We're in all the same classes and training."

"Yeah, but I had a life before Will Shaw, hard as that may be to believe. I'm not a raw recruit."

That stole the wind from my sails.

I'd never really thought about Thomas going on missions before we met. We hadn't talked about what he'd done in the navy, other than his working for the Office of Naval Intelligence and receiving basic medical training. I'd been thankful for that last bit after a bad night on the basketball court with some rowdy opponents.

"Can you talk about any of it?" I asked tentatively.

We walked a good ten paces before he spoke. "I can tell you some, sure, but it's not exciting, mostly domestic stuff."

"Domestic? As in, inside the US? You're in the navy, you're not allowed—"

He scoffed. "You'd be surprised. We *definitely* need to be in your room for that conversation though."

Our pace quickened as my mind tried to wrap itself around the possibilities of Thomas's past. What had he been involved in? Maybe he spied on others on a military base, searching for enemy agents. Surely he wasn't involved in anything with civilians. That would go against at least a few laws professors had drilled into my head in my freshman year.

Thomas was only a few years older than me. He couldn't have been *that* much more experienced, could he?

We stepped inside my room and the door clicked behind Thomas as I tossed my copy of our mission packet onto my desk. Thomas leaned against the door and was staring at me when I turned around.

"Okay, no more hiding. What did you do before we met? You've got me curious."

He stepped forward and reached up, gripping the top button of my shirt with his fingers.

"Thomas, come on. We have a lot to—"

He leaned down and dug his teeth into my neck, sending a jolt from the top of my spine to my toes. Then his tongue crawled up my neck to my ear, where his teeth attached themselves to my earlobe. The last of my shirt buttons popped free before I was able to find my voice again.

"Thomas—"

He eased back and stared into my eyes as he yanked my shirt off and tossed it across the room. All ten of his naughty digits grazed my bare chest, one teasing the sensitive tip of my nipple.

"Shit, Thomas—"

"You're asking for stories I shouldn't tell. That requires payment ... in advance." His voice was a low rasp that sent a shiver across my arms.

Then his lips smothered whatever sharp reply I was going to make, and all thoughts of missions or pasts—or even the future—gave way to the beautiful friction of skin and sweat.

Chapter Six

Will

I really wanted to talk. We'd just been given an overview of our first mission as spies, and Thomas had hinted at a past life with the navy ... and I was curious ... and then he bit my nipple.

His lips teased mine as he ran his tongue across the bottom of my teeth. Tiny centipedes of pleasure tap-danced with their hundreds of feet across my gumline. When he pinched both of my nipples and held them like a vice, I thought the lightbulb in the ceiling had exploded all over the room.

"Fuck me!" I shouted.

He pulled back, a feral gleam in his eyes. "Careful what you ask for. You know I've been wanting to do that."

My face must've shown instant panic. I know my butthole puckered harder than a baby eating a lemon.

"Shh. Relax," he said, pressing a tender kiss to my mouth. "We'll only do that when you're ready. If it never happens, that's okay too. I love feeling you inside me."

I breathed again.

Without parting our lips, his fingers released my nipples and trailed down my stomach, where they began unbuttoning my trousers.

"Boxers? You're actually wearing underwear?" he said, looking down.

"We had a big meeting. I don't know ... I didn't want to be flying free in the middle of—"

His laugh cut me off. "Flying free? Was your dick going to grow wings and start dive-bombing Manakin? Is it one of the birds now?"

His fingers dug into my now naked sides, and an uncontrollable fit of laughter swept over me. While I was disabled, the fucker grabbed me by the arms and shoved me so I fell onto the bed, where he dropped to his knees and began unlacing my shoes.

"You're mine, Will Shaw. You know that, right?"

I propped myself up on my elbows. "Yeah. I tried to run away, but you're a fast fucker."

His hand reached up and squeezed my balls.

"Ow!"

"Be a good boy or get punished. It's up to you." The psychopathically cute gleam in his eye told me this afternoon would be a romp for the ages. I could feel my heart thumping harder and faster.

Once my shoes were tossed safely across the room and my pants lay in a heap on the floor, Thomas leaned up and took my cock in his mouth.

"That feels so damn good, Thomas."

He bobbed up and down, his lips gentle while his tongue curled and stroked with vigor. Every so often, he pulled off completely and traced his tongue around the tender underside of my head, sending shivers down my legs and up my stomach.

I leaned up and gripped his shoulders. "Time to get these clothes off."

While I usually tore at his clothes with the reckless abandon of youth, that day I savored every button and snap, pulling his shirt slowly over his shoulders, letting the fabric drag across his perfectly unmarred skin, revealing him slowly. By the look in his eyes, the slow reveal was as exciting for him as it was for me.

When I slipped my hands beneath his pants on either side of his hips, a smile curled his lips.

"My puppies like to fly. Let them be free."

I pulled his underwear-less pants down and watched as his cock sprung from beneath, thumping against his stomach.

"Looks like he's very happy to see you."

I rolled my eyes, but couldn't suppress a grin. "It's good to see him too," I said, pressing my mouth to his tip and coming away with a salty lip for my effort.

"Hmm. Thomas tastes like fries today."

He chuckled. "You calling my cock a potato? I'm not sure how to take that."

"Oh, you'll *take it* how I give it."

"Damn right about that," he said in a hoarse whisper as I swallowed his dick like he'd done mine.

He let me devour him for long moments as I removed his shoes and pants, then grabbed my shoulders again and forced me onto my back on the bed.

"There's something we haven't done yet that I want to try."

I raised a brow.

He didn't answer, simply spun his body so his balls smacked into my nose and his dick flopped against my cheek. Never one to miss a hint, I took him into my mouth again. I was a good suck or two into things, about to get my rhythm, when my dick vanished in a blanket of warm moisture. I chanced a glance to find his eyes closed and his tongue swirling around my cock. I couldn't decide which felt better, having him in my mouth and knowing I was giving him pleasure, or the ripples of pleasure thrumming through my body every time his tongue and lips dragged across my most sensitive skin. Having both at once was amazing.

"Shit, Thomas, if you keep—"

He stopped. "Not a chance, fast boy." He pulled himself free of my lips and spun around so our lips met again. "I think it's time you experienced interrogation training."

My eyes flew wide. "What?"

His hands clamped around my wrists and he hauled my arms above my head. Smooth ropes I hadn't noticed were tied to the metal frame. Before I could resist, so were my arms.

"Thomas, what are you—"

He held a finger to my lips. "You're my captive. I'm going to make you confess."

I didn't know how to respond to that.

He gripped my nipple again, then twisted it hard.

"Ah!" I shouted, as the pain morphed into pleasure that seeped from my skin into my chest.

He reached down beside the bed, and I heard the familiar sound of a jar lid unscrewing. When his hand returned, his fingers were coated in clear jelly. He took a small amount and began massaging it into the tip of my dick.

I squirmed. Every touch, every tease, brought me closer to release. I could feel it welling inside me. It felt like my whole body wanted to explode.

Then he stopped again, his eyes locking onto mine. "I love you, Will, more than anything in this life. I will always love you."

With that unexpected declaration, he kissed me again, this time more passionately than before. The next thing I felt was my cock slipping inside him as he pressed down against my body.

Still, he kissed me.

His other hand found my hair, and his fingers dug into my scalp.

He held himself there, sitting atop me, me inside him, unmoving. We were one person. One passion. One love.

In that moment, I knew we would never be apart. All my fears about being separated or living in other worlds were little more than the silly notions of a frightened boy. This man, this beautiful man, was my life now, and I wouldn't let anything—not even a war—come between us.

I poured my soul into those kisses without realizing I'd begun pressing myself deeper into him. He moaned into my mouth and lifted himself then pressed down again.

We kissed as one. We moved as one. We thrust as one.

I tried to reach down, but the ropes wouldn't budge. Thomas didn't open his eyes, but I felt his stupid smirk against my lips.

He quickened his pace, rising and falling faster, driving me deeper and harder. My legs twitched and thunder rolled through me as I pulsed inside him.

He must've felt my stomach tense, because he pulled our lips apart, straightened, and began stroking himself as he ground his ass against me.

"I'm coming, Thomas," I cried, yanking against the ropes.

He stroked faster, thrust me into him faster. He grinned as I squirmed against the bindings, but still he drove me deeper.

I saw his abs flex and hold. His hole squeezed around my shaft. Pinpricks of light danced in my vision as his body drew cum out of me. One shot after another flew from me. I opened my eyes to see his head thrown back, his body tense, and his cock hard and raw. I'd barely shot the last of my load when he began, the first of his cum reaching my chin, followed by several shots to my chest and stomach.

When we were both spent, and our breathing slowed, he reached down and freed my wrists, then carefully edged his body to lie atop me, keeping me inside him as he moved.

"Just lay here a minute," he said. "I want you to live inside me a little longer."

I stroked his hair and kissed the top of his head.

How had everything changed so much so quickly? Only a few years ago, I thought I would meet a girl, get married, have children. We would live outside the city, maybe on a small farm, where life would be carefree and peaceful. My parents would love …

I would still have my parents. There would be no war.

But war came. And so did this beautiful man.

I kissed his head again. He'd fallen asleep. His sweat-slicked body smothered mine, and I couldn't imagine a more perfect blanket. The world had gone to hell, and I had lost so much; yet here, in the arms of Thomas Jacobs, I'd found my calling and my comfort.

I'd found my future.

Chapter Seven

Thomas

On June 3, 1943, I woke with Will's head on my chest, his warm puffs of breath tickling the tiny hairs and sending warmth into my soul. Arty had left for the lab an hour earlier, leaving us one last morning alone.

I watched as Will's lidded eyes darted at the call of peaceful dreams. His face held a stillness and placid beauty I sought to etch into my memory. I wanted that morning, that moment, to live forever.

I trailed circles with my fingers across his back, savoring the smoothness of his skin. That's when he finally stirred.

"Hey, you," he smiled up, his voice a hoarse whisper of the sunrise.

"Hey." I craned forward and kissed his head.

He blinked himself awake, and I thought he might rise, but his arms tightened about my body as he nuzzled deeper into my chest.

"This is my favorite place in the whole world."

I kissed his head again.

"Do you think we'll have mornings like this again?"

My fingers stilled. "What do you mean?"

"With me on your chest, waking with the sun, and no one around to care? I wish the whole world would just fade away and leave us alone. I think I could be happy, just you and me, like this."

Will and I had been together for over a year, yet his words still pricked my heart. No one had ever spoken to me from such a place of love or vulnerability.

When I didn't respond, he said, "I'm scared, Thomas." His arms tensed. "I'm scared ... we won't come back, or that I'll come back and you won't. I can't lose you, Thomas. I can't."

When his hot tears rolled onto my skin, my resolve crumbled, and my own fears trickled down my face. "I can't lose you either, you hear me? Don't you dare die on me."

He released his hold and pushed himself up to stare down at me. I didn't recognize the first few emotions that flitted across his eyes, but confusion, then compassion, settled in them as his fingers reached out to wipe my face.

"I promise to not die or lose you in this damn war. I will come home with you, and we will have a life without fear or shame. We will be together for the rest of our days. I swear."

I could barely breathe.

This man loved me so, and I was so unworthy of it. I felt so small in his gaze, yet knew he saw me as some invincible protector. What had I done to deserve this amazing creature?

I reached up and cupped his cheek, and he covered my hand with his. "I swear to come home alive with you, Will Shaw, to love you and care for you, to protect and nurture you, to give you everything I have and everything I am, for the rest of my days."

Our tears were flowing freely then.

Will leaned down and pressed his lips to mine. His kiss wasn't hungry or passionate. It wouldn't lead to a sweaty roll in the hay.

It was the purest ray of light breaking free of dark clouds as a storm's fury faded away.

A long moment later, he released our lips and rose so our breaths still mingled.

"You know, what we just said sounded a lot like vows. I mean, we can't actually do *that* ... but if we could, it sure sounded ..."

I stared into his eyes. There wasn't a hint of humor. His statement was a question.

And that's when I returned to myself and held up my hand, wiggling the finger with the ring from Arty's lab. "Guess it's a good thing the OSS gave us rings. Looks like Uncle Sam blessed our union after all."

Horror flooded his face, then retreated as his body shook with laughter. He fell sideways to lie beside me, howling so loud those in the yard probably heard him. There was such boundless joy in his eyes, my bitter tears turned to beads of heavenly bliss.

"Only you," he spat through gasps, "would claim a ring with a suicide pill for a wedding band, you sick fuck."

I grabbed his hand—the one that bore his OSS ring—and held it up next to mine, then locked eyes and batted my lashes. "They're not a set, but they're perfect. Our whole lives are shadows, why shouldn't our rings be too?"

"God, you're *terrible*!"

"Hey, it really does work. Nobody will look twice. They won't know."

He barked another laugh, then froze. The silence was so sudden, so jarring, I thought he might've hurt himself somehow.

"Will?"

He turned and propped up on an elbow, his words tentative and halting. "Thomas ... I wasn't joking. I gave you ... my word, my ... *vow*. I know you might not've meant it—"

As I placed a finger to his lips and leaned closer to kiss him, I whispered, "Shut up, *husband*."

———◆———

We ate a last breakfast in the dining hall, then bid adieu to Will's dorm. As the door to the house closed behind us, Will turned and pressed his palm against its wood and held it there for a long moment.

"It feels weird walking out, knowing I'll never sleep here again. Like starting a new chapter."

"A whole new book is more like it," I said through a tight smile.

He nodded soberly, and we strode across the yard.

Manakin and Arty waited on the steps of Loeb House. The others had yet to arrive. A small bus that looked like a police wagon waited nearby, its driver leaning against the side as he smoked a cigarette.

"Come over here, guys, just for a minute." Arty stepped forward and motioned to the side of the building, away from Manakin and the driver. His voice shook in a way I recognized as nerves.

The moment we rounded the corner, Arty barreled into Will, nearly knocking him off his feet, as his spindly arms wrapped around him in a grip any wrestler would envy.

"Easy there, buddy," Will said, rubbing his back. "What's this all about?"

He let go and stepped back. Tears streaked his face. "I wish you could stay, both of you. Will, I …" He struggled for air before calming. "Just come home, okay? You're family. I mean it. You're my brother, and I love you."

Will choked down his own emotions and pulled Arty back into a hug. "I love you too, little brother. So much."

When they finally parted, Arty looked to me. "You come back too, and keep Will safe. He gets hurt easily … and isn't that smart."

"Hey!" Will protested.

I laughed and surprised Arty by grabbing him roughly and pulling him into my chest, then whispered, "I'll give my life for his, Arty. I swear that to you."

His sobs racked my chest, and I lost track of how long I held him. Will stepped closer and placed a hand on his back. For one brief moment, we truly were family.

"Alright, guys, time to load up," Manakin's voice called.

Arty wiped his face and shuffled back. When we started toward the bus, he held up a palm. "Hang on. I have something for you." He dug into his coat pocket and produced a letter with Will's name scrawled in elegant script. "Janie couldn't come to see you off. She wanted to, but she ... Just read her letter. You'll understand."

He handed the letter to Will, then turned and led us back to where the others stood.

Manakin nodded to Arty, and our friend disappeared through Loeb's doorway. Then the OSS recruiter turned back toward our group. "Emu, Condor, Egret, Sparrow, what you are about to do will make a difference in this war. You will save lives. Never doubt that. I'm proud of each of you, and look forward to raising a glass when you return home. From this point forward, your code names do not exist. You are your alias, even to the Brits. We know there are spies in their ranks, so giving anything other than your alias could put you at greater risk. Understand?"

Four heads nodded.

"Good. You've got a long flight ahead, then an even longer one. Use that time to learn each other's legends. The three of you"—he pointed to Will, Egret, and me—"are all Germans. Coming up with a connection should be easy. Sparrow is French, so you'll need to get creative. When you land, an SOE handler will review your story and offer to smooth any rough edges. He will give you the code name Falcon. Trust only him."

He started to turn away, then grinned up at us. "Sorry about the lousy accommodations. The air ferry isn't exactly a luxury liner, but it will get you to England. Godspeed."

He eyed each of us one final time, nodded, and pointed toward the van.

We settled into our seats, and the engine roared to life. Manakin waved like a father watching his children leave for school. We waved in return.

"What did Janie have to say?" I asked across the seat, noticing Will's face fall as he read. He stared at the page, then handed it to me.

My dearest Will,

I'm so sorry for not being there to see you off.

You and Thomas are such wonderful friends; brothers to me, really. I wanted to be there, truly I did, but my heart began breaking the day I learned you would go overseas.

I couldn't bear to watch you leave.

But it's more than that, really. I need to beg your forgiveness. Not long ago, I lied to you. I lied to everyone.

I was in such a dark place, Will, and I didn't know how to find my way back. I've never felt so lost and alone.

My fiancé was an attorney in town, that much of what I told everyone was true, but he didn't leave me because I fell into a bottle or lost myself with other men. I did those things because I lost him. He asked me to marry him the day before the army sent him to fight. He said he didn't want to leave without knowing he would return to a life with me in it.

That morning, in the dining hall, when I showed you all my ring, he was boarding a ship. Some days later, he was on that ship headed to some island, he couldn't tell me which, when a German U-boat found them. I don't know how many were lost that day, but I count myself among them. I've never felt such unrelenting pain.

I still feel it: his absence, this pain.

I never told you he was in the army, ~~or that he~~ or any of this because I knew you would soon leave to join the war, and the last thing you needed was to be burdened by my grief and the fears that kept me from sleeping most nights.

I'm so scared for you, Will. I'm scared I'll lose you too.

God, I sound like such a wilted flower. I'm sorry. You don't need to hear this now.

I love you. Know that you both are in my thoughts and heart every moment of every day.

Come home to me, Will. Come home safe.

All my love,

Janie

Chapter Eight

Dr. Lang

Jÿrgen Vogt stormed out, leaving two men in white coats slumped at a small table, mugs of tea steaming into their faces as they stared at the hypnotic ripples in the liquid's surface. The lab's perpetual movement had been unnerving in their first days, but they'd become used to its incessant shifts.

The door opened, snapping the men's heads up, and a third scientist entered.

"Jesus, Manfred. We thought you were Vogt again."

Chemist Manfred Lang shook his head and stepped to a sink where he grabbed a mug, poured hot water, and dunked a tea bag. "I saw him leave not long ago."

"Thank God. That man is insufferable," Adal Köhler said before taking a sip.

The third man, Felix Bauer, sat back and stared up at the ceiling. "They expect miracles. Does he not understand how *unstable* sarin is? We cannot rush the tests."

Lang sat in the remaining chair at the table and cradled his mug in his hands. "He does not care. I think he would use the gas on our own people so long as it killed the British."

"Manfred!" Köhler hissed. "Do not say such things aloud."

"Look there and tell me it is not so." Lang pointed to the glass wall of the test chamber where the bodies of three test subjects lay unmoving. Two workers had entered to clear the chamber and prepare for the next test only to fall prey to sarin's insidious touch. "Lethality should have diminished since that test was conducted, at least to the level that our workers could cleanse the chamber without need of a full suit. It may be a week before—"

"Yes, yes. I know," Lang said, waving a dismissive hand. "But I have no new ideas to stabilize the compound. Without an answer, we become ... how do they say ... expendable."

Bauer's gaze returned to meet Lang's. "We could tell them it is ready, simply give them what they want."

"Now *you* are mad. What is in that tea?" Köhler snapped. "We must do all we can. There must be a solution. They give us unlimited subjects, so we keep at it. Period. No more talk of failure or doing something stupid that would kill an untold number of our own people. Understand?"

The three men's gazes fell to their tea, and silence loomed over the lab.

Chapter Nine

Thomas

N ervous excitement reigned as we boarded the bus to head
to the airport. Manakin had failed to specify which airport housed our ferry. We'd assumed Boston housed a significant military presence, so this would be a quick trip. An hour
into the slowest-moving bus trip ever conceived, we learned our
destination was Grenier Army Air Base in New Hampshire.

We chatted quietly, joking about how the bus ride couldn't
possibly be prophetic of our flights to come. We knew long
hours above the clouds lay ahead of us, but hoped this well-es-
tablished route for men and material would go smoothly and
quickly.

Hope proved a fool's errand.

Nearly three hours after climbing into the bus, we ascended
the steps of a drably painted Douglas C-47 Skytrain. There were
no markings on the plane's exterior beyond the familiar star
designating it as an American craft. Two seats barely the width
of a starving man's shoulders on either side of an even narrower
aisle allowed for twenty-eight passengers. Six of those seats were
already occupied by uniformed soldiers when we boarded. They
eyed our civilian dress, but said nothing, merely nodding in
greeting as we passed.

Unrehearsed, Will took the window seat on one side of the aisle, and I folded myself next to the opposite window. To anyone watching, we were just two members of a team who wanted extra space on a long flight. We knew how sitting together might send a very different signal to observers. Still, looking across the aisle and two empty seats, I longed to press into him and hold his hand as we traveled. The look in his eyes and the slight curl to his lips told me his mind traveled the same path.

Sparrow and Egret mirrored our arrangement in the row behind us. I was fairly sure they just wanted extra leg room.

A major, yet to remove his stiff coat, sat two rows in front of Will. As he turned and leaned against the back of his seat, sweat beaded his brow, and his eyes struggled to settle in one place as he spoke.

"How far are you lot going?" he asked.

Will glanced across at me, as if mentally asking how much we should share. This was, after all, our first clandestine mission. We'd been trained and briefed but had no real notion of what to expect.

"Great Britain," Egret said from behind us before I could answer.

The major looked past me and nodded. "Oh, okay. That's a long trip. I'm off at Stephenville."

"Stephenville Air Base is a ferry staging field in Newfoundland operated jointly by the US and RAF military forces," I said in response to Will's blank stare.

He nodded, but kept his lips tight.

"Good thing they got the error rate down," the major said as he turned to face forward.

"Error rate?" Sparrow asked, popping up from her seat behind Will.

Egret shrugged and looked to me. I shook my head.

"Major." Will leaned forward as the man began to turn away. "What do you mean by error rate?"

His eyes narrowed. "First ferry flight?"

Our four heads bobbed.

He blew out a sigh. "If the skies could get worn like a road, these ferry routes would be little more than rubble. Some of the planes are so exhausted they actually do fall apart. FDR started sending equipment with his Lend-Lease program a few years ago. They used to lose about ten percent of those flights. Between the weather, especially around Greenland and Iceland, and all the wear on these birds, it's a wonder any of them stay in the air. Some pencil-pusher in the Pentagon came up with the name for those losses."

"Didn't they just open the Pentagon this year, back in January?" Egret challenged.

The major nodded. "Yeah, guess the guy wasn't actually in the building back then, but he works there now. He's one of the clerks on the Joint Chiefs' staff."

Anyone working directly for the new unified command of US forces wasn't to be taken lightly. Bile rose in my throat as the plane lurched forward and began taxiing down the runway.

"I'm sure we'll be fine," the sweaty man said. "I've never done the Atlantic crossing, but this is my third time between Grenier and Stephenville. I'm sure it'll be fine."

He turned away and settled into his seat.

Will's head fell back, and his eyes drifted to stare into the bare metal of the plane's sparse interior. Paint had scraped away in places, likely from passengers bumping packs and luggage against it. Still, the man's reassurance failed to instill confidence, especially after the major's admonition.

"We'll be fine," I said, hoping my voice didn't betray the terror threading its way through my chest.

Egret settled back, appearing unaffected. Sparrow vibrated with anxiety. Will remained stoic and silent. I just tried to breathe.

Sparrow slept through most of the trip, but Egret insisted Will and I play cards with him to pass the time. He posited that adding some wear to the deck would enhance their authenticity when we dropped behind enemy lines. He was probably just bored, but his reasoning was sound enough to have us gambling possessions we didn't actually possess.

It was during those long hours I came to genuinely like our resident explosives expert. Egret had a quick wit that belied the Cro-Magnon forehead that gave the impression he would be slower than our bus to New Hampshire. His humor was sharp, and he didn't spare anyone or any topic. Everyone was fair game to be offended by his dark jibes. It became clear, however, that his jokes were truly made in jest and represented little more than a desire to pass the time and win over his new comrades.

I hoped Sparrow would prove collegial. A four-person team could ill afford dissention within its ranks, and, while I never expected to bond as kin, I did hope the four of us would share a friendship born of more than necessity.

The hardest part of the flight was being stuck in a confined space with Will. We were so close, yet society's invisible barrier rose between us like a barb-tipped coil dividing front lines. I wasn't bitter or angry about it. We both understood how the world worked in that regard. We shared occasional glances when our heads fell below the seat and no one could see. He'd smile and wink, just to let me know we shared one mind, but I still longed for the warmth of his touch. I ached to press my lips to his, to taste his breath and feel its warmth against my skin … to cup his cheek and stare into his eyes.

Restless sleep allowed me those moments, as Will consumed my dreams.

———◄O►———

Aside from a patch of gut-wrenching turbulence on the leg from Greenland to Iceland, our flight had been smooth and un-eventful. After more than nineteen hours in the air, seventeen hours on the ground, and eight stops at way stations along the route, we touched down at Prestwick Airport in Scotland.

"I don't ever want to fly again," Egret grumbled as he placed his palms on the ceiling and twisted to stretch his stiff back.

Will chuckled. "Guess you won't be joining us on the rest of our vacation then. Should we leave you at the beach? Give you a good book to read?"

Egret grinned. "I hate fucking reading. What's the point when I can be outside blowing shit up?"

"Boys, can we not kill things until it's absolutely necessary?" Sparrow chimed in.

"It's war, sweetie. Killing is the order of the day," Egret said, earning a sharp look from our radio operator.

We hadn't brought any bags, so exiting the plane was a quick affair. A lean man in a neat gray suit stood at the base of the stairs.

"Mr. Richter, welcome to Scotland," he said to Will, the first of us to set foot on British soil. The man's accent was decidedly English.

It took a moment for Will to recognize his legend after our mind-numbing travel, but he recovered quickly and smiled. "Thank you. This isn't our final stop. Why are you greeting us here?"

"It is now," the Brit said without explanation.

Will's face betrayed the same alarm I felt in my gut. We were supposed to fly to London and be driven to middle-of-nowhere England.

"Washington and London love change. I assure you, this is part of your new itinerary."

Will's shoulders relaxed. "Okay. And who are you?"

The man grinned and inclined his head. "I am called John Milton. I will be your host."

"John Milton?" Will's mouth twisted, then he attempted a terrible British accent. "Fancy writing, do you?"

"Please stick with American. You wound my sensitive British ears." Milton grinned, and I found myself warming to the man. "You have your birds. We have our scribes. Rather fun, don't you think?"

Will's mouth opened, then closed, and I could hear his thoughts screaming about this man knowing our code names—the first thing we were told to protect from everyone, even our allies.

"You Americans think you are so clever. We have been at this game much longer. Besides, we are friends; *cousins*, really. Family should not keep secrets." He made an exaggerated gesture, as though pondering something deeply. "You know, we would be closer relatives if you hadn't rebelled against your King and all. Terrible mess that was."

None of us knew what to say.

The last of the passengers deplaned and flowed around us like we were rocks in the middle of a bubbling brook.

Silent rocks. Stunned rocks.

Then Milton laughed and slapped Will on the shoulder. "I'm giving you the business. That's what you call it, is it not? Come on. Let's get you lot settled. You're only here for a couple of days, and I suspect you might like a shower and a good meal. The Crown may even buy you a pint or two."

"God, yes please," Egret said, summing up my thoughts.

Milton led our team off the airfield, through a monstrous hangar and out to a small parking lot. Sparrow climbed into the front seat, while "her three boys" crammed into the back like sardines. Egret winced as shoulders shoved against each other, but I enjoyed the moment of closeness with Will. There hadn't been a single moment alone since we'd left the States, much less an opportunity to sit so close to one another. I breathed in deeply, feigning annoyance, but truly relishing the scent of his two-day-old musk.

Milton drove through the Scottish countryside for twenty minutes before pulling off the road and onto a dusty driveway that stretched for hundreds of yards. At the end of the drive, a massive stone mansion lorded over lands that spread for hundreds of acres in every direction. To my young American eyes, the castle-like estate appeared to be an ancient structure of immeasurable age, yet the stones that comprised its walls held fast and showed little sign of wear from the harsh highland weather.

We were greeted at the door by a middle-aged man in a neat white shirt and black tie. His bulky biceps caused the fabric of his shirt to strain, hinting that this man was more than a demure domestic.

"Welcome," he said in the richly accented notes of a local. "Your rooms are prepared. Please, come in."

As we strode the length of richly paneled halls, the man introduced himself as George Eliot, earning yet another round of American teasing at the British spy organization's nomenclature.

We ascended a grand staircase whose walls were lined with portraits of men and women from centuries past to arrive at yet another long, elegant hallway.

"This is the residence," Eliot explained. "Each of you has been assigned a room. Inside, you will find a go-bag with clothing, toiletries, and other essentials. Dinner will be served at six o'clock, so you have a couple of hours to clean up and rest. Should you choose, you have free rein of the house and grounds. Feel free to look around. Locked doors are restricted, and we ask you respect our privacy. I'm sure you understand."

His smile as he spoke those last words failed to meet his eyes, and I knew "privacy" was the man's polite way of saying whatever was kept behind those doors was classified and intruders would not be looked upon kindly.

The others entered their rooms, as Eliot showed me to mine last then vanished down the hallway. There was, indeed, a duffel on the large bed in the center of the room. I took a moment to rifle through the clothing and remove the toiletries. Each item, no matter how small, was of German manufacture and carried well-worn tags or maker's marks. The diligence of the British was remarkable.

Satisfied, I tossed the bag aside and peeled off the clothes I'd worn since leaving the States. Outside the days of hand-to-hand combat training at Camp X, I couldn't remember a bath so refreshing as it felt that afternoon. The irony of water reviving my spirit after days of travel across an ocean of the darned stuff wasn't lost on me as I toweled off. I chuckled to myself as I dressed in one of my new outfits: a faded sky-blue shirt and gray trousers.

Days of being cramped on a plane had stolen any desire to remain indoors, so I wandered downstairs, pausing briefly to examine each portrait or vase or other work of art in this extraordinary home. It almost felt like our plan had not simply transported us across the globe, but back in time as well. I'd always loved anything with historical significance, so the simple descent down the staircase whose onlookers' eyes had witnessed the shaping of this land thrilled my mind in ways I hadn't felt since ...

Since Will and I strolled the streets of Boston. A smile tugged at my lips at the memory.

Will had been like a child visiting a zoo for the first time, enthralled at the size of a lion's head and thrilled to pet a friendly goat. Each building we passed, each story I relayed, filled his eyes with a delight I craved seeing every day of our lives. That was the day I knew I loved him. It hadn't made any sense at the time. We were men, after all, and men simply didn't love each other—not in *that* way, not if they hoped to live respectably in society, or even as free men outside of an asylum or prison cell. No, our world was not kind to those like us.

And yet, Will was a gravitational pull I simply could not repel.

I may never understand how one person can infect and consume another's thoughts, their waking dreams, their sleeping mind. That's what Will had done to me. With that first glance in Harvard Yard, that first half-smile that was more of a smirk than a grin, Will Shaw had entangled himself within my soul in ways that could never be unwound. My heart thrilled at the thought.

"You must really like that painting." Will's voice nearly knocked me down the staircase.

"Shit, you scared the life out of me," I said, involuntarily grasping the banister for support. "Give a guy a little warning next time, okay?"

He chuckled, and his eyes danced with the unbridled merriment that made my skin tingle. He wore a gray woolen shirt that made the blue of his eyes glow brightly in the dim light of the stairs. His hair was still wet from his bath, and he smelled of the same citrusy soap I'd found in my room.

"Should I carry a little bell to ring? Oh, I know, we could get me a collar with one of those tiny balls that jingle, the kind you'd put around a cat's neck. Although, we might have trouble finding a collar to fit—"

"You're an ass, you know that, right?" I shoved his shoulder playfully.

He nodded. "Yep. Absolutely." Then he leaned in toward my ear and whispered, "And you love me for it."

My head whipped around, eyes scanning for anyone nearby who might've seen us whispering, or worse, overheard.

"Easy, soldier," he whispered again. "I checked. It's all clear. No Nazis—or anyone else, for that matter."

I shook my head. "Will, we have to be more careful. I know it feels different, being so far from home and all, but still—"

"Careful. Got it." He nodded, though his tone spoke of one who didn't care about "getting it" in that moment. A worry creeping into my mind was forestalled as he punched my arm and said, "Come on. Let's go check the grounds. After all that flying, I need a good walk."

With that, he bounded down the stairs like a preteen boy headed to steal dessert pies from the kitchen. I shook my head, unable to suppress a grin, and followed him down and out the back door of the manse.

Cool air, not quite crisp, greeted us as we stepped out onto the sprawling stone patio attached to the back of the mansion. Several tables and chairs huddled together, ringed by a neatly stacked stone wall.

There were no gardens or paths, no neatly trimmed hedges or lawns. The untouched grounds, with their rolling hills and stone-strewn grassy plains, were as wild and free as Scotland herself. A small grove of trees several hundred yards in the distance broke the beautiful monotony of the landscape.

Will was down the patio's steps and racing across the field before I'd a moment to savor the clean highland air. I shook my head and chuckled as I strode after him, like a parent chasing a child as he raced toward the ocean's edge for the first time.

He crested a hill and paused, scanning the horizon beyond. I arrived to stand by his side, our breathing still labored from our run. There were no other structures within sight, only a few animals grazing in the distance, and not a single human to be found. The breeze, a constant companion, caused the grassy field to glisten in the setting sun's light, and played mournful notes as it caressed time-worn boulders strewn about. Verdant mountains ranged in the distance, framing the world in hues of green and gold.

"God, that felt good. I think my muscles were about to rebel if they didn't get some exercise."

A twinge in my legs agreed with him.

"This place is amazing. Even the air tastes sweet, feels ... *fresher*. How is that possible?" He sucked in a deep breath and held it, throwing his arms out wide. "We're in Scotland!" he shouted into the wind. A wild laugh trailed after his call.

I was still staring into the distance when he started off again and I had to jog a few dozen yards to catch up. The glow of the sky faded as a canopy of ancient trees enveloped us in their shady embrace. The wind's song trilled as it navigated untold numbers of leaves and limbs. I reached up and placed a palm on the trunk of an aged oak whose girth was easily five times the width of my waist. I wasn't paying attention when Will's hands gripped my shoulders, spun me around so my back pressed against the massive tree, and his lips moved within a breath of my mouth.

"Will, we can't—"

He leaned in and stole my breath.

God, I loved this man.

We'd barely brushed shoulders as we casually passed on the plane. We hadn't kissed since leaving Boston. I'd wanted to hold him, to feel his skin against mine, to taste his breath and lips … but our path would never be an easy one. Our life would never be open and free. Our very existence was borne of shadows.

But in that moment, against that tree, within Scotland's embrace, I wanted to forget the world, forget the war, forget the eyes forever staring over our shoulders. I wanted to love this man and draw his passion into my soul.

And so I poured myself into that kiss.

He leaned forward and pressed his body against mine, pinning me against the tree. I felt his excitement grow in both the timpani of his heart and the throbbing below his belt. The warm wetness of his tongue teased my mouth, and I moaned at the ecstasy of his touch.

"Will, we need to stop," I breathed.

He kissed me harder.

"Will—"

He roughly kneaded the muscles of my chest, and I groaned as my hunger for him gnawed in my gut. This man … this beautiful man … he would be the death of me.

"Will, stop." I found the strength to push him back, my hands thrilled to feel the hard muscles of his arms as I held him away. "Someone could see us. We need to be more careful."

His eyes explored mine, as if searching for some mystical realm, then fell to my lips. "I know. I just ... I need you, Thomas. I need you so much." His whisper tugged at my soul.

"We'll find a way. I promise." I brushed his hair away from his forehead. "I love you, Will Shaw. We'll find a way. Just not out in the open like this, okay?"

Reluctantly, he nodded and stepped back.

I brushed my shirt, failing to smooth the wrinkles his aggression had embedded in its fabric. When I looked up, his gaze was still fixed on me.

"What?"

He reached up and cupped my cheek, as I so often did to him. "I love you, Thomas, more than anything in this world. I'm terrified of what we're walking into, but just being with you gives me hope. Is that weird?"

I held his gaze and thought. "Yeah, probably a little, but I get it. And you do the same for me. We're going into a world where we can't trust anyone. Hell, we can't even trust our team with who we really are. It's just you and me. We're it. We're all we can trust with everything we are. So, yeah, it's weird, but it also makes sense ... in a weird way."

He pressed his forehead to mine and held it there for a long moment before smirking. "You didn't have to call me weird three times. That was kind of rude."

I couldn't help the laugh. It just tumbled out. "You're so weird, Will, so fucking weird."

He shoved me back against the tree, then strode away.

"Come on, we'd better get back before anyone notices we've been gone so long."

I brushed myself off for a second time and shook my head as I watched him head out of the grove and toward the house. My heart filled at the sight of him.

How could I love anyone so much?

Chapter Ten

Will

D inner that night was a welcome respite from the sparse food we'd eaten along the ferry route. While wartime rationing limited the amount of meat on offer, the variety of vegetables spread across the table seated for twenty was impressive, especially since there were only nine of us dining that night: our four-member team, John Milton, and four others who wore civilian clothing but had the clean-cut hair and sharp jawline of British military or other operatives.

As we helped ourselves to the family-style delicacies, one of the strangers stepped forward and extended a hand to Thomas.

"Arthur Doyle," the rugged man, who looked more like a linebacker than a writer, said without a hint of humor.

A typical Thomas-like smirk played at one corner of his mouth. "Wilhelm Müller."

Doyle's brows raised, and the others in his group turned to eye Thomas. "A German? Here?"

Thomas shrugged and thickened his American accent. "I have to be somewhere, don't I?"

Doyle eyed him a moment, then turned away and loaded his plate with roasted potatoes. The others took that as a cue and resumed their quiet conversation at the other end of the long table. There were no further introductions, which I thought a bit odd, but was something for which I was grateful. They would only give us more dead poets, and we would return fake foreigners. There really was no point.

Dinner continued, with each group clustered at opposite ends of the table and Milton neutrally positioned by himself in the middle. Conversations were hushed, and the sound of utensils clanking against plates was louder than any voice. When the British team of whoever-they-were finally rose and bid us goodnight, Milton grabbed his plate and scooted toward us.

"That went well," he said before shoving another forkful of brussels sprouts into his mouth.

Egret actually laughed. "If you mean neither of us caused an international incident that threatened our alliance, sure. Beyond that, I believe silent détente is about as close as a description might get. They really don't like our German leader here." He patted Thomas on the shoulder and winked across at Sparrow and me. Thomas chuckled and shook his head, unable to speak due to the buttered roll he was chewing.

"Well, that's fine. Détente is a rare thing these days, don't you think?"

It seemed Milton was a peacemaker who would not be deterred. We let him have his moment and finished our meal in silence.

"Now that we are alone, we need to chat," he said, after washing his final bite down with a spot of tea. The shift in his tone from amiable host to steely operative made all four of our heads snap toward him. "Please refill your beverages and join me in the study. We will need privacy for this conversation."

I met Thomas's gaze, but he simply shrugged and rose to follow Milton, saucer and cup in hand.

The room we entered was as much a study as the mansion was a country cottage. Thousands of books, most bound in leather with faded titles embossed in gold or silver, filled shelves that rose to a ceiling twice my height. Several rolling ladders standing watch allowed readers access to the upper shelves. Richly appointed chairs surrounded tables adorned with decorative vases and crystal trinkets. A massive hearth stood empty on the far wall, and a part of me wished we'd visited this place in winter so I could feel its warmth.

"Please sit," Milton said as he settled into a chair by the hearth. As soon as the door clicked shut behind Egret, he began, his tone even more serious than it had been in the dining room. "The original plan was for you to remain here for two days so you could recover from your journey and receive operational training from our SOE man responsible for your target area. Unfortunately, events in theater have advanced your timeline. You leave tonight."

We were too professional by that point to gasp at the unexpected news, but I caught both Egret and Sparrow shifting uncomfortably in their seats.

"Over the past week, the Germans have successfully neutralized most SOE radio operators operating in Paris and the surrounding region. The elimination of our pianists has effectively blinded us to resistance efforts, and the PM has ordered all teams with communications capabilities to be inserted as quickly as possible."

He took a sip of his tea, then slowly returned his cup to its saucer.

"I understand you have your own mission, and that OSS leadership has decided not to share its details with us. As unfortunate ... never mind." The irritation that flashed across his face was quickly smoothed. "You will do what you must while in France, but Britain *needs* your help once again."

"Are there no other SOE teams to move into the area?" Thomas asked.

Milton's features tightened. "The Germans intercepted two landings this week. Three other teams were killed dropping into the countryside. In each instance, they were waiting for our people. We have teams midway through their training, but they are not ready, especially with the possibility of a new German intercept capability. I do not believe your government understands just how thin our ranks have become."

The room fell silent. In that interminable moment, I longed for the crackling of a fire, for anything that might've filled the void created by Milton's obvious despair.

Finally, Thomas leaned forward, his eyes intense with resolve. "What do you need us to do?"

Milton eyed him a moment, then a tight smile crept across his lips, and the tension around his eyes relaxed, if only a bit.

"Our last report from Paris was three days ago. We have heard nothing from the outlying towns in over a week. We fear the Germans are up to something, and we have no idea what that might be. We cannot order you to assist us, but His Majesty's government must know what the Germans are planning if we have any hope of countering it. Moreover, we need to learn how the Nazis are finding our radio operators so quickly."

"Does Washington know you are asking for our help?" Thomas asked.

"No," Milton shook his head. "This comes from one desperate spy to another."

Thomas thought a moment, then said, "Your fight is our fight, and so long as helping you doesn't compromise our mission, we'll do everything we can to help. You have my word."

Relief flooded Milton's face as he set his cup and saucer on a side table and stood, extending his hand to Thomas. Once their hands clasped, the Brit grabbed him with his other hand and pulled him into an embrace.

"Thank you, son. God keep you safe."

There was so much Milton wasn't telling us. I could feel it. There was no way the British government would ask for our aid without even advising the US government unless the wheels had truly fallen off the cart. This whole conversation felt unrehearsed, rushed even, as though, at the last moment of some lengthy act, the playwright had decided to add a scene.

It was only then, as emotion nearly overcame the stoic Brit, that I realized just how desperate the situation had become.

Chapter Eleven

Will

F ive walked onto a rugged airstrip that was little more than a patch of ground whose foliage had been scraped away to reveal bare dirt and sparse patches of gravel. The air was unseasonably crisp for a mid-June night, and the sky, which I'd expected to be clear and bright, remained blackened by a curtain of clouds so thick even the brightest stars shed no light. As we followed Milton across the aviator's yard, the silhouette of a plane resolved in the distance.

"Uh, Milton," I called above the howl of the night's bluster. "Didn't you retire the Lysander?"

He glanced back over his shoulder but didn't slow his stride. "Yes, from combat missions, but these have proved our best assets in reconnaissance and strategic deployment."

As we neared, I saw the pilot walking around the plane, working through whatever preflight sequence was standard for his tiny craft. I squinted, straining to see inside the glass bubble, and could only make out one seat behind the pilot.

"Where are we all going to sit?"

Milton stopped walking and turned to face us. "This will be a very tight thing, not just the seating but the whole insertion. These planes were never meant to carry four passengers. In fact, the most we've attempted is three plus the pilot. Should your team be successful, you will establish a new record."

Should we be successful? That sounds ominous.

By the pale faces staring back at him, I could tell the rest of our team shared my thoughts.

"Is there no other way into the country?" Thomas asked.

Milton shook his head. "Not that will get you into position quickly or with less risk. The German air force patrols the skies north of France, and their U-boats control the Channel and seas above Scotland."

"Fine. What can you tell us about the insertion itself?"

The pilot walked up as Milton began to speak, his hands resting on his hips, as though our last-minute briefing interfered with his schedule.

Milton ignored him. "The flight will be rough. With four of you in back, you will literally be on top of each other. The added weight will also slow your progress. Should you make it to your landing zone, the plane will touch down and you will have five minutes to scramble out before the pilot takes off again. If he lingers longer, the Germans will find and destroy him."

"Dear God," Sparrow whispered.

"If all goes well, you will be greeted by a host who will take you to a safe house. From there, you will make your way to wherever your mission requires."

"How will we identify our host?" Thomas asked.

"She'll be there to greet you at the landing site." Milton's grin was tight. "She goes by Anais."

"We need to go before we lose this cloud cover," the pilot grumbled.

"One last thing," Milton said, stepping to face Sparrow. "I know your training tells you to keep transmissions brief and move immediately. I suggest you prepare your messages in advance, write them down, then keep your radio on less than fifteen seconds."

"Fifteen? That's less than half—"

"I know. Work quickly. Until we know how the Germans are finding our people—"

"Okay. I get it," she said, her voice shaking with each word but her eyes hardening with determination.

Milton eyed each of us one last time, then clapped us on the shoulder. It seemed an oddly personal gesture for a man who kept his distance, but the sincerity of his gaze made me appreciate it all the more.

"Godspeed, my friends," he muttered, before striding down the runway toward his car.

Milton didn't tell us of the failures of previous Lysander missions, how nearly a quarter of all spies who flew from the isle to the mainland were captured or killed. He didn't speak of the anti-aircraft and night patrols the Nazis employed, or how troops on the ground of occupied France were ever vigilant, with eyes always cast toward the skies. He didn't frighten us with the odds of our journey's success, burdened with one more occupant than any sense, common or otherwise, allowed.

He didn't need to stoke our fears. They were a raging tempest inside each of our chests, and only the safety of the ground and a well-concealed countryside home would begin to ease them.

As the plane coughed, at first belching and stopping, then sputtering again before roaring to life, every terror I'd ever experienced, every childhood nightmare or horror-filled dream, became real and present in my mind. My only comfort was in feeling Thomas's chest pressed against my back, and his arms wrapped securely around my chest. I tried to ignore the weight of Egret shoving me backward, though it also offered a strange sense of comfort. Sparrow, the slightest of us, sat atop the birds in our nest. At first glance, I was jealous, then I saw how her knees and shins ground against the hard metal of the pilot's seat, and was thankful for my back-of-the-sardine-can position.

We'd flown nearly the whole length of the British isle before the plane began to descend. Two lights on the ground appeared, then two more. The outline of a small airfield came into view, and the pilot slammed us into the packed earth. Egret's body rocking into mine knocked the air from my lungs, and I'd barely begun to breathe again when the plane came to a halt.

"Quick refueling stop. You have a few minutes to stretch. Don't wander off," the pilot called above the dying engine, as if we knew where we were and had some inkling to take a midnight stroll.

Thomas had to shove me out, as Egret hauled me by my arm from the front. There was no way my flattened form would've made it out of the plane otherwise.

"Dear God, everything hurts," I said, stumbling as my feet touched the ground. I realized Thomas wasn't behind me and turned back to find him slowly climbing out of the plane, Egret keeping him from tumbling to the ground. He took a tentative step, then grabbed Egret's shoulder to brace himself before attempting another.

"Fuck me. How are we going to get out of that thing and escape with our host without falling apart?" Thomas asked, his first words of protest since our journey began.

Egret gripped his shoulder. "We'll do it together, alright? We'll make it work."

If I'd liked the man for his sharp wit before, I loved him for his fortitude in that moment. Manakin might've been an odd bird, but he clearly knew how to knit together a solid team.

Sparrow had walked some feet away and was staring into the distance. I stumbled to her side. "You okay?"

She continued staring over the cliffs I hadn't noticed. The pounding of waves against rock heaved hundreds of feet below.

"It's beautiful," she said, her voice small.

"What is?"

"This place. The cliffs. The sea. All of it." She breathed in deeply, as if to suck the whole of England into her lungs.

I drew in a breath of my own and savored the tang of ocean salt.

"You and Condor should be cautious."

The air whooshed out of me. "What?"

Her voice lowered. "You two need to be more careful. He may not appear so, but Egret is strong-minded. He sees the world his way; I learned this in our training together. Surely, you saw it. I don't know how well he would take the notion of two ... *birds* ... sharing a nest."

My mind raced, and a wave of dizziness and scorching heat flooded through me. I nearly staggered back. If I hadn't been so astonished, her use of our code names might've brought a laugh to my lips. But ...

I tried to speak, but my mouth refused to open ... or close, I wasn't sure which.

She turned to looked into my eyes. "I see how you love each other. Your eyes declare it each time they meet. It is perhaps the most beautiful thing I've witnessed on our journey, truly, but it is also the most fragile of all our possessions. If I see it, others will too. I can't imagine how the Germans would react ... Actually, we *know* what they would do. Guard it better, please, for all our sakes."

She placed a hand on my cheek, as any mother might, then stepped away from the cliff and returned to the plane.

I don't remember sitting or tucking my knees to my chest. I don't even remember how I got back to the plane or safely wedged into position between Egret and Thomas. We were high above the waters of the Channel before I returned to myself and began worrying about our landing once again.

———◦○◦———

As we entered southern France, a German anti-aircraft position spotted us. Flares soared into the skies, and powerful guns fired into the air. The pilot took the plane higher, turned it sideways, right then left, slamming us against the sides of the plane and into each other like baggage tossed haphazardly in bins.

By the time we approached the outskirts of Paris, I'd lost all feeling in my legs. My torso was not so forgiving, and I felt every twitch and turn deep inside my chest. Egret's bulky frame squashed me flatter with each shift, and I was sure my manhood might never recover from the persistent pinch against the cushion-less seat. I didn't even want to think about the surging pain in my balls every time the plane lurched and Egret's bony ass slammed into them. I longed for the numbness of my legs to travel northward.

Thomas never complained. His arms never left my sides.

On occasion, his fingers would squeeze into my stomach or sides, and I knew he was offering reassurance and strength. More than a few times, his lips risked discovery as they found my exposed neck.

Sparrow's words echoed in my mind, sending a chill across my skin, but in those simple moments, those precious, tender glimpses of passion and compassion, I found the strength to believe we would survive.

Then the pilot thrust the plane's nose downward and Sparrow flattened between the pilot's seat and the three of us as we slammed into her back.

"Landing," the pilot called back, the only word he'd spoken during our four-hour flight.

Thomas's hands squeezed into me, and I felt the muscles of his arms bunch as they tightened around me. His breath tickled my ear as he whispered, "As soon as Egret is up, I'm going to shove you upward. We need to move fast. Are you ready?"

I nodded, leaning my head back so it touched his forehead. He squeezed again.

One tiny light flickered to life below us. It looked like the flicker of a candle, but I knew was likely a torch of some kind. A second light appeared a moment later, some distance away.

"So short," I thought I heard Egret say over the howl of the engine. As the ground came fully into view, I understood what he meant. The strip on which we were to land looked more like a home's driveway than a place for a plane to touch down. My stomach found its way into my throat.

The plane wobbled, its wings rising and dipping as the pilot fought for control. We slowed to an interminable crawl I was sure would send us to a fiery death, yet the bird continued her flight.

The ground was mere feet away. I could taste the grassy air.

The wheel slammed into the ground, and the plane bounced, then slammed down again. We hurtled toward a thick grove of trees, barely slowing.

The pilot was pulling at a stick, leaning one way, then the other. The plane turned and slowed, and we all breathed as it came to a halt.

"Out, now," the pilot yelled.

The light at one end of the field winked out, and a woman's form raced toward us.

Sparrow scrambled down the side of the plane, then Egret. I felt Thomas's hands against my back, and before I could think, my body was hurtling upward. I braced myself, then took Egret's outstretched hand and scampered to the ground. As Egret helped Thomas, the woman ran by us, her breathing labored.

"Get to my car now. The Germans are coming!" her thickly accented voice called in an urgent half-whisper, half-yell.

We ran after her. She doused the second torch.

The engine of the Lysander sputtered. The pilot cranked again. Still, it didn't catch. On the third attempt, the rotor spun, and the engine groaned awake.

In the distance, another engine snarled, smaller yet angrier than that of the plane.

We raced through the trees after the woman to find a waiting car. She leapt inside and flashed her lights once, then extinguished them.

I fell into the back seat and slammed the door shut as a search light panned the field behind us.

Shots rang out. Then a second gun joined the first. Then a third.

The plane lifted off. I held my breath.

The gunfire came faster, the staccato clang of metal on metal filling our ears as the bullets found their target. Then a deafening explosion caused us all to start, and a fireball lit the black night like a sun painting the sky.

Still the woman drove, her lights doused, until the echo of the guns and the light of the blaze faded into the distance.

Chapter Twelve

Vogt

SS-Sturmbannführer Jÿrgen Vogt's boots clicked against the hard pavement as he strode across Prinz-Albrecht-Strasse. He would normally stop cars with a stiff palm to allow his crossing, but at half past midnight, the only cars intruding on his path bore officials of the Reich. No one, not even a member of the state's vaunted secret police, delayed men on missions for the Führer.

Globed lights held aloft on artistic wrought-iron poles cast a dim yellow glow at oddly spaced intervals on the street and sidewalk. No light touched the imposing five-story stone building that housed the leadership of the SS.

Despite wearing the uniform of a mid-level officer of the organization, Vogt presented his identification to one of several guards standing watch at the base of the steps leading into the building. As one man scrutinized his papers, two others eyed him with interest, searching for any hint of spy or saboteur.

Once inside, Vogt climbed the stairs to stop before another set of guards at the entrance to the third floor, where the offices of the senior-most officers were housed. The guard holding his papers peered up, only the tops of his eyes visible above the identification card.

"Who are you seeing?"

Vogt stiffened. "That is none of your concern. Verify my papers and let me pass."

The guard's eyes narrowed, and one of his partners stepped to Vogt's side, a hand rising to rest on the rifle slung over his shoulder.

"Who. Are. You. Seeing?" the man asked again, this time punctuating each word like a drummer's taps.

Vogt hesitated, his eyes quickly darting to the man beside him, then back to the guard who held his papers. There was a time for strength, a time for bravery, and then there was a time to know one's limits. This was such a time.

"SS-Oberführer Fuchs," Voght answered with the name of the senior colonel who'd summoned him to a late-hour meeting.

A third guard sitting behind a small desk scanned papers on a clipboard, then nodded to the ID checker.

"Second office on the right." The guards pointed behind the desk as he handed back Vogt's papers. "Knock and wait before you enter. The oberführer does not like surprises."

Vogt offered a crisp nod and strode past the men. After two raps and five minutes of staring at the bare wooden door, a gruff voice finally barked, "Enter."

The first thing Vogt noticed was how heavy the door was. He actually had to muscle it open. As he stepped inside, he found the modestly sized office bereft of furniture, save for two chairs positioned before a wooden desk and a tall metal filing cabinet in the corner behind it. The only light in the windowless box came from a banker's-style desk lamp that currently illuminated a stack of folders thicker than the width of his palm. The severe, pale face of a man who'd likely never seen the sun peered up, his angular jaw and sharp nose adding ferocity to his raptor's gaze.

"Sit," the man said, pointing to one of the chairs with his pen. He scribbled a few notes on papers in the open file before him, then slammed the folder shut and tossed it into a wire basket as though it had offended him somehow. He eyed Vogt, steepling his fingers, then looked down to flip through the folders until he found the one he sought.

"Operation *Gorgulho*?" Fuchs asked bluntly.

Vogt couldn't hide his surprise. He'd understood the operation code-named Weevil to be classified at the highest levels, restricted to Hitler and only a few others, all of whom were well above this man's pay grade. How had he—?

Is this a test?

The SS was without parallel in enforcing loyalty and ferreting out those who might harbor the slightest dissent, but why would *he* be tested? And why now? He'd been nothing but loyal. He'd been loyal to the point of fanaticism—which didn't preclude him from suspicion. The only reason the SS boasted of a spy-proof headquarters was their perpetual vigilance where moles were concerned.

Still ...

"You may speak freely. I know all about your discovery on the farm, that laboratory you were instructed to oversee. Such a facility would be a ripe target for our enemies. Quite ingenious, the ideas you floated to hide the place."

Dear God, the man knows everything.

Vogt's mouth opened, but words failed him. He wasn't often rendered speechless, but Fuchs had managed the impossible twice this night, without even rising from his chair. "Sir—"

"Take a breath, Jÿrgen." The casual use of his first name sent a thrill of terror through Vogt's chest. "The Führer is pleased with your work with the weevils." Fuchs chuckled, his chair screaming in protest as he leaned back. "I spoke with him this morning. He would like to meet you soon."

Terror shifted to patriotic fervor at the mention of the Führer.

He knows who I am ... and he wants to meet me!

Vogt thought his heart might beat out of his chest. He leaned forward, placing a hand on the oberführer's desk. Fuchs's brow twitched, and Vogt snatched it back.

"So," Fuchs continued. "How goes the research?"

Back to the questions. How should I answer? Should I answer?

Fuchs rose from his seat, unfurling a man nearly six-and-a-half-feet tall with a broad chest and trim waist. Vogt's eyes widened slightly as he stared up at the giant.

"Jÿrgen, when we leave my office, we will walk to the end of this hall, where SS-Brigadeführer Heinrich Schulz will replace your shoulder boards with those of an obersturmbannführer. You are being promoted for your work. That is how pleased Hitler is—how pleased we all are—with you."

Vogt leapt from his chair and snapped to attention, extending his arm in a crisp salute. "Heil Hitler!"

"Yes, yes. Heil Hitler," Fuchs said with a smug grin, raising a lazy palm. "But we cannot leave this office for you to receive your new rank until I have a full report on *Gorgulho*. Sit down and start talking."

Both men sat, and Vogt finally relented.

"We have three scientists working around the clock. It has only been one week since we left the farm, and it took two days to establish and equip the lab, so there has been little time for progress. Their first few attempts to weaponize the substance went ... poorly, but the research goes well. They advance with each new attempt."

"Stop," Fuchs ordered. "Define poorly."

Vogt cleared his throat. "All test subjects passed quite ... violently, which was expected. However, the substance should have cleared more quickly than on the farm. It did not. In fact, it remained as lethal on the second day as on the first, killing two of our workers assigned to reset the test chamber."

Fuchs stared past Vogt and strummed his fingers against his desk.

"Sir, this is a very volatile substance. I want to bring it to bear on our enemies as much as anyone, but until we can ensure our troops—"

"I am familiar with the risks." Fuchs thought a moment, then muttered so low Vogt thought he might not have meant to speak aloud, "Hitler shares your fondness for safety."

"Sir?

"Nothing." Fuchs waved a hand. "Continue. What is the problem?"

"Uh, sir, I am no scientist. I am there to ensure the work of the experts. We would need to speak with—"

"When will we have a solution?" Fuchs's lips tightened as he spoke, and an uncomfortable flush of color entered his cheeks.

"I ... uh ... Sir, this will take some time."

"Dammit, Vogt!" the senior man bellowed with sudden furor, his hand slapping loudly against the desktop. "The Russian front is not ... We *need* this solution. Now."

Vogt knew better than to trust the German newspapers, but all internal reports he had seen stated German forces were winning the Russian war, pushing the communists toward their capital, which should fall any day. Russia was not his arena, but he wasn't so far removed as to receive false reports. Was he?

"I understand, sir. I will—"

"You will do *nothing*!" Fuchs barked, standing to round his desk and tower over his guest. "I need someone who understands what the hell he is working on, someone who can give us a weapon tomorrow, not months from now when our fucking troops are frozen to death."

Fuchs's neck was bulging against his collar, and the light flush in his cheeks was now a four-alarm fire. "This is what you will do, Sturmbannführer. You will accept your promotion tonight with gratitude, shaking hands and smiling like the good soldier you are. Tomorrow, you will take a train into France where you will assume temporary command of our assimilation efforts outside of Paris."

"But sir—"

"The resistance has proven ... challenging. Our own men are disorganized and unreliable. You will relieve those in command who are ineffective and restore order within our ranks. You are a blunt instrument, Vogt. I have every confidence you will find a way to stop the vandals from harassing our efforts to pacify the country. Show them we are liberators, even if you must use your fist to do so." Fuchs waited for a response that didn't come, so he decided to offer a small olive branch. "You are only a temporary solution. Your orders are to return in six weeks and resume your work. With luck, our scientists will have a solution, and your focus can shift to plans for use of this new weapon."

Vogt slumped back. Heat flared in his chest. His head spun.

How had the conversation turned from a celebration of his success with the operation to virtual banishment from both his work and the fatherland? Sure, someone had to quell rebellion within German-freed Europe, but he had discovered a vital weapon that could end this war and ensure Nazi dominance for generations. The Russians might even capitulate under the threat of such a blight. Why would he be sent far from the Führer's favor now?

Fuchs's glare had only grown more intense the longer he sat and thought. There was no more time. There was only one choice.

"I will free all of France if that is my Führer's command. Thank you for the honor, Oberführer Fuchs."

Fuchs stared a moment longer, his eyes riveted into Vogt's skull, until, at last, he nodded once and stepped back. "Good. Now, let's go see to your promotion."

Chapter Thirteen

Thomas

The drive from the landing site might have been more harrowing than the plane flight over the Channel. With no lights, no moon, and only the barest hint of a road before us, our driver barreled forward as though she was traversing a well-lit racing track, occasionally veering off the graveled strip to jar our teeth and aching heads. Despite being packed into the back of the car almost as tight as we'd been on the plane, we turned to look behind almost as much as we faced forward. I dreaded the sight of headlights or the sound of an irate German engine.

Yet none came.

Still, no one spoke. Fear saturated the air within the car.

Will rolled down a window, relieving some of the sweltering heat. Our terror remained.

The car turned only twice, taking long stretches of unbending paths. Darkened fields I knew to be farms surrounded us. My bearings were still scrambled from our desperate escape, but I could tell we were not headed toward any town. The only buildings we passed were the rare cottages or farmhouses dotting the landscape.

The world around us slept.

The car left the comfort of the gravel road, bouncing across uneven land for a minute or two, before pulling to a stop in front of a lonely barn at the desolate end of a barren pasture. With the car still running, the woman turned the lights on, hopped out, and raced to open the barn doors, then returned and drove to park inside. Once the engine quieted, she stepped out to secure the doors behind us.

None of us moved.

"You may come out now," the woman said through the open car window. "I believe we are safe."

We climbed out, each stretching as we did so. For the first time, I got a good look at the woman's face. It was streaked with tears, her eyes rimmed red.

"I am Anais," she said.

"Wilhelm," I said, then pointed to the others in turn. "Anny, Heinz, and Tobias."

The woman eyed each of us, then wiped her eyes and nodded once. "Come."

She led us to the back of the barn where a small table was surrounded by simple chairs. As Anais lit an oil lamp and set it on the table, she motioned to a crate near the far wall. "There is wine over there. I will bring you food in the morning. We should not risk leaving the barn tonight."

"Thank you, Anais. Wine will be welcome," I said.

Anais retrieved two bottles, while Egret returned to the car and killed the lights.

"I am sorry, but there are no glasses here. We will have to drink from the bottle."

Egret chuckled, the first sign of mirth since our departure from British land. "I think we'll be just fine with the bottles, ma'am."

Anais nodded, but a smile failed to reach her lips.

"You knew him, didn't you? The pilot?" Will asked, causing everyone to pause.

Anais met his gaze, and a tear returned and fell down one cheek. She nodded and choked out, "Yes, very well."

We sat and drank in silence for a time. The sound of the wind howling outside and the rattling of the shutters in the loft above were our companions.

Finally, Sparrow spoke. "We lost our radio when ... our radio is gone."

"We have nothing but what we're wearing," Egret said.

Anais awoke from her daze. "I can help with clothing and such, but the radio is a problem."

Thomas leaned forward. "Is there an operator within the resistance who could pass on a message for us?"

Her eyes were hollow as she shook her head. "The Germans have destroyed so much ... there is no one I know now. I am sorry."

"It's alright, Anais. We'll figure it out. Thank you for helping us tonight."

"I will leave you to rest now. There are pallets with blankets upstairs. You should not burn the lamp more than is necessary."

"Where will you go?" Will asked as she rose.

"My home is not far. I will walk across the fields. The Germans will not bother a lone woman walking her own land." Her declaration sounded more like hope than a statement of fact.

"Should one of us—"

"No." Anais cut Will off. "Two would draw more attention. I will be fine, but thank you. *France* thanks you for the risks you take."

A moment later, we found ourselves staring at two empty bottles and the dim glow of a dying flame, unable to move from the table and unwilling to give voice to our fears.

———◇———

Sleep proved impossible, as I lay on a pallet whose stuffing ground more knots into muscles than it eased. Every creak of the barn's aged wood had me bolting upright, wondering if Nazi agents had discovered our hideout. On the few occasions when my eyes surrendered and lids closed, images of the plane limping into the air then bursting into flames haunted my dreams.

An hour before the sun rose, I accepted that sleep was an unwilling partner. I stood and stretched my aching back. The others didn't stir. Will mumbled, fighting some demon of his subconscious mind as he kicked and thrashed against a blanket now fully twined about his legs. My first instinct was to go to him, to unravel his covers and try to calm his sleep, but one glance at Egret and Sparrow stilled that inclination.

One day, I thought, as I watched Will's eyes twitch beneath his lids. His lips pursed, then smoothed. My heart swelled at the sight of him.

I descended the ladder as quietly as possible, then carefully opened the door a crack to check the surrounding fields. When Anais had left the night before, the hinges remained soundless. Unfortunately, I didn't have her touch and the darn things cried out in pain, a squeal loud enough to wake the dead.

"*Wilhelm, sind Sie das?*" Egret's whisper bounced off the barn's wooden walls. *Wilhelm, is that you?*

"Yes. Sorry. I didn't mean to wake you. Go back to sleep."

Egret's face appeared as he looked down the ladder's length at me. "I'd rather not dream again. I'm coming down."

"See anything?" he asked as he descended.

"No. Just empty fields as far as I can see."

He sat at the table and rubbed his eyes. "That's good."

"The others still asleep?"

"Yeah, they're knocked out. I'm surprised Sparrow didn't stir, but Emu could probably sleep through anything."

I grunted agreement. If he only knew.

"We have no radio, no explosives, no supplies of any kind. Our only contact is Anais. What are we going to do?"

I thought a moment. "Anais may prove more helpful than we think. I need to talk with her, find out how connected she is to the resistance. She may also have access to more supplies." I held up my ring with the garrote button. "We have a few gadgets." Each of us had our suicide pill. While Will's and mine were in rings, Sparrow's hid in a pendant around her neck and Egret's was in the back of his watch. "But weapons, explosives, and a radio are a problem. London won't even know we're alive, especially after we lost our plane."

"Yeah, I was thinking that too. They might think we died in the crash."

"We need supplies."

"Supplies? How would they even buy them?" Egret asked.

"We may have to steal what we need; although the SOE did manage to sneak a fair amount of money in my shoes." I reached down and removed my right shoe, then pried the heel off with an old knife Anais had left on the table.

"Well, shit," he said, as I removed folded notes. "You have expensive feet."

I grinned, and held up ten one-hundred-franc notes. "Not the same as greenbacks, but they'll help. The SOE boys said a franc is worth about two cents to us."

"So, we've got twenty bucks?"

"Give or take. Who knows what it's really worth with the Germans in charge?"

He nodded thoughtfully. "That might get us a handgun."

"Maybe. Let's see what we can scrounge up before spending anything first. This is all we've got."

"Nothing in your other shoe? Mom didn't send you off with baked goods in your boot?"

I chuckled at his lopsided grin. "The other shoe is just a shoe. I asked the same thing, but the boys wanted me to be able to hand the Germans a legitimate heel if I ever got caught. They called it a last attempt at subterfuge."

"Sounds like bullshit. I'd rather have the cash."

I chuckled again. "You might be right."

"What's for breakfast?" Will's voice rasped from the top of the ladder. Egret and I glanced up to find his eyes puffy and his hair disheveled. "I heard eggs and bacon were on order, but the chef didn't show. Bastard."

Egret choked back a laugh. "Get down here, asshole. Condor is a rich man, did he tell you that?"

Will's eyes bugged wide, then he scampered down the ladder like a monkey on a rope.

I held up my shoe and the cash, and relief flooded his face. He must've thought Egret had learned about my real family.

"Oh, right, *spy* money," Will said as he sat. "I would give anything for some spy coffee."

"Is there coffee down there?" Sparrow's lilting whisper drifted down.

Will called up, "Yeah. Omelets too. They're amazing."

Sparrow's face poked over the ladder as her eyes darted, searching for the aforementioned food. For a brief moment, she actually resembled a hungry bird, beak snapping from side to side in search of a worm.

"Fucker," she said, glaring at Egret.

"Whoa." He held up one palm and pointed at Will with the other. "That was bedhead over there. Don't blame me for the poor service in this diner."

The first slivers of sunlight shone around the edges of the door as Sparrow filled the last seat at the table. After a moment of silence, she looked up. "What do we do now?"

All eyes turned toward me.

"Our first priority is still discovering what the Nazis are up to. Egret and I will head into town and check it out, while you two search for supplies. Emu ... I mean, *Tobias* ... your primary goal has to be finding a connection to the resistance. Just be careful. We're new in town, so we're automatically suspicious. Plus, we know the Germans have moles on the inside. Don't drop cover, even for a moment."

Will nodded. "Got it."

"And me?" Sparrow asked.

"Same as Tobias. Locate supplies and a connection to the underground, but don't act on anything. We're just doing reconnaissance at this point."

The door creaked open, and I nearly knocked the table over jumping up.

"Sorry," Anais said, as she entered and closed the door behind her. "I brought you some bread and cheese, and a small thermos of coffee. It's all I could carry across the field."

"This is great. Thank you, Anais," I said, helping her with the woven sack in her arms.

"It is light outside. I cannot stay here long. There is clothing in the wooden chests upstairs. Take what you need." She reached into a pocket and unfolded a crudely drawn map and began pointing. "We are here. The town is there, along the Grand Morin river. It will take you a half-hour, maybe more, if you walk a straight line through these fields. If you walk along the road, expect to be stopped and searched. Your contact is Claude Petit. He owns a small bakery on the corner of Rue de la Halle and Place du Marché. When you speak with him, order *le kouign amann*. He will ask what you would like to drink with your pastry. Request a *café noisette*."

Her hands shook as she refolded the map and stuffed it into her pocket.

"We can't—?"

"*Non*! You must not be seen with maps. Did they not teach you anything?" she muttered to herself as she turned and grasped the door handle. "Trust *no one*. Many Germans have arrived in the last weeks. They are everywhere."

I wanted to ask what she thought brought so many to this small village, but she'd darted back into the field before I could speak.

Chapter Fourteen

Will

Anais had been right. The walk from the barn to the edge of town took roughly thirty minutes. Thankfully, it hadn't rained recently, so the fields were firm and dry. Sparrow reached up and straightened my tie then smoothed my lapel.

"You're a handsome man, Tobias."

"You're not so bad yourself, dear wife-to-be."

She grinned and threaded her arm through mine. "How did we meet?"

"What?"

"We practiced our covers the whole walk here, but never talked about how we met. Anyone could ask that."

We'd already passed the first row of houses marking the outskirts of the village. Rue Deshuiliers lay just ahead, which meant we were only a couple of blocks from our destination. I stood frozen, unable to think of a reasonable explanation for a young German to fall in love with a French girl almost the moment he arrived in France.

She patted my arm. "You arrived in Paris six months ago, just before the new year. We met on the street under the lights of celebration."

"Did they celebrate the new year in occupied Paris?"

"Oh, right. How terrible." Her face fell. "If you were a German national, you would have stayed in a proper hotel, which meant there would have been some sort of celebration, at least by the Germans. What if I was working in that hotel?"

"Alright." I turned that scene over in my mind. "That's it. It took some time to convince you I was a good German, but you fell in love with my smile."

Her grin returned. "That could happen."

Heat flooded my cheeks, and her grin exploded into barely controlled laughter.

"What?""Did you forget I know ... about Wilhelm?" She dragged out Thomas's cover name like she was pulling taffy. "I was only teasing. Though if you were, how should I say this ... aimed in my direction—"

"Anny!" I hissed.

"You have a nice smile. That's all I meant." Her giggle grew. "Husband-to-be."

"Jesus. I have to be on this trip with him, now you? This is no way to work."

Her giggle vibrated up my arm as she gripped me tighter.

We strolled the rest of the way in silence, partly to mask my lack of French-speaking skills, but mostly because I didn't trust my foot to stay out of my mouth.

As we strolled down Place de Marché, the clear air of the farms was replaced by a murky smell that reminded me of the rancid aftertaste from nearly spoiled milk. It wasn't quite disgusting, but it was getting there.

"The Grand Morin must be close. I'd know a river's stank anywhere."

"River's stank?" She grinned up at me, batting her eyes dotingly for a passing couple.

"*Oui*, stank. *Le stank*, if you prefer—or is that *la stank*? Perhaps *un petit poo-poo*?"

Her melodic laugh sang off the ancient walls of the town, drawing the eyes and a few smiles from locals walking nearby.

"Look." She pointed to a long building on the corner where two streets met. The center doors were crowned by a faded yellow sign that read, *Boulangerie Petit.*

Two soldiers passed on the opposite side. One of the men made eye contact, so I smiled and casually called in German, "*Hallo. Ein schöner Tag, nicht wahr?*"

Hello, beautiful day, isn't it?

The man's face beamed at being greeting in his native tongue. I was suddenly struck at his youthful face. He couldn't have been older than twenty, and had likely never traveled so far from home. He might've been on the wrong side of the war, but he was still just a boy. What had the world come to?

"*Hallo,*" he called back, smiling broadly.

Sparrow stepped ahead, reaching back to pull me by the hand. "*Une boulangerie. Je voudrais quelque chose de sucré.*"

A bakery. I would love something sweet.

I shrugged back at the soldier and grinned. "*Ich habe meine Befehle. Schönen Tag noch.*"

I have my orders. Have a good day.

He waved and walked on.

Sparrow tugged me by the hand the rest of the way into the shop. The tables we passed outside were filled with guests, but there were only two other people sitting alone at tables at opposite ends of the bakery. A merry bell tinkled with the opening of the door, and an impossibly short, rotund man in a white smock peered above the counter. His balding pate and eyes were all that were visible until he climbed onto a box to elevate himself nearly to my shoulders.

"*Bienvenue, bienvenue. Venez voir. Qu'est-ce qui plairait à la dame?*"

Welcome, welcome. Come, have a look. What would the lady like?

She made a show of pursuing the pastries held within a large glass case, then paused, her face scrunching into a mask of disappointment.

"*Madame?*" the baker asked. "*Rien n'attire votre attention?*"

Is there nothing that catches your eye?

She stepped away from the case and lowered her voice. "*J'avais vraiment envie de le kouign amann.*"

I really had my heart set on le kouign amann.

The skin around the man's eyes twitched, but to his credit, his broad smile didn't falter. "*Je crains de ne pas faire cette pâtisserie particulière.*"

I'm afraid I do not make that particular pastry.

Sparrow leaned down. "*Un bon ami nous a dit que c'était le cas.*"

A good friend told us you do.

He eyed her a moment, then glanced back to where I stood, then asked in a level tone, "*Voulez-vous boire quelque chose avec votre pâtisserie?*"

Would you like anything to drink with your pastry?

"*Café noisette, s'il vous plaît.*"

The man's eyes darted toward where his other patrons sat. Neither looked up from whatever they were reading.

"*Il faut que je sorte certaines choses du four. Suivez-moi et goûtez-les pendant qu'ils sont chauds.*"

I need to pull some things out of the oven. Follow me and have a taste while they are hot.

Chapter Fifteen

Thomas

E gret and I tromped across the fields. He'd changed into farmer's overalls and a dingy blue cap, while I wore the stifling formality of a threadbare coat and tie, each of some indeterminably drab color that reminded me of the business end of a baby's poop tract.

"Looking dapper there, Herr Müller," Egret smirked, as I stared jealously at his loose-fitting, collarless shirt. It wasn't exactly hot, but the summer sun wormed its way into my skin as we trudged across the uneven land.

"*Danke*, asshole."

He laughed.

A few strides later, I shifted into mission tone. "When we get within sight of the edge of town, we'll need to split up. You go around the eastern side of town, see what's coming in and out from that direction. I'll go as far west as I can. Look for checkpoints or anything out of place. Like Anais said, we shouldn't be seen together at any point."

"Right. I can't exactly grab your arm and play the doting couple like Sparrow and Emu."

I nearly stumbled. The amused quirk to his lips told me he was being his usual unabashed self, but it still threw me for a moment.

"Might want to watch where you're walking, boss. That ground'll reach up and grab you."

I chuckled along with him, but couldn't stop my mind from spinning about how close to the mark he'd hit, if unwittingly.

The first buildings appeared in the distance, and I could just make out a small line of German military vehicles stopped on the road ahead.

Egret squinted and covered his brow with a hand. "Looks like a supply convoy. Two leads, one trail, one troop truck, four box vans. And … there's a motorcycle."

"Time to split up. The cycle will be their chase man. Take a wide arc to avoid that group." I scanned the area, noting several soldiers gathered around one man. From that distance, I couldn't make out any of their uniforms, beyond the shades of midnight denoting a few SS officers mixed in with regulars. Four guards had fanned out around the convoy, sunlight glinting off their rifles as they turned one way, then another. "I have a bad feeling about this."

"Could just be routine supplies this close to Paris, but I doubt it. Somebody's taking security a little too seriously for those vans to be hauling sauerkraut or beer."

I grunted in agreement. "Wide berth. Let's move." As we stepped apart, I turned back and whispered, "*Denken Sie daran, dass Sie erst ab diesem Punkt Deutsch sprechen.*"

Remember, German only from this point.

He nodded once, then headed east. I watched him stop when he was a few hundred yards away and inspect something on the ground.

Playing the farmer. Good man, I thought.

The Germans remained standing in the middle of the road, their vehicles unmoving, so I turned and made my way toward the Paris-facing side of Crécy.

Chapter Sixteen

Will

T he smell of freshly baked pastries had tickled my nose when we entered the building. Walking through the kitchen, it slammed into my senses like a tidal wave—a very pleasant, sugary wall of water.

"Mein Gott, können wir diesen Ort nie verlassen?"

My God, can we never leave this place?

I devoured the scent with an inhale worthy of a drowning man whose head finally rose above the swells.

"Tobias!" Sparrow chided while swatting my arm playfully. Her infectious smile had the baker chuckling as we passed a set of ancient ovens I imagined feeding the masses in the Middle Ages.

We entered a storeroom lined with shelves laden with sacks of flour and other staples. Petit closed the door behind us, then lowered a bar to seal the entry.

"You may speak English now," he said through a French accent almost as thick as the cakes we'd seen in his case. "Your accent is ... a nice try. That is how you Americans say it, no?"

I blinked. I'd thought my accent was solid.

"It cannot be helped. Come, we only have moments before I am missed." He squeezed around us, pressing my back uncomfortably against the wooded shelving, then led us to the far end. "Move those, please."

I reached down and moved the dozen sacks of flour stacked on a low shelf. Once clear, Petit shoved the shelf out of the way, then pulled one of a dozen rusty rings, most of which held spoons, spatulas, or other cooking implements. The wall groaned, and the outline of a door appeared where only dust had settled a moment before.

"Help me pull this, would you?" Petit said, his face reddened with strain.

Once the door was opened wide enough to pass through, Petit pulled a chain to illuminate a narrow staircase that led into a cellar. Again, shelving lined the walls of this room barely larger than a coat closet, but there were no sacks of flour. Rifles and pistols stared back at us. There were no explosives, no grenades, not even one of the Resistance's signature cocktails with their telltale kerchief sticking out of the bottle. My heart sank as I scanned the mostly bare room.

"My instructions are to give you whatever assistance you require. Unfortunately, the Nazis have become quite effective at taking out our people. Only a few weapons remain." He motioned to the shelf with the pistols. "You must expect to be stopped. Anything standing out will go poorly for you."

Sparrow stepped past Petit and lifted a pair of palm-sized binoculars likely used in the last war. I nodded, and she stuffed them into her pocketbook. I took a couple of knives, but left the guns.

"As much as I'd like to take the pistols, you're right about concealment. If our mission changes, we may be back for those."

Petit nodded.

We turned to leave, but the baker's chubby fingers closed around my forearm. "You need money, yes?"

I nodded thoughtfully. "We have a small amount, but yes. That would be helpful."

He struggled to his knees and dragged a weathered box from beneath the bottom shelf, reached in, and handed Sparrow a bundle of hundred-franc notes. "There is ten thousand."

Sparrow's eyes widened as she shuffled through the bills. "Where—?"

"Our dead have no need of money. We do our best to collect what we can before the Nazis find it." His eyes struggled to meet hers before he slid the box back into place and braced himself against the shelf to stand. "I must go back. If soldiers enter and I am not present—"

"Thank you, Monsieur Petit," Sparrow said as she divided the cash between us and began hiding small sums in shoes, pockets, and, finally, her blouse.

On our way back through the kitchen, Petit stopped at a metal rack that held a dozen shelves filled with pastries. He snatched two, tore off part of each, and handed the rest to us.

"It looks like you have been eating them now. Please, take a bite so you are chewing when we enter the café."

"*Monsieur, c'est le paradis,*" Sparrow said through a mouthful as we reentered the bakery proper. Her eyes rolled back as she moaned in pleasure.

His merry chuckle brought a smile to my lips despite knowing it was all an act. In another life, the man would've been a beloved fixture for us. "*Laissez-moi vous apporter votre café, madame.*"

Let me get your coffee, ma'am.

We found a table outside the boulangerie, sipped our coffee, and enjoyed a very French morning of leisure observing the passage of strolling couples and patrolling men wearing crimson and black bands.

Chapter Seventeen

Thomas

It had taken most of the morning to walk all the way around the western edge to the river and then cut east into town. By the time I stepped onto the cobbled streets of Crécy, the sun had reached her peak. It was a bit jarring to see Sparrow and Will enjoying their day on a café patio as I reconnoitered the town. Sparrow and I made brief eye contact from across the plaza, but she quickly turned back to Will and pretended to laugh at something he'd said. The doting couple routine looked good on them, and I knew her hand drifting casually to his hair was part of their cover. Still, an uncomfortable spike of jealousy found its way beneath my shirt.

I stopped before a few storefronts, peering into the reflection of the glass to check my surroundings and ensure the ever-present soldiers weren't watching my movement. This wasn't my first time operating undercover, but it was my first mission in hostile territory during a war. The unceasing waves of anxious tension ebbed and flowed each time soldiers came into view then passed with little more than a disinterested glance.

For a town under foreign occupation, there was a strange air of normalcy. Everywhere I looked, villagers moved about their daily routines, tending street-side markets or hanging out laundry to dry in the summer sun. Occasional empty bins and handwritten signs were the only indication of rationing, and most of the sellers I passed appeared to be well stocked by the surrounding farms. I knew better than to believe the French were happy to be under the Nazi heel, but few offered less than warm smiles or polite nods to their occupiers when they passed on the street.

Was that their cover? Was that how ordinary citizens survived? Were they truly accepting their fate under the Nazi banner, or were they playing the dutiful serf only to later resist and rebel? It was hard to tell, and those thoughts frightened me more than the soldiers and their weapons.

I walked south and crossed the narrow bridge. Water from an aged paddlewheel splashed nearby, drawing my eye and making me pause to enjoy the simplicity of its movement. There was a peaceful feel to this town that warred against the internal tension that consumed me.

Eglise Saint-Georges-et-Saint-Louis rose ahead, her weathered gray stones and rusty, sun-kissed shingles a monument to French architecture from some bygone era. Thick trees surrounded the cross-shaped structure, and a tall tower centuries older than the building proper rose above the northern end. I squinted up at the inscription etched into the facade and struggled to interpret the Latin phrase: *Temple of Reason and the Supreme Being*.

The repetitive, sharp sound of clippers echoed off the stone, and I turned to find a middle-aged man in the frock of a friar stooped low, with fallen leaves and limbs scattered on the ground around him. His head snapped up at my approach, and the snicking sound ceased.

"*Mon dieu!*" he exclaimed. "*Vous avez failli arrêter mon cœur. la prochaine fois, donnez un petit avertissement à un homme.*"

You nearly stopped my heart. Give a man a little warning next time.

His features bunched as I stared blanky, and I worried I'd angered him until a broad smile crept across his face. He straightened to his full height and brushed himself off, and spoke in thickly accented English. "Where are my manners? Welcome, son. What brings you to God's house today?"

I painted on my best German-accented English and replied, "Forgive me, Father. I did not mean to startle. Your church is so beautiful." I let my eyes travel upward to the stone cross that adorned the roof.

"It is, is it not?" Pride sang in his voice. "Have you walked the grounds? Seen the bell tower? Would you like to see inside?"

I looked back to the man and shook my head. "No. I have not, and I would love to see everything."

He beamed, and his bony fingers reached out to grip my arm. "I will be your guide today, but it will cost you."

I raised a brow.

"Carry these while I gather my clippings." He handed me his shears with a wink.

"May I help—"

"No, no. You will soil your suit. Just carry those, and I will clean up here. If you would like to go inside, I will join you in a moment."

"Thank you, Father," I said.

As I pushed open the heavy oak, a rush of anticipation I hadn't expected coursed through me. The air was still, and a hushed reverence hung like a velvet curtain over the threshold. The flickering candles along the nave's walls cast shadows, beckoning me deeper inside.

The vaulted ceiling soared, its intricate ribs reaching toward the heavens in a silent plea for grace. As I gazed upward, the soft, filtered light poured through stained glass windows, bathing the interior in a kaleidoscope of colors. It was as though the divine itself had painted the very air with hues of devotion.

Chapels branched off from the main nave, each a hidden alcove of devotion and grace. Here, statues of saints gazed benevolently, their stone eyes watching over the faithful with eternal compassion. Floral fragrances filled the air, mingling with the soft rustle of ancient scrolls and the whispers of pilgrims seeking solace.

The stained glass windows came alive with stories of faith and miracles, their colors dancing in a silent symphony. As the sunlight played upon their intricate patterns, I felt a connection to the divine, a love story between earth and heaven that transcended time itself.

My gaze drifted to the ceiling, a masterpiece of architectural wonder. Ribbed vaults intertwined like lovers in an eternal embrace, while flying buttresses reached out like outstretched hands.

"Beautiful, is she not?" The priest's voice jarred me back to the present.

"She certainly is."

"The tower dates back to the 1300s, though much of the rest was restored following terrible destruction inflicted during the Hundred Years War."

I shook my head in wonder. Everything he'd just said predated my country's entire existence, and it had rolled so casually off his tongue; immeasurable pride mingled with the smoothed edges of centuries past.

"Are you a believer, child?"

It felt so strange to be called "child."

"I want to believe. Does that count?"

"Of course it does." His smile bore a hint of melancholy. "Come, let me show you the altar. It is original and worth more than all of Crécy combined."

An hour later, I'd received the most in-depth tour of any building I'd ever visited. Even with my love of history, I had to fight to stay awake through some of the priest's descriptions. My family had never been particularly religious, but I couldn't deny the pimpling of my skin as my fingers traced the ancient stones that held so much faith aloft.

"Could we walk the grounds?" I asked.

I hadn't thought the priest could smile more broadly than he did in that moment. His love of his church was infectious.

"I love the Grand Morin. This church sits on an island, you know. The river embraces her on all sides. There is something lovely and symbolic in that, I think, as though God has wrapped his arms around us for all eternity through the flowing waters."

We passed rows of ancient tombstones, weathered and worn yet obviously cared for with diligence and respect. The priest paused to point out a few of Crécy's more prominent citizens of the past, offering drawn-out tales of their heroism or leadership in days long gone.

At last, our stroll brought us to the river's edge. I made a show of kneeling down to revel in the languid water's flow and breathe in the tangy air that was far from refreshing. When my host turned to stare up at his church, I rose and scanned the land beyond the opposite shore. A lone wooden building, some two stories high, hung nearly over the river, with its massive paddle-wheel turning slowly in time with the lazy brook. The clipped sound of German drifted from the far side of the structure, and I could just make out a few helmeted men with rifles slung over a shoulder strolling along the side.

"They have been quite busy over there of late." For the second time in as many hours, the priest's voice nearly scared me out of my shoes. He chuckled. "Forgive me. I did not mean to startle."

I turned toward him and grinned. "Do all priests step so quietly?"

"It is an old habit." An odd distance crept into his eyes as he stared across the water. "The Germans have been here so long now, many of our people believe this is our new life."

"Is that what you believe?"

His eyes lingered on some indistinct point in the paddle-wheel. Its rhythmic sloshing was mesmerizing.

"There are more of them now," he said so quietly, I almost thought he spoke only to himself.

"More?"

"In the last few days." His head barely nodded once. "There are always trucks passing through on the way to Paris, but none stay. Dozens have remained recently. They sleep in homes, but return to that building throughout the day. Multiple patrols guard it day and night. That is also new."

I was caught by the priest's observations, but more by his openness in sharing them.

"Crécy seems so peaceful," I said.

He nodded again, this time even slower. "It appears so, yes."

"Appears?"

He stared a moment longer in silence, then glanced up. "I am afraid this is the last of our tour. I must wash up and prepare for evening services. We will only have a few tonight, but they will expect me to smell more of soap than sweat."

In another time and another place, this man might have become a dear friend. I saw it in his smile and the warmth of his voice. He wore his passions plainly and opened his arms freely.

"Thank you for showing me around, Father. You turned an accidental find into a wonderful afternoon of discovery."

As we strode back toward the front of the church, he placed a hand on my shoulder and leaned close. "Perhaps the next time you come to peer across the Morin it will not be so … accidental?" His voice reduced to barely a whisper. "God works in mysterious ways. I, too, enjoy *le kouign amann* from time to time."

I nearly missed a step.

"They go so well with *café noisette*, do they not?" He smiled, his eyes piercing mine.

We'd been trained to find local resistors, to recruit assets and use them to execute our missions, but I'd never expected to be approached by one.

Could I trust this man? Was he truly offering to help? What if he was a German sympathizer guessing at my true allegiance? Had we already been discovered by our enemy?

How had he known …

"Tonight's service ends at nine o'clock. There will be no one here after the keeper leaves at ten." He clapped my back, and shoved me lightly toward the bridge, calling over his shoulder as he vanished into the church. "Farewell, my child. May God guide your path."

Chapter Eighteen

Thomas

"I don't like it," Will said, stuffing the last bite of his dinner into his mouth.

The basket of cold meats and cheeses Anais brought for our dinner had been our most substantial meal since arriving in France, though I worried I might've chipped a tooth on the bread's crust.

"This is our best chance to see what they're up to. The priest—"

"The priest you *think* is on our side. For all we know, he'll have a pack of wolves in black waiting for you inside that church."

Sparrow's eyes darted between us, but she said nothing.

"The baker put up a brave front, but he was scared. The Germans have really stepped up their efforts lately, and if the priest was telling the truth, they're all over that building. Are you sure sneaking around at night is the best idea?"

"We need to know what they're up to. It's why we're here. I'd rather sneak in the dark than the daylight." I tried to keep the annoyance out of my voice. I knew Will was just nervous and worried, but he'd been at it since we sat down to eat. His questioning in front of the others was wearing thin.

Egret grunted and stabbed the air with his fork. "Every mission is a risk. Your call, Condor."

I gave the plan one last thought. "Egret and I go tonight. You two, assemble the map and try to find us a route to the outskirts of Paris. We need a radio. From what the baker told you today, Crécy's run dry. The resistance in a larger town is probably our best shot."

Sparrow dug into her pocket, pulled out the deck of playing cards, and began examining the corners.

Will glared at me.

I stood, dusted off the crumbs, and turned to Egret. "Grab the binoculars. I wish we had one of those miniature cameras they showed us back at Harvard."

"I'd settle for a gun or block of putty," Egret said.

"Always want to blow something up," Sparrow chided, a smile teasing her lips.

Egret shrugged. "Can you think of anything better to do with a building full of Nazis?"

Sparrow's lips smoothed. "Just be careful, okay?"

Egret grinned. "Aw. Mom is worried about us."

"Fuck off, Egret." The heat in Will's voice turned all our heads. "What? He was being an ass."

I checked my watch. It was nearly ten.

"Let's go."

———◆———

The island was a darkened jewel in the inky setting of the slow-moving river.

Nothing stirred. Even the air was still.

Despite the earth's slumber, the heavens churned. Thick clouds drifted across the full moon. One moment the land was illuminated by her yellow glow; the next, everything was plunged into darkness.

A thick row of trees and scruffy brush obscured where we lay, only a dozen feet of water drifting between us and the building. The paddlewheel barely turned, the groan of its gears louder than the endless dipping of its blades.

"Two patrols, two men each," Egret whispered in the clipped manner of a seasoned soldier.

"That's at the rear side. What about the front?"

"I'm blind. Building and trees in the way." A moment of silence passed, then he muttered again, "Rotation at fifteen-minute intervals. Static patterns. No variation at all."

"Bored or alert?" "Heads on swivels."

He handed me the binoculars, and I watched the choreographed movements he'd described continue like the perfect clockwork of a German watch. "Shit. They're tight."

"Something worth guarding inside."

I handed him back the goggles. "Yeah. Just what I was thinking. We need a look inside. Ideas?"

"They'll have the front buttoned up. The back is a no-go unless we can take out both patrols without getting caught. That's unlikely." He raised the glasses to his eyes a moment, then pointed. "The river side—there, by the paddlewheel—is flush with the water. Looks like it hangs over some. If we could get across, we might get a look inside that window. Unless one of the patrols walks to the river's edge and looks down, they wouldn't see us."

"Have they walked the edge?"

He shook his head. "Not once. There's no door on that side, so they probably think it's secure."

"Fuck, I hate cold water," I grumbled.

Egret smirked. "A squid who hates water. Now I've heard it all."

"We have ships, dumbass. We don't go floating for fun."

"Tonight you do."

"Fuck." I rose to my knees and peered into the darkness that was the Grand Morin, more a stream than a river where we stood. "Let's get this over with."

Egret's hand on my shoulder stopped my foot from entering the water.

"Remember, go slower than you think you should. Noise carries over water, and that wheel isn't turning fast enough to help."

I nodded and stepped in. Chilly fingers clawed up my leg as water rose beyond my ankles to my waist, then edged against my chin. It might've been the middle of summer with sweltering nights back home, but the French countryside offered little in the way of warmth, even less so within the river's flow.

Egret barely made a sound as he entered the Morin behind me, and we waded forward slowly. Thankfully, there was no point where the river rose beyond chin height. The last thing I wanted was to dip my head, losing what little warmth was left within my scalp.

Moments later, we were staring at moss-covered boards beneath the building. The paddlewheel's blades plunged so close to my head I fought the urge to duck each time it spun.

Egret appeared at my side. He motioned to a pair of planks that jutted from beneath the house wide enough for him to stand with half a foot atop them. The window was directly above our heads. Its glass looked like it hadn't been cleaned in half a century, and I worried we wouldn't be able to see inside—until I realized the bottom third was fully opened, and muffled voices drifted out. I couldn't make out more than the guttural tones of spoken German.

I scanned the side of the building for anything we might use as handgrips to climb out of the river, but before I could speak or signal, Egret had braced himself, then reached up and grabbed one of the paddlewheel's blades as it lumbered out of the water and lifted him out of the river. The wheel moaned, but didn't hitch or halt, its plaintive movement progressing despite the man's added weight.

Just as I thought he'd missed his opportunity and would plunge back into the river, Egret stepped lightly down onto the half-shoe perch, teetering precariously before bracing himself by a few fingers in the knot of one plank.

The beam of a flashlight peered across the water, darting back and forth like the eye of an unsettled beast.

Egret flattened his body against the wall. I pressed myself beneath the building, lowering my head so only my nose and eyes were above the chilly line.

"*Ich schwöre ich habe etwas gehört.*"

I swear I heard something.

The brassy voice chilled my heart far more than the Morin had my skin.

Neither of us dared move. I tried not to breathe.

"*Verdammter Fisch. Das ist alles was Sie gehört haben.*"

Fucking fish. That's all you heard.

The beam spun away, and the river slumbered once more.

I remembered to breathe.

Egret waited another moment, then craned his head to peer into the open corner of the window.

His hand flashed. Five. Another five. Then three. *Thirteen people inside.*

A closed fist. *Stay still.*

Egret pressed himself back to the wall, out of view of the window, as two voices grew from a blanketed murmur into words that tickled the river's surface.

"... *n'ont pas réussi à la faire disparaître en moins de deux semaines.*"

Have not been able to make it dissipate in less than two weeks.

The first voice's French was thickly laced with German tones, while the second spoke with the richness of morning *café.*

"What agents have been tried? Do you have notes? Photographs of test results? Anything that might help me understand what is being tried? Surely your people have run tests—"

"Of course we have run many tests!" the German voice snapped, then calmed. "I am no scientist, Dr. Bernard. I cannot tell you all the compounds, or combinations, or ... whatever ... they have used, but I can convey any ideas you have to my people."

The Frenchman scoffed. "I would be only stabbing in the darkness. Surely, you know better than to ask for a scientist's help without allowing him to work directly on the substance. Why did you not bring any with you?"

"You think the Reich would allow our most important work to simply drive across the border? Have you no concept of security?" The German laughed.

"No, security is not my area, but science is, and I cannot help you without something to actually work on, to perform tests with. Forgive me, but this is a waste of time."

"This is *not* a waste of anything, Doctor. This project is the war; the *entire* war." A pause, so uncomfortable I felt it beneath the water, settled inside the building.

The paddlewheel's dips and splashes echoed off the banks of the lazy river. Crickets trilled.

When the German spoke again, his sharpened voice pierced the night. "You will return with me to Berlin."

"Herr Vogt ... my value to the Führer is greater inside France. There is no one better positioned—"

"We will not need your eyes and ears in Paris once the weevil solution is complete. No one will defy us then. Do you understand?"

Another pause ended in French. "*Oui, Herr Vogt. Comme vous l'ordonnez.*"

Yes, Herr Vogt. As you command.

We waited, breathless, for another long moment, but heard nothing more from the pair. Egret motioned for me to stand beneath him and help him lower back into the water. I braced one leg as he released his hold on the knot, then he eased down, trying to grip the smooth planks. He'd nearly made it down when his foot slipped, and his weight fell backward. I pushed upward, desperate to help him break the water's surface as quietly as possible, but a loud splash echoed off the building and across the river.

We huddled in the paddlewheel's shadow, our heads nearly submerged, as a golden beam returned, panning back and forth. A heartbeat later, a second beam stabbed into the water near the front of the building.

The clouds chose that moment to scatter, and everything around us brightened beneath the nearly full moon.

Chapter Nineteen

Thomas

When the guards first heard us in the water, the light of their flashlight had drifted slowly across the river's surface. Now, from either side, yellow beams darted in frantic scans. Twice, the eyes of the guards passed before where we hid, the building's overhang and the paddlewheel's shadow providing our only protection from their piercing gaze.

Egret's head rose so his mouth breached the water's surface, opening to speak. My eyes widened in panic, and I shook my head as firmly as possible without disturbing the river's flow. His lips clamped shut before he dropped back down.

Staccato shouts pierced the night as more soldiers arrived on the banks and more lights joined the dance.

Adrenaline kept my heart racing, though the Morin's chill seeped into every pore. I had to fight to keep my teeth from chattering, and Egret's face was turning pale.

We couldn't stay hidden in the river's embrace much longer. Still, we dared not move.

A splash sounded near the far bank, and four beams snapped toward the rippling waters. The shell of a massive turtle sank as the last of the soldiers' lights arrived on scene, then winked out.

"*Idioten. All das für eine Schildkröte, die wir nicht einmal essen können?*" an irritated voice barked.

Idiots. All that for a turtle we can't even eat?

Two more lights vanished, leaving one stubborn beam still searching where the turtle had been. A few heartbeats later, it extinguished, and the clouds took their cue from the soldiers and veiled the moon, once more casting the land in shadows.

We waited a few more minutes before drifting at a sloth's pace across the shallow water. Once safely concealed behind the church bank's shrubs, Egret stripped down and began wringing out his clothes, never once looking up to see if his sudden nakedness might be seen. I shrugged and followed suit, surprised at how much flowed from my soaked shirt and trousers.

Before our swim, I'd thought the night's air chilly against my skin. Temperatures barely reached above fifty. Now, after feeling the Morin's touch deep within my chest, Crécy's breeze felt like a warm kiss.

Reluctantly, we redressed in our damp clothing and crept across the yard, past the church, and across the bridge into town. I guessed the time around two o'clock, well past the curfew imposed by the German occupiers. We clung to shadows and alleys, conscious of the ever-present patrols hunting for any sign of resistance or even simple disobedience.

Despite it all, the hardest part of our flight from the river that night was holding in the myriad questions hammering against my mind. Egret had seen inside the building. He'd heard the conversation, possibly others, that I couldn't catch from my position beside the constant turn of the paddlewheel, but we didn't even speak once the ground of a farmer's well-turned field crunched under our boots.

The door to the barn creaked open when we were twenty yards away, Will's head peeking out.

Our eyes met, and I could almost feel his shoulders loosen. Sparrow's head appeared comically above his, her eyes roaming up and down our nearly dried clothing.

"Egret and I decided to go for a swim. The water was a little chilly, but it felt great," I deadpanned as the door closed behind us.

"Fuck you. My balls are still tucked up beside my lungs." Egret flopped into a chair. "Any chance you guys have—"

Sparrow handed him a steaming mug, and he threw it back with a groan of pleasure.

"God, that feels good," he said, cupping his hands as they drank in the mug's warmth.

I took a mug from Will and sat.

"So?" Will asked, sitting opposite me. "Did you learn anything?"

Egret took another long sip, then looked to me. "Nothing good. The building is stacked full of crates, floor to ceiling, several rows deep. Rifles and explosives, from the markings. Looked like enough to arm all of Paris."

"They must be beefing up their suppression efforts," I muttered into my mug.

Egret nodded. "I only had a few seconds, but I thought I saw a couple of tables where uniformed men sat at radios. It was too quick to tell if they were sending signals or hunting for them."

"Probably both," Sparrow said. "Standard radios? Could you see anything odd about them?"

Egret shook his head. "Didn't get that good of a look."

"What about the conversation with the Frenchman?" I asked.

"Frenchman?" Will asked.

"Yeah," Egret said, then recounted the parts of the conversation he'd overheard. "The German was the same officer we saw on the road before, SS patches and all. Real asshole from the sound of it. I think the French guy was a scientist spying for the Germans, but he never said where."

No one spoke for a long moment when he finished.

"A weapon that '*is* the war?' Those were his words?" Will asked. "You think he was talking about some kind of explosive? Some new bomb?"

"No. The German said they were having trouble making it dissipate, like it's some new gas or liquid."

"Shit," I said. "The gas they used in the last war was bad enough."

"The way he talked," Egret continued, "this could end the war. Maybe he's full of himself, but he sounded pretty confident. Whatever it is, it's important enough for him to pull the French spy out of whatever he's been doing and drag him back to Germany."

"We need a radio," Sparrow said.

I nodded. "There's no way we're getting into that building, and based on what you two learned today, I doubt there's much hope of finding one outside of the Paris resistance."

"You're not thinking of going into Paris—?" Will's eyes widened.

"No," Egret snapped. "No, our mission is that building, the munitions. That's why we're here."

"It was why we were sent here, but command might not know about this new gas. If it's half as bad as the German made it sound—"

"So, you don't want to risk going into Paris, but you're thinking we should chase down this rumor in the heart of the fatherland? Really?" Egret's mug thunked against the table as he rose and began pacing.

"We may be the only ones with a shot at—"

"At what?" Egret hissed. "We don't even know it's real."

Sparrow stood. Her voice was a shadow. "We have to try. We know enough. If it's real and we do nothing ..."

"I agree," I said. "Will?"

Will's eyes bore into me, then fell to his hands. "We ... we have to try."

"Fuck it. Fine," Egret said, smacking the back of his chair so it slammed into the table, tipping his mug and spilling the last of his coffee. "I was dreading taking that cross-Atlantic flight again anyway. This'll definitely save me that trip."

It took a second for his lips to curl upward.

There wasn't anything funny about what we were proposing, but humor was his shield and I didn't dare rip it from his grasp. We needed our team whole and committed.

Sparrow leaned against the back of her chair, her eyes distant.

I sucked in a breath, eyed each of them one last time, and nodded. "Alright, here's what we're going to do."

Chapter Twenty

Will

S everal hours before dawn, we rose from a restless sleep.

Egret trekked across the fields, through town, then crept across the bridge that led to the side of the river where the paddlewheel building stood. He skirted the road and hid in a thick stand of trees opposite the short driveway that led to the structure. Four soldiers, rifles at the ready, stood at the entrance, their heads on a constant swivel.

Egret's job was to observe, to discover which route the German took with his scientist, then report back. He was not to engage in any way, simply hide and watch.

We'd spent hours debating which route the Nazi officer might take to get back to Berlin. The drive would take at least a dozen hours. With checkpoints and military convoys clogging France's narrow arteries, it would likely take many more. If this new weapon was as important and powerful as the man claimed, he would want to return as quickly as possible. That meant flying. We knew the Allies had begun chipping away at the Luftwaffe's control of Europe's skies in recent months, but the Germans still maintained flight paths to and from their capital. That meant a drive into Paris or to a larger town to the east where our target could acquire passage.

I bet on Paris.

Thomas said our real challenge wasn't following them—that was impossible. Getting ourselves into Hitler's homeland alive was now our virtually impossible mission. Our secondary aim was finding a way to advise command on what we'd discovered and how we were proceeding. I thought it odd that he never once suggested we ask command for instructions on how to proceed. He knew we had to follow, to learn what was afoot, to stop whatever evil the Germans were cooking up before they could serve it to our troops.

Shortly after sunrise, Sparrow and I headed back into town to speak with our baker again. As we crossed the road that separated farms from the edge of town, I whispered, "Not a single soldier. That's odd."

She scanned the road in each direction, squinting against the morning's rays. "Very. This town's been crawling with them since we got here."

"Keep your eyes open. I have a really bad feeling."

"Worse than the whole 'they're developing a mystery gas that could end the war' feeling?"

My head whipped around. Sparrow rarely cracked jokes or made light of a situation. Her lips remained tight, and she didn't look up at me.

"Yeah, that too," I said, unsure how else to respond.

We walked through town arm in arm, as any couple would. Sparrow carried a basket filled with potatoes Anais had given us for the baker. Barter wasn't a common currency in Crécy, but gifts from neighbors who knew the other's family might be struggling were. No one would look twice at a woman carrying goods for her friends.

That was our theory.

The tables outside the boulangerie were filled with men and women enjoying their morning *café* and pastry. Two Nazi soldiers sat near the street and nodded as we passed.

Sparrow smiled and nodded, offering a friendly, "*Bonjour.*"

Monsieur Petit's eyes widened briefly, then darted away as we entered his shop. A young woman I hadn't seen before bustled beside him, handing pastries and drinks to diners as Petit collected coins. We took our place in queue behind three others. Only one table indoors sat empty.

"Looks like we came at the busy hour," Sparrow whispered in French.

It took me a second, but her eyes roaming meaningfully at the crowded dining area helped her words sink in.

"*Oui*," I said, nearly exhausting my French vocabulary.

She actually chuckled, and I raised a questioning brow.

"*Votre accent*," she said, batting her smiling eyes.

I wasn't sure which was more unnerving: her calling out my accent when I'd only spoken one word, or her smiling. I'd become used to her stoic expression.

The woman ahead of us chanced a glance back. When she saw the flirtation in Sparrow's eyes, she leaned in and whispered, "*C'est ce qui arrive lorsque des Allemands essaient de parler français.*"

That's what happens when Germans try to speak French.

Sparrow and the young woman giggled together, as though schoolgirls laughing at a silly boy, both eyeing me, then turning back toward each other to share in their private laughter at my ignorance.

"She said you have a nice voice," Sparrow translated into German.

The woman spat out another laugh and stepped up to the counter to order her pastry.

I realized in that moment how odd life was in Nazi-controlled France. The people here hadn't suffered the same brutal destruction of their cities and towns as had their neighboring nations. They'd surrendered in the face of overwhelming odds, saving the children of the revolution that fate. Now, with their occupiers committing unspeakable atrocities and ever vigilant for those who might struggle against the boot on their necks, the

French clung to the simple pleasures of life. More than simply injecting moments of normalcy in an impossibly abnormal era, they sought to preserve their every moment, live each day, as though life simply continued regardless of the blood streaking their flag.

I knew most hated the Germans for what they'd done—for what they were doing. No sane Frenchman wanted another country to rule them. And yet, that was their reality. The Germans controlled most of Europe and were rolling into Russia. There was no clear path to liberation—little hope of freedom from Hitler's yoke. As badly as any people might wish for freedom, empires fell—and others rose. The Nazi banner might fly over every capital, castle, and palace for centuries to come.

Life had to go on. They had to live every day, to find happiness and joy where darkness reigned. They had to preserve *themselves* even if their beloved nation faded into history.

By the time Sparrow's conspirator gathered her cherry-filled puff and cup of chocolate-laced coffee, my mood had darkened. I should have taken pleasure in the playful exchange of two women finding companionship in a simple moment, but I couldn't shake the shroud that surely clung to this land.

"Ah, it is good to see you, my friends." Petit smiled warmly up at us. I nodded and smiled as though understanding, despite catching only a few words. "Would you like your usual again? I believe I have some of those lovelies coming out of the oven any moment."

Sparrow leaned across the counter and exchanged kisses like they were old chums.

"That would be wonderful. You do know how to work magic into dough." She turned and patted my chest affectionately. "Tobias woke this morning with a craving, and not the kind I had hoped for."

The baker feigned surprise and chortled at her suggestiveness. "A man with priorities. I like this one."

"You boys always stick together." Sparrow squealed in protest and playfully slapped Petit's hand that rested on the counter. "At least I'll get a tasty treat—even if I didn't get the one I wanted."

Petit hooted, and I didn't think he was acting. Whatever the two were prattling on about had amused him greatly. Was Sparrow actually funny? Had she cloaked a sense of humor all this time, only to whip it out when our cover demanded it?

"Come, I will check the oven for you." Petit waved us back.

As we rounded the counter, we passed the woman who'd been in front of us in line. She'd been dressing her coffee and listening to our conversation. Her hand reached up and comforted Sparrow's shoulder, as her eyes darted down to my trousers then back. Sparrow followed her gaze, then the pair broke into more girlish laughter.

I let out an uncomprehending huff and pressed a hand into the small of Sparrow's back to urge her on. "Do I want to know?" I muttered in German.

Sparrow snorted once more, then shook her head. "*Definitiv nicht.*"

Definitely not.

A woman slightly shorter than the shop owner—and nearly as round—slapped at dough on a board as we passed through the kitchen. She glanced up, grunted, then returned to beating and folding the pastry dough. The scent of baking dough and cinnamon made my stomach roil.

"Ah, here we are," Petit said, reaching to the top shelf of a trolley and snatching two golden sweets that looked like muffins whose tops had been shaped into a four-pointed crown. Flakes of deliciousness crackled and tumbled off as he handed each of us one.

Petit smiled proudly as I took a bite and closed my eyes, groaning at the perfect confection. "I began making a tray of these each morning in hopes of seeing you again."

"I could die back here and have lived a happy life," I said in muffin-muddled German.

Petit's rumbling laugh bounded off the stone walls of the ancient building.

"I wish we had time to stay," Sparrow cut in. "Anais asked us to bring you some potatoes from her farm. She says the harvest is quite robust this year."

When Petit took the basket, Sparrow pulled back the cloth and shifted a few of the vegetables to reveal a hint of paper buried beneath. Thomas had crafted a coded message in hopes the resistance had radios in operation and could pass along its contents. Petit was our best hope of getting the note into the hands of someone in Paris while we worked our way east into Germany. It was a thin rope, but it was one we clung to.

"I am sure we will put these to good use. Please give her my thanks. Was there anything she needed in return? Perhaps a few baguettes?"

Sparrow forced a smile. "I'm sure she would love that."

Petit pulled a few arm-length baguettes from another tray and filled a basket of his own.

"Will I see you tomorrow morning?" he asked.

Sparrow hesitated, glancing at the woman and her dough. "Perhaps. We may have to travel soon. The Germans seem to be acquiring antiquities at a rapid pace, and Tobias is needed to assist with the influx."

"They certainly are." Petit's eyes betrayed a sadness. "Please travel safely. I will make more of these little gems for you when you return."

Sparrow surprised the man by stepping forward and wrapping him in a tight embrace. "*Merci, Monsieur Petit. Merci,*" she whispered.

Chapter Twenty-One

Will

Thomas, Egret, and Anais were sitting around the table when we walked into the barn.

Relief flooded Thomas's eyes as they met mine, and I fought back the desire to wrap him in my arms right there. Being together had been the greatest blessing of our wartime service, but maintaining our distance was even more challenging than it had been back at Harvard. Our whole world now revolved around a handful of people with whom we spent virtually every waking moment—the sleeping ones too. And yet we had to maintain this barrier, this curtain of iron, all in the name of social propriety.

To say falling in love with Thomas had been unexpected would have been the understatement of all understatements. I hadn't even known I was attracted to men. At least, I hadn't consciously acknowledged or accepted it. Somewhere, deep inside, I probably always knew, but growing up in the 1930s, two men being more than pals wasn't just frowned upon, it was a criminal offense. America wouldn't take us beyond the walls and stone us, as some religions taught, but we could be imprisoned or institutionalized. Worse, the scarlet letter we'd wear for the rest of our lives would mark us as outcasts, as deviants unworthy of social standing or common decency.

When I looked at Thomas, though, all I saw was the strength of a man determined to risk his life for all those people who would see him jailed. When he set his stubbled jaw, and his eyes fixed on a point somewhere in the future, nothing shook him from his course. I couldn't imagine a better man, or one I would ever be more proud of.

My heart danced as our eyes lingered.

"Move, *Tobias*." Sparrow groused as she bumped into me. Then she hissed in my ear, "Look away. Egret is watching you two."

I blinked myself free of Thomas's grasp, then singsonged toward Egret, "So, how was your day, dear?"

Thomas spat a laugh, and I was sure I heard Sparrow roll her eyes behind me.

"The Nazi and the scientist are on the move," Egret said, his expression grim despite my attempt at humor.

"Shit," I said, then looked to Anais. "Sorry."

She waved a hand and offered a tight smile. "We are in a war. I hear worse in the market."

Sparrow moved around me and sat. "What do we do?"

"We've been discussing that," Thomas said. "We can't beat them back to Berlin. They'll probably catch a transport flight. Despite the Allies' recent efforts, the Germans still control the skies. Unfortunately, we don't have that option."

"You're not thinking of driving all the way to Berlin?" Sparrow was incredulous. "The checkpoints at the border will be brutal, and that doesn't account for all the stops along the way. With all their troops moving west, we'd be lucky to only run into convoys every twenty miles."

Anais unclasped her hands. "It is not nearly that bad, but you are correct. The Germans do move many troops and weapons through France. You would be stopped often."

"Every stop is another risk of detection," Egret grumbled.

"Alright, we can't risk a twenty-hour drive—or whatever it is. How do we get there?" I asked.

Thomas looked to Anais, then back. "We can't do this part on our own. We need help. Anais has agreed to take us into Paris."

"Paris? Like *into* the beehive?" I asked.

"Berlin is the beehive. Paris is a walk in the park." Thomas grunted. "The resistance might be able to help us get into Germany. At the very least, we should be able to find a way to radio London."

The creak of the wind battering the barn's planks was the only sound for the longest moments of my life. None of our eyes had the strength to lift from the table. It felt like we stood on the edge of a cliff with a pack of rabid wolves at our backs, and we knew our only path was into the unknown.

Thomas finally broke the silence. "We leave tonight. Get packed. We won't be returning to Crécy."

Chapter Twenty-Two

Thomas

A hand gripped my arm.

Without turning, I knew Will's touch. It was insistent yet gentle. His fingers pressed through my sleeve as though begging to find skin rather than cloth. My own need for him flamed beneath his grip.

"Can we talk—alone?" he whispered.

We'd both packed quickly. Egret and Sparrow were still in the loft, moving bedrolls and crates to return the place to the unlived-in state we'd found upon arriving. The last thing any of us wanted was to leave a trail that might lead the Nazis to us, or worse, cause them to suspect Anais of resisting.

"We really shouldn't leave the barn," I said, still without turning to face him. If I looked in his eyes ...

"*Thomas*, please." He hadn't said my name since we'd left Harvard, and his voice trembled. My heart willed my body to turn. His eyes burst with watery blue, like some overflowing ocean cresting the shore. I could *feel* them deep inside my chest as he stared up.

"Okay," I croaked out. "You want to step outside?"

He nodded, a clenched smile threatening one corner of his mouth.

"We're going to walk the perimeter," I called up to Egret. "You two stay in here. We're well out of sight, but still shouldn't go out in more than twos."

"Aye, aye, boss." Egret's head hung over the loft's railing, and he gave a snarky two-fingered salute. I shook my head and wrestled the urge to offer him only one finger in return.

The door thudded shut behind me, and I saw Will standing some twenty paces away at the edge of the field of barley. The golden fronds were blackened by the night, barely visible beneath the moonless sky. They rustled in the persistent wind, giving the sprawling field an oddly comforting quality.

Will watched me approach. When I stood an arm's length away, his hand rose, almost as tentatively as the first time he'd cupped my cheek. I watched in silence as he repeated that favorite gesture and his fingers traced the line of my jaw. A shiver trilled through me at his touch.

"I'm scared, Thomas," he said, his eyes pleading.

I reached up and pressed his hand into my cheek. "Me too."

"Really? You are?" Something flickered in his eyes. "You seem so ... I don't know ... sure."

"Being sure is my job." An uncomfortable laugh escaped. "But of course I'm scared. Will, we're already in enemy territory. Now we're heading into the capital of occupied France to find a way into Hitler's backyard. How could I not be pissing myself?"

His mouth twitched, then a grin formed.

"More than me getting killed or hurt, I'm terrified something might happen to you. God, I don't know if I could live—"

"Thomas, stop. No—"

"Will, I love you with everything I have. *Everything*. Sending you out on missions is like ... I don't know ... tossing a part of me into a fire and hoping it doesn't get burned."

"You can't protect me—"

"I know that," I snapped, not meaning to sound so defensive. "Sorry, I know. It's our jobs, and a lot of people depend on us. I'm just saying—"

"You don't have to say it."

"I think I do. Either you need to hear it or I just need to get it out so it stops clawing at my chest. I'm not sure. Sometimes I don't know ... I just don't know."

Will eyed me a moment as I pulled away. I turned and took a few steps into the field.

"I wish you were back home and safe," I said into the wind, unable to see whatever might be in his eyes. "I can handle risking my own life, but every choice I make puts you in danger, and that's killing me."

Will's hands gripped my shoulders, and he spun me to face him again. He stared as moisture threatened the corners of my eyes.

"I wouldn't be anywhere else in the world," he said.

"Than in war-torn France?"

"No, dummy, than with you, wherever you are." I had to swallow hard at that. His fingers dug into my arms as he spoke. "Thomas, if we live through tomorrow, we'll do it together. If we die, we do that together too. I'm not worried about one of us outliving the other because we're on a four-man team in hostile territory. We'll either make it, or the Nazis will kill us all."

He caught his breath, then continued. "I know it sounds nuts, but that's comforting to me. Whatever happens, we'll never be apart again. And ... and that's how I want it to be."

I stared into the eyes of this beautiful man and wondered how I could've ever been so lucky he walked into my life. The tear that tickled my lid streaked down my cheek before Will's thumb gently wiped it away.

"Will, I ... I know you wanted to come out here and talk, and I've rambled on ... and ... I'm sorry ... I don't know—"

"Would you shut up and kiss me already? We don't have much time."

Desire and need overcame caution. Our arms wrapped around each other, hands grasping, clawing, desperately clinging to the life we longed for. Our lips met, and I swear stars that weren't there a moment before exploded in the infinite sky.

For one brief moment, there was no war. The meadows of France fell away. The barn vanished, and all thoughts of missions or countries or *anything* vanished.

There was only Will.

In another universe, where men didn't crave power or harbor hatred, I would lose myself in this man's arms and never wrest free. I would live in his heart, his eyes, breathe his every breath. As our tongues brushed against each other, I drew him into me and filled my lungs with his essence, holding him there, feeling his warmth inside me.

God, I loved this man.

"We'd better get back," he whispered, breathless.

I kissed him again.

The carefree smile I'd come to crave spread across his face, and I thought I might die right there. "I love you too, Thomas Jacobs."

He cupped my cheek, then reached down and pressed his palm into my back, urging me toward the barn. "Come on. You have a team to lead."

Chapter Twenty-Three

Will

T he stars I'd seen when Thomas and I stood outside the barn were unwilling to watch our approach into Paris. The moon must've shared their fear, because the sky remained the deepest shade of black. On the one hand, darkness was our cloak. On the other, Anais couldn't see the road without using her headlights. We couldn't have announced our passage more loudly if we'd blared the horn the whole way.

Thankfully, Anais knew tiny dirt roads used by farmers and locals that kept us off the better-maintained routes favored by German military convoys. The narrow lanes required more turns and added an hour to the one-hour drive, but I was grateful to be some distance from the hunters who sought any who dared violate the curfew.

At three o'clock, thirty minutes into our drive, we'd not seen another car or any sign of a waking soul. We slowed to make an especially sharp turn onto yet another dirt road when a pair of headlights and one large beam of yellow fire blazed to life.

"*Halt!*" a voice steeped in German barked, and I could just make out the silhouette of three men pointing rifles in our direction from behind the lights.

"Shit," Egret said.

"Listen to me," Anais ordered. "Do not speak. This is a checkpoint, and they will question us about curfew. I will handle this."

I watched Thomas debating her instruction from the back seat. As the sound of boots on packed dirt grew louder, he nodded once, and Anais leaned forward to dig through the glove box.

One soldier approached the driver's side, while another stood just in front of Thomas's seat on the passenger side, covering his door. Their rifles hadn't lowered, and the set of their jaws told us everything we needed to know about their intentions.

"Why are you out after curfew? Where are you going?" the man asked as Anais lowered her window. The man had a neck thicker than a tree trunk, and I swear his arms were almost as wide. Scars crisscrossed one cheek and above the opposite brow, marking him a veteran of brutal battles—or, at least, some nasty fights.

Anais handed the man a paper. The spotlight's beam poured through the windshield, so I caught the Reich's eagle and swastika stamped on the page as it passed from her hand to the soldier's. The man glanced at the paper, but scanned the back seat where Egret, Sparrow, and I were crammed as Anais spoke. "We are headed into Paris."

"Why? Who are they?" He waved the business end of his rifle at us.

"Doctors, and one nurse. They are German Red Cross. Except for the nurse. She is French."

The soldiers exchanged a look, and the one on Thomas's side barked, "You! Out, now! Hands up so I can see them."

Thomas made a show of his hands, then reached down and slowly opened the door.

"Get out!" the soldier barked. "Keep your hands up. Shut the door and turn toward the car."

Thomas slowly did as instructed. The soldier slammed him roughly against the car frame, his rifle digging into Thomas's side as he patted him down, pulling out a stethoscope I didn't know had been secreted into his pocket. His search complete, the soldier stepped back, his rifle still set on Thomas, and held up the instrument to his partner.

The man with Anais nodded slowly, then looked down at her again.

"Where are you taking them?"

"Nouvel Hôpital Beaujon," she said without hesitation. If I'd been impressed by Anais before, I sat in awe of her composure when faced with a rifle and sharp questioning. The woman never flinched, and her story rolled almost as smoothly as her accent.

The soldier eyed Thomas, then leaned down to get a better look at those in the back. "Why are you taking them in the night? Long after curfew?"

I couldn't tell if the man believed her or not. His tone never shifted, persistently hostile gravel swirling with each word.

"I do not know," Anais said, and I had to fight to keep my eyes from widening. "I only follow orders. I was told to get these people to the hospital immediately. I know better than to delay when an officer issues a command."

Her last words struck home, and the soldier's jaw relaxed. He glanced up at the other man keeping Thomas pressed against the car, then straightened and handed the paper back to Anais. "Heil, Hitler."

"Heil, Hitler," she echoed.

The rifles lowered, Thomas was allowed to regain his seat, and the soldiers waved us through.

The lights winked out behind us as darkness shrouded the Germans once again. It was only then, some fifty yards from their position, that I remembered to breathe.

"Good God," Sparrow muttered.

"Anais—" Thomas started.

She waved a hand. "We live with checkpoints and random stops. I am prepared for them."

"Prepared? What if they don't believe you? Or don't trust your papers? And where did you come up with that story about the hospital?" Sparrow placed her hands on the headrest and leaned forward. Her breathless questions tumbled out, along with her anxiety.

Anais smiled back to Sparrow through the rearview mirror. "My papers are in perfect order. We 'liberated' the stamp used on them from a high-ranking officer."

"But ... the hospital? You said it so ... I don't know ... like you'd practiced it." Sparrow sat back.

"That is because I had practiced it. I spoke with the contact you will meet earlier today by telephone. It was a risk, but a necessary one. He gave me the Red Cross covers and detailed the hospital. It is a new one, opened in '35, so staffing would be an issue, especially given the war. Our people are very good at what they do. You will be in good hands."

I was just about to take a deep breath and let her words soothe my frayed nerves when I noticed how her hand trembled as she shifted it on the steering wheel. She'd managed to fight that back from her voice, but her body betrayed the fear still thrumming through her—the fear I was sure we all felt.

It was terrifying to learn her bravado was only a thin veil, but oddly reassuring that she shared our trepidation yet found a way to power through and offer confidence to others. I glanced to Thomas and caught him staring at her fingers too. He never missed a thing.

We were stopped three more times.

One might think a numbness to interrogation would set it, but it never did. Each set of soldiers asked the same questions, though in vastly different tones. Two shared the venom of the soldiers at our first stop, but the last approached the car with a warm smile and a holstered handgun.

I think he unnerved me the most.

Through it all, Anais hid her fears and presented our story with the seasoned skill of a Hollywood actress. The tremble in her hands returned after each encounter.

Nearly two hours after leaving the barn, as hues of yellow and orange began peeking over the horizon, Anais pulled into an alley beside a series of brick buildings crammed together on a lazy lane. She parked in the first open spot, then turned to face us.

"This is the dangerous part. We must walk two blocks without being stopped by a patrol. We are nowhere near the hospital, and our story will not hold. My papers would not save us from ... We must not be stopped. Understand?"

We nodded and climbed out of the car. Egret walked to the trunk where our packs lay, but Anais placed a hand on his arm and whispered, "Leave your bags. No one will bother the car. The one thing the Germans are good for is preventing crime."

We crept in the shadows of the buildings, careful to remain in the alleys as long as possible. No cars passed. No soldiers marched by. We remained alone as we approached a café with bright blue wooden doors and a sign above that read, *Le Bon Georges*. A small British flag painted above a case displaying a menu was even more out of place than we were—if that was possible. I wanted to ask how they'd managed to keep the banner of the Nazi's enemy on the storefront, but Anais's two raps on the door stilled my tongue. A long silence followed, then she rapped twice, waited, then rapped three times.

The door crept open a few inches. All I could see from where I stood was the outline of a crooked nose. Anais muttered something. The owner of the nose replied, then the door swung open and we hustled inside.

"You made good time." A man who'd seen at least seven decades gripped Anais by the shoulders and kissed each of her cheeks. His smile made it clear the gesture was more than a formality. There was great affection between these two.

The man spoke in English, but his accent wasn't precisely French. Other languages, perhaps Italian or Spanish, were muddled in. It was hard to pinpoint where he might've hailed from, something I appreciated more with each passing day.

I glanced around the darkened place, a typical pub or restaurant one might see on any street corner in Paris. Wooden booths lined the walls, while rickety tables filled the center. Each booth contained a sconce whose light had been extinguished before our arrival. Paintings of men in regal costumes filled the walls above the sconces. They felt so familiar. Then I realized they were depictions of English monarchs of the past. I looked from one painting to the next and recognized each was of one of Britain's King Georges, whichever number they might've been. The name above the door suddenly made sense, though I still couldn't fathom how an English-themed establishment had escaped the scrutiny of the ever-vigilant Nazis.

"We were only stopped four times," she said. "It is so good to see you too."

"Only four—" Egret muttered. I was too shocked to speak.

Wisps of white hair flew as the man, standing barely to Thomas's shoulder, trudged with the knees of an aged man toward the table that sat closest to a long, polished bar whose marble top swam in the light of an oil lamp that burned dimly atop it. I couldn't remember the last time I'd seen an oil lamp in use.

"Come, sit. Would you like something to drink?" he asked in English, again startling us into silence. "I have fresh *café* prepared."

I realized then that he hadn't asked our names or begged an introduction from Anais—nor had he offered an introduction.

"*Café* would be wonderful. *Merci*," Thomas answered for our group.

The man hesitated, as if considering, then moved behind the bar, where he filled cups and handed them across the bar for Anais to pass to each of us.

The man studied us as he rounded the bar with his own cup and reclaimed his seat. His bushy brows, like tiny peaks atop a mountain, twitched, as if his mind was processing all the data our faces and clothing offered. He might've played the affable old fellow, but this was a keenly intelligent septuagenarian.

Anais leaned against the bar, sipping slowly and allowing the aromatic steam to drift across her nose. She watched closely, but didn't speak.

"You are birds, yes?"

I almost fell out of my chair.

The creaking of Egret's as he jerked back startled Sparrow nearly as much as the man's question had me.

Thomas's stare hardened. "Forgive me, but we do not know you."

The man cocked his head and said, "I am Andi," as if his name explained everything.

Thomas barely moved, his etched features giving no hint of what he thought of the man or his query about our affiliation, though I could see his mind spinning even harder than Andi's had a moment earlier. Their staring contest lasted until my skin began to crawl, then Thomas finally answered, "Yes."

Guess we're trusting the old guy.

Andi glared a moment longer. Then, in a tone he might use with his favorite patron, he asked, "Do you enjoy pastries?"

I wanted to run out of the café. *What the hell—?*

"Very much," Thomas said. "But I have a particular weakness for *le kouign amann*. And yourself?"

Oh! The damn pass phrase? I guess that made sense with Anais involved. But why wasn't the fact she was with us enough—?

"Goes best with *café noisette*, does it not?" Andi saluted with his coffee.

Thomas nodded slowly. "*Oui. C'est le cas.*"

Andi took a long sip, then carefully set his cup on the table. "Anais tells me you need assistance. Our resources are limited, but we will do what we can. I am sure the Americans ... *your* Americans ... will return the favor ... eventually."

Thomas's eyes flinched for the first time. "We will. With all the fury and might we can muster."

Thomas startled when Andi reached out and patted his forearm. "That will be good. We have seen the might and fury of the Germans. I would love to compare it to that of the Yanks before I die."

Andi's repeated implication about America's foot-dragging was as obvious as the snow-white critters above his eyes. It had been equally obvious when Anais had grumbled, and when the baker had expressed his frustration.

Something in my gut twisted as Janie appeared in my mind's eye. She had argued that our nation should leave Europe's war to Europe, that we didn't have the strength or the national will to help, that we deserved to enjoy a moment of peace and prosperity after everything the first war—and the Depression—had wrought. Then there was Arty. He overheated every time another atrocity went unanswered. His passion and conviction were the reasons I ultimately enlisted. I hadn't known what to think—or how we should react—but his winnowing of right from wrong had opened my eyes, had spurred me to action.

In our own ways, I supposed the three of us represented America's embattled conscience.

Seeing the fight first-hand, doubt no longer prickled in my chest. I only hoped we hadn't waited too long.

Thomas's voice brought me back to the present. "We need two things. First, to pass a message to London."

Andi nodded slowly. "And the second?"

"To travel to Berlin without getting killed or captured."

The snowy peaks nearly shot to Andi's receding hairline, then Andi burst into a deep-throated laugh. When none of us joined in, his wide smile fell, and his eyes widened. "You are serious."

Thomas nodded.

"*Mon dieu*," he mumbled, looking back to where Anais stood. She shrugged and nodded, as if it was the most normal request one could make. When he turned back to face Thomas, all humor had left his features and pale fear colored his cheeks.

"Please, you cannot be serious. Berlin?"

Thomas leaned forward and grasped the old man's arm as he'd done a moment before. "I would not ask if it were not vital. Everything may depend on this mission. *Everything*."

Andi stared, then finally closed his mouth and let his eyes fall to his coffee.

"I will have your message sent tomorrow, but Berlin ... that is beyond me."

Thomas didn't remove his hand. "Andi, we must get to Berlin soon. It may already be too late, but we have to try."

Their eyes were locked in an embrace I thought might never end, each searching the other's soul.

Finally, Andi let out a deep sigh. "Come with me."

Andi rose, turned from the table, and walked toward the far end of the bar. He lifted the bar's back counter, pinning it into place with a hook on the wall, then knelt down and tossed an old rug aside, revealing the outline of a trap door.

"Open that, would you?" he said over his shoulder, then stepped aside.

Thomas dropped down and pulled a small ring, lifting a handful of planks. Light flickered from somewhere below.

"Let me go first," Andi said. "All of you, follow."

Chapter Twenty-Four

Will

W e followed Andi down the ladder into a large cellar lined with shelves laden with vegetables, sacks of flour, and other staples. Casks and large barrels were stacked at the far end, where the shelves mostly contained bottles of various wines and liquors. The storeroom wasn't musty or disheveled, but it was a typical, almost claustrophobic chamber someone had scooped out of the ground to use for storage. Its rough-hewn walls told of picks used centuries ago to hollow out the space.

Andi walked to the middle of the room, then turned to face the center shelf. He reached up and placed both hands into the handles of a large crate and pulled. The entire shelf swung outward as hinges I hadn't seen groaned at the effort. Once the shelf was fully open, he pulled up a tattered cloth that hung nearly the full length of the room behind all the shelves, revealing a half-door. He retrieved a key from his pocket, unlocked the door, then ducked and passed through.

"Come," he called back when we didn't immediately follow.

Thomas glanced back, then led us forward.

The brightness of electric lights nearly blinded us as we entered a large room. The walls were lined with bookshelves, and vacant leather couches and plain wooden chairs huddled about several small tables, each holding their own electric lamp. I was immediately struck by how comfortable it felt, almost cozy despite its size. There was room for thirty or so people to sit in the large space, though only one rose to face us as we entered.

"*Bonjour*," he greeted us, his timbre so rich and smoky I immediately longed to hear him speak again. His eyes flitted from Andi to Anais, then to Thomas. "You must be very tired traveling into Paris in the dark of night. Please, come sit with me."

If Hollywood sought to cast a caricature of a Frenchman, our host would've won the part a dozen times over. Thick, slicked-back black hair with a perfect part on one side that looked laid with mortar rather than hair gel. Thin, neatly trimmed brows framed deep-set brown eyes, and a pencil-thin mustache, as perfectly manicured as his brows, sat atop equally thin lips. He was handsome, almost strikingly so, in the way one who represents the qualities of his entire people must be. The crisp maroon bowtie that clung to his neck, which might've been comical on another man, only added to his continental allure.

Andi leaned in from behind the man and whispered something in his ear. The man's eyes brightened, and he turned back toward us.

"Please forgive our secrecy. The Germans would love nothing more than to find us out, and I doubt they plan to award me one of their little crosses they are so fond of." He smiled at his own joke, a grin that widened as each of us shifted uncomfortably, unsure how to react. "How rude of us not to make introductions. I am George Creuset. Please, call me George."

Thomas extended his hand. "I am Wilhelm. This is Tobias, Anny, and Heinz. We are in great need of aid to—""You *Amerloque* are always so direct," he said, waving a hand. "Please, no mission is so dire you cannot enjoy refreshment. Would you like a drink? Perhaps some meat and cheese?"

For the first time that night, Thomas blanched, and I could almost hear the tiny voice in his head chirping about the silly man sitting before him. I think a curl formed at the corner of my mouth as I watched.

"Uh, well, yes. That would be wonderful. We are all tired, and Heinz is always hungry, but I really do need—"

Before Thomas could finish, George was across the room retrieving a tea cart filled with charcuterie, glasses, and several bottles of wine. He rolled the cart beside us and motioned us forward. "Please, take what you like and have a seat. If you prefer *café* at this hour, I am sure Andi can bring some down from the restaurant."

"Oh, no, wine will do," Egret said, bounding around the table to grab a small plate. Thomas glanced back, but had to look away as my grin widened. We were in the heart of the French occupation, likely near to German soldiers who would love to capture or kill us, and I couldn't stop my amusement. He really was flustered by this mustached Frenchman and his wine.

Once settled in our seats, plates in our laps and wine in our hands, George smiled up at Thomas. "Now, how is it you need help?"

"We need to get to Berlin as quickly as possible."

George's smile fell, and his perfectly coiffed brows rose. He glanced at Andi, then Anais, both of whom nodded soberly.

"And why would you want to do something so ... suicidal?"

Thomas set his plate on the table at the group's center and downed the last of his wine before fixing his eyes on George's.

"We believe the Germans have developed ... well ... are working on something terrible—"

George held up a palm. "You believe? They may be? Do you know anything for certain?"

Thomas hesitated again, then shook his head. "We overheard an SS officer talking with a scientist. We only caught pieces of their conversation, but the officer was certain they were close to a breakthrough. He forced the scientist to return to Germany with him to assist in their research."

"A *French* scientist? This man is helping the Nazis?"

Thomas nodded. "We heard enough to know he has been spying for them for some time. He sounded reluctant, but only for the travel into Germany. He had no qualms with helping the Germans."

"*Mon œil* ..."

Silence clawed its way into the room as George wrestled with the implications.

"We do not wish to believe it either," Sparrow said, leaning forward. "But we cannot sit by and do nothing. We have one lead—a thin one, to be sure—but if we have any hope of stopping this, we must act."

"You are brave, I will give you that. Would that we had more of you here ..." George eyed each of us, then his troubled features smoothed. "Berlin? Truly?"

Thomas nodded.

"Alright," George said. "The sun is rising. I will need to think and see what can be done. Andi will take you upstairs to my apartment, where you may rest.""Thank you, George," Thomas said, standing and taking the man's hand again. "Thank you."

"Do not thank me until you return home alive. Until then, I am not sure I do you any favors."

———◦○◦———

George's apartment above the restaurant turned out to be a sprawling complex of well-appointed rooms that spread above most of the shops and restaurants in the block-sized building. I wondered at how wealthy he must've been before the Germans decided to go on holiday across Europe.

Anais and Andi led us upstairs, then returned to offer their assistance with whatever George might need. Sparrow took a bath and curled up beneath the covers of a plush bed in one of George's several bedrooms. Egret found a liquor cart and made himself a morning cocktail, then promptly passed out in an overstuffed chair. Thomas and I found a small study where we could talk without being overheard.

"What's your thoughts on Andi and George?"

I slouched in a wooden chair whose stiff back refused to give. "I like Andi. George ... I don't know. There's something about him I can't wrap my head around."

"You think he's lying?"

"No." I sat forward. "No, I think he means well. It's just ... that mustache."

Thomas blinked, then smirked for the first time in too long. "With everything going on, you're hung up on his mustache?"

"Thomas, it looks like something out of a bad Hollywood film where a bad actor ties an overly panicked woman to train tracks."

"Would she really be *overly* panicked if someone was tying her to train tracks? Isn't she allowed to panic any way she likes in that case?"

A laugh slipped out. "Fuck off. You know what I'm saying."

"Oh, no, you're on your own with this one. I have no idea just how dastardly you think our man is here."

I found a throw pillow and made to hurl it. Thomas cocked a brow and held up a finger. "Not our place, remember?"

Then his fucking smirk widened.

"I really hate you. You know that, right?"

He darted across the room and pressed his lips to mine. "No, you *love* me within an inch of your life, just like I do you." His words were rasps wrapped in growls tied with moans. My whole body yearned to rip off his coat and—

"Seriously." He shattered that illusion by stepping back and sitting. "What do you think?"

I blew out a frustrated sigh. "Well, he's all we've got. I say we hear him out and go from there."

Thomas nodded thoughtfully. "Yeah, guess that about sums it up."

He stared into the barren hearth for a long moment, then muttered without looking up, "I wish we could curl up and hold each other while we slept. I miss holding you."

My heart leapt into my throat. "Me too."

***

The four of us stared blankly toward each other; not at, just toward. Despite each attempting to nap throughout the day, none of us had slept well and were barely coherent as we waited. An hour past noon, Anais entered the apartment with a tray of sandwiches, nuts, and dried fruit. We'd been left alone since, and it was nearly ten o'clock in the evening.

"God, I'm hungry," Egret groused.

"Yeah, I'm not even going to give you shit this time," I said. "I'm pretty much starving too."

Sparrow's mouth opened, and I was sure she was about to scold us, citing how many people across Europe knew hunger far more than we did, when the door opened and Anais, Andi, and George entered. Andi fought to smooth his wispy hair as it swirled in all directions. George looked like he'd just walked off set. Nary a hair on his head—or mustache—was out of place.

Thomas stood. "So? Do you have a plan?"

"So fucking direct," George grunted. "Yes, Wilhelm, I have a plan. It is ... how do you say ... a shitty one, but it is a plan."

Thomas chuffed. "Shitty is what we do. I don't think we'd have it any other way."

"Speak for yourself, fearless leader," Sparrow snarked.

"I like shitty plans. They're fun," Egret chimed in.

"Children, please," I said in my most mocking, matronly tone.

Andi and George turned to Anais. She grinned as she shook her head and said, "Americans," as though that one word explained everything.

George's shoulders rose, then fell, then he turned back toward us. "We should not talk up here, and the restaurant is filled. Once the patrons and staff have left, we will meet in the cellar. You leave for Geneva tomorrow afternoon."

"Geneva?" Thomas spoke the question in my head.

"Yes. I will explain later. Anais and Andi will bring you dinner. No one will look twice at a tray of food coming upstairs. I will speak with you soon."

With that, he and Andi spun and vanished back downstairs. We fell back into the chairs they'd found us in.

"Geneva. What the fuck?" Egret asked no one in particular.

"It has to be part of a larger plan. We'll know soon enough," I said, hoping to end his moaning before it grew too loud.

Anais had remained with us, and I noticed Thomas whispering with her at the far end of the room, so I stood and joined them.

"... have known him for many years. He is a very good man."

Thomas scratched his chin. "And George?"

"George is ..." She looked down, as though searching for the courage to finish her answer. "One of the leaders of the resistance movement in Paris. You could not have a better ally in your mission."

Thomas's eyes widened slightly. "Thank you, Anais. We can't say that enough. We would already be dead at least once without your help."

"And you will likely die with my help now. This mission is insane. You know that, don't you?" her voice pleaded more than asked.

"I know," Thomas said.

When the silence stretched between them, I finally asked something that had nagged at me all day. "Anais, how has an English pub survived the occupation?"

She startled at the change of subject, then a thin smile formed. "George has the Nazis convinced he is an agent for them. He also gives their officers free alcohol. It is amazing what a man will do for free wine."

"A double agent? And you trust us with that?" Incredulity threaded Thomas's voice.

"You go to Berlin. What harm will that knowledge do?" She shrugged in the way we'd seen a hundred times since entering France. "I will go find you dinner now. Try to get some rest."

We ate roasted vegetables from the kitchen and sipped on wine from George's bottomless barrels. At any other time, our stay at Le Bon Georges would've been a postcard memory, something Thomas and I would remember fondly for many years.

But this wasn't any other time. This was war.

Andi poked his head in the doorway shortly after midnight and bade us follow him down to the cellar. Once comfortably seated with another round of glasses filled to the brim, George began.

"Let's start with the easy part first. I had your message transmitted to London today."

Thomas stiffened. "Did they reply?"

George shook his head. "Nothing beyond acknowledging receipt of our transmission. The Nazis have become skilled in finding our radios. I doubt they would send more than a few words anyway."

Thomas sat back, his eyes distant but hard.

"You cannot cross the border from France into Germany. It is too heavily guarded. Besides, convoys move constantly on the main roads. You would be stopped too many times." George placed a set of thin spectacles on his nose. "One of the few non-military organizations the Nazis allow free passage into and out of Germany is the Red Cross. If you walked the streets of Paris, you would eventually see their people. The Germans hope to win the hearts of the French people by healing the wounds they inflicted."

Andi's voice faltered, "There is a delegation of leaders from the Swiss Red Cross headed to Berlin in two days. The Nazis plan a tour of one of their camps to show the world they care for their captives with compassion and humanity. It will be scrubbed clean of their horrors, to be sure. I have arranged for you to join this delegation."

"Red Cross *again*?" Egret blurted.

George nodded. "We find the cover of aid workers to be most helpful. The German Red Cross has fully aligned itself with the Reich. You must not trust them, especially their leadership."

I finally looked past Thomas to a stack of uniforms folded neatly on a table near the door. I hadn't noticed them when we'd entered. A few looked like standard Nazi blacks, but their stark white armband with its blood-red cross was unmistakable. Near the bottom of the stack lay a pure white outfit I assumed was for Sparrow.

"Anais and Andi will drive your team in two separate cars. We cannot risk so large a group traveling together. Our contact in Geneva will give you further instructions. Wilhelm, this is your team. How do you propose using this cover?"

Thomas thought a moment, then spoke, his words like tempered steel. "I have fairly comprehensive triage training. Anny was a nurse in a former life." Thomas cleared his throat, then pointed toward Egret. "Heinz, you and Tobias will pose as corpsmen. If challenged, you are actually security for our Red Cross team, a function the Germans will understand and respect, especially since we'll be returning from an aid mission in *liberated* France."

I knew that's how the Nazis described their conquests to the German people in newsreels, but hearing Thomas refer to a country under an oppressive boot as "liberated" still ground my nerves.

George winced. "It is such a terrible thing to say."

"I know. It is," Thomas said, his gaze locked on George. "But it's how we have to speak until this is over. We keep the backstories created for us … back home. The chance for a slip with new identities is too great, given our short amount of time to learn them. The one difference is that each of us answered the Führer's call and joined the Red Cross to support the war effort."

"Wait." Sparrow leaned forward. "I'm French. How does that work?"

Andi stood and rifled through the uniforms, unfurling the white one. It reminded me of a nun's outfit, pure white complete with a habit that draped past the shoulders. The only color was a tiny red cross and elegant script that read, *Croix-Rouge Française*.

"You will still be French. You met Tobias in Paris and fell in love."

She groaned.

"Hey!" I shoved her playfully, briefly forgetting the seriousness of the conversation. "You were just my fiancée. The least you can do is follow me back home to Schnitzel-land."

Her hands flew up and covered her face as a snort escaped. "We're so fucked," she muttered.

Thomas and Egret's eyes popped wide. In all the time we'd known her, Sparrow almost never cursed. Not even once.

Sparrow sat back and crossed her arms. "This is awfully thin. Why would a crew of rank-and-file Red Cross workers be pulled from Paris to travel to Switzerland to *then* travel to Berlin to attend a high-level Nazi parade? It doesn't make sense."

"She's right," I said. "This is weak."

George's voice remained patient, though I could tell he wasn't a man who liked being tested. "Flights from Paris to Berlin have all but halted. The Allies have focused their bombing on the submarine ports, but their fighters still battle for control of the skies—and all the talk is about how the Americans will impact the air war … if they ever arrive."

He muttered the last words just loud enough to be heard. The whole of Europe had begged for assistance from across the Atlantic since the Germans first rolled tanks into Poland. If Japan hadn't provoked America, they might never have awoken from their slumber.

"And the Germans won't object—or just shoot us?" Sparrow added.

George leaned in. "Our people are well embedded in the Swiss government. The Germans want to show the international community how well behaved they are. They might not roll out a red carpet, but they *will* ensure this delegation's safe passage. I know this is tough, but it's the best we've got."

When no one spoke, George stood and removed his spectacles. "I will have breakfast prepared for you tomorrow morning. You should travel in daylight to lower suspicion, which means leaving before noon. Get some rest. You're going to need it."

Chapter Twenty-Five

Thomas

Anais and Andi brought trays filled with simple fare for breakfast. Meat was a luxury, but with numerous farms surrounding Crécy, eggs were plentiful. The coffee from George's press was like drinking silk, and each sip made me long to stay another day in his care, if only for the *café*.

"I packed some food for the trip," Anais said, setting two flour sacks on a table. "It would normally take us five or six hours, depending on how many times we are stopped, but I expect a much longer drive with the Germans checking papers near every town."

"Did you hear from London?" I asked Andi.

He shook his head. "We have not received a reply, but that may mean nothing. Our pianists move constantly. They may not have had time to send word of London's message, even if one was received. Such things are handled with great care.""I'd hope so," Egret snarked as he shoveled his third helping of eggs into his mouth.

Sparrow punched his arm. "Behave."

"Yes, Mom." He grinned like a rebellious youth, displaying a disgustingly full mouth of half-chewed breakfast.

I pinched the bridge of my nose and released a chuckle. God, it felt good to laugh. We risked our lives every moment we remained in Europe, and much of that time was fraught with tension and fear. If Egret's boyish antics lightened the mood, who was I to complain? Besides, I knew Sparrow enjoyed his torment. She might play the prude, but she was nearly as cheeky as he was when she let her hair down—albeit in the style of a librarian who'd just lowered her evening's tome to crack a joke.

I glanced over to find Will lost in thought. His eyes were distant, staring somewhere between the books on a short shelf and the other side of the ocean. To anyone else, he looked contemplative, but I knew his furrowed brow bore more than simple reflection. Worry creased the corners of his eyes, and I couldn't blame him. While it was the best plan we could muster, this venture into the heart of Hitler's capital was insane, and the odds of success—and our survival—were less than I could calculate.

As though sensing my gaze, he looked up. I offered a tight smile and quick nod, then turned back to Andi. "What do you think we should do if we get separated?" I asked.

Andi didn't hesitate. "We *will* get separated, either at a checkpoint or somewhere else along the road. We cannot be seen to travel together, so it is imperative one car not wait for the other if we are stopped. In fact, being separated may be best for our cover."

"But we're part of the same Red Cross team. Wouldn't it make sense if we drove together?" Sparrow asked.

"Don't use logic with Nazis. It will not work, and your head will hurt," Andi said with a smile that didn't reach his eyes. "Our cover will not work so well until we enter Switzerland. You will each receive Red Cross credentials once we arrive. Without them, you have no story to tell."

"Well, shit," Egret said. "Why didn't we get those before leaving?"

This time Andi's grin was warmer. "You only arrived in Paris yesterday. There was not time, and we do not have the material needed to create such documents. The Swiss do.""So, how do we pass checkpoints without them?" Sparrow asked, leaning forward.

"The same way we always do. Let us speak and remain silent unless a soldier addresses you," Anais said. "There are many small roads that connect farms. We have mapped a route that avoids known checkpoints."

I resisted the urge to join in Egret and Sparrow's questioning—they needed to see my confidence—but I felt the same trepidation they expressed. This was the first leg of our journey and already the thread was frayed thin.

"Other questions?" I asked my team.

When no one responded, I said, "Fine. Tobias, you and I ride with Andi. Heinz and Anny, you ride with Anais. We leave in twenty."

Egret's attention returned to the last of his breakfast.

Sparrow shook her head and sipped her coffee.

Will stared into the bookcase in silence.

⸺◆⸺

"What's happening?" Will jolted awake as Andi slowed and turned onto a gravel drive. He'd slept in the back seat since we left Paris, while Andi and I chatted quietly up front. We hadn't seen a single German soldier along the winding paths that crisscrossed France's farmland, though we had lost sight of our other car a few miles into the trek.

"We need petrol, and my back needs to stretch," Andi said. Then, reading my thoughts, he added, "The others will be along shortly. Anais knows to stop here."

I looked back to find Will rubbing his bleary eyes with his palms. A cowlick had formed where his head had pressed against the window. It might've been the cutest thing I'd seen in months.

We pulled up to a large house in the center of a golden field that stretched beyond my sight. The driveway was the only path to the house, and it must've extended more than a mile. Andi drove the car around to the back of the house and parked.

"We are far from anything, but it's best we keep out of sight as much as possible. It would be strange to see more than two cars in front of one farmhouse," Andi explained before opening his door and unfolding himself.

A short, thin woman with leathery skin and a tangled mass of black hair stepped out of the back door, then waved us in without a word. Andi barely looked up when she introduced herself as Gardiner, making it clear this was the closest thing to a name we would receive. Twenty minutes later, the second car with Anais and our remaining team arrived.

Gardiner refueled our cars while we ate a quick meal of freshly made crusty bread and an assortment of cheeses and meats. As simple as lunch was, Gardiner beamed when I told her it might've been the tastiest food I'd eaten since arriving in France. A woman of few words, she prattled on about the freshness of each item, and how she'd grown every ingredient.

A half-hour after the second car arrived, we waved goodbye to Gardiner via a small dust plume behind our car.

Thirty kilometers from the Swiss border, our luck ran out.

"Is that a checkpoint ahead?" I asked.

Andi grunted and nodded, as we both squinted into the distance at what appeared to be two large vehicles and the quickly resolving outline of a half-dozen men in uniform. We entered a queue behind two other cars and watched as an officer questioned the first driver while two soldiers inspected their vehicle. Several soldiers remained at the checkpoint, their rifles hanging lazily across their shoulders.

The car driven by Anais pulled in behind us before we were waved forward for inspection. Chancing a quick glance back, Will and I locked eyes before he settled in to pretend to be asleep, part of the checkpoint drill we'd rehearsed a dozen times during the trip.

I couldn't help the flutter that clawed at my chest as the officer approached Andi's window. The sun was low on the horizon. Still, light streamed through the windshield as Andi handed over his papers. The officer scanned them once, then glanced up at Andi, then returned his scrutiny to the papers.

"*Steigen Sie aus dem Auto aus,*" the officer ordered.

Step out of the car.

A spike of fear stabbed into my gut.

Andi fiddled with the handle, then made a show of using the door to lever himself out of the driver's seat. Once standing outside, the officer shut the door behind him and walked him a few paces away. Two men who'd been inspecting the car took up positions facing my door and Will's on the opposite side. From one of the trucks at the checkpoint, a third man joined them, and all three spun their rifles off their shoulders into the ready position.

I couldn't hear what the officer asked Andi, but our guide was feigning poor hearing and even weaker German language skills, making the interrogation painful for the German. I wondered if his tactic was wise, given the Nazis' proclivity for shooting first and asking later, especially when locals annoyed them, but Andi stuck to his legend, and the officer, clearly more frustrated than annoyed, eventually handed back his papers and waved us forward.

I breathed even more deeply when our other car encountered only cursory inspection and passed quickly through the checkpoint. They wouldn't drift too far behind now that we were almost within sight of the Swiss border.

"I thought I might throw up," I said as our rear bumper whisked past the German line.

"You?" Will said, sitting up behind me. "You never show nerves. Besides, you could see what was happening. I had to just lay there and hope everything would work out."

"Sounds familiar," slipped out before I could stop myself. I could practically hear Will blushing, though he had the good sense not to reply. Andi shot me a glance with one raised brow, but also remained silent.

"What now? We've got to be close," I asked, desperate to distract myself.

"We are not far now. There will be a checkpoint at the border, then we head into the city to meet our contacts. Switzerland may be neutral, but remember, every nation on earth has spies here, *especially* the Germans. They are on every street corner, in every café, in every business and organization. You must assume they are listening at all times and never break cover."

"Even in the Red Cross?" Will asked.

Andi chuckled. "Especially in the Red Cross. They would not have been invited to Berlin for this ridiculous side show if Hitler had not riddled the cheese with holes."

A Swiss cheese joke, really? I resisted the urge to groan.

"Come on. That was a good one, no?" Andi chided with an affable smile.

"No. Really ... no," Will answered drolly.

"Before we go further, I need to finish your briefing for this leg of your journey," Andi said, his voice turning serious.

Finish our briefing? What had they left out, and why would he wait until now to tell us everything? We had been holed up in the privacy of a safe house. Now we were traveling through Nazi checkpoints into yet another country whose loyalty was questionable at best. My mind reeled as Andi gathered his thoughts.

"There are three members of your delegation: Victor von Steinbach is the president of the Swiss Red Cross. He's a bit uptight, but has worked for the organization for many years and is well respected. He has remained frustratingly neutral in all conversations regarding the Nazis. Second is Dr. Alexander Emile. He is a psychiatrist who will help evaluate both prisoners and your escorts."

"A psychiatrist?" I asked.

He nodded without looking up. "The Nazis are masters at deception. We know of two instances in which they set up entire towns to fool inspectors. They brought in Germans and dressed them in prison garb. Dr. Emile's primary role is to ferret out deception the untrained eye might miss."

"Huh," I grunted, unsure how to feel about having my head examined during the mission.

"Finally, one of the Red Cross's most significant patrons, Baroness Isabella von Hohenberg, has insisted on attending. She is ... how shall I say ... quite a character. I do not know why she wanted to be part of this inspection, but her political and social influence made refusing her impossible. We believe she and von Steinbach have known each other since childhood, but have no insight into her loyalties beyond her affinity for wine and jewelry."

"A socialite wants to go into Germany during the war? And we're letting her?" Will asked.

Andi chuckled. "I believe you will soon find that no one 'lets' Baroness von Hohenberg do anything."

The conversation died as a line of stopped cars appeared a few hundred yards ahead of us. Andi's face remained smooth, but his knuckles whitened on the steering wheel. This was the checkpoint we most dreaded.

⸺◇⸺

We could barely believe it. The guards at the Swiss border were surprisingly friendly, barely glancing at Andi's papers before welcoming us into Switzerland. Fifteen minutes later, the familiar sight of a white flag with a crimson cross snapping atop a building came into view, and our car rolled to a stop.

Avenue de la Paix 19 in Geneva, Switzerland, presented an elegant and dignified facade that blended seamlessly with the surrounding buildings, most of which had been labeled with bronze plaques marking them as diplomatic or governmental enclaves. Smooth, cream-colored stone walls rose several stories high, exuding an aura of history and importance, while vines of ivy clung to the walls, as if nature itself sought to embrace this bastion of diplomacy and humanitarianism.

Large arched windows framed in ornate molding punctuated the building's facade. Behind these windows, delicate curtains hinted at the presence of life and activity, though the true nature of the building's interior remained hidden to the casual observer.

"Wow, that's a big headquarters," Will said.

"It houses more than just the Swiss Red Cross. You will see," Andi said, his lip curling with hidden knowledge.

When our second car pulled up behind us and Anais's door opened, Andi began to exit. "Time to dance. Remember, trust no one. Never drop your cover, not even in private."

Chapter Twenty-Six

Will

"**G**od, it feels good to stand up," I said, stretching my arms high over my head and arching my back.

Andi grunted his agreement as he took a few steps around the car.

Thomas gave me a quick smile, then turned and headed quickly toward the other car where Egret and Sparrow were climbing out. A moment later, the four of them joined us at the front of Andi's car, and Thomas leaned in to whisper, "Anais gave them the same speech. We're all good."

I wasn't sure "all good" was how I would've described our team in that moment but took comfort in us all having received the same information.

The grand double doors to the Red Cross building swung open and two figures emerged. An elegant woman, her hair awash with the ebb and flow of the current style, drifted down the stairs as would the highest royal entering her court. Three strands of pearls descended from her neck to her breast, and the sheen of her emerald gown glimmered in the waning sun. Behind her, a bald man with a thick salt-and-pepper beard stood stiffer than a Nazi soldier at inspection, his eyes roaming, never settling on one of us for longer than a heartbeat.

"*Willkommen in der Schweiz,*" the woman said as she approached Andi, then kissed each of his cheeks, allowing him to do the same.

Welcome to Switzerland.

Her every movement held the grace of every dancer to ever grace a stage, and I found myself mesmerized by her presence. She wasn't beautiful in the way of a Hollywood pinup, more classically handsome as a woman of middle age, but the air seemed to warm around her as she greeted each of us in turn. I found myself a nervous boy receiving his first kiss when she alighted before me and smiled.

"You must be Tobias," she said in beautifully accented English that reminded me of lilies and a gentle breeze. "I must scold my advisers for understating how handsome you are."

The blush burned to the tips of my ears as my head fell forward in an unintended bow. My eyes averted, I caught the sun's brilliance refracted in the facets of a boulder-sized diamond on the Baroness's hand. Two other fingers held bands embedded with pearls and other precious stones whose value likely exceeded the wealth of entire towns we'd passed earlier in the day.

She laughed, and I swear the sunset blazed across the sky at her call.

"I am Baroness Isabella von Hohenberg, your hostess for the duration of our travels. This"—she turned and extended an open palm toward the stoic, bearded man still standing atop the stairs near the doors—"is Victor von Steinbach, president of the Swiss Red Cross. He is a lovely man who leads our most worthy cause."

She leaned toward me and whispered behind a gloved hand, "He's exactly as rigid and boring as you are thinking, but he is a good man nonetheless."

I stifled a laugh. She didn't, and the sound of her mirth echoed off the building's walls.

Von Steinbach scowled, as if knowing exactly what she'd just said.

"Come," the Baroness waved. "You must be tired from your long drive. I will have the staff show you to your rooms. Dinner will be served in the executive dining room at eight. I am sure our president will choose to speak then."

She gave me one last conspiratorial grin, then wheeled and glided up the staircase, where she shooed the president inside.

"President Stiff Back," I muttered to myself.

Thomas and Egret, standing on either side of me, spat a laugh.

"Steinbach," Egret said. "You behave. We're guests, remember?"

"Yes, Mom," I groused, though my smile spoke more of amusement than abasement.

We entered the building, and I was at once struck by the spacious, marbled foyer adorned with graceful chandeliers that cast a warm, inviting glow.

A young man with bright blond hair stepped forward as we stepped to the foyer's center. His crystal blue eyes flared against the deep navy of his uniform. Golden buttons formed two rows across his chest, and a band of pure white with the familiar red cross adorned his arm. He couldn't have been more than twenty years old, yet his eyes held a keenness that somehow belied his age.

"Steven, would you show our guests to their rooms so they might refresh themselves before dinner?" the Baroness asked, receiving a smile and shallow bow.

"Of course, Baroness von Hohenberg." Steven turned toward us, warmth radiating through his features. "Follow me, please."

He led us down a series of wide, richly paneled hallways whose walls were decorated with tasteful, muted artwork depicting scenes of compassion, resilience, and the organization's history. Polished wooden doors with subtle brass plaques denoting various offices were recessed in the walls between each piece.

"I will be your personal attaché throughout your stay. If you need anything, please ask," Steven said over his shoulder as we walked.

We descended below ground level, entering a hallway that resembled a typical hotel. Rich carpets covered the floors, and the names adorning plaques on the doors were replaced by simple numbers.

"I am afraid we cannot offer each of you your own room. With the war, we remain overcrowded, even using offices to house refugees. I am sure you understand."

Anais spoke before any of us could answer. "Of course. It is the same in Paris, and I expect we will find Berlin experiencing a similar strain."

"Yes, of course," Steven said, his smile effortless. "Your rooms are here. Two of you are assigned to each. Numbers twenty-one, twenty-two, and twenty-three. I will leave you to refresh yourselves, but will return a few moments before the dinner hour. This building can be quite the labyrinth without a guide."

He handed Anais our keys, then offered a crisp bob of his head, wheeled about, and vanished down the hallway.

"I think Heinz and I should room together," Sparrow said, a quirk forming on her lips.

Egret's brows rose. "Really? And why would I want—"

Sparrow stepped close and placed a hand on his chest, her voice low and raspy. "I haven't slept in a comfortable bed in far too long, and I haven't had a handsome man beside me in far longer. It's time I taught you how to roll your Rs properly." Her French accent was somehow sultry *and* playful.

Egret nearly staggered back, and I thought Thomas's eyes might fly out of their sockets. None of us had seen this side of Sparrow, and we certainly hadn't seen this coming.

Egret stared down at her, then his eyes fell to her hand still pressed against his chest. "I ... uh ... think that ... would be fine."

I'd never seen the man so flustered. It took everything I had not to spit laughing right there in the hallway. Sparrow spun, snatched a key out of Anais's hand, then grabbed Egret by the lapel and dragged him toward the room matching the key fob's number.

"We have enough time before dinner to ... how did Steven say it? Refresh ourselves?" Sparrow called over her shoulder. "I plan to be fully refreshed."

Egret cast one last glance back at Thomas and me, and I couldn't decide if it was more plea, pleasure, or panic. Whatever it was, I lost my battle with self-control and laughter echoed down the hall. As the pair of lovebirds vanished into their room, the rest loosened their own laughter and shook their heads.

"In the middle of all this, they managed to find ... whatever that is," Thomas said.

"Andi and I will leave early in the morning, so we should room together. Here is the key for you two," Anais said, handing Thomas a key. My heart fluttered at the realization that Thomas and I would share a room together—a private room—for the first time since leaving the US. Suddenly, Sparrow's taunting about "refreshing herself" sounded tame in my ears, and heat flooded places it had abandoned over the past weeks.

Thomas stared down at the key as if Anais had handed him a bar of gold, finally glancing up and nodding.

"Try to get some rest tonight. Tomorrow begins a challenging mission," Anais said, a warning in her tone but a smile on her lips.

Does she know about Thomas and me? Panic replaced lust, and a spike of fear shot through my veins.

Anais must've noticed, because she leaned forward, gripped my arm, then whispered, "Calm yourself. We are not so uptight as you Americans. The love between you is as plain as the sun in the sky. There is too much suffering these days to not enjoy happiness where you may."

I could barely breathe. Words definitely wouldn't come.

Thomas sputtered, "Thank you, Anais. Both of you, for everything."

With those words, Thomas turned and opened the door to room twenty-two.

Chapter Twenty-Seven

Thomas

I stepped inside the kind of well-appointed room one might find in a mid-tier hotel. The furniture was more utilitarian than luxurious, but the linens were crisp, and the air smelled of lilac or some other fragrance I couldn't quite identify. A pair of twin-sized beds consumed the center of the room, separated by a small table whose lamp welcomed us with warm light. Images of men and women in Red Cross uniforms giving aid adorned the walls, a perpetual reminder of the building in which we would sleep.

I tossed my coat on a chair next to the window and turned as the door clicked shut. Will stood there, motionless, his eyes following my every move.

"It'll be nice to sleep in a bed for a change," I said, suddenly self-conscious for no good reason.

Will nodded, but remained still.

"Are you okay?"

He finally stepped forward, closing the distance between us. My heart leapt as his hands rose to grip my face, and his lips found mine. I'll never fully understand what type of magic that man possessed, but his kiss made Geneva and Europe and the war—all of it—fade away. There was nothing in that moment but his love for me, his desire to be close, to feel safe, to be wanted.

And I more than wanted him. I needed him.

I wrapped my arms around his waist and pulled him into me, squeezing him as though he might vanish if I let go. At the first taste of his tongue, my senses reeled.

"I love you so much," his breathless words uttered.

"You're wearing too many clothes."

He snorted, wrenching our lips apart. "You're so fucking romantic."

My lips quirked. "You know it. Now, get naked. You have nipples that need my teeth."

His brows rose, and his eyes popped wide. "Who am I to refuse our fearless leader?"

"Follow orders. That's exactly what you need to do, *Tobias*."

His head cocked, as though processing his cover name, perhaps deciding whether its use had killed the mood, then his hands left my face and he began to strip off his clothes.

"We don't have much time. Let me help." I began to unbutton his shirt.

"Romantic and impatient. I love it," he taunted.

His only reply was to yank my shirt off my shoulders and toss it against the wall. I'd barely sucked in a breath before his fingers were working the buckle on my belt.

"Shit, your hands are cold," he said.

I pressed a palm into his chest and received a wince for my effort.

"Fucker."

I grinned, and shoved him down onto one of the beds. "Soon enough."

He snorted as I began unlacing his shoes, then pulled his pants and underwear off. We'd only kissed for a dozen heartbeats, yet he had already stiffened. The beautiful blue pathways pulsed as his shaft twitched against his flat belly.

"God, I missed him," I growled, leaving his socks in place to climb atop him and run my tongue up the length of his cock. His whole body shuddered, and his fingers reached down and dug into my shoulders.

"Why aren't you naked?" he grumbled.

I swallowed him as far as my throat would allow, cupping his balls, pulling gently. I looked up the length of his torso, reveling in how his head fell back, eyes closed, and elation painted his features.

Nothing drove me more mad than this man's happiness.

"Fuck, Thomas." His fingers kneaded my shoulders through my shirt.

I pulled back and repositioned myself, straddling his legs so I could remove my shirt. He reached for my belt, but I swatted his hand away. "You, be a good little boy and just watch."

His smile ignited my soul.

I had to roll over to remove my shoes and trousers. His hand trailed along my back the entire time, keeping us connected.

Fully naked, I laid beside him so we faced each other and scooted us both up so our heads rested on the pillow. The bed was a tight fit for two grown men, but neither of us cared. We pressed our bodies together, and the pulsing I'd seen before writhed against my own hardness.

I cupped his cheek, and he leaned into my touch, as he so often did. Our eyes locked, and I thought the world might spin away.

"I love you, Will Shaw, more than anything in this world."

"We already established how hopeless you are. Now, what was that nipple thing you mentioned earlier?" he asked with a quirk of his lips.

I poured myself into our next kiss. If I could've climbed into him and lived forever, it wouldn't have lasted long enough. His hands gripped my back, pulling us together, nearly pressing the air from my lungs. Still, I wanted more.

I kissed his cheek, then trailed my teeth down his neck.

He shivered again.

So I bit into his skin, just enough to earn a moan, then worked my way to his ear. He had the cutest lobes, a little too small for his ears, but they were perfect. My teeth latched on, and I ground back and forth, enamel grazing tender flesh.

He groaned deeper and arched his back.

A kiss to the raw lobe, then onward.

I trailed my teeth down his neck again, kissing his collarbone, then chest, then hovering above his right nipple. Like his lobe, it was tiny, too small for his corded muscle, but it was Will's, so I loved it.

My tongue played around the edges, circling, teasing, taunting.

He squirmed again. He was so sensitive.

When I brushed the hardness of my teeth against his perky skin, his whole body jerked.

"Oh, fuck, that feels crazy."

I clamped down.

He gasped. "Thomas!"

I bit harder.

"Oh, shit. Ow. Fuck."

"Too much?"

"Hell no. Do it again."

So I did, harder.

By the time I moved to his other nipple, the first one was more crimson than pink, and even the slightest flick of my finger against it made his cock twitch. The first drops of pre-cum were already slickening our bodies as we moved against each other.

I took my middle finger and moistened it, then reached down while his eyes were closed and grazed the outside of his hole.

Another spasm ... and a gasp.

"Yes, please, Thomas ..."

I pressed against him, barely entering. His back arched again.

I ran slow circles just inside him, widening, loosening, testing; all the while, my tongue licked at his other nipple. The combination had his eyes clamped shut and his head thrown back.

Then I pressed in deeper, and his moan filled the room. I shot upward and covered his mouth with mine, suddenly conscious of how sound might carry between rooms but not wanting to stop.

Will barely noticed.

I pulled my finger back, then drove deeper, searching, finding that place within that sent a jolt through him. I pressed against it, again and again, smothering his whimpers with my mouth and tongue.

"Get inside me, now. Please. I need you, Thomas," he begged.

Reluctantly, our lips parted, and I freed my finger, then repositioned myself so his legs could rest on my shoulders.

"We couldn't exactly bring ... equipment. Spit will have to do," I apologized.

"I'll spit on your hand if it'll help. Just get in there."

I grinned at his insistence, and lathered up my cock as best I could, then pressed my head against his rim. His hand flew behind me and pulled me forward. Before I realized what he'd done, I was fully inside him, the warmth of his body consuming my cock, sending a tremor of pleasure up my spine. His hand held me there, kept me still, as his other hand reached up and pulled my head down toward him. When our lips met, his fingers dug into my butt, and I began rocking slowly, pulling myself almost out, then pressing deep again.

Cautious of a lack of lubricant, I steadied my pace—until he pulled his lips away, tossed his head back again, and ordered, "Harder. Fuck me harder."

So I did.

The bed creaked beneath us. Our bodies slapped against each other.

I leaned over him, forcing his legs higher on my shoulders as my hands pressed against the wall above the headboard.

There was nothing but Will in that moment. His need for me. My desire for him.

I thrust harder, drove myself deeper, as if heaving all the years of love between us into his body with each push.

Pressure built, growing from deep within and flowing forward, so I gripped his cock and began to stroke. He was so damn hard. Feeling him throb in my palm drove my need, quickened my pace, and I knew I wouldn't last much longer.

"Will, I'm close. Fuck."

"Me too. Stroke me faster. I want to ... shit!"

Warmth struck my chest as his first wave shot toward me. His ass clenched and his abs tightened, again and again. As the last of him streamed out, I felt my own control vanish and I poured myself into him.

"God, Will. Fuck. I love you, dammit."

I slammed into him harder, faster, draining every drop from my body before flopping over onto my side next to him.

"I wish you could stay inside me as we sleep," he said, reading my thoughts.

I smiled and brushed the hair from his forehead. "I would live inside you if I could."

"You do, Thomas. You already do."

Chapter Twenty-Eight

Will

Two sharp raps on the door jolted me out of my thoughts. Thomas reached up and fastened the top button of my uniform, then ran a palm over my chest to smooth the wrinkles. It was such a simple gesture, but something in its intimacy conveyed more than any words could.

"Must be dinnertime," he said in a near whisper that begged to preserve our private moment for a few heartbeats longer.

"Must be." I reached up and smoothed a lock of his hair, then cupped his cheek. "As much as I'd like to never leave this room, I really am starving."

He turned and grabbed his coat off the bed. "So ... Egret and Sparrow?"

I laughed. "Yeah, who knew?"

"I guess he's handsome, but ... Sparrow? She's more of the naughty librarian type than I thought. I mean, I had the librarian part down, but the naughty?"

I grunted. "Bet she's a wild one. Egret might be begging for mercy before it's all over."

Thomas chuckled. "That I'd like to see. Mr. Bravado brought to his knees."

"Literally."

Thomas missed a step laughing. "Stop that! You're going to blow our cover."

"Almost like I just blew you—"

"Will!"

I laughed and gave him a last peck on the cheek. "I love you, Thomas. Now, let's go get food before I start gnawing on your leg."

"Ooh. That sounds—"

"Shut up and move," I said, shoving him toward the door.

Egret and Sparrow were the last to arrive in the hallway. She was as put-together as ever, her hair sweeping in perfectly tight curls. He looked like someone had run over him with a car, his hair wet from the shower and flaring in all directions. His eyes weren't exactly rimmed red like he'd not slept in days, but there was clear exhaustion staring back that wasn't borne of our travels.

Sparrow's face belied nothing, then our eyes met and her lips quirked, ever so slightly.

I leaned in. "You and I need to talk."

She nodded once, then her lips smoothed, and the mask of her cover returned.

Steven's eyes darted from one of us to the next as though searching, or trying to interpret the hidden messages in our gazes, I wasn't sure which. "Please, follow me. You will be dining in the executive suite. President von Steinbach wishes to have a moment of privacy with you this evening."

"Will you be joining us?" Andi asked.

"Oh, no," Steven said. "I will dine in the main dining room with our other guests and staff."

He led us up three flights of stairs, then down two long hallways before opening an unmarked door to reveal a richly appointed conference room. Two dozen polished, high-back chairs lined an equally polished table that spanned the length of the room. At the far end, where a larger chair held court, six dinner settings had been placed at the chairs nearest the head where von Steinbach sat. He rose as we entered.

"Ah, there you are. Thank you, Steven. That will be all."

Clearly dismissed, Steven bobbed to von Steinbach and exited, as we stepped down the table's length.

The smell of roasted meats and garlic made my mouth water. I had to hide a chuckle as Thomas's stomach agreed. We hadn't had a proper dinner in ... I couldn't remember how long. It was only after we had sat and begun to serve ourselves that the extravagance of the meal struck me. In the midst of a war, with rationing more prevalent than ever, we ate at a table set for royalty whose wealth knew no bounds. I couldn't help the pang of guilt and I wondered what Steven and the others ate in the main dining hall.

Von Steinbach must've seen the inner battle scrawled across my face. "We do not eat this well often, but this delegation is of special import, and we thought you might enjoy a small luxury before we depart."

I'd barely taken my first bite when the door opened and Baroness von Hohenberg swept into the room. She'd changed into a crimson gown, her strands of pearls replaced by delicate golden chains embedded with diamonds on each link. Her hair now rose in a chiffon barely an inch taller than the glittering tiara that rested easily on her brow.

I didn't know whether to greet her with words or drop to one knee. She was breathtaking.

The president popped from his chair and bowed deeply. "Baroness, you are a vision this evening."

She tittered as though never having received a compliment. "Oh, Victor, you are such a flatterer."

Egret, Andi, Thomas, and I rose, and she smiled at each of us.

"Please, sit. Don't let me interrupt. This looks delicious," she said, gliding toward the empty chair to the right of von Steinbach's throne. For a moment, I thought the president might insist she take his seat at the table's head, but the moment of indecision passed when she motioned for him to retake his seat and settled into the one by his side.

A uniformed member of the staff entered, filled our wine glasses, and deposited several extra bottles before vanishing through the side door and leaving us alone for the next several hours. I had hoped we would have an opportunity to ask questions and learn more about our mission, but the Baroness clearly entered the dining room with other plans. She began with Anais and Andi, peppering them with questions on conditions in France, then turned her raptor-like gaze to the rest of us, asking so many questions that I feared she might discover the limits of our cover stories. More than a few times, Thomas and Sparrow had to create additional friends or family from their past to satisfy her curiosity.

The Baroness was a force of nature that would not be denied.

Through it all, President von Steinbach remained silent. It wasn't as if he tried to interject and was shot down; his mouth never opened in the attempt. If his eyes hadn't been constantly roaming, perpetually seeking, I might've thought he was disinterested. Instead, I began to wonder if his role in this play was to assess and scrutinize as the Baroness distracted. The uneasy feeling I'd felt earlier in the night when Steven showed us to our rooms rumbled once more.

"Victor," the Baroness said, turning to von Steinbach. "Would you be a dear and find someone to bring us another bottle or two? We appear to be empty, and these poor boys look thirsty."

So hard was his gaze, for a moment I thought von Steinbach might refuse and berate the poor woman. Instead, a quiet détente settled between them, and he rose and slipped out of the room. Egret gaped. Sparrow looked like she wanted to run, and Thomas quirked a brow in my direction. All I could do was shrug in bafflement. If there was a social game afoot, I didn't even know the rules, much less how to read the players.

"Listen to me. We only have a moment." The Baroness shot to her feet and leaned across the table. Her voice had lost all its frivolity, as she now spoke with the urgency of a hardened military commander. "Do not trust von Steinbach. He sympathizes with the Nazis and is determined to make this 'tour' of their camps a public relations success for Hitler. Steven is his protégé. You must assume you are being watched and that any conversation in this building is listened to."

The woman's sudden shift from vacant socialite to clandestine shepherd had me so thrown I nearly forgot to breathe. The frozen stares on the others' faces told me they shared my disbelief.

The Baroness glanced toward the door, then continued in a rapid, almost breathless whisper, "When we arrive in Berlin, you will be taken directly to the Ridermark Cathedral. This will be your home while in Germany. There are seven priests. I do not know the loyalty of each, but you must assume most support the Nazi cause. Trust *no one* but Lehmann. Others will watch your every move. You must never let your—"

The door flew open.

"... couldn't believe the theater would put such cheap swill in my delicate hand!" The Baroness's deep-throated laughter filled the room as she switched gears more easily—and far more abruptly—than a racer.

My head spun as my eyes flew to where von Steinbach entered with Steven, each carrying two bottles of wine.

"So, you like our wine?" Steven said, raising a bottle held in each hand. "We cannot let your throats run dry."

Sparrow's eyes darted from Steven to von Steinbach. Thomas and Egret maintained placid expressions, as I raised my empty glass and painted on a smile. "Steven, you're a lifesaver. Thank you so much."

The Baroness snatched her glass from the table and shoved it in front of Steven. His eyes rolled as he looked down at the nearly full glass, but he topped her off without protest.

Thomas placed a palm atop his glass. "None for me, thank you. We have a long day ahead tomorrow."

Sparrow took her cue and similarly covered her glass. Undaunted, Egret held his glass across the table, then knocked back a third of his refill.

"What?" he said with feigned innocence when Thomas glared. "I was thirsty."

Thomas shook his head and leaned back.

Von Steinbach set the bottles he carried on the table, then cleared his throat. "I will leave these with you. Please enjoy your evening. Tomorrow, we will see if your German camps are as humane as the Nazi leadership claims."

For the briefest moment, I'd forgotten that, except for Sparrow, our covers were of *German* Red Cross officials.

"You will be pleased, I am sure," Thomas said with the disinterest of a Nazi who expects compliance.

Von Steinbach eyed him, then nodded crisply. "I will see you in the morning. Breakfast will be served in this room at eight, and we leave for the airport at nine."

"I believe we will follow your example, President von Steinbach. I am exhausted, and your wonderful wine has put my mind in an excellent place for sleep." Thomas stepped forward, took the Baroness's hand, and kissed the back of it. "My lady, you are a most gracious and beautiful host. Thank you for receiving us with such grace."

For the first time since we'd arrived, the Baroness appeared genuinely thrown off as a blush crept into her cheeks. "Oh, my boy, you are too kind."

Thomas kissed her hand one last time, earning a girlish giggle that was at odds with the formidable woman we'd seen all night, then nodded to von Steinbach. "Good evening."

Egret gulped down his wine as I set my untouched glass on the table and followed his lead in paying our respects to our hosts.

That night, I surrendered to the unknown, forgoing dreams of Nazis and what might happen when we entered Hitler's lair. I slept peacefully with my head on Thomas's chest, enjoying the steady rhythm of his heart and the warmth of his breath on my neck.

Chapter Twenty-Nine

Thomas

We bade farewell to Anais and Andi the next morning. We'd only known the pair a few days, but our time in Crécy-la-Chapelle, followed by a harrowing drive fraught with Nazi checkpoints, bonded us in ways no time could measure.

Our flight from Geneva to Berlin was a far cry from the metal seats and turbulent seas of the trip across the Atlantic. The Baroness, wearing her most sensibly sequined ivory gown, climbed the stairs and immediately demanded champagne for the delegation. By the time we settled into plush leather seats, we each had a flute of bubbly in hand and were offered our choice of canapé.

The white of Sparrow's uniform dress, stockings, shoes, and cap stood in odd contrast to the black of the German army uniform Egret, Will, and I wore. Our only saving grace was the band on our arms: white and red rather than blood and black.

President von Steinbach avoided eye contact with each of us as he stepped past to take a seat near the back of the plane. For one who ran a globally respected organization designed to aid those in need, he might've been less interested in human interaction than any man I'd met.

As we entered German airspace, the door to the cockpit opened, and a pilot whose nose bent unnaturally in two places emerged, greeting the Baroness with a bow and kiss on each cheek then turning toward the rest of us.

"We are about to enter Germany. We have advised Allied Command of our mission and do not expect any aerial combat this morning, but this is war. The fighters that ordinarily accompany their bombers do not discriminate between military and civilian aircraft. For that reason, we will fly at a far lower altitude than usual. Unfortunately, this will extend our flight time to nearly two and a half hours. Please try to relax and know we will get you to Berlin safely."

He nodded to the Baroness one last time, then turned and disappeared back into the cockpit.

"Well, that inspired confidence." Egret's voice couldn't have dripped with greater sarcasm. The fact he spoke in German with the thick Dusseldorf accent only underscored the sentiment.

A half-hour later, we settled into a cruising altitude low enough for us to still clearly see barns and houses dotting the edge of farms. Our eyes barely left the windows as we passed over towns and cities.

"My God," Sparrow muttered when the outskirts of Berlin finally came into view.

Plumes of black smoke rose from the ruined shells of several massive buildings that now lay in rubble thanks to the efforts of Allied bombing campaigns. Once proud bridges now sank in the depths of rivers, their girders rising above the water as disjointed monuments to the war's destruction.

At our low altitude, the people of Berlin were visible, many moving about their daily tasks, but more than a few working to clear rubble and debris.

"This is only a taste of what Hitler is doing in Russia, what he has done in other countries," the Baroness said, her voice devoid of its usual cheer. "When all this is over, we will rebuild these cities, but the number of lives lost will be uncountable."

No one responded. I doubted any of us knew what to say. My heart had certainly stilled at the thought.

"When we land," President von Steinbach's voice cut through the gloom, "we will be taken immediately to Theresienstadt. It should be a three-hour drive, but will likely take longer, given road conditions. Our purpose is to inspect conditions of the prisoners of war held there."

To Sparrow, he said, "Nurse Bedeau, please be alert for signs of malnourishment, dehydration, and recent injuries that might indicate physical abuse." He turned back toward the rest of us and continued. "Obviously, we will be shown only locations the Nazis believe will best support their claims of proper internment. Our minders will watch and guard our every movement. Do not stray from the group, but alert me to anything amiss. I will arrange to follow up on anything we cannot fully inspect today. Any questions?"

"Will I be allowed to treat any of the prisoners?" Sparrow asked.

Von Steinbach shook his head. "Doubtful. You may ask, but do not be discouraged if you are refused. The Germans prefer to handle the prisoners themselves."

Handle.

The word would have been comical if it hadn't made my stomach threaten the loss of its contents. The Nazis certainly did *handle* their prisoners with classic German efficiency, if news reports were accurate. Part of me couldn't wait to see the horrors for myself, to confirm why so many Americans now donned uniforms and left families. Another part dreaded whatever we might find, knowing my mind and soul would forever be marred by the experience.

"You okay?" Will whispered near my ear.

"What? Oh, yeah. I guess. Why?"

His lips formed a tight smile. "You've been staring out the window since von Steinbach gave his motivational speech."

I grunted. Motivational. That was a word for it.

"I'm okay. Just thinking about what we might see, that's all."

Will gripped my forearm. "This part's for Arty."

A lump lodged in my throat, and I thought tears might explode from my eyes. I hadn't thought of our friend in weeks; yet here we were, headed into the heart of enemy territory to inspect one of the camps where Jews were ... We didn't know that for certain. I refused to believe any people could be so evil as to ...

Arty.

His face flashed before me, his toothy grin and floppy hair. His innocent gaze, hardened by the worth of the world's wickedness. He was goodness incarnate, and on more than one occasion, our moral compass.

"Yeah, for Arty," I agreed.

"Wheels down in five," the captain's voice called over the speaker. Our attendants scurried about to secure the cabin and ensure each of us was buckled in. The tremor of the plane as it slowed in its approach mirrored that of my chest. I doubted the bees bouncing angrily around my ribs would settle until we returned safely to Allied lands.

The president of the German Red Cross stood at the foot of the stairs as we descended onto German soil. He was flanked by a small group of doctors and nurses, all of whom were surrounded by a bevy of rifle-bearing Nazi soldiers. Whether the latter were our protectors or our wardens remained unclear.

A motorcade of several elegant black cars, flanked by numerous army vehicles and motorcycles, whisked us away before we had time to get our bearings. The airport faded to memory as we snaked our way through the heart of the capital, then north on rural roads toward the camp. The Baroness and President von Steinbach rode in the car with the head of the German delegation. Egret and I were in the car behind, while Sparrow and Will brought up the rear of the caravan. A Nazi driver guided each car, while one German Red Cross representative played host to the guests in their respective vehicles.

Everything moved so quickly as we deplaned that I missed which car Steven climbed into. A quick glance down the line confirmed the only other vehicles were those of the German military. Steven traveling with soldiers might've raised alarm had the Baroness not warned us of his true loyalty. I wondered at what report he must be giving even as we rolled toward our destination.

Nearly four hours later, we'd crossed into Czech territory. Our cars halted before a long cobblestone walkway that led to an archway in a massive redbrick wall whose stones were painted alternating black and white, like horizontal stripes on a prison uniform.

Our hosts ushered us through a set of solid metal doors beneath the arch. I wasn't sure what I'd expected, but a wide, open plaza where children laughed and played was nowhere in my imagination. A long building stretching more than a hundred yards on our left looked more like a small town apartment than a prison. To the right, several market-like stalls offered drinks and fruit. Everywhere we looked, men, women, and children appeared well fed and well dressed. Each wore the golden Star of David sewn above their upper left chest.

I scanned the grounds, stunned that I didn't see a single guard. There were no Nazis carrying machine guns or soldiers standing erect at doorways. They had to be there, watching their charges—and us. It was impossible such a place operated without the vigilance of jailers, but the Germans had clearly done an expert job of hiding any sign of heavy-handed surveillance.

A small girl, no more than six, raced up to Will, extending a daisy she'd picked a moment before. He kneeled to receive the offering, a broad smile parting his lips, then stiffened as the girl wrapped her arms around him and kissed his cheek before racing back to where her mother watched.

"It appears at least one of our guests has taken a liking to you," one of our minders said to Will, loud enough for all to hear. He nodded slowly, watching the girl from across the plaza.

At the opposite end where we entered stood another archway. This simple arc bore not paint, only a simple sign that read, *Arbeit Macht Frei.*

Work Sets You Free.

The Red Cross presidents, the Baroness, and our lead minder strode forward at the head of our disorderly mass, through the humble arch and into yet another plaza, this one surrounded by smaller buildings, each with windows adorned with brightly colored flowers growing from boxes beneath their bottom sill. A few older Jews sat in chairs outside their "apartment," one knitting, another whittling a hunk of wood. It struck me as strange that a prisoner would be allowed a knife, but the man's age and obvious infirmity chased those questions from my mind.

As we walked past each building, narrow alleyways offered a brief glimpse into what lay beyond. Again, I was struck by the most commonplace sight: gardens, lush with leaves and stalks. Shirtless workers labored, weeding and harvesting, going about the usual chores of tending crops. None of the men appeared malnourished. If anything, they appeared hearty and strong.

I stopped walking and stared, unable to resolve the dissonance between what my eyes saw and the stories we'd been told. These gardens were something I was sure could not have been planted simply for our visit. Mature vegetation required the whole summer to grow, which made me wonder if Nazi claims might actually have more merit than we'd originally allowed.

"Please, continue," the minder behind me prodded gently, his voice friendly yet firm.

"Oh, sorry. It's just ..." I pointed down the path between two buildings.

"Ah, yes," the soldier said. "The soil is quite rich here. You should try the vegetables before you leave. They have a sweetness you find in few places."

Sweetness? We stood in the middle of an internment camp for people the Nazis deemed "socially unacceptable," and this man wanted to talk about the way its vegetables teased the palate? I wasn't speechless often, but words failed me as I turned to see the man who'd spoken.

He smiled warmly. "We are falling behind. Should we rejoin the group?"

As if refusing was an option.

"Yes, thank you," I said, shaking myself free of my fog of disbelief.

———◆O◆———

"Did you notice the textbooks in the school?" Sparrow asked as we neared the cars.

"Yeah, they weren't new, but they also weren't worn out," Will answered. "It's as though they were actually used by students and not staged."

She nodded thoughtfully.

I stepped between them. "Did you find any signs of disease or malnutrition? Any bruising or odd cuts? Anything?"

She shook her head. "I really looked. If the place is fake, they've done an incredible job of hiding what's underneath. ""Or they brought in Germans to play the role for us," Egret chimed in, his gravelly voice barely a whisper on the wind. "You don't actually believe this shit, do you?"

Will looked to Sparrow. Her brow rose then fell, then they looked to me.

"All I know is what I saw. Let's wait until we have some privacy and can discuss this with the others."

Ten minutes later, we'd folded ourselves back into our cars and were driving north. The sun was setting, and an eerie orange halo had formed above Theresienstadt, as though the heavens themselves warned of believing the lies we'd just been told.

Chapter Thirty

Vogt

SS-Oberführer Bernard Fuchs downed the last of his brandy and flicked the short-stemmed crystal brandy balloon across his desk. The glass, with a stylistic swastika etched in the middle of an elegant crisscross pattern, clinked against the dull metal of his desk lamp.

The liberation of Russia was well underway, though most of the world had yet to realize it. Between rumors of an Allied landing somewhere on the Western Front, the unexpected beating German troops were taking in Africa, and the opening of the new Russian campaign, the SS general command was driving everyone who worked in the headquarters past their already war-thinned limits. Exhaustion combined with frustration over the African campaign was putting the normally surly men in even more volatile moods.

Fuchs had been holed up in his office for nearly eleven hours, only escaping long enough to relieve himself or retrieve another bottle from the secret storage known only to the elite officers among the SS—and perhaps the cleaning staff. They went virtually unnoticed and knew everything, a thought that chilled his veins, especially given the secretive nature of his work.

He watched his glass wobble, then settle, as though the outcome of the war hung on whether or not it righted itself. His meaty fingers rose to rub his reddened eyes, whose lids had begun sagging hours earlier.

Two sharp raps banged against his door.

He groaned inwardly, but slowly raised his head and sat back. "What?"

"Forgive the intrusion, SS-Oberführer," the staccato of one of the young floor wardens called through the thick wood of his door, sounding more like the firing of an automatic rifle than a human. "There is an SS-Obersturmbannführer Jÿrgen Vogt here insisting you want to see him, but he is not on the day's list."

Fuchs pinched the bridge of his nose. He had resolved to leave the building once his drink evaporated. The last thing he wanted was a visitor, especially one he thought he'd exiled for another few weeks.

"Send him in," he said, resigned to having to face the man before earning an evening's respite.

A moment later, another pair of raps sounded, but this time, the knocker didn't call out. He simply turned the knob and entered.

Arrogant bastard.

Fuchs straightened in his chair, but didn't stand.

"Heil Hitler," Vogt barked crisply, clicking his heels and saluting.

"Yes, yes. Heil Hitler." Fuchs cocked his head. "Why are you in Berlin, Obersturmbannführer?"

"Sir, while I was—"

"Was I not explicit in my orders? It has not been six weeks. Were you able to wave that ego of yours around and pacify the whole of France in less than a month?"

Fuchs had to fight the urge to smile as a blaze flared in his subordinate's eyes.

"Sir, there are Americans in Berlin."

The chair screamed as Fuchs leaned forward and placed his elbows on his desk. "Americans?"

"Yes, sir. One of my men believes they are posing as part of a Red Cross mission."

"Believes or knows?"

Vogt's gaze faltered slightly. "Believes, but is fairly certain. They are staying at Ridermark for the night and returning to Geneva tomorrow. We must act now if—"

"Act now? You mean barge into the most significant cathedral in the fatherland? On a hunch? Or a rumor?" Fuchs barked a laugh. "Obersturmbannführer, the world may believe we act on anger or passion, but I assure you, in this building, we make decisions based on fact. What you *believe* is of no importance to anyone."

"Fine ... sir." Vogt's lips twitched at the sarcasm dripping from Fuchs's voice.

"Was that all? I would like to leave before the sun rises again."

Vogt hesitated, then spoke slowly and deliberately. "I also found a French scientist who may have a solution to our ... weevil problem."

"Go on. Who is this scientist, and where is he?"

"His name is Bernard, and he is downstairs, sir."

All tiredness vanished as Fuchs's head snapped up. "*Hugo* Bernard?"

Vogt cocked his head. "Yes, sir. He worked—"

"You *fucking* idiot." Fuchs shot to his feet. "Do you have *any* idea what you have done?"

"Sir, he can help with the weapon—"

"Vogt, I sent you to Paris with *one* mission: to handle the resistance. I did *not* ask you to pull our most highly placed asset off the board so he could play chemist on a scheme that has little chance for success. Bernard has a *code name* known only to the Führer, Reichsführer Himmler, and me." Fuchs's voice rose as he invoked Hitler and the head of the SS. "You just put years of work in jeopardy."

"Sir—"

Fuchs rounded his desk to stare down at Vogt, his extra six inches and sixty pounds adding to the authority already pinned to his shoulders. He glared down, his jaw clenching and nostrils flaring, and he thought of the many ways he wanted to kill the man standing before him, to crush him like the conniving cockroach he was.

Vogt didn't look away. He didn't flinch. The bastard had the gall to lift his chin in challenge to Fuchs's squared shoulders and snarling eyes.

"You …" Fuchs sucked in a breath, struggling to calm himself. "You will take *your scientist* to join the others. Stay with them. Find a solution or die trying. I truly do not care which, though your death would almost be more satisfying than winning this war. Your access to this building is revoked. If I see you here again, your blood will paint these walls."

Vogt's eyes widened slightly—just enough. "Yes, Oberführer," he shouted.

"Get the fuck out of my sight."

Vogt's heels slammed together, the clack echoing off the paneled walls, then he bellowed, "Heil, Hitler," saluted, and stormed out of the office.

The door thundered shut behind Vogt.

Fuchs stared blankly. His breathing refused to slow. His pulse pumped fire throughout his body.

Ten, perhaps twenty, heartbeats later, he launched into action, racing out the door and past the startled guards.

Chapter Thirty-One

Will

It was half past eight when we finally stopped before our evening's destination, the Ridermark Cathedral in the heart of Berlin. I stared in awe, the grandeur of her towering stone matched only by the intricate carving of her columns and facade. Three magnificent dome caps towered heavenward like green-tipped fingers pointing toward God. Beautifully artistic statues set deep within recesses of the stone became passersby.

"I still can't get used to every building we see being older than our whole country."

I turned to find Thomas staring over my shoulder at the remarkable building. "Yeah, but this ... this is something else ... and right here in the heart of—"

"The fatherland," Thomas finished, ensuring I didn't trip over my German-tainted tongue.

I nodded slowly, noticing the carving of a mother and child near the two grand doors at the church's center.

"I don't know about you, but I am famished," the Baroness said, her voice a tinkling bell against the clamor of the city streets around us. "They had better have good wine or the Führer himself will regret admitting me into his country."

I couldn't help the chuckle that slipped out. If anyone could make Hitler squirm in his own home, it would be this formidable woman.

Three priests appeared through the cathedral's doors as the last of us climbed out of the cars. White hair crowned two of the men, while the third, positioned in the middle, appeared to be in his mid-thirties, his wavy brown hair at odds with the stoic set of his jaw. They waited patiently on the top step, their posture indifferent, but their eyes never settling as they scanned the guests they would host that night.

"Father Lehmann." The President of the German Red Cross strode forward and grasped the young priest's hand. "It is good to see you again. Thank you for hosting this delegation."

Lehmann's lips parted, and it felt as though the sun had returned to the sky. "You are most welcome," he said. "These days are too often consumed by war. It is a pleasure for us to celebrate guests for a change."

The two priests flanking Lehmann nodded grimly, as though mere mention of the war darkened their souls.

Lehmann turned toward our group and motioned. "Please, you must be exhausted. Our brothers have a meal prepared, and I am sure Rector Schmidt will welcome your company."

As we climbed the steps, the car doors clicked open and slammed shut. I turned to watch our uniformed minders driving away.

"They're leaving?" I muttered, a bit louder than intended.

Lehmann gripped my forearm and waited for me to take his outstretched palm. "You are in the care of the Catholic faith. Our friends in the government trust you will be well tended."

Something in the man's eyes communicated far more than his words. Did he offer encouragement? Was he an ally? Or an agent of the regime, simply cloaked in a different uniform?

I'd been so taken by the young man's greeting that I'd failed to notice his two older brethren watching the exchange with unguarded interest. It was only when Egret nudged me to move forward that I looked past Father Lehmann to catch each of his companions quickly look away.

I'd never been one for church-going. My parents weren't terribly religious, and since their deaths, I'd found myself more bitter toward a God who would steal parents from a child than eager to shelter in his arms. Maybe I was being harsh or cruel—or stupid—or a bit of each. For whatever reason, I rarely darkened the doorways of a cathedral and had little experience witnessing the grandeur that was Catholic architecture.

As we passed beneath the capstone of the doors' archway, my eyes widened. Ridermark was impressive on the outside. Beyond her entrance, she was magnificent.

The central nave was a spacious, grand area, with high ceilings and towering stone columns that stretched toward a ceiling I could barely see in the dim candlelight. Colorful stained glass depicted Jesus breaking bread, or healing the lame, or working some other miracle. Each panel was a work of exquisite art, relics of a past designed to inspire and guide worshippers toward faith and a life of selfless sacrifice. The panes were darkened due to the nighttime beyond, but I couldn't help imagining their brilliance if light was to stream in from outside.

Small alcoves set beneath each window contained statues of saints whose outstretched arms awaited a loving embrace. As the others filed down the central aisle, I found myself drifting toward a carving whose aged bronze plaque read, *Saint Christopher*. In one hand, he held a tall branch like one might a walking stave. He braced a small child on his shoulder with his other hand. The expression on his face was etched with such care, I almost forgot it was stone capturing my attention.

As my fingers trailed across the cold stone, a gentle voice spoke from behind. "Blessed are those who travel, yes?"

I yanked my hand from the statue and nearly leapt out of my shoes.

Lehmann's teeth shone in his broad smile. "Forgive me. I didn't mean to startle."

The man's eyes glittered, and his grin touched something deep within my chest. Somehow I knew there was kindness deep within his soul. He was no friend of the Nazis or agent of Hitler. This was a good man, a deeply good man. How I divined that, I will never know, but I could *feel* compassion and kindness in his gaze.

I returned his smile as my breathing returned. "I think I lost a year or two of life just then."

"Perhaps we should pray for your lost years?" He chuckled and placed a hand on my arm, guiding me back toward the central aisle. "Let us rejoin the others. A little refreshment will do you good."

He lowered his voice and leaned toward me before turning. "Ask me for a tour of the cathedral after your meal. You return to Geneva tomorrow. There is much you must know, and we must act quickly."

——— ◄O► ———

Dinner turned out to be more of an ordeal than I'd imagined possible in a house of worship. Seven priests, our four-person team, the Baroness, Steven, President von Steinbach, Dr. Alexander Emile, and the German Red Cross president crowded around a table designed for eight and reached across to help themselves in a family-style free-for-all.

No one complained about the close quarters until the portly Father Fischer's elbow collided with the Baroness's plate, sending potatoes and a vinegary slaw across the table and into the German president's lap.

The Baroness sat frozen, her mouth hanging open with one hand inches away, apparently keeping flies from entering. Three priests, attempting to help, reached across and knocked over a bottle of wine, which also drained into the lap of the poor man. President von Steinbach leapt to his feet, and, in an uncharacteristic show of emotion I hadn't known the man capable of, screamed as he dabbed at his German counterpart's trousers. The pompous, wine-and-vegetable-coated man barked for von Steinbach to step away from his potatoes, sending whatever happened to be in Egret's mouth at the time hurling across at Father Lehmann.

"He's sure sensitive about who touches his taters," Egret proclaimed through his now empty mouth. How he managed to get the Americanized abbreviation of potatoes to translate into German was a wonder but added to the ridiculousness of the situation.

Thomas's eyes widened as he took in the scene, but he remained still. I thought Sparrow might crawl under the table, though that would likely have given Egret more ammunition—and he rarely needed encouragement.

A solid ten minutes later, the German president had excused himself, with von Steinbach following closely on his heels, simpering the entire way. The Baroness had regained her composure, refilled her wine glass from an untipped bottle, and taken her leave.

Egret had barely taken a breath between jokes, forcing Thomas to wipe tears from his eyes.

Sparrow still looked like she wanted to crawl under the table.

Lehmann leaned toward me with a smirk, his black frock marred from whatever sauce Egret had fired across the table. "You folks certainly know how to brighten a dark room."

I chuckled. "That's one way to put it."

A couple of the other priests leaned in and were obviously listening to our conversation. Lehmann ignored them and spoke in a clear, friendly tone. "You took quite an interest in St. Christopher earlier. Ridermark has a wonderful store of historical artifacts and relics. If you would like a tour, I fancy myself something of an amateur historian."

"I would like that very much," I said, taking a sip of wine, then pointing at Thomas with my glass across the table. "Wilhelm is our resident art lover. I bet he would love to join us."

Lehmann nodded. "Absolutely. My brothers have heard me drone on for years. It will be nice to have a fresh audience."

"Nice for us all," one of the other priests added dryly, raising his glass and earning a clink and a grin from his brother.

"I would love to join, if you do not mind."

My head snapped up to find Steven leaning forward on his elbows.

"Of course," Father Lehmann said without hesitation, his smile never faltering.

"Please, no one else," the priest sitting next to him said. "If his audience grows any larger, we will not be able to live with him on the morrow. He is almost unbearable as he is."

The glass-clinking clerics laughed between themselves as Lehmann rolled his eyes.

"We live, dine, work, pray, and sleep together. I would say that forms a unique bond, but with those two, perhaps dancing on one's last nerve is more apt." His words were sharp, but the smile radiating through his eyes belied any ill feelings. These truly were brothers, poking and prodding just as playfully as I remembered Arty's doing during my holiday stay with his family.

That recognition caused my mind to drift back to that time, to Harvard, to our simpler days when studies and tests were the most threatening challenges we faced. I didn't have to close my eyes to see Arty's face, nearly split in two by his ever-present smile, and the bright twinkle in his unfairly keen emerald gaze. There was such innocence in that boy—man, I corrected. Still, it was hard to think of Arty as an adult. He'd been so naive when we'd met our freshman year. My life turned upside down when my parents died, and Arty stepped into that void, offering quiet strength and comfort so I did not shatter completely. I hadn't seen it then, his unwavering courage and fortitude, but that gentle soul possessed a stronger backbone than anyone I'd known. He proved it time and again, and even more when he decided to enlist—an act that stirred something in my own soul and called me to act.

I wasn't sure where I would be had I not been randomly paired to room with him. Life had a funny way of shoving one in the right direction, if only we let it.

"Where did you go?" Father Lehmann asked. I'd been so lost in thought that I'd missed almost everyone standing to retire for the evening. Lehmann had slid into the seat beside me and was watching me.

"Just remembering a friend," I said quietly. I glanced around at the majesty of our surroundings. "He would love this place."

An unfettered laugh escaped as I realized what I'd just said. Arty, my Jewish friend, would love a Catholic church in the middle of Nazi Germany. What a ridiculous thing to say. And yet, staring up at the domed ceiling and the moon's rays filtering through the panes of multifaceted glass, I knew it to be true. Arty would immerse himself in the history and beauty of this building, Jesus-centered or not, and walk out spouting more details than any human should be able to remember.

I found myself smiling again, horror replaced by bemusement.

"You were close, this friend?" Lehmann asked.

"Like brothers. He was my roommate at … university." I barely caught myself from saying *Harvard*.

Thomas wasn't looking at me, but I could feel his attention.

Steven was engaged with one of the priests who was trying to escape for his evening's rest.

Egret and Sparrow stared through me as though boring holes in stone.

A stab of fear pricked my gut as I realized just how close I'd come to blowing our covers. One simple slip, one turn of phrase, that was all it would take for the Nazi machine to snuff us from the board, and our role was far too important to be wiped from this game by careless musings.

We walked a knife's edge every moment we breathed German air.

"Ah, to be young again," Lehmann said, oblivious to my near misstep. "Shall we begin our tour?"

"Yes." I nodded, desperate to hide the nerves that now prickled my skin. "As much as anything, I think I need to walk off some of that dinner. Thank you for the wonderful meal."

Lehmann laughed easily. "We take vows of poverty, not starvation." He patted his burgeoning belly, and his laugh grew. "Perhaps we should consider adding that to the list of holy commitments."

The man was infectious. His smile, his bearing, his easy humor. Compassion wafted off him like heat from pavement on a summer's day. I could feel his empathy each time our eyes met, and his humor lifted my spirit.

He stood, tried to brush the crusty stain from his frock with a napkin, then tossed the cloth aside with a rueful shake of his head.

Then he glanced toward me and smiled. "Shall we start our tour?"

Chapter Thirty-Two

Thomas

S ince I was a child, art had fascinated me. How someone could start with a blank page or block of rough stone and breathe life into it was a wonder.

Thus far, we'd viewed tapestries depicting miracles, relics in glass cases from hundreds of years before, and paintings by masters whose brushes stroked more emotion than paint onto the canvas. Father Lehmann's own brushstrokes rendered events and lives in vivid detail. I already knew the man's magnetic personality and kind heart made him impossible to dislike. Now, hearing the passion and elegance of his words, I understood why Berliners flocked to hear him each time he took to the pulpit.

Will hadn't spoken since we'd risen from the dinner table. His eyes grew impossibly wide with each statue or painting. My heart swelled watching this small boy on his first visit to a zoo, reaching toward the monkeys or lions in their confines. We hadn't been away from the States for more than a month, but it already felt like a lifetime. Seeing the glimmer return to his eyes reminded me of our days at Harvard when we'd first fallen in love.

Steven cleared his throat, and I quickly looked back toward the statue Lehmann now described.

"... about Edmund are known, as the kingdom of East Anglia was devastated by the Vikings, who destroyed nearly all contemporary evidence of his reign." Lehmann placed a hand reverently on a sword the statue held with two hands, point toward the ground. "Edmund was killed in 869 after the Great Heathen Army advanced into his country. There is great debate over whether he died in that battle, or was killed following the battle because he refused to renounce his faith in Christ. Either death fits his moniker: Edmund the Martyr."

"Why is his crown tied to his belt?" Will finally broke his silence.

"Excellent question." Lehmann brightened further. "The artist feared presenting a king within the house of God, for He is the only king to reign here. You will notice, even in the paintings and tapestries, none of the monarchs of the past wear symbols of their office."

"Interesting," Will said, his head wheeling about to check some of the pieces we'd already passed.

"Father, forgive me." Steven covered his mouth as a yawn escaped. "These are beautiful, but history and art have never been my forte, and it has been a very long day. I will leave the rest of the tour to you three."

Lehmann smiled. "Rest well. Our brothers will have breakfast ready when you wake."

Steven nodded his thanks, then locked eyes with me. It was strange, as though he was seeking something, but he didn't speak.

As the echoes of Steven's footsteps receded, Lehmann gently gripped Will's elbow and guided him toward the front where the cathedral's grand altar stood, but rather than launch into the history of the gilded box, he led us around it. Barely visible on the marble wall beside the lower pulpit was the threadlike outline of a half-door. A tiny handle was set in the stone so one had to push the top for the bottom to extend and be tugged.

The door was completely obscured from view of anyone not standing directly behind the pulpit and in front of the wall.

Lehmann's voice fell to barely a whisper, and, for the first time since we'd met, his tone held none of his usual lightheartedness. "Come. Close the door behind you."

The small door swung easily, though its hinges groaned in protest, and dim light trickled from somewhere below. Lehmann folded himself into the opening and descended, glancing back one last time before disappearing into the near-darkness.

Will's hand found my shoulder, and his eyes asked the same question that filled my mind.

I reached up and squeezed his hand, then nodded and turned to follow the priest.

A moment later, the door clicked shut as Will climbed down.

Shallow steps led us deep below the cathedral into a narrow hallway whose walls were as smooth and polished as the marble of the building above. There were no markings, no etchings, no artwork or statues, just smooth stone on either side for dozens of paces. Tiny bulbs attached to ornate silver lamps sputtered like candles and cast flickering globes of light every few yards.

Lehmann opened a door at the end of the hallway, releasing an odd ethereal light that clawed its way toward us. Cooler air joined the glow, prickling my skin.

"Come on," the priest said, motioning for us to speed up.

If the smooth walls and dim light of the passage had been a surprise, the massive chamber we entered, nearly as large as the church's nave above, was staggering. Unlike the highly polished walls of the hallway, the lifeless gray stone in this chamber was rough, as though time herself had raked her nails, marring its perfect surface. Faded etchings, more interpretations of alcoves than actual recesses, rose halfway to the ceiling that towered above.

Save for the thundering of our footfalls, the silence that shrouded the chamber was absolute.

I approached one of the carvings and traced my fingers over barely visible letters.

"Each niche contains the remains of a court of past kings." Lehmann's voice bounced off the harsh stone.

I snatched my hand back, as though ghosts might strike me down for disturbing their rest.

Lining the far wall were several ancient coffins, most intricately carved and gilded, each adorned with a crown above where a head surely rested.

"The Prussian kings," Lehmann said, following my gaze. "These are the most prominent since the sixteenth century. Others rest in adjoining chambers."

Then I remembered the eerie light that beckoned us into this room, and my eyes lifted to the ceiling where a full moon smiled through a large oculus.

"We are beneath one of the crypts behind the main building," Lehmann explained. "The oculus illuminates both that small chamber and this one. Ingenious, don't you think?"

At the center of the room, well-lit by a full moon streaming through an oculus high above, a massive sarcophagus stood atop a two-tiered dais, which was surrounded by an ornately carved stone railing. Lifelike engravings of dozens of people filled the sides of the coffin, while the top was adorned with equally artistic renderings of shields, their stars and beasts clearly visible in the moonlight. The whole thing looked more like medieval partygoers riding a palanquin than a box in which a person was interred. Still, the artistry was breathtaking.

"Frederick the First, first king of Prussia," Lehmann said, then pointed toward the far wall. "His wife, Queen Sophie Charlotte, lies in the golden box over there."

Will crossed the room to examine the Queen's confines.

"It feels irreverent speaking in this place," I muttered.

Lehmann nodded. "I have heard similar words many times."

"Father, why did you bring us down here?"

He stared a moment, as if debating—or deciding—then turned. "Follow me. Sound carries in these chambers, and our words may be heard clearly in the crypt above." He pointed to the oculus.

We exited a door on the far wall, a few coffins down from Frederick's beloved, walked several paces down another narrow hall, then climbed stairs that led to a plain room the size of two or three coat closets. Hundreds of etchings on each wall offered names and dates of those interred. A metal door consumed much of the far wall.

"This door leads outside. We prefer no one uses this entrance without our knowledge," Lehmann said. "We must not linger. One of my brothers informs the Nazis, though I do not know which."

Shock flooded Will's face as he turned back toward us. "A priest? Working for the Nazis?"

"I know," Lehmann said, his head bowed. "It is unthinkable given what they are doing, but Hitler's voice is powerful, and many wish to believe the tale he weaves." Lehmann lost himself in thought for only a second before returning to the present. "I was informed of your visit and told that your mission is of vital importance, but offered no details. What do you need from me?"

"Have you heard rumors of the Germans working on a new weapon?" I asked, unsure how to start.

Lehmann chuckled wryly. "They are always working on new weapons. Each more terrible than the last."

"This would be one ... where they run experiments ... on people."

Lehmann's head cocked as though a child had asked a silly question. "That still does not narrow it down. There are rumors of many such terrible trials: bending the mind, bombs of every kind, new vehicles or planes, poisons, you name it."

"Poisons," Will interjected. "What have you heard about those?"

Lehmann's brow rose. "Nothing specific, only stories of people killed or missing thanks to tests performed on crops or in laboratories. Most were originally loaded in train cars bound for the camps, but redirected to labs or other facilities. It is a terrible business."

"Have you heard of a weevil solution?" I asked.

"Weevil? The vermin?"

I nodded. "We overheard a conversation between an SS officer and a scientist discussing some new weapon. At the end, the Nazi referenced their weevil problem."

"I know the pests have riddled farms in the east." Lehmann scratched his head as he thought. "The papers compare them to the plague of locusts, but this is nature, not Nazis at work."

I glanced to Will. Disappointment filled his eyes as he shook his head.

Our one contact knew nothing of the weapon. The SS officer had vanished, and we didn't even know his name. We had no leads to chase, and our flight would return us to Geneva in hours.

I blew out a breath. "Father, can you think of someone we might speak with tonight? Anyone who might have heard something, anything?"

Again, Lehmann rubbed his temples. "I am sorry—"

The sound of the lock turning in the metal door sent a jolt through my chest, and all three of us turned. Lehmann flipped a switch on the wall, casting the small room in darkness, then grabbed my arm with one hand and Will's with the other, yanking us back toward the stairs.

The door swung open, and the outline of a uniformed man shone in the moonlight.

Chapter Thirty-Three

Will

"Stop!" A dark voice bounded off the stone walls.

The three of us froze, unsure how well the man could see in the blackness.

"Father, I need confession. *Now*," the voice commanded.

Lehmann released us, and his next question sounded stiff, almost mechanically rehearsed. "What troubles you?"

"My soul bears many scars," the man replied.

Lehmann's shoulders relaxed, though the stress in his voice hadn't ebbed. "Kreuzotter, what are you doing here?" he hissed. "You should *never* come here."

"There was no time," the man said, urgency threading his words. "We must speak now, before it is too late. Your American friends are in danger."

Lehmann clicked the light back on, and the man stepped into the room. His eyes narrowed as he scrutinized Thomas and me.

My mind reeled. He'd just called us out for being American.

As I looked closer, three things leapt out: first, the combination of his severely angular jaw with his ghostly white skin made me wonder if he belonged more as a resident of the catacombs than a guest. His broad shoulders spoke of a powerful frame beneath his coat. I briefly wondered if the three of us could even match his strength if it came to a fight.

Second, he wore the black of the Schutzstaffel, the Nazi security service whose iconic double S was feared across Europe.

Finally, I had to scrub my memory for the symbol of rank that marked him as an oberführer, a senior colonel. This man was as high-ranking as an officer could get before entering the elite inner circle of Hitler's most trusted leadership.

The pistol holstered on his belt—and our complete lack of weapons—only added to the fear I'd felt when the lock first turned.

Then I mentally translated the name Lehmann had called him: *Kreuzotter*.

Viper.

Lehmann stepped between us and the newcomer. "What is your news?"

The oberführer looked past him toward us, then returned his gaze to the priest with a meaningful glare. "I do not know these men."

"They are friends. Besides, as you said, we have no time. Speak." Lehmann's stance squared and his voice took on an edge of command I hadn't heard before—or thought possible—from the demure man.

After only a moment, Kreuzotter nodded once. "Fine. The SS suspects two American spies are part of the Red Cross delegation. I do not believe they know for certain, but suspicion may be enough—"

"They would not *dare* enter the cathedral." Lehmann's proclamation brooked no argument, and I was stunned to see Kreuzotter's head lower in submission.

"No, I do not believe even they would tempt God here, but they *would* plant teams outside and apprehend the entire delegation the moment they leave your grounds."

Lehmann scratched his chin. "They leave tomorrow. Can you hold them off until then?"

Kreuzotter nodded. "I think so, but we have a larger problem than your guests."

"What now?"

"Some scientists working on a pesticide—"

"For weevils," Thomas interjected, causing Kreuzotter's eyes to widen.

"Yes. How—"

"It doesn't matter. Keep going. What happened with the scientists?" Thomas pressed.

"The gas is unstable; extremely so. It lingers for weeks, sometimes months. Our chemists continue to fail at stabilizing it or helping it dissipate more quickly." His hardened eyes fell as he spoke the next words, and his voice lowered. "They have killed many test subjects, likely thousands."

"Thousands?" Lehmann covered his mouth with a hand.

"Even the Führer fears its use—so much so, he ordered the lab be removed from Berlin and refuses to allow its use until a solution is found."

"If he will not allow its use, what is the urgency? Why do we not have time—"

"There is an officer, Vogt, he is determined to use this gas, to secure its advancement. I sent him to France to get him away from the project. He should not even know where the lab is, but I fear he does. He will stop at nothing to advance, even using *Gorgulho* before it is stable."

"*Gorgulho*?" Thomas asked.

"That is the project's code name. It is known only to a few at the highest levels of command."

"If Hitler barred use of this gas—" Lehmann began.

"Sarin."

Lehmann cocked his head. "Sarin?"

"That is what the scientists call the gas."

"Okay, fine. If Hitler has barred use of this sarin, why would Vogt continue pursuing it?" Thomas asked.

"Because his desire for advancement and power rivals that of the Führer, and he is without scruples."

It was almost laughable for a high-ranking SS officer to talk of scruples, but I kept my mouth tightly closed. The man was an asset.

"Where is the lab?" Thomas's voice hardened.

Kreuzotter stared so hard I thought he might lunge forward.

Lehmann reached out and placed a hand on the man's swastika armband. Kreuzotter stared down at his hand as he spoke. "Please, Kreuzotter, you would not tell us any of this if you did not hope we could stop its use."

The silence of the tomb rang in my ears as the two men searched each other's souls.

Finally, Kreuzotter spoke. "Emden."

Then his chest jolted twice as one bullet, then a second, slammed into him. Twin fountains of blood leaked across his field of black, and our eyes met just before he fell.

I turned to find Steven standing behind us, a Walther P38 pistol pointed where Kreuzotter had stood a heartbeat before.

Thomas wheeled and charged.

Another shot fired, and my ears rang from the blast filling the tiny chamber.

Thomas fell as I shot forward, driving a fist into Steven's stomach.

He reeled back, but his grip on the gun held. He raised it toward me, and I chopped down on his wrist.

He fired again.

I slammed my elbow into his wrist, finally dislodging the gun, but he kicked out, his boot slamming into my gut.

Stars filled my vision. I staggered back, holding my stomach, struggling for breath.

Steven charged forward, punching the side of my head and knocking me into the wall. I tried to move, but I'd crumpled to the ground and could barely draw air.

Thomas got to his feet and threw a right hook at Steven's ear. Steven wobbled, but kept his feet.

Then Thomas kicked. The blow missed Steven's groin, but was strong enough to slam him back. Steven staggered a step, then his foot slipped on the top stair, and his whole body tumbled backward.

Thomas surged after him as Lehmann dropped to my side. "Are you—"

"Get the gun!"

The priest scrambled to retrieve the Walther.

The sound of scuffling rang throughout the catacombs. I heard a punch, then the grunt of someone slamming into a wall.

Thomas cried out. Boots scraped against stone. Frantic scraping. Desperate breathing. Panting. Wheezing.

Then something hit the floor. And silence.

"Wilhelm?" I called out. "Wilhelm!"

No answer.

"THOMAS!" I screamed.

"Tobias," a weak voice echoed up the stairs. "I'm alright."

Lehmann vanished down the stairs, returning a moment later with Thomas draped over his shoulder. My eyes flew over his body, searching for blood or a bullet hole or stab wound. His face was cut and would be more purple than tan, but I couldn't find anything else.

I wanted to fly off the floor and wrap him in my arms, but Thomas fell to a knee and began turning my head back and forth, searching my eyes.

"Are you alright? Where are you hurt?"

"I'm fine, just got the wind knocked out of me," I wheezed.

"Don't you *fucking* scare me like that again, you hear me?" he growled.

"Me scare *you*? I thought—" I was too relieved to be truly incredulous. Then I remembered who watched, and my eyes shot behind him to where Lehmann stood.

Thomas's eyes closed, then opened. He released a sigh.

Lehmann spoke in a measured tone. "I assume the name Thomas was a childhood friend or family member, shouted in shock or pain, and has no relation to either of you."

"Thank you, Father," Thomas said over his shoulder without taking his eyes from mine.

"I am here to help with your mission, nothing more; though ... I am always happy to take confession, should you seek it."

Thomas almost grinned. "Thank you again, Father."

A moment passed before I thought to ask, "Steven?"

He held up the watch Arty had made for him. The button to wind its mechanism was missing. "The garrote works," he said grimly. "That was ... the first time ... my first time—"

Lehmann cut him off. "Talk about that later. We need to move quickly. The catacombs are solid stone, but those shots could be heard outside." He pointed to the partially open door just past Kreuzotter's unmoving body.

"What do we do now?" I asked. "Steven ... he was part of the delegation."

Thomas turned to Lehmann. "Father, there are a lot of boxes down here. Is there an empty one? Maybe a king who'd want some company?"

Lehmann gaped.

Thomas stood. "If you have a better plan, I'm all ears. But, like you said, we need to move."

"I do not." The priest shook his head, then crossed himself and muttered, "God forgive me."

Chapter Thirty-Four

Thomas

Hiding a body is far more difficult than it sounds, even when doing so in a graveyard or catacomb. That's a life lesson I never expected to learn. By the time Steven and Kreuzotter were safely tucked into two separate resting places, and we made it back to our room, it was nearly half past two in the morning.

The second life lesson learned that evening was that a human body does not enjoy falling down stairs while fighting an enraged opponent. I had bruised and sore muscles in places I didn't even know muscles existed.

"So, what do we do now?" Will asked as he eased my shirt over my shoulders. I tried not to wince.

"Nothing tonight," I said. "Tomorrow, we fly back to Geneva and find a way to contact Command. I'd wager the Baroness has plenty of ways to communicate with anyone in the world. That woman is a force of nature."

"That's an understatement," he grunted as he unbuckled my belt. "What about Steven?"

Lehmann and I had discussed this briefly, but not agreed on a course of action.

"I think Father Lehmann is probably right. The Germans won't let the delegation stay longer than planned. We'll fly back on schedule, and they'll assume Steven will show up at the cathedral at some point. If we're lucky, the SS will waste some manpower looking for him."

"I hadn't thought about them chasing their tail hunting for a dead man. That makes tonight a little better." Will chuckled. "What do we tell the others?"

"What do you mean?"

"Thomas, have you looked in the mirror? You're going to be bruised and probably swollen in the morning. I didn't fare much better. They're not going to believe you and I spontaneously decided to spar in the catacombs after our tour and ended up beating the shit out of each other."

I groaned. "With von Steinbach's questionable loyalties and Dr. Emile's expertise in spotting lies, that's a problem."

"We should've talked with Lehmann. I didn't even think about it until now."

"I'm not sure Lehmann could do much about our faces turning purple."

I stepped into the steaming bath and dunked my head to wet my hair. Will shifted from squatting to sitting by the tub, his hand never leaving my back. This was our first mission and we'd already come precariously close to one of us—

"How do you feel?"

I turned to meet his gaze. "Sore."

"I mean about Steven."

I turned back and laid my head against the rim of the tub and stared at the ceiling. Will didn't know much about my service before we met. My job had mostly involved boring analysis and desk work, but he probably wondered whether that was a cover story, especially given what we were doing with the OSS.

I'd never killed before. Not hunting, and most certainly not a person.

The rush of the fight and the panicked cover-up that followed hadn't left much time for thoughts. Soaking in that tub, I almost wished my brain would stay in neutral and let me never replay the events of that night.

But I knew Will needed to know what happened, and I probably needed to get it out. It already weighed on my heart.

"By the time I got to the bottom of the stairs, Steven was almost on his feet and scrambling to find his gun. I managed to ram an elbow into his ribs, then slam him into the wall." I closed my eyes as if to see the scene better in my mind. "He was strong, Will, a lot stronger than I'd thought. He knew how to fight too. If I hadn't taken so many punches and kicks back at Camp X, there's no way I would've survived."

Will's hand drifted to the back of my head where his fingers gently tangled in my hair.

"He got a few solid hits in, but I was able to grab him by his shirt and toss him into the opposite wall. I think it stunned him for a second, just long enough for me to remember the garrote watch and pull out the cord. He struggled ... kicked ... I just leaned back, threw my weight back. I could feel him—"

"It's alright. You don't have to talk about it." Will sat up and leaned over the rim of the tub, cupping my cheek. Tears trickled toward his palm.

"Will, I felt when ... when he wasn't there anymore. I felt it, like a shudder, and then ... just ... nothing. I let go and—"

My throat caught.

Will was leaning over the tub in an instant, his arms pulling me into his chest as I sobbed.

My fingers were pruny by the time I squeaked out, "You're getting your shirt wet."

His body shook with sudden laughter. "You're an idiot. You know that, right?"

I grinned against his warmth. "You may have mentioned that before."

"I love you so much that tonight scared years off my life." Will was suddenly serious again, though I had a hard time ignoring the soap bubbles marching down his nose. "Is this our life now?

Always in danger? Always wondering if tomorrow will be our last day ..."

"Will, look at me," I said. "We are not going to lose each other. Not tonight, not ever."

"That's so easy to say as we sit here." He blew out a breath. "It's just ... we came so close tonight. If Steven had fired his gun again after killing that SS guy, or if he'd had the garrote instead of you ... it was just so close."

I pulled his hand to my lips. "I know. I was scared too. But we made it—at least, until the next scary thing."

"Next thing." An exhausted laugh slipped out of Will's mouth. "Next thing. Is that a technical spy term? What do they call it in the pictures? Tradecraft? Should we radio Washington to let them know we can handle a *next thing* now?"

I splashed water in his face. "I'm done being sweet with you. It gets me nowhere."

I stood and reveled in his eyes roaming my body. We were both too tired and sore to do anything more than sleep, but it still felt good to be wanted, especially by a man I loved so damn much.

He reached up and flicked my penis, making it bob like some carnival game. "Hey, little guy."

"Little?" I feigned offense.

"The water *is* cold," he smirked. "Get dried off before he gets all big and angry. I'm about to fall asleep in this tub and don't have the strength to fight him off should he try to attack me. He can get pretty aggressive."

"When I'm rested and moving doesn't hurt, you'll learn what aggressive means, mister."

"Promises, promises."

His snort as I dripped my way to a towel and into the bedroom sent a familiar warmth through my chest. I just hoped my dreams would be filled with him and not garrotes and guns.

Breakfast was awkward.

All seven of the priests ate quietly, their eyes darting up to glare at either Will or me, desperate to ask but afraid to intrude.

The Baroness entered in her usual grand style, the satin of her ruby gown rustling with each step. Her eyes widened briefly as they fell on my face, but she schooled them quickly and plastered on a smile.

"I don't know about you, but I am ready to get home. The bombing last night nearly shook my bed." She plopped into a chair and held out her mug for a serving boy to fill with steaming tea.

"Bombing?" fell out of my mouth before I could catch it.

Von Steinbach cocked his head. "How could you possibly sleep through that? It was terrifying."

Will and I exchanged a look.

"I think the day exhausted me such that I could've slept through a train crashing into my room."

Von Steinbach stared, his fork halfway to his mouth. Then he set it down. "What happened to your face?"

Here we go.

"Wilhelm and I ... had a disagreement," Will said, leaning forward and displaying his own shining jaw. "It has been settled."

Von Steinbach gaped. I wasn't sure if he suspected a lie or was simply horrified by the prospect of members of his delegation brawling in a cathedral while on foreign soil. Either way, he grabbed his fork and didn't speak another word throughout the meal.

Sparrow spoke for the first time since beginning her meal. "President von Steinbach, you will have to forgive Wilhelm and Tobias. They often have a ... contentious relationship. I think the war has brought out the worst in many."

Von Steinbach considered as he chewed, then nodded slowly, as if dismissing the subject from his mind.

Steven did not make it to breakfast, nor did he appear for their transportation to the airport. The delegation did not wait.

This enraged the Baroness. "I cannot believe we would leave one of our own in that ... that land. Who knows what those people will do when they find him," she fumed. Von Steinbach had patiently listened to her argument, then summarily dismissed it, stating the mission was complete, and the Nazis expected their plane to take off precisely at noon.

The Germans were, above all else, precise.

I fell asleep the moment the wheels lifted off the runway. Our several-hour flight drifted by my dreams without notice, and, while Steven had not made the flight, he did manage aboard my sleeping visions. I saw him fall, again and again. I felt the garrote tighten and my weight heave backward. I felt his strength wane and his resistance slacken. I saw the garrote fall, bloody and empty, from my hand to the cold stone floor.

I saw and felt it all.

Twice, Sparrow shook me awake, claiming I hollered or was muttering nonsense. Sweat soaked my shirt and slicked my neck. Will kept his distance, sitting several rows behind, but I caught Sparrow glance back a time or two and offer a compassionate smile.

Staring out the window as the plane descended over Geneva, I wondered how long Steven would travel with me.

Black cars whisked us from the airport. Ten minutes into the drive, I realized we had yet to cross through the city.

I leaned forward and asked the driver, "Where are we going?"

"The Baroness instructed me to take you to her estate."

I sat back.

"Sounds like fancy food tonight," Egret said, focusing on the one thing that always captured his attention.

"As long as the bed's comfortable. I'm beat," I said.

Egret's eyes narrowed, and he glanced over without turning his head. We had yet to brief him or Sparrow on our evening's activities. That kind of secrecy within the team would've driven me mad, so I couldn't blame his annoyance.

"Why don't we take a walk when we get there too. The Baroness mentioned her gardens, and I know how you enjoy horticulture."

Egret snorted. He hated anything to do with dirt unless it involved tossing it into an opponent's eyes. "Yeah, that'd be great. Think she grows her own tomatoes?"

I nearly choked on a laugh. "That's *exactly* what I bet she has in her garden. Maybe okra or cabbage too? Think she wears one of those flashy gowns while she's weeding?"

"Definitely. Gotta make it look good." His grin widened, and I knew he understood.

The driver peered back through the rearview mirror, his eyes widened in horror. "This is the Baroness. Surely you do not think *she* toils in the earth with vegetables?"

Egret looked over, and we burst out laughing.

Moments later, our car turned off the road onto cobblestones that stretched across rolling hills. Meticulously trimmed box-wood hedges hemmed us in as the car approached a massive fountain at the center of a circular drive. I'd been so taken by the water flowing from the mouth of the massive swans that I'd barely noticed the mansion behind them.

The facade was made of finely crafted sandstone blocks carved with masterful depictions from Swiss folklore and history. Tall arched windows with leaded glass panes and ornate ironwork grilles added to the mansion's opulent charm. The entrance featured a large, richly stained wooden door with iron accents, flanked by imposing stone pillars, while a colossal clock tower rose from the center of the mansion, topped with a copper-sheathed dome that gleamed in the dying sunlight.

The blend of Gothic and Baroque architectural styles was impressive. The estate's grand scale reminded me of a humbler version of my extended family's home back in the States, but I didn't dare show anything other than awe at the mountainside manse before us.

"Jesus, Mary, and Joseph," Egret said as he climbed out of the car and stared up at the clock tower.

I snorted. "I'd never taken you for a religious man."

"Funny, it took a Baroness to make me see the heavens."

On cue, the door opened and our hostess appeared in the entrance, her silver gown grasping at the sunset's hues and tossing them aside with a brilliance and grace that almost matched her smile.

"Hello, boys. I'm so glad you could visit."

I shook my head and returned her grin. This woman was … something.

"Come along. The others should be here shortly. You only have a few minutes to refresh yourselves before dinner is served. The staff has worked tirelessly to make this an evening to remember." Her command to follow issued, she wheeled about and swished back into the manse.

"Enjoy the tomatoes," our driver said. I glanced back to find an amused quirk to his lips as he tipped his cap and folded himself back into the driver's seat.

"Is it just me, or is everyone here lost in their own strange picture show?" Egret muttered.

"Oh, it's not just you," I said, taking the stone stairs one at a time. "I've felt like I've been walking in a dream for weeks now."

The moment we entered the foyer, Egret's steps faltered. "Jesus Christ."

The grand foyer was a testament to art and history. The walls were adorned with paintings by masters even Egret recognized, priceless works of the caliber rarely seen outside of museums—or homes of the ultra-wealthy. Antique tapestries, likely passed through many generations, provided a backdrop to rich furniture upholstered in brocades and velvets. The mosaic floor was inlaid with rare marble and intricate patterns, many of which contained thousands of pieces no larger than the tip of my little finger. Crystal chandeliers hung from the vaulted ceiling, casting the place in a warm, inviting glow.

Somewhere down a hallway, the gentle notes of classical piano drifted toward us.

"Have you ever seen anything like this?" Egret asked, his head upturned as he gaped at the ceiling.

I wanted to say "yes," to invoke the family I'd eschewed in service to country, to tell this awestruck man I'd grown up surrounded by far greater wealth, but covers were covers, even among our team. Perhaps *especially* among our team. That was one of our first lessons at Camp X, and I wasn't about to ignore it.

"It's pretty amazing, that's for sure," I said. "Which way did the Baroness go? She said for us to wash up, but—"

"Gentlemen, if you would follow me, please." A tall, painfully thin man who looked older than the mountain behind the mansion stepped into the room. His perfectly tailored crimson tailed waistcoat and the gilded crest embroidered on his chest declared him one of the Baroness's household staff. "I am Bisch. My lady bade me show you to your rooms."

Egret's brow rose. "Well, if she bade you, lead on."

I had to bite back a laugh.

Bisch simply bowed, then strode up the grand staircase that encircled the foyer.

I shrugged to Egret, then followed.

Once in the bedroom assigned by Bisch, I sat on the end of the bed and unlaced my shoes. The temptation to fall back onto the pillowy soft covering almost overrode my desire to bathe, but I worried I might fall asleep and miss the opportunity. A quick glance around the room revealed yet another surprise

from our illustrious host: a black tuxedo hung from a wooden
stand. Behind it hung a stiff white shirt I knew would fit me
perfectly.

My rational mind knew I should focus on our mission and
what steps should be taken next, but I couldn't help but ponder
how the Baroness had managed so many details since our return.
She couldn't have arrived at her home more than a half-hour
before us. How was *any* of this possible?

I shook off those questions and began stripping off the German uniform I'd worn for two days. Tossing the coat on a chair,
the Red Cross armband drew my eye. That had been a clever
play, one that worked beautifully to get us into Berlin, but what
had we actually accomplished? The Germans were still working
on their weapon. All we knew was that their lab might be in the
port town of Emden.

That assumed the SS man wasn't lying. If Steven hadn't shot
him—

The thought of the Arian poster boy froze me in place. He'd
been close—too close. He could've easily shot any of us, especially since he'd clearly snuck after us into the catacombs. If the
oberführer hadn't been there to take the bullets, was he going
to aim for us? Were we his targets until a better one came along?

My heart nearly stilled.

Even if we hadn't been shot, Steven could've tipped the Nazis
off to our presence. Given what the oberführer said, he might
have already done so. How close had we come to being captured? Steven's bullets might've been a welcome release compared to the embrace of the fabled SS.

I forced myself to move again, dropping the last of my clothes
onto the chair then padding into the bathroom. Hot water
blasted from the shower the moment I turned the knob. I
pressed a plunger, redirecting it into the tub. After the past few
days, I needed to soak and think.

Dinner would have to wait.

Chapter Thirty-Five

Thomas

I lost track of time as the blessed heat of the bath unwound sore muscles and eased my troubled mind. By the time I stood and reached for a towel, the water was cold and my fingertips felt like prunes. Angry marks and a few gashes stared back at me in the mirror, but I was still in one piece. A win was a win.

A light tapping at the door startled me out of my self-examination.

"Wilhelm, may I come in?" the Baroness's voice slipped through the cracks around the heavy door.

"One minute," I called back, as I darted across the room for the proffered tuxedo hanging in the opposite corner of the suite. Pants and undershirt donned, I stepped to open the door.

Our host looked even more regal than when we'd arrived, now dressed in a ball gown of pearl and jade, complete with a matching tiara.

"Baroness." I stared, openmouthed. "I feel like I should bow or something. You are breathtaking."

Her girlish giggle somehow brightened the dim lighting in the room, and the blush that flooded her cheeks spoke of a woman who missed the affection of a partner. It was as if she'd transformed from a statue to flesh and blood before me with one simple compliment.

"If I was ten years younger," she said, batting her eyes. "Okay, maybe twenty."

She had to be fifty if she was a day, but I played along.

"My lady is as beautiful as she is charming," I said with mock flourish and a bow.

She giggled behind her gloved hand again. "May I come in? Perhaps you need help with that shirt?"

The glint in her eye warred with the playful twist to her lips. She was enjoying this far more than I might have expected.

"Please, come in. Why don't I try the shirt on my own before asking for help from royalty."

She nearly doubled over. "Royalty? Now I know you spread the jam too thick."

I was pretty sure being a baroness marked her as a member of some royal family, but as an American, what did I really know? It made her smile, and that was all that mattered in that moment.

The moment the door clicked shut behind her, all humor drained from her face. "What happened beneath the cathedral?" She shot forward, and her hand reached toward my bruised face. "And are you alright? Do you need attention?"

"I'm fine, a little banged up, but okay," I said, taking the stiff shirt from the hanging stand and snaking my arm through a sleeve. "Father Lehmann took us into the catacombs. I don't think he had any new information, but was instructed to offer assistance. While we were down there, a senior SS officer who was spying for Lehmann showed up. A few minutes later, Steven stepped out of the darkness and shot him."

"Dear God," she gasped. "And Steven?"

My eyes fell, and my fingers froze around the first of the shirt's buttons. "I ... had to ... He fought hard."

When I finally looked up, kind eyes enveloped me in warmth, but the Baroness said nothing.

"I've never killed anyone before. I've trained to, and practiced, but doing it is—"

Her hand gripped my arm. "I know. It is terrible."

"You know?" My eyes widened.

She nodded slowly. "I have served my country for many years, Wilhelm. We are called to do many things in her defense. I do not regret them, but that does not make living with the memories any easier. Life is still precious, even that of our enemies."

Our enemies? Even the Nazis who assigned no value to life?

That concept jarred my senses, but I was too wrapped up in the image of Steven's lifeless form falling onto cold stone to fully absorb it.

"You will heal, in all the ways that are important. For now, we must focus on what lies ahead." She squeezed my arm and stepped back so I could finish dressing. "Tell me what this SS officer said."

I replayed our conversation, remembering each word as if they were etched in my memory.

"Emden? That is a northern port, only a few miles from the border with Denmark."

I nodded. "He said Hitler wanted this substance far from Berlin, that the Führer was afraid of it."

She scoffed. "Afraid. That man would slaughter the world if it meant his own power grew."

"That's what I thought, but it sounded like this officer spoke with personal knowledge, like he'd been in the room when it was discussed. He used the code name *Gorgulho* and even knew the name the scientists used for the gas. He called it sarin." I turned to tuck in my shirt. "He said Hitler feared the poison lingering and killing his troops. He said it was highly unstable, which is why their team of scientists is working around the clock for a better formula."

The Baroness took a couple steps back and lost herself in thought.

Then I remembered something that hadn't registered before. "Lehmann said something about a pesticide, about a weevil problem. He already knew about the gas."

"Perhaps that is why he led you into the catacombs, to relay that information?"

"Maybe." My gut churned. Everything felt wrong, tainted, like no truth existed without the cloak of a lie. "But ... we were together for a couple of hours after ... after everything happened. Why wouldn't he have said anything then?" "It does not matter now. If he worked for the Nazis, we would be in prison—or worse." She shook her head. "Come with me. We need to send word before the others gather for dinner. My staff has been with me for decades, but do not trust them. If you need privacy, walk in the gardens. Do not trust the walls to keep your secrets."

I couldn't help but admire the brutal efficiency of her words. She was all frills and lace to the outside world, but as cunning as any when her mask fell away. In another time, when war did not rage about us, I could see the good lady become a close friend.

As impressive as her words may have been, her forethought and actions were even more remarkable. I straightened the coat and was shocked by how perfectly everything fit. It was as if the suit had been tailored to meet my body's every curve.

The Baroness strode purposefully down the hall, and I nearly had to run to catch up. At the end of the passage, she stopped before a door, retrieving a small key, then unlocking it. A circular wrought-iron staircase greeted us. She began to climb, the hem of her gown brushing either side of the railing as she took each step.

Halfway to the top, I realized we were in the clock tower I'd seen from the driveway. While the exterior matched the rest of the mansion's gray stone, the interior facing was red brick, feeling more like ascending a wide chimney than a clock.

The clicking of hands and groaning of gears grew louder as we neared the clock's mechanism at the top. When we entered the final room, I ducked to peer beneath the clock's face. The whole of Geneva spread before me, the crystal water of Lake Geneva rippling miles away. I turned to find the back a solid wall of brick and found myself wondering at the snowcapped mountain view that lay beyond.

A loud thunk spun me around. The Baroness had dropped a large metal case onto the ledge of the clockwork. When she opened the case, I recognized a mechanism we'd spent endless hours mastering back at Harvard.

"What message would you send?" she asked, a pencil hovering over a plain white pad beside the transmitter's code key, the device we called "the tapper."

"You know Morse code? In English?"

She cocked her head, as if about to scold a child.

"Who will receive this?"

"An operator who works directly for the head of British military intelligence. Unfortunately, I do not have a contact within American intelligence."

"That's fine. The Brits trained us." I scratched my scalp, thinking. "Please send this: 'Nazi program code name *Gorgulho* discovered.' No, strike that."

She scratched a line through the phrase as I wrestled with words.

"Nazis discovered new chemical weapon called sarin. Project code name *Gorgulho*. Lab in Emden. Weapon not yet operational. Flock returned to mountains. Request instructions."

Her pencil paused as she waited for more. When I didn't continue, she glanced up with a smirk. "Flock? You Americans and your silly names."

Then she began tapping.

We entered the dining room ten minutes later, though banquet hall might've been a more apt description of the space. Richly paneled walls rose twenty feet toward an arched ceiling that towered above. Crystal chandeliers like those we'd seen in the foyer hung from impossibly long chains.

But it was the table that stopped me in the doorway.

Long enough to seat forty people comfortably, the table's surface was adorned with a mosaic of intricately carved designs, showcasing the remarkable craftsmanship of Swiss artisans. The edges were laced with carvings of grape clusters and vines that wound down and around the massive pedestal base. Fierce griffins, with broad wings outstretched, flew within the base's vines. Each of the high-backed chairs lining the table bore the cluster and bunch carvings, and were crowned by a regal griffin where one's head might rest.

"Pretty impressive, isn't it?" Will's voice snapped my head to the side. He wore a tuxedo similar to mine, but his coat bore a different cut in the front and had tails. I tried to keep my eyes from widening, but his smirk told me I'd failed.

"There are a lot of impressive things in this room," I agreed, allowing my eyes to drift down his torso without lingering too long.

He flushed the most adorable shade of pink, as his eyes fell to his shoes. "Yeah, I kind of noticed that too."

Sparrow and Egret chose that moment to enter, Egret's shoes tapping like a dancer. His tux was a deep navy with the traditional cut and no tails. Sparrow practically glided toward us, her floor-length gown shimmering with faux diamonds with every step.

"Anny, good Lord. You look amazing," Will said, his mouth agape.

"Do I not usually look amazing?" she asked, one brow cocked.

Egret darted behind us. "I'm getting out of the line of fire. That's a no-win question, and I've seen her with a gun."

Sparrow's other brow rose. Her eyes hadn't left Will's; clearly a challenge.

"You two are having a little too much fun. Can you at least wait until we taste whatever hundred-year-old wine the Baroness pours before firing on one another?" Egret placed a hand on Will's and my shoulders. "I bet she's got a thousand bottles of something stashed below this place."

"Nearly two thousand actually, but one does lose count after a while." Our host's smile was filled with proud amusement as color raced up Egret's neck. I wasn't sure I'd ever seen the man embarrassed. My respect for the Baroness leaped tenfold.

Servants scurried by, filling water glasses and placing a centerpiece of fresh-cut flowers at the far center of the table where I assumed we'd sit.

The Baroness leaned into the center of our circle. "Do not speak here, even when the servants leave. I will insist you take a stroll through the gardens then feign exhaustion and excuse myself."

She looked to me. "While you are in the gardens, I will await a reply to our message. Join me after your stroll."

She straightened and her smile reappeared. It seemed her whole aura shifted as she reached for a wine glass and turned toward a waiting servant. "The Château Raymond-Lafon 1929 tonight. What do you think? Three bottles? Oh, we need a good laugh after such a boring trip, bring four."

"Yes, Baroness," the man said with a respectful bow before hustling out of the room.

It felt almost redundant, my wonder at the woman before me. She flitted about the room, a shallow dilettante more concerned with the placement of dishes than the fate of the world. Yet, I knew that act for what it was: her own cover.

My mind strayed back to Steven; not his death, but his deception. He'd been playing false as well.

Then the baker in Crécy flashed before me, Claude Petit. He, too, wore a false face.

Still others played in my mind like an endless reel.

Was anyone who they claimed? Did we now live in a time when everyone had a cover, an identity designed to mislead and deceive? Could we ever truly know—and *trust*—anyone?

Had the world truly gone mad and forced us all to hide our true selves?

That question brought me back to Harvard—and Will.

My heart sank as it answered: yes. We would always have to hide. There would never be a day in which we could simply be. Society had weighed us on their wretched scales and judged us unworthy, simply for who we loved.

I glanced across the table to where Will sat chatting quietly with Sparrow. He was striking in his tuxedo, his hair longer than at any time since I'd known him, unruly despite all the effort I knew he put into making it lie down. His smiles were so easy, an extension of the beautiful man I knew within.

He looked up, catching me staring, and cocked his head, as if to ask if I was alright. I gave him a tight smile, which he returned before looking back to Sparrow and laughing at something she'd said. My heart fluttered at the tenor of his happiness.

I turned to stare at one of the many paintings adorning the walls. Two lovers lay naked on a chaise in the middle of a wooded meadow. Where they got living room furniture from in the woods, I didn't know, but that was the artist's interpretation, and who was I to question art? The man's hand stretched up to push a curl from the woman's forehead. Her gaze on him was filled with adoration.

Unbidden anger simmered beneath the surface of my skin. I felt the heat reddening my neck and clawing its way up my cheeks. Why could they be immortalized, yet we must hide? Their naked forms did not offend, but put Will and me on a wall and the earth would shake with humanity's wrath.

I hadn't thought about any of this in so long. Before meeting Will, it hadn't even bothered me much. There'd been no reason. Now, the idea of anyone finding Will *less than* anything or anyone made my blood rage within me. Think what you would of me, but deride him at your peril.

"You okay? You look like you want to throw your knife at that painting." Egret's hand on my shoulder jolted me back to the present.

"Oh, yeah, sorry. Got lost in thought."

He eyed me a moment, then grinned broadly as servants trickled in bearing platters laden with meats and vegetables. My stomach howled as the aroma flooded my senses, even before my eyes could take them in.

The priests had done their best, but the Baroness and her staff were in a league of their own. Wartime rationing had clearly not impacted the home of this ultra-wealthy woman.

By the time the last of the wine was poured and dessert had arrived, I thought my pants might burst. Egret barely slowed, reaching for a bowl filled with a fruity concoction with whipped something throughout.

"You're a beast," I said.

He gave me a disgusting, full-mouthed grin. "Growing boy's got to eat."

I chuckled and shook my head.

A massive yawn sounded above the din of the table chatter, and I looked up to find the Baroness standing. "I believe the wine has served its purpose. I am exhausted. Wilhelm, I know you wanted a tour of the grounds, but I fear I might pass out before we get to the roses. Please feel free to wander anywhere you like though."

"Thank you, Baroness. I might just do that."

She inclined her head slightly, then yawned again. "I bid you all a good night. We will arrange passage for you tomorrow."

Arrange passage. She hadn't said where we would go. I scanned the room and wondered if the presence of servants had stilled her tongue, or if she truly did not know where we should head next. Then I laughed inwardly at the thought of that woman being in doubt of anything—ever.

The air was crisp and clean. The mountains that loomed beyond were barely visible, mere shadows of outlines, in the sliver of a moon's light. Still, their majesty was undeniable.

"I've never seen anything like this place," Sparrow said, staring at the top of the tallest peak. "It's like they go on forever."

The overpowering scent of roses shattered our reverie, and I looked around to find nearly closed buds of every color spreading like eggs waiting for their charge to spring forth. I'd never seen so many roses in one place. I immediately thought of fields in Holland with their endless waves of tulips, but with a far stronger, sweeter smell.

"Alright," Will said, ending our moment of peaceful bliss. "Fill us in. What is the Baroness up to?"

I couldn't help but chuckle. I wagered she was *always* up to something. "We sent a status to British intelligence."

"What? How?" Sparrow's eyes narrowed.

"The Baroness has access to a transmitter," I said vaguely, unsure how much I should say about the woman's on-premise operation. I trusted our team—as much as I could trust anyone—but we could still be overheard, and I didn't want to put anyone at risk, especially the Baroness.

"Okay, what did London say?" Egret asked.

"We're still waiting for a reply. She said it could take hours for them to coordinate with the Americans and get back to us with instructions."

"They could at least confirm receipt," Sparrow groused.

"I doubt operational security allows for conveniences like that. You all know how skilled the Nazis are at finding transmitters."

"We're in Switzerland. They can't—" Sparrow began.

"You think that would stop them from killing someone they thought was violating Swiss neutrality and helping the Allies?" Egret said. "They'd make it look good because of who she is, but she'd be dead inside a week if they caught her."

"The Baroness can take care of herself," I said with more conviction than I felt. "Our mission will be to find out where the lab is and, if possible, disrupt or destroy it."

"We don't even have a way back into the country. How are we supposed to do that?" Will crossed his arms.

"We're working on that. Emden is on the northern coast, near the border with the Netherlands. We have friends there. We'll find a way. We have to."

Chapter Thirty-Six

Will

*T*he sun's warmth kissed my skin on a cloudless day, as a light breeze tickled the hairs on my arms. Thomas's laughter filled my ears and warmed every corner of my soul. I glanced over as we walked, but his eyes were fixed on a familiar fixture: the statue of John Harvard. His hand drifted up to touch the yellowed toes of the founder's shoes. The black paint coating the rest of the piece had long since worn away thanks to countless touches of students and visitors alike. As a sailor assigned to train on campus, Thomas wasn't technically a student of Harvard, but our traditions had wormed their way into his heart.

He turned toward me, the depth of a thousand oceans welling in his eyes, and grazed his fingers against my cheek. I leaned into his caress, then turned my head to kiss his hand. His eyes brightened.

As if magically frozen in time, the world halted around us. Leaves drifting on the breeze stilled as though caught in an invisible web. Students on distant sidewalks paused mid-stride. The ever-present whistling of the wind between the buildings and the echoing calls of resident birds ceased.

Nothing moved—nothing existed—except Thomas and me.

His eyes, so full of promise, widened with his smile. He cupped my cheek and leaned down, pulling my lips into his. The world vanished as our lips met, as I felt the magnetic force of his love.

The terrifying bellow of gunfire shredded the blessed silence.

Our lips parted, and Thomas looked down, his eyes suddenly wide.

A smattering of blood marred the pristine white of his shirt. As his face paled, twin plumes formed across his chest, growing, crawling, as his life leaked onto the fabric.

Another shot rang out, the peel of a horrific bell whose toll heralded a last breath. I followed the bullet's path to a man in black, his arm wreathed with the blood and black of Hitler's men.

His eyes were fixed on Thomas. He fired again.

"Go!" Thomas shouted at me, shoving me away from him. "Go! Save yourself. I'm done."

I couldn't move. I could barely breathe.

This couldn't be real.

He couldn't—

My eyes fluttered open as someone banged on the door. "Tobias?"

That was Thomas's voice. He was alive. Dear God, he was alive.

I blew out a breath, then scanned the darkened room. I was in the Baroness's home. There were no Nazis on Harvard's campus. It had all been a dream.

The door opened then shut as Thomas entered. He was fully dressed in a gray business suit, complete with a navy tie. I briefly wondered where he'd gotten new clothes, but all thought fled as he sat on the bed beside me and wiped my face.

"Why are you crying?" he asked.

My hand flew up. I *had* been crying. It had felt so real.

"I ... I don't know. I had this dream ..." Memory of the sleeping world faded, and I struggled to grasp the reason for my tears.

Thomas pulled me toward him and kissed my forehead. "I want to hear all about it, but Command responded about thirty minutes ago. We need to gather the others and get moving."

"Where are we going?"

"London, for now."

I was halfway out of the bed, but froze. "London? How are we supposed to—"

"Just get dressed. We'll talk about it with the group. The Baroness is waiting for us in her study."

He spoke with the authority of our team leader. There was no time for intimacy or questions.

"Where'd you get the suit? You look nice, by the way."

He reddened as he glanced down. "The Baroness, where else? You should have several sets of clothing in the armoire over there."

I'd been so exhausted after dinner the night before that I hadn't given the ornately carved piece a second glance. I opened the door to find three suits. I shook my head. "She thinks of everything."

"That's an understatement," Thomas grunted. "I'd love to stay and watch you change, but I need to get the others moving. See you downstairs in ten. The study is the door opposite the dining room. The staff is already up and preparing breakfast if you get lost."

Thomas gave me a quick smile, then turned and vanished out the door.

Precisely ten minutes later, the four members of our team sat in comfortable leather chairs. The walls of the study were lined with bookshelves holding ancient, leather-bound tomes, most of whose spines bore gilded lettering. A small tea tray in the corner held a variety of bottles, glasses, and decanters. The Baroness's desk consumed much of the far end. It was even more of a work of art than the dining table we'd marveled over the night before.

"Ah, excellent, you are all here," our host's voice sang from the doorway.

It was barely four o'clock in the morning. I suspected the woman hadn't been to bed yet, since she'd been waiting for a transmission from London. Still, she appeared as fresh and elegant as every other time I'd seen her. She'd even found time to change into a mesmerizing cobalt gown one might see in any court across Europe.

The Baroness swept into the room and stood with one hand on the mantel like some perfectly formed mannequin in a store for the rich and famous.

"I must say, your little flock has presented me with quite the challenge," she said, though the glimmer in her eyes told me it was a challenge she relished. "You may have performed a miracle in this war: London and Washington finally agree on something. You are to travel to Scotland to join a team whose mission will be explained once you arrive."

"How are we supposed to get all the way to Scotland? By the time we drive across the continent—"

The Baroness cleared her throat, cutting Egret off. "Getting you from Geneva to Scotland was the greatest challenge in our plan. The government has ceased all commercial flights from Switzerland. Diplomatic flights, like the one used for our visit to Berlin, are still active. You board one such flight in three hours."

"Three hours?" Sparrow sat forward.

The Baroness nodded. "Hence, this early meeting. It should take you roughly three hours to fly to Lisbon. From there, three routes travel to England. You are ticketed on the five o'clock flight this evening. That trip will take a little longer, perhaps three and a half or four hours, depending on weather."

A moment of silence passed, then Thomas asked, "How? I mean, what names and identification did you use? Surely the Nazis have spies in both airports."

She nodded again. "Absolutely. There will be spies in each airport, and you should expect to be observed the entire time. We could not use your German identities for obvious reasons, nor your French one, Anny, so you have each been assigned Swiss names. As French and German are two of our official languages, we have assigned you a Swiss address based on the language you have been using so far. Your new passports should arrive shortly. Questions?"

We stared blankly at one another. I wasn't sure if it was the early hour or the travel plans just unveiled, but none of us found the ability to speak. This was the point in most briefings where Egret cracked some inappropriate joke, but even he sat dumbstruck.

"Alright then. Let's get you something to eat before the cars arrive. You can't start a dangerous journey on an empty stomach now, can you?" She sounded like a proud, cheerful mother sending her children off on a school field trip.

———◆◇◆———

The rest of the morning was even more of a blur than our initial briefing. Following a quick breakfast, the Baroness bade us farewell, breaking with tradition and pulling each of us into a hug and kissing each cheek.

When she reached Egret, her eyes brightened as she said, "I've been wanting to get my hands on you for days."

Her comment and his squirm in her embrace nearly brought tears to Thomas's eyes, he laughed so hard. Anxiety had run amok, and the Baroness's antics offered exactly the moment of levity we needed as we embarked on the next leg of our journey.

There was never an opportunity to spot hidden Nazis at the Geneva airport as we were whisked directly onto the only concrete runway there, where our plane waited, rolling stairs at the ready. The others settled into their seats and slept nearly the entire flight to Lisbon. I stared out the window and watched the clouds roll by, wondering at what lay ahead. I understood why we had not been told of our mission that would begin in Scotland, but anxious curiosity still riddled my thoughts.

We landed as the Baroness had predicted, exactly three hours after taking off. Her typical Swiss precision was the first topic of conversation when the others woke. Her crush on Egret and his brilliant blush was the second. Our banter quieted as the pilot stepped out from the cockpit. He glanced back to where the flight attendant busied herself, then rapped on the overhead railing to get our attention.

"Welcome to Lisbon." His hushed tones were nearly as startling as his thick British accent, the first we'd heard since our harrowing entry into France. "The man at the foot of the stairs is a Nazi SS officer. At least a dozen others throughout the airport, at the counter or cleaning the floors, work for the Germans or Italians. You have five hours until your next flight. Godspeed."

He didn't tell us to stay alert or maintain our covers. He didn't have to. The mere mention of SS officers lurking in our midst sent a spike of fear through my chest in ways that no other warning could. While Portugal proclaimed neutrality, and the Nazis would be loath to cause a scene in public, there was no question they would try to intervene if they knew who we truly were.

As we ambled across the tarmac from the plane to where a uniformed attendant held the door, I could practically feel the enemy spy's eyes searching for any hint of subterfuge. Then I looked up at the man holding the door and wondered at his lingering gaze. Two mechanics walked past and nodded toward us, one's eyes locking onto mine, and I questioned if he might be Italian or—

"Hey, you okay?" Thomas stepped up beside me and asked in whispered German.

"Oh, yeah. Guess I'm a little jumpy."

"Breathe. We're just catching a flight, nothing more. We go in, grab some food, maybe a beer, then hop on a plane."

And that's exactly what we did. Well, Egret had three beers.

Twice, as we sat chatting quietly, random passengers strode up to our table. One asked for the time. The other said Sparrow looked familiar and asked where she was from. Neither looked extraordinary nor worthy of a dark cloak and cane, but I supposed, neither did we. That would defeat the purpose of being undercover.

They were probably enemies testing us. I was sure of it. Almost. I think.

"Will it always be like this?" I asked Sparrow.

She cocked a brow.

"Wondering which direction the knives will come from? I mean, did you see that woman who asked Wilhelm for the time? She *had* to be SS."

Sparrow snorted. "You need another beer. She was eighty if she was a day. Her grandson might be a Nazi, but she's just an old woman."

"She could be an informant. Who'd suspect her?"

"She could be the tooth fairy in disguise too, but I doubt it." She reached over and patted my arm. "You haven't been jittery a single day since ... well, ever. What's going on?"

I blew out a breath. "I don't know. It just feels like it's all closing in, the whole world just folding tighter and tighter around us. I'm being crazy, right?"

Her smile was tight, but genuine. "Yes and no. I get it. Just try to ignore the world around you and enjoy the trip. The part after this is what I'm more worried about."

I grunted and let our conversation drift, though my mind screamed every time a new person walked by.

At four forty, we joined a short queue near the number-two counter, where an attendant had posted a wooden placard with stenciled letters reading, *London*.

The old woman who'd asked Thomas the time stood ahead of us. The moment she turned and recognized Thomas, her hand wrapped around his arm and she prattled until the line began moving forward. For a blessed moment in time, I smiled, forgetting my suspicions, and simply enjoyed watching the man I loved make an aged woman a little less lonely.

There were twelve passengers on the plane: the four of us and eight suspected spies. Two flight attendants added to my list. Then the pilot and co-pilot took a moment to introduce themselves, and I found reasons to suspect each of them too.

Thomas, Egret, and Sparrow appeared unconcerned.

The weather up the coast and into the Channel was brutal. Harsh winds and pelting rains caused the plane to bob like a fisherman's cork in the sky. For once, Egret was the green one in our group, as the bouncing plane wrecked the last of his normally iron stomach's defenses. At five minutes before nine, our wheels touched down in London, and I breathed deeply for the first time in days.

I peered out the window, confused by the rows of British fighter jets on the tarmac and in nearby hangars. I was no expert on London, but the thought of fighter jets parked all over Heathrow seemed odd.

"We're at Luton Airport, about thirty-five miles north of London proper, in Bedfordshire," Thomas said, reading my thoughts.

As we exited the plane and were enveloped by the watery arms of London's stormy welcome, two black cars rolled to a stop about twenty yards from the staircase. A uniformed Brit emerged from one of the cars, popped open a black umbrella, then waved. The passengers in front of us, a couple of stairs below, glanced over, confused. Thomas didn't hesitate, raising a hand in return salute.

By the time the doors closed and our cars drove away, we looked more like soggy puppies than highly trained operatives.

The cars turned off the main road onto a dirt and gravel stretch. A moment later, a large, two-story farmhouse came into view. The cars pulled around behind the house, revealing a smaller, single-story replica of the main home a dozen yards away.

"Welcome to The Cottage," our driver said before lumbering out and opening Egret's door.

We waded through puddles and onto the porch, tugging off shoes and coats to minimize what we might track inside.

An elderly man with sagging eyes and blotchy skin introduced himself as Bruce and explained that he would be our host for the evening. There were three rooms: two in the main house and one in the outbuilding he referred to as "the dependency." Before anyone could speak, Sparrow chirped, "I would like my own room."

Egret raised a soggy paw. "Dibs on the other one."

"Looks like you two are dependents," Sparrow said with a smirk.

"If we're depending on you two, we're in trouble," Thomas groused in good humor.

Sparrow locked eyes with me for a second and smiled, ever so slightly. I gave her a quick nod of thanks.

Bruce stepped into the foyer and braced himself against the wall. The poor man looked like he might blow over in a strong wind. "There's fresh clothes in those trunks over there, ladies' outfits to the right. Take whatever fits and leave your old clothes. I'll have them cleaned for the next lot to come through. Breakfast will be on the table at eight, and your cars should arrive at nine. If you need anything, I'll be around."

We rummaged through, holding up various articles to guesstimate a fit, then headed in the direction of our respective rooms, which meant Thomas and I had to brave the storm to cross to the outer house.

The room we entered was a large, open sitting area with a sofa, two chairs, and several side tables. The light of a lonely lamp in the corner lit the space with a cozy hue. Thomas led us to the only door of the main room, stepped inside, then halted. I'd barely made it two paces past the doorway before he turned, grabbed my face in both hands, and pressed his lips to mine.

I could feel how much he needed my touch, how much he craved our connection, but his kiss wasn't ravenous or insistent, as it often was. It was deliberate and tender, somehow passionate yet gentle. His hands held my head with the care one might a frightened bird, barely touching but offering comfort and safety. His body leaned into mine, but in a way that begged to be close, to join in spirit more than flesh.

His eyes fluttered open, and I dissolved beneath his gaze.

There could be no greater love in all the world. It wasn't possible. My heart—no heart—could swell so large without slipping beyond a body's bounds.

A single tear slipped free and trailed down my cheek.

Thomas froze and pulled back, wiping the tear with his thumb. "Babe?" he breathed. "Are you okay?"

I tried to nod, but shivered instead. "Yeah ... I'm ... God, Thomas, I love you so much."

His smile was the brilliance of a thousand suns, and my heart found yet more room to expand. "Mind if I help you out of those wet clothes?" he asked.

This time, I actually nodded, though my voice cracked as I spoke. "Sure."

He sank to his knees and, one button at a time, reached up and opened my shirt. I couldn't remember a time when his fingers had moved so slowly. It was as if he wanted to remember each movement, each tiny revelation of what lay beneath, as though he sought to extend that night beyond the realm of time. When the last button popped free, he opened my shirt and let it hang from my shoulders. Warm fingers tickled my collarbone, then snaked their way down my chest and across my stomach.

"You are so beautiful, Will. How did I ever get so lucky?"

The heat of my pleasure and embarrassment flooded my cheeks and neck. I wanted to tell him I was the lucky one, that no man had ever been more fortunate in the history of men, that he was the greatest part of my life, and I would love him forever. But all I could do was lean down and kiss his forehead.

Somehow, he understood. He always understood.

He stood and gently pulled my shirt over my shoulders and let it drop to the floor behind me. I returned the favor, in exactly the manner and speed with which I had received it. Thomas's eyes never left mine. With each button, I glanced up to find him staring and smiling, warmth and love flooding through his features. I had to remind myself that he was real, that *we* were real. It felt like an impossible dream.

When his shirt joined mine, and we stood with our chests a breath apart, Thomas leaned in and kissed me, and I felt the force of a thousand butterfly wings against my soul. More tears welled in my eyes, but before they could escape, he pulled back. "Stay here. I'll be right back."

He had a glimmer in his eye that I couldn't quite identify, but I did as instructed and stood, half naked, teary eyed, in the middle of a farmhouse bedroom. It suddenly sounded comical, and I barked out a laugh. Then another. Before he returned, I had dropped onto the floor and was giggling incessantly.

"Uh, Will, should I be worried?" he said, standing over me.

"I was just ... we're in a farmhouse ... and ... oh fuck," I gasped, another bout of laughter making my side ache. "It's just so ... so much."

He shook his head and smiled, then gripped my shoulders and pulled me upright. "Come on, we both need to warm up."

He led me into a small bathroom, where a cast-iron tub consumed most of the space. Steaming water gushed from the faucet so quickly the tub was already half-filled. Thomas felt the water, then adjusted the knob. "Let me finish what I started, then I want to bathe you."

The last giggle chirped out like a baby bird right before its mother shoved a worm in its mouth.

Thomas chuckled reflexively. "You're an eight-year-old boy. You know that, right?"

"Am not. You are." I stuck out my chin.

He snorted again. "Shut up and take your pants off before you earn a spanking."

"Oh no, Daddy, not a spanking," I said with mock fear, slapping my hands to my cheeks and pooching out my butt toward him. He slapped it playfully.

"Abuse!" I shouted.

"I'll show you abuse if you don't get naked before that water gets cold."

"Yes, dear." I blew him a kiss and unfastened my pants.

When the last of our clothes fell away, he climbed into the blessedly hot water with his back to the far wall. I started to step in facing him, but he reached up and grabbed my forearm, gently turning me so my back would be against his chest. When I settled into the tub, his arms wrapped around and pulled me against him. My head rested against his shoulder, and he kissed my temple. "I want to hold you for a while. Is that okay?"

My whole being wanted to scream that he could hold me forever and never let go, but I just said, "Yeah, that works."

His fingers found mine and entwined loosely, rubbing up and down, as though searching but not wanting to lock into place. He held our hands up, and we watched them dance.

The water began to cool before either of us spoke—or even moved.

Thomas reached up and turned the hot water on, then whispered, "I don't want to lose this."

"Lose this?" I turned my head. "Thomas, you're never going to lose me."

His arms tightened briefly, and he kissed my neck, sending a thrill through my chest.

"I know. That's not what I meant." His chest swelled as he drew in a breath, pushing against my back. "It's just ... I don't know any details, but I think our next mission ... Will, this one's going to be bad."

"Bad?"

"Yeah."

I waited, but he didn't go on, so I shut off the hot water and worked my body around so we faced each other with our legs scissored in opposite directions. For the first time that night, he struggled to meet my gaze.

"Babe, what aren't you telling me?"

His eyes closed, then opened, and he looked up. "I honestly don't know what's coming next. They haven't told me. But think about it. If Command really does know where the sarin lab is, they'll want to destroy it. That means going back into Germany, probably into a heavily defended port, and planting mines or bombs. Their navy is huge, and they have more U-boats than we can count. What are the odds we could actually get in, blow shit up, and get out alive?"

A heartbeat passed in silence as we stared into each other's eyes. Thomas's held such desperation, such pleading, as though he hoped I would have some answer or hope.

I had nothing.

"Why us?" I asked.

He cocked his head. "Huh?"

"Why send us? We're spies, not special forces. I guess it makes sense to send us if they want someone to sneak in and out, but this sounds like it needs a team of ... I don't know ... somebody trained to attack a port or something."

Another moment passed, then Thomas laughed.

"What?"

"Attack a port or something? Is that a new mission term? Should I call the navy and inform them?"

I splashed water at him like the eight-year-old I was. "Fuck off. You know what I mean."

He laughed harder. I splashed more.

Before I knew it, we were both laughing and splashing, the floor and walls were soaked and dripping, and the tension of the coming days had drifted away.

God, we needed that.

Chapter Thirty-Seven

Will

We toweled each other off, then dried the walls and floors. Thomas chuckled as he wiped, and I slapped his naked ass in response, which made the fucker laugh more.

How can I hate and love someone so much? I thought, as I draped my wet towel over a hook on the wall.

Thomas pulled the covers back, and we fell onto the bed. The day hadn't been physically taxing, merely two plane flights and some waiting in an airport, but the constant fear of surveillance, and the threat of detection, had worn on my last nerve. Laying down for the first time, I realized just how exhausted I was.

Neither of us moved for a long moment, then I felt Thomas turn as the bed creaked.

I looked over to find him staring. His hand reached up and his water-wrinkled fingers brushed my cheek.

"You haven't shaved in days," he said quietly.

I glanced to where his own five o'clock shadow was thickening. He'd have a beard to rival a dwarf if he let it grow out.

"I've never really liked hair on a guy's face, but yours looks really good. It makes your jaw sharper." I reached up and tickled the stubble on his neck. "We'd need to clean that up though."

"Grooming me now?" He grinned. "I like it on you too. It makes you more manly."

"Manly?" I pulled my hand back, my eyes suddenly wide. "What are you—"

He grinned. "You're plenty manly. This just adds to it."

I relaxed. "Oh. Good."

His fingers left my cheek and found my lips. An electric tingle trailed his touch.

I kissed as he started to pull them away, and he pressed them toward me.

My arm stretched out, and I pulled him into me.

Our lips met again. His were so soft. I brushed mine back and forth, savoring the gentle friction. His hand pressed to my head, fingers kneading beneath my hair.

Our movements held longing, but remained as gentle and tender as when we'd first entered the room. Lust and need so often drove our bodies together, but in the midst of war and the uncertainty of life, we craved intimate fondness above primal passion.

Thomas's kisses washed away the day's journey and a lifetime of doubts. They filled me with joy and hope, and were somehow innocent, like the first gaze of a newborn babe on her mother.

His hands fell to my arms, and strong fingers dug into muscle.

I kissed him deeper, longer, unwilling to let our lips part for even the briefest moment.

He edged forward, enfolding our naked bodies, and I felt his cock slick against mine. I'd always loved how pre-cum coated his head, but this felt like he'd already enjoyed his last moment of bliss. Curious, I pulled us apart and looked down. He was thoroughly coated in beautiful slickness.

He smiled as our eyes met, and the pressure of his hands turning me sent my heart pounding. We'd traveled with nothing, and we couldn't exactly leave the safe house to shop for lubricant. Thomas's body had shopped on our behalf.

He rubbed himself between my cheeks, teasing my hole. His hand reached around and teased the tip of my cock.

He bit into the back of my neck. My body shuddered, and I groaned.

It felt like a lifetime since he'd been inside me. I could feel his cock's warmth just beyond, the oily wetness threatening to seep inside.

I craved him. I needed him. I wanted him to fill me and never leave.

He pressed forward, and his head barely breached my hole.

"Oh, God, Thomas. Yes."

He pulled back and teased against me again.

The inside of my cheeks was fully wet now, and pre-cum seemed to pour from him in an endless stream. I didn't take the time to think how that was possible. I didn't care. All I wanted was this man inside me.

I pressed my butt backward and he slipped inside, tentative at first, the pre-cum not quite working its magic as I hoped it would. His body shifted, and I heard him spit in his palm, then felt him move to add water to wetness.

Then he slid inside again, and my eyes flooded with stars.

As slowly as our kisses, as tenderly as his lips against my skin, he drifted more than pushed himself deep inside my body, not stopping until his stomach pressed with force against my rear. He pulled back just as slowly, taking forever for me to feel his tip barely hanging on inside me, then ground forward again, even slower than before.

Each time he eased forward, my breath flooded out, leaving me gasping in pleasure.

His fingers drifted down my shaft and teased my balls, then reached up and gripped me, sliding up then down in time with his thrusts.

He kissed my neck. Then bit into it. Then pressed inside again ... and stroked again.

The room began to spin. "Thomas ..." I groaned.

He drove deeper, this time harder.

I could feel his heart beating through his chest against my back. His grip tightened around me, and his strokes quickened. His stomach muscles clenched, and I felt their definition grasp at my back.

The image of his abs flexing flashed before my eyes, and my excitement welled, begging to surface, to be released.

He thrust deeper, now faster, his body tensing with each push.

My mind reeled as my body trembled.

His grip tightened. His arms flexed around me. His teeth sank deeper, surely marring my skin.

I didn't care. I wanted more.

He gave me everything. His body roared, and all the pent-up passion we'd been refused flooded out of him in waves, one after the other. I felt him fill me with his essence a moment before my own burst forth.

"Fuck! Thomas, I'm coming!"

He squeezed tighter and stroked harder. His cock dug deeper.

I shot again and again.

And then we stilled.

The clutch of his arms loosened, but he didn't let go. The clench of his stomach eased, but he didn't pull back. The pulse of his cock ebbed, but he didn't pull out.

"I don't want to move. Ever." His breath brushed against where his teeth had been a moment before.

"Then don't. Please don't," I said, begging to every god that man had ever dreamed of to make it true.

He kissed my neck, then kissed it again.

And the darkness of peaceful slumber swept the world away.

Chapter Thirty-Eight

Thomas

I woke early the next morning. The sun had barely begun peeking over the horizon.

I watched Will sleep. His breathing was slow, and the movement behind his lids was languid, matching the peace scrawled across his face. As much as I hated the thought of untangling our bodies, I knew the day waited for no one, we needed to get cleaned up before any of our team came calling.

I carefully freed my arm, then stood and stared down at Will's beautiful body. A slightly angry spot on his neck reminded me of how much my teeth had enjoyed his skin last night. I smiled as I leaned down and kissed it, then padded into the bathroom.

Not long after, we strode into the main house to find that Sparrow had been the first to arrive. She sat at the kitchen table cradling a mug in her palms.

"Morning, boys," she singsonged. "Sleep alright?"

Her bemused smirk made me wonder if she'd tried to walk in on us at some point—or if she'd been outside and heard some of our louder moments. I was fairly certain we hadn't screamed or shouted—it hadn't been that kind of passion—but the look on her face gave me pause.

Will didn't flinch. "Best rest I've had in weeks."

She winked at him, and his grin broadened.

Bruce strode in from outside, his coveralls streaked with grime. I wondered at how the old man had managed to do any manual labor without tumbling over. He looked like a strong wind might snap him in two.

"Ah, good, you're gathering. I'll wash up and get breakfast ready."

"Thanks, Bruce," Will said.

"Egret sleeping in?" I asked.

Her eyes rolled. "Never. He's out walking the grounds. Boys need to explore everything—at least, that boy does."

"I saw him out by the pond," Bruce called from down the hallway. "Said he'd be up in a few."

Breakfast was simple fare: buttered toast with marmalade, eggs, and bacon. Egret ate like it was his last meal. Then again, he did that with every meal. I'm not sure why it continued to surprise me.

Our cars arrived midway through our meal. A half-hour later, we were climbing out beside a small airplane bearing the markings of the Royal Air Force. A man in a flight suit bearing silver wings and an embroidered crown stepped from around the plane and waved in our direction.

"You the birds?" he called in a cockney accent I knew hailed from the eastern side of London where regal feet rarely trod.

I nearly missed a step. How many Brits had been told of our covers? A rush of anger filled my chest, then I realized they couldn't exactly call us by our German covers. That could get us shot or mobbed on Allied soil. Besides, what harm could it do? Even if the enemy knew I was called Condor, what could they do with that information? The heat in my chest suddenly felt silly and I let it evaporate.

"That's us," I answered.

"One ferry to Glasgow, coming right up." His easy smile and sloppy salute made me like him instantly.

As we climbed the short ladder to board, Will muttered behind me, "Glasgow? What are we doing up there?"

I shrugged. "No idea. Probably not visiting castles."

Egret snorted. "Castles. Good one, boss."

Great, he's calling me boss now. Please, don't let Sparrow have heard that.

"Boss, I like it. Condors are kind of bossy, aren't they?" she called from the back of our line.

"The bossiest. Bitchy, even," Will answered.

I groaned inwardly. "I hate every one of you," I said dryly.

Then I noticed the name painted on the plane, and my face fell.

Bossy Bitch.

The others burst out laughing.

"Don't worry, mate. I named her after my old lady, not you," the pilot said as I ducked to enter his bird.

Egret, Sparrow, and Will doubled over in laughter as I slunk toward a seat.

A little over an hour and a half later, we touched down in Scotland. The Brits maintained their streak of efficiency, as a car arrived by the stairs before we could set foot on Glasgow soil. A five-minute drive dropped us at a ferry port, where a uniformed sailor escorted us onto a Royal Navy boat that looked more like a small yacht than a ferry.

The four of us stood at the railing and watched the land streak by. The air smelled of salty sea, and the wind whipped against my skin. Egret spread his arms wide and screamed toward the sun. I'd almost let myself share in his exhilaration when I noticed something poking above the water's surface in the distance. We drew closer quickly, and a British submarine resolved before us, its unusual bulbous head staring at us from the port end of the craft. I'd seen subs before, but never one like this. Will and Sparrow's widened eyes told me they hadn't either.

"Oh shit. Holy mother of fuck. No, no, no!"

Sparrow's sudden stream of profanity rose to a near-shrill cry and whipped all our heads about.

"I ... no ... God, Condor, please. Tell me we're not ..." She covered her mouth and stepped back from the railing.

"I have no idea," I said calmly. "I honestly don't. They haven't briefed me on any of this."

Her arms flew around her body as she hugged herself for comfort. I'd never seen the brave woman so pale.

Will stepped up and wrapped an arm around her, something I'd only seen him do once before. She leaned into him and pressed her head against his chest.

I heard her mutter, "I can't do this, Emu. I can't."

He held her tight and glanced up at me, as if asking for help.

I sighed, and shrugged with my brows. I had no help to give.

Chapter Thirty-Nine

Will

We sailed past the sub toward a small village whose largest structure appeared to be a naval dock that housed several massive warships. A smattering of houses and other buildings dotted the mostly untouched landscape. Had there not been two heavily armed behemoths floating beyond the beach, the town might've been among the most picturesque places I'd ever visited.

Our ferry squeezed itself between the ships to tie-off at a small pier close to the shore.

"Welcome to Holy Loch, lads ... and miss." The ferryman inclined his head toward Sparrow, then pointed to a two-story building just beyond the shore. "Head to that building over there. Warrant Officer Landry is who ya want."

We hopped onto the bobbing planks of the dock, then headed across the sandy beach toward the building. As we approached, the door flew open and a young sailor who couldn't have been more than sixteen was hurled out. He landed on his back and rolled to a stop at Egret's feet.

"... don' wanna see yer fookin' face ag'in till it's done!" a leathery voice boomed from inside the building like a shot from one of the battleships. The Irish accent was so dark and thick,

I was sure the country's famous stout was dripping from the speaker's mouth.

"Aye, Warrant Officer." The boy scrambled to his feet and ran across the beach, struggling against the sand all the way.

Egret and Thomas traded a glance, then Thomas stepped up to the doorway. He froze halfway in.

"Who the fook are ye? This be a navy yard, not a damn tourist station," the voice belched.

Thomas hesitated.

"Well? Ye got a voice? Or are ye one o' them mutes? I ain't got all fookin' day."

"Uh, we're from—"

"Dear God, Mother Mary, and Joseph, ye be th' fookin' American birds. Ye flown all the way to fook up my yard, I see."

I'd never seen Thomas so completely at a loss for words. The back of his neck was crimson, and every attempt to speak came out a stammering garble. If the Royal Navy man shouting at him hadn't sounded like he wanted an excuse to shoot someone, I would've doubled over onto the sand right there.

Sparrow had actually covered her mouth, and Egret was on the verge of losing his battle with laughter.

Thomas righted himself. "Yes, sir. That's us. The birds."

"Don't fookin' call me 'sir,' ya idiot Yank. I'm enlisted. I sweat oil and seawater, not perfume and lace like fookin' officers."

Every time he said "fookin'," Egret's shoulders shook, and I knew this was about to get worse before it got better.

"Don't fookin' stand there in the sand. Get in here. All o' ye. And don't fookin' get sand on my floor or ye'll clean it up."

That's when it happened. Egret lost it. Sparrow followed a second later.

Thomas whirled, horror etched on his features, and I stepped back, unwilling to meet his gaze—and unsure whether to laugh or cringe.

The next thing I knew, a towering beast of a man whose chest was nearly as wide as the doorframe peered over Thomas's shoulder. Egret looked up and bit back his laughter, but the sight of the sailor with his bushy mustache turned upward so its ends almost curled to touch his nose sent him straight to the ground. Egret wasn't a man to shed tears, but they flowed freely as he howled.

Sparrow gasped for breath.

Warrant Officer Landry's eyes narrowed, shifting from Egret to Sparrow, then to me.

I shrugged and, for absolutely no reason, took another step backward.

Thomas finally felt the man's breath on his neck and stumbled forward out of his reach.

Landry stepped into the doorway, planted his meaty fists on his hips, and did the last thing I expected: he began to laugh. Like a gentle shower growing into a hurricane, Landry's laughter swelled until I thought the walls of his building might rattle.

A moment later, Landry quieted long enough to ask, "Why are we laughin'?"

And that sent Egret into a whole new fit.

Thomas stared up at me, but I had no words. Absolutely no words.

Welcome to Holy Loch, indeed.

———◆———

Landry finally gathered himself long enough to order another sailor to show us to the mess hall at the rear of the building. We ate a simple meal surrounded by sailors, dock workers, and others who likely built or repaired ships. Their hands were rough and their faces rougher, but they offered a warm smile and tip of their hat as we passed.

At one o'clock, we gathered, as instructed, in a training room on the second floor. A few dozen chairs arranged in neat rows faced the front, where large blackboards covered the wall. A

British flag hung from a golden pole resting in a golden stand in the corner. The image of the King hung framed on the opposite wall.

Ten men sat scattered throughout the room. Every head turned when we entered. Nods were exchanged, but none spoke.

We took our seats in a row together, as one team. Something in the simplicity of our unity comforted me. We'd only been together a few short months, but we were so much more than operators thrown together on a mission. We were family.

Thomas leaned across Sparrow to say something, but was interrupted by footfalls smacking against the floor. The men who sat slouched around us shot to their feet and stood at attention. I turned to watch a Royal Navy officer enter, his uniform crisp, though his tie was askew.

A circle crowned two thick gold bars that sandwiched one thin one on his cuffs, marking him as a lieutenant-commander. His smile was broad, his steps sure. The man exuded confidence and charisma. The men standing stiff about us relaxed as their leader spoke.

"Sit," he said, taking up an easy stance at the front of the room.

"Roth, shut that door, would you?"

A man sitting behind us leapt up and did as he was asked.

"For the new guests in the church, I'm Lieutenant-Commander Drake Raines."

The sailors chuckled and turned to eye us.

"Men, our new friends will be joining our grand adventure. None of them have heard the ocean's call, at least not from inside her belly. I doubt they've ever seen a cockle, much less tried to keep one afloat on rough seas. We need to make the most of the next two days. Understood?"

I had no clue what he was saying, but the men in uniform nodded and grunted their assent. None of them looked happy about us tagging along.

"Alright, let's get down to it," Raines said. "We set sail in two days. There will be a full mission brief one hour before the *Tuna* leaves harbor, so save your stupid questions until then." A ripple of laughter and amused grunts rolled through the sailors, who'd clearly heard their commander use that line before.

"We have two days to train on the Mark-Twos." Raines eyed his men, gathering his thoughts. "Each of you have spent time in a cockle, but our guests have not. You have no other priority than getting these folk up to speed so they don't fall in the drink. Here are your assignments."

He grabbed a clipboard off a table and began flipping through pages before stopping on one. His finger scrolled down the page.

"MacLeod and O'Connor, you're together. Your kayak is *Cachalot.*" He glanced up with a smirk. "Sounds like a damn Irish jig. Try to stay sober at sea."

The men laughed and one shoved the man in front of him, clearly either MacLeod or O'Connor, earning a faux scowl.

"Thompson and Smyth on *Catfish*. Davies and Mitchell will take *Conger*."

Raines paused, then looked past his men toward us, and his gaze hardened. He looked at Thomas, then me, finally settling on Egret. "Foster," he said, shifting toward a tall man sitting in the front. "You take that big Yank back there."

He glanced down at the paper, then back up, and pointed his pen at me. "Ward, you've got that one. And you"—he finally pointed toward Thomas—"will be the guest of Roth here. God bless your soul."

The sailors enjoyed another round of laughs and jeers aimed at a scrawny guy sitting in the middle of their group, clearly one of the more popular men by the way they all joined in teasing him. I briefly wondered at how the commander had chosen to pair us, then realized one member of our team had been left out.

Sparrow sat quietly, staring at the blackboard behind Raines.

"Now, get out of here. Cockle training in thirty minutes on beach one. Dismissed."

As the men rose and chatter filled the room, the commander's voice shouted above the din. "Americans, stay, please. I need a word."

We waited for the Brits to file out, each giving us appraising glances as they passed. I felt like some infinitesimal germ under the all-seeing glare of a microscope.

When the door slammed shut, Raines stepped to where we sat and propped himself against the back of a chair. "We don't have time for me to play nice. Washington insisted you join my crew, and the Crown is mighty grateful for your country's help of late. Despite that bit of cross-pond appreciation, I don't like this, not one bit. This team is the best trained in the Boom Squad, but I doubt most of them will make it back. That's how insane this mission is. Throw you lot in, with virtually no training or experience at sea, and our odds just dropped into the shitter."

His jaw flexed as he thought through his next words.

"You have two days to learn the cockles. Don't waste them, or you'll have zero chance of surviving what's to come. If I think you are putting my men in danger, I will toss you in the ocean and sail away without a second thought. Fuck what Washington thinks. Any questions?"

Raines's stare was a sword slicing into my eyes. I couldn't hold his gaze. Even Egret looked to his shoes.

After a moment of excruciating silence, a small voice asked, "What about me?"

I looked up to watch Raines's gaze snap to Sparrow. His lips played at a grin, then tightened into an angry frown. "You're a pianist, right? You'll stay here and help with our comms team."

Sparrow nodded, and her shoulders relaxed.

Raines looked at his watch. "Your training starts in less than half an hour. You'll learn the basics during the day, but the real training starts tonight once the sun sets. Darkness is our friend, but also our worst enemy. You'll understand that soon enough. Warrant Officer Landry has clothing and gear for each of you. Now, get out of here and try not to die."

Chapter Forty

Thomas

"What's a cockle?" Egret asked as we filed out of the training room.

"Some kind of boat, I'm guessing," I replied.

Egret groaned. "Hope it's not one of their experiments. They've come up with some good stuff over the years, but the first few versions usually don't work so well."

That sent another thrill of fear through me.

"Let's just see, okay," I said, trying to keep from sounding annoyed. "We've got two days to learn whatever this is, so keep focused."

We made our way to the first floor, where Landry was barking at another pair of sailors. I'd been around navy men most of my adult life, and I don't think I'd ever heard one curse as often as that man. It was like watching a very real, very menacing cartoon character berate everyone who walked by. It was terrifying and hilarious at the same time.

"Yanks, over 'ere," he barked after dismissing his last victims. "Yer fookin' packs are over there. Gear up and meet the team on beach two in twenty minutes."

"Where is beach two?" Will asked.

"Bloody fookin' hell. I'm not yer mam. Ask one o' yer fookin' mates. Now, go on."

As we stepped out into an overcast day, Sparrow whispered to Will, "I was going to ask him where the comms room was, but I was afraid he wouldn't fookin' tell me."

The pair tried to keep their laughter quiet, but it quickly rippled through Egret and into me. We were still laughing as we caught up to James MacLeod, one of the Royal Marines from our briefing. MacLeod pointed us to the barracks where we'd likely be assigned bunks, then gave directions to beach two, on the western side of the inlet known as Holy Loch.

Sparrow asked about comms, but MacLeod shrugged and told her to ask Landry. The blank stare she gave him elicited another round of chuckles from Will, Egret, and me. MacLeod glanced from one of us to the other, confused.

With two minutes to spare, the three of us managed to change into our too-loose wetsuits and trudge our way across the sand to beach two. All nine of the Royal Marines were already assembled, chatting in a wide circle. In their tight-fitting gear, they looked like a pack of lean sea lions preparing to leap into the ocean.

"Come on, lads. Step up, and let's meet ya. I'm O'Connor, Sean O'Connor. You met James." He pointed to MacLeod, who nodded toward us. Then, one at a time, the Marines barked out their full names: last, then first and last together, as though children ensuring their new teacher had their names listed correctly in the roll.

Then all eyes turned toward Will.

He froze, and I guessed he was struggling with which name to offer. He glanced toward me, and I gave him a reluctant shrug.

"Shaw," he said. "Will Shaw."

It was the first time we'd used our real names since entering the program. Egret and Sparrow had never even heard them.

Egret's eyes bore into Will as he considered what he'd just heard. Then the scrutiny of the pack turned on him, and he made his own decision. "Booher. Charlie Booher."

Huh. Charlie. Guess I'd never heard his name either. He looked more like a Billy or Butch to me.

I looked toward the men. "Jacobs. Thomas Jacobs, US Navy."

"Look, boys, we've got us a bona fide squid," MacLeod declared. The pack hooted and made squishy noises that sounded more like wet farts than any creature I'd ever known.

It was an odd relief to use my real name. And yet, I suddenly felt naked and exposed in a way I hadn't known for months. A name was such a simple thing, yet they contained power over us. I'd never realized that before. Regardless, these men and I prepared for battle together. I was glad they knew who I was.

"Welcome to the team, lads," MacLeod said, quieting the flatulence. "I'll be leading this rabble through training. Welcome to cockle school."

The Marines hooted in what I assumed was their equivalent of the US Marines' *oorah*, though with the Scottish, Irish, and English accents muddled together, it came out more like notes of a song than a battle cry.

MacLeod led us around a stand of brush to six boat-like things that looked to have been flattened with a massive iron. The boat's sides were canvas, but the bottom looked flat and rigid. MacLeod and Davies marched to one, each man grabbing an end and popping it up, forcing hinges to snap into place and expand the vessel into a full-fledged, fifteen-foot kayak.

"Meet the cockle," MacLeod said, looking toward the three of us. "Don't worry, they float ... most of the time."

A few Marines nodded and chuckled in a way I knew meant they'd bailed water more than a few times. Sailors were alike the world over—and very easy to read.

"Pair off, pop up, and push off," MacLeod ordered, and the men began to move.

I watched Egret and the lanky Daniel Foster snap their boat into place and haul it into the water. Of the three of us, I'd expected Egret to have the toughest time on the water, but he climbed aboard and the pair paddled out into the loch with the others with ease.

Adam Roth, a broad-shouldered man with pale blue eyes and breezy brown hair, stepped up. "Ready for this?"

I shrugged. "Don't really have a choice, do I?"

"Nope," he said with a lopsided grin. "Try to stay in the boat, and I'll show you how to maneuver."

"Stay in the boat. Got it." I returned his grin with the tip of the hat I wasn't wearing.

As our cockle drifted from shore, I glanced back to find Will and his partner, Christopher Ward, struggling to get their gears to snap into place. The Marine had stepped one foot into the boat to hold the bottom down and was yanking with all his strength. Will looked like he wanted to toss the boat into the loch and walk away.

Fortunately, the yanking mechanism finally gave, the boat formed, and the pair followed the teams into the sea. Will's face was a mask of stone.

After hours of paddling across the loch and back, MacLeod led us back to beach two, where we flattened our boats and stashed them in a wooden shack where the sand met vegetation. The Marines chatted and joked like they'd just spent a day playing ball at the park. Will, Egret, and I walked together in silence.

"I can't feel my arms," Will said.

"Lucky you. It's my ass I can't feel," Egret groused.

"At least we stayed upright. Think how miserable this would've been if we'd tipped over and had to spend the day wet," I said.

"Yer a fookin' ray o' sunshine," Egret said, invoking the accent of our resident warrant officer.

"Why did that sound more Chinese than Irish?" Will asked, grinning for the first time since we'd boarded the kayaks.

"Fook you," Egret said, offering a finger with his curse.

"Now, children, why are we misbehaving?" The voice of Adam Roth turned my head. My kayak partner strode behind us and had likely heard our whole conversation. "And it's none too kind t' be makin' fun o' fookin' Landry. Right, lads?"

The other Marines barked laughter at his perfect imitation that put Egret's garbled attempt to shame.

Roth tossed his arm around my shoulder. "You boys did alright today, a lot better than the commander let on, but the real test'll be tonight. There's a storm coming our way, so the water's going to get rough, even in the loch."

"Great. So much for staying dry," Will muttered.

Roth grunted. "That's for fookin' sure," he said, then released my shoulder and jogged up to where the others had nearly reached the barracks.

The skies were already darkening and thunder rolled in the distance.

Three hours later, following a meager meal of stringy corned beef, mushy potatoes, and something one Marine called pudding that looked more like baby poop, we'd donned our gear and once more stood by our cockles on beach two. This time, however, Lieutenant-Commander Raines stood at the top of the beach, and every Marine's mouth was clamped tight.

"Two exercises tonight, men. For the first two hours, take our baby squids on a tour. Let them get a feel for the rain and the waves. Head toward Fyne." He pointed at MacLeod like a teacher might a child who wasn't paying attention in class. "Nothing too crazy, MacLeod, just training."

Raines glanced toward us, then back to the others. "Once our squids have their sea legs, sneak your arses into Loch Fyne and steal the flag off the *Kilmartin*. It'll be attached by a magnet where we'd normally slap a limpet. There's three patrols out looking for you. Get caught and you lose. Capsize and you lose. Don't return with my flag—"

"And you lose," the Marines said in unison.

"Right. Arseholes." He shook his head, but grinned. "Don't lose. That's an order. Now fuck off, and keep our babies safe."

He didn't look at us as he strode away, but there was no doubt in anyone's mind who "our babies" were.

As we broke into pairs and began shoving off, I heard Will ask Ward, "How far is it to Loch Fyne?"

"Oh, about thirty-five, maybe fifty miles, depending on where the *Kilmartin* is anchored. Not too far."

"Fuck me," Egret said. "We won't be back until sunrise."

"Nah." Ward shook his head. "The water pushes us. We'll get there in three. Coming back will take a little longer, maybe four hours."

Seven hours in a pop-up boat on rough seas in a storm. The Marines seemed to take it all in stride, like it was just another day on the job. Will, Egret, and I looked like we already wanted to jump overboard.

The moment the last cockle reached the middle of the loch, thunder boomed like a thousand bombs, and lightning brightened the sea for miles around. The boat bobbed on waves that rose above the bow, but somehow managed to not take on water.

And then the rain began.

A light mist became occasional drops, which quickly grew into gusts of angry, icy sheets. I paddled with my head bowed to avoid the cutting rain from scraping like fingernails into my skin. Had the top canvas not snapped into place over our legs, I was sure we all would've been dropped into the sea.

"The water's a lot colder up north," Roth shouted over the roar of the sky and sea.

"Not helping," I yelled back.

Roth laughed into the wind like a lunatic. "Don't lose sight of the others," he called. "Use the lightning flashes to spot them."

We'd already become separated, a set of six floating tarps with oars drifting farther apart with each roll of waves. How the hell were we supposed to work as a team in all this?

———— ◆◇◆ ————

At four o'clock in the morning, the last of the cockles ground against the sandy beach. Ward hopped out, landing lightly in shallow water, then tugged the kayak forward. Will poured himself out, practically crawling up the sand onto higher ground, before flopping onto his back. The worst of the storm had passed a few hours into our exercise, but a light rain still fell. Will didn't seem to care. He just closed his eyes and let it fall.

"Come on, Shaw. Let's get you out of those wet clothes," Ward said, reaching down and offering a hand to help him up. I couldn't help the irrational spike of jealousy at the sound of another man offering to get Will out of his clothes, though I knew that wasn't what Ward meant.

We staggered our way to the barracks in the midst of Marines who, while as soaked as we were, still walked with a spring in their step and snark on their tongues. They weren't laughing like before, but they didn't hesitate to toss barbs about the mission.

"You idiots got caught before Fyne's mouth even came into view. Next time, just wave a torch around so they don't have to look so hard," MacLeod shot at Smyth.

"You're one to talk, Mac. You made it, what, ten more minutes? Dead is still dead, even if we beat you to it," Smyth shot back.

"At least we didn't fall in the drink like Davies and Mitchell. We got caught going back to pull their drowned arses out," MacLeod said.

The Marines roared at that one.

"Rookie and I got the flag. Fuck all you guys," Roth said, slapping my back in congratulations. I was too tired to respond.

"Inside, now!" barked Raines's voice from inside the main building. A groan replaced the banter as the group turned from the barracks. We'd hoped to get dry and enjoy a little sleep before the mission debrief, but our boss had other ideas.

Our second day began at five o'clock in the morning. That's when Raines finally let us leave the training room and head to the barracks to peel off our clothes and get some rest. Even the Marines were starting to grumble by that point.

Just before noon, Warrant Officer Landry entered and barked for us "ladies" to wake up. He shouted something about "sleeping near' till noon," but I couldn't make out most of it through his accent. Will and Egret looked like they wanted to throw something at the man, but the Marines rose without complaint.

Following a lunch that bore a frighting resemblance to dinner the night before, we followed Landry onto the beach and boarded a motorboat large enough to carry the entire team into the loch.

It was time to meet the *Tuna*.

Chapter Forty-One

Will

T he *Tuna* was about as ugly as a fish—or a sub—could be. With a bulbous head that looked like a birth defect and inlets near the bow that reminded me of nostrils flared too wide, the gray ship was a mockery of modern underwater vessels. At least, that's what I thought as we pulled up alongside her.

The Marines huddled around me spoke her name with affection.

We scurried aboard like ants climbing up the side of a can, then descended a vertical staircase into the belly of the beast.

Since we'd arrived to the sight of the sub, my imagination had crafted images of the interior. Reality did not disappoint. The long hallway down the center of the long tube was lined with pipes of every size, most colored gray to match the walls, but a few painted red. I had expected it to feel cramped, but nothing could truly prepare me for the overwhelming claustrophobia that cloaked me as we ducked and squeezed further into the vessel.

On top of everything, the *Tuna* was anchored in the loch, one of the most peaceful places for a boat outside of a landlocked lake. Still, the darn thing swayed as often as it sat still. I couldn't imagine what the ocean would feel like when the ship was underway.

The tour took all of five minutes, and we were back topside, gathered about the conning tower where Lieutenant-Commander Raines sat. He looked like he couldn't have been more at home atop the beast.

"Men, welcome to the *Tuna*. She's ugly as shit, and has a German heart, but she works as hard as any ship out there. I've had to kick a few of my normal crew off for our mission, but we'll make it work. We'll talk more in tomorrow's mission brief, but I wanted to give you an introduction to this lady today. Treat her with respect and she'll bring you home."

A few of the Marines placed a hand on the conning tower, as if soothing a nervous dog.

"Your next training starts in thirty minutes. Back to beach two."

With that, we piled aboard the motorboat and headed back to the shore.

That afternoon was spent in our cockles, working on rowing and navigating. While MacLeod explained that the exercises were for the entire team, I was fairly certain they were aimed squarely at the three of us, ensuring we knew just enough to not obliterate the efforts of our Marine partners. They were the ones in the back of each kayak, with more control over direction and steering. We were raw muscle in open water. It was a little more complicated in tight spaces, but not much.

When the sun set, Raines gave us another war game. "Gents, tonight you go ashore to reach your objective."

This excited the Marines. They loved the water, but going amphibious really lit their fuse. They were a brave, utterly insane bunch of men.

"You'll paddle up Long Loch, turn left into Loch Goil, and find a place on the western shore to land and hide your boats.

You will then approach Carrick Castle on foot. Your objective is the same flag you liberated last night. It will be attached somewhere on the outer wall of the castle."With each word from their commander, the men's excitement grew. It was palpable. And for some reason, it was contagious. I found myself elbowing Egret and Thomas, like some kid who just got picked for a sports team.

"Tonight, each of you must carry a pack and rifle. Even you three," Raines said. "The packs are weighed down to simulate wet gear. Get them wet, and they'll be even more fun to carry. The rifles aren't loaded, so don't try shooting deer."

Amused grunts flowed through the group.

"There are five patrols this time: three on water, two on land. If they spot you, you lose. If you capsize, you lose. If you fail to return with my flag—"

"You lose," the men chorused, clearly a ritual from more than just our two nights together.

"Don't fucking lose. Bring me my flag."

"Aye, Commander," they shouted as one, then started toward their boats, but Raines added, "And take care of my babies, arseholes!"

The Marines cackled as only adult-age, testosterone-enhanced children could.

———————◆———————

"So? Did you get it? The flag?" Sparrow asked, leaning forward on her elbows like a girl listening to her grandpa as he finished an exciting tale.

"We did, Foster and me. Everybody else got caught." Egret puffed out his chest. "Even Captain America over there."

Thomas glared, but a smile I knew held more pride than annoyance soon appeared. Egret had proven himself time and again, but he hadn't taken to the water very well. The overnight victory had given him back his swagger, something I noted gave Sparrow's smile a bit more brightness.

"When is your mission briefing?" she asked, her change of topic freezing any cheerful banter.

"In just a few minutes," Thomas said. "Commander told us to come with our gear, which means the clothes on our back and our wetsuit, since we'll be sailing in a tin can with no space."

"I still can't believe you're taking a submarine. And kayaks? Are you seriously using kayaks?"

"They're cockles," I said in mock seriousness. "Be respectful of the cockle."

"Oh, I have zero respect for your cockle," she shot back.

"My lady, that mouth!" I said in alarm. "And I'll have you know, my cockle is amazing."

"Yeah, I saw two men riding it just a few hours ago," Egret chimed in.

We all laughed, but I caught Thomas's uneasy gaze out the corner of my eye. Egret was just joking, but he'd hit a lot closer to home than he realized—except for the *two* part of his joke. There was only one man for my cockle.

"Let's go, ladies," Warrant Officer Landry bellowed. "Enough eatin' and chattin'. Get those pretty fookin' arses moving. Mission brief in five."

We stood and I turned to Sparrow, but before I could speak, her arms wrapped around my waist and she kissed my cheek. "Take care of our boys, okay? You come home."

I kissed the top of her head and squeezed her tight. "Yes, ma'am."

"Proctor," she said, smiling. "It's Sarah Proctor."

She repeated the hug with Thomas, then Egret, or Charlie, as he insisted we call him now. He kissed Sparrow's lips rather than her forehead, a kiss that lasted long enough to catch the attention of the Marines. Hoots and whistles filled the dining hall until they pulled apart.

Sparrow didn't reward them with so much as a blush.

Exactly five minutes later, the last of us strode into the training room to find Lieutenant-Commander Raines standing in the front of the room wearing his navy shipboard uniform. The golden buttons running up the center looked like they'd been freshly polished.

"Take a seat, men. Let's get started."

He waited until we'd all settled, then began.

"This mission is classified, and will remain classified upon your return until the Crown falls off the King's royal head and rolls down the streets of London."

The men laughed at another joke I was sure they'd heard a hundred times.

"The Germans are working on a new weapon. It's a gas of some kind, and it's nasty stuff. They'd be able to hit the Soviets again, even though Joe's winter kicked their arses." The men hooted until he said, "They could land on our shores and take the whole of England, Ireland, and Scotland, with none of us alive to stop him."

The mood in the room sobered as he let that sink in.

"From reports we've received, this weapon is so dangerous, Hitler had the lab and all his scientists moved from Berlin to the northwestern coast of Germany to prevent accidental catastrophic loss should something go wrong."

He turned and pointed to a large map that now hung over the blackboard.

"The *Tuna* will sail from Holy Loch, over the northern tip of Scotland, to the mouth of the Dollard bay. Technically, we'll be at the Ems because the German navy will have Dollard bottled up. The six Mark-Twos will put to sea and paddle into the bay, keeping to the western shore, until you reach this point." He stabbed at the town of Delfzijl on the Netherlands side of the bay. "You will cross to what is now the northern end of the bay. We believe our target is a freighter anchored just outside the harbor at Emden. The Americans will graciously assist our mission by bombing the port of Emden back into the Stone

Age, but you can expect German patrols, especially on foot on either bank of the river. Your job is to slap limpets onto the target and any nearby boat bearing the Nazi flag. Once you have visual confirmation the target has been destroyed, you will return to the *Tuna* so we can head home. Questions?"

MacLeod raised his hand.

"Mac?"

"If the Yanks are bombing, why don't they just take out the target?"

Raines nodded. "They might get lucky and do just that, but this is too important to leave to a camera snapping photos in the dark. If you get there and confirm a kill, great, but we have to know for certain this weapon, and all their research, has been destroyed. There's no room for maybe."

Charlie surprised me by raising his hand.

"Booher?" Raines said.

"Sir, is this purely a kill mission? Do we not want their research?"

Raines shook his head. "Under no circumstances do any of you board that ship or attempt anything stupid. Washington and the Crown have made that crystal clear. You take that fucker out and get your arse back to the sub. Kill only."

"Anything else?" Raines's eyes scanned the men. "Good. The code name of this operation is Falkirk. Sorry to you Irish lads, the Scots won the naming lottery this time."

"Fookin' rigged lotto," MacLeod growled, thickening his usual accent and earning a round of teasing from the rest.

"Assuming we don't run into any Nazi interference, the trip should take about three days, maybe a little more with the extra weight of your fat arses. We could make it in less if we stayed topside, but I doubt any of you want to waltz up to the German shore with your fly down."

The men grumbled, but there was an undercurrent of laughter. Raines was good. He knew how to grab his squad's mood and pull or push where needed.

"That's it. Ferry leaves the dock in twenty. See you on the *Tuna*."

Chapter Forty-Two

Thomas

As a kid, one of my favorite adventures was going spelunking in the caves of Middle Tennessee. I clearly remember my uncle taking me to Cumberland Caverns, and the pair of us squeezing our way through one tight tunnel after the next. The utter blackness and confined space sent most people screaming, but I found an odd peace beneath the earth.

When the *Tuna* descended beneath the waves for the first time on our voyage, my idea of peace beneath the natural world changed. First of all, with the caves, I could leave at any time. Once the sub left Holy Loch, there was nowhere to go. We were trapped. The ship was our life. Once the floating tube sank beneath the surface, it morphed into an oxygen-filled life raft on which my every breath depended.

I didn't mind the dimly lit corridors or bunks crammed above mechanical devices or torpedo tubes. But the constant creaking and groaning of the hull under pressure of the ocean's grip was a constant reminder of the unparalleled forces at play around us. It was surreal and eerie, like being inside a living creature whose stomach never settled. The occasional crackling of a radio might've been comforting if I'd been able to hear the words, but the distant garble of unintelligible speech only added to the otherworldly atmosphere.

Looking out the few circular windows scattered about the ship didn't help either. Glimpses of murky water and occasional shadows I knew to be various sea life filled my mind with fears of the unknown.

Charlie seemed undaunted, spending most of his time around a table playing cards with Smyth and the two Irishmen, MacLeod and O'Connor. Will kept to himself, reading a small book Sparrow had found before we left, something about a boy who found a ship in a bottle that took him on a magical adventure. He tried explaining it to me, but I lost interest the moment he mentioned magic.

Most of the Marines took the whole thing in stride, but a few failed to hide their own fears of the deep. I was surprised to find Roth among that number. The hardened veteran, who couldn't have been older than twenty-five, had never shown fear of anything. Even in the midst of torrential rains and billowing seas, the man had joked and teased.

But not now. We were at Poseidon's mercy, and Roth knew it.

"I've never liked subs. Fuckin' tin cans. There's too much that can go wrong," he muttered as I flopped down on the bunk next to his above the engine room. It was the noisiest place on the ship, but the sounds of machinery turning offered their own comfort as we sailed through nature's strange land. "I keep waiting for the next sound to be a whale biting us in half or a shark slapping us with its tail."

I chuckled. "I don't think sharks do that, Roth. They're more into teeth than ass."

"Fair point," he grunted. "Still, the whales are a thing. We'd be a tasty snack."

"Oh, I'm sure. Nothing says 'fish food' like a solid metal tube filled with torpedoes and oil."

He sat up, grabbed his pillow, and smacked me with it. "I liked you better when you were just trying to fit in."

I laughed. "Who says I'm not still trying?"

He pressed his pillow into the hull and propped himself against it. "You fit in just fine. Hell, you'd probably make a good Marine if you had the good sense to be British."

"Thanks, I think. You know, we were British until we kicked your asses."

"You're still British. We never fully accepted that little independence thing you tried. All you need to do is bend the knee and I'm sure the King would welcome you back." He grinned. "Oh, and I think you owe us a few crates of tea too."

I shook my head. "Fair enough. I'll brew some as soon as we get back."

A long peel sounded throughout the ship as the pressure shifted. Roth stared into the pipes that ran along the opposite side.

"Where's home, Roth?"

"Oh, home. Right. Birmingham, born and raised."

"Birmingham, that's in the center of England?" I asked.

"Sort of, but you're not too far off."

"You have family back home?"

He hesitated, then nodded. "My mum and baby brother. He's nineteen now, but still a baby to me. He just signed up. I don't know where they're sending him yet."

The damned war. It took everyone.

"I'm sorry, man. That's got to be hard, especially for your mother."

His head dropped. "She's a mess. Both her boys in uniform. We already lost my dad."

"Shit."

"Yeah."

We sat in silence for so long I thought we might just call it a night and get some sleep, but Roth finally spoke again. "What about you? You got family? A girl back home?"

And there was the question. Time to duck again.

"No girl. My folks are back in the States, near Boston. My ... uncle ... is the closest family to me. He's too old to fight, so

I know he's okay." I couldn't exactly tell him James was our driver, a servant to our family for decades. That begged far too many questions. Uncle seemed to fit.

"That's good. Keep 'em safe."

"Yeah."

I liked Adam Roth. He was a good man; solid, decent. Something in the moments where we shared our fear of the sea bound us together far more than the exercises and war games. In another time and place, he'd become a brother. I could feel it.

"You ready for this mission?" he asked.

"Don't really have a choice, do we?"

He grunted. "Not really, but that's not the same as being ready. I get the feeling you three have seen a thing or two before you got to Holy Loch."

"Yeah, we have."

He shifted to face me. "How long have you been a team?"

"I guess that depends on how you think about it. We went through a ton of training together before they formed us into a team. We ... deployed ... for the first time a few months ago."

I struggled with how to talk about being sent on a mission. The language we used in the OSS was entirely different from that of the traditional military. If I slipped ... I wasn't sure it would matter though. Roth was part of an elite special force within the British military. He likely understood keeping secrets better than any of us.

"It's okay to be scared," he said. "I'm scared. This is a hell of a mission."

I hadn't expected the tough Royal Marine to go down that path.

"Uh, yeah, I guess. I mean, it really is."

He huffed a chuckle. "Don't try to be tough. It's just us talking. Odds are most of us won't even make it to the target. Between the sea, patrols, and bad luck, there's just too much that can go wrong. Mac was right. They should let the Americans bomb the shit out of everything floating near Emden and be done with it."

"Maybe," I said. "But ... what if the one boat with the lab got away and the Germans had that weapon?"

"You think it's as bad as Raines said?"

And here we were, another decision on how much to say, how much to hide. Roth was right, most of us wouldn't make it back alive. He was risking his life to save thousands, tens of thousands, maybe more. He deserved to know why he might die. I would want to know.

"It's worse."

He stared at me for a long moment. "That's why you're here. You know what this is, don't you?"

I nodded slowly.

"Who are you guys?" he asked, a question every military man was trained never to ask, but I couldn't fault him for it, especially given ... everything.

"I'm a US naval officer assigned to the Office of Naval Intelligence," I said, sticking to my script.

He eyed me. "I can see that. The others aren't navy though. Charlie nearly threw up in his cockle the first day."

I chuckled at the thought of Egret, our rough giant, getting seasick every time he boarded a boat.

"Yeah, he's a real sweetheart with a tender stomach.

"Roth grinned. "A *green* sweetheart. You sure he's from this planet?"

"I've wondered that a few times over the last few months." I returned his smile, thinking back over our adventures across Europe.

"I'm gonna get some sleep. Good talking, mate."

"Same here."

Chapter Forty-Three

Will

T he officers' wardroom was a cramped space with a shiny silver table surrounded by benches bolted to the floor to seat eight. Framed photos of past crews stared down from where they'd been screwed to the walls. The twelve of us packed around the table, practically sitting in each other's laps. Royal Marines weren't known for being dainty, making the space feel even smaller than it actually was. The constant sound of our wetsuits grinding together sent rounds of, "Don't get fresh with me," "Why are you so happy to see me," and every other kind of juvenile reference to farts or men being on top of each other about the room faster than any ship could sail.

"Glad to see you men took team bonding seriously, though I'm starting to get worried. Should I just leave you alone a while?" Raines teased as he appeared in the doorway.

The men responded immediately, filling the space with cat-calls and shouts of protest

Someone yelled out, "Mac is mine. Have you seen that arse?" sending the cacophony to a new level.

"Quiet down," Raines said, in a strange combination of shout and whisper. "We're on a submarine, remember? Sound carries. The Allies did their best to get the Germans out of this area, either through bombing or luring them out into open water, but I'd still rather not risk it. From here on out, nothing above a whisper. Got it?"

A low murmur of assent offered their compliance.

"We'll be in position in about an hour. You deploy the moment we get there, then the sub is going to leg it back home."

Shock ran through the room. We thought we were escaping back to the sub.

Raines repeated the mission brief, then added a few new twists. "Your target is the *Gnade*."

Will's head snapped toward mine. He mouthed, "Grace?"

"For those of you who don't speak German, that means 'grace.' Hitler put his lab on a German Red Cross ship. You need to forget how this looks and execute your mission. There are no doctors or nurses on that boat, no wounded soldiers or injured civilians. The only thing aboard is a deadly compound that could wipe out whole cities."

The thought of destroying a mercy ship sent waves of nausea through my system. How could we be sure this was the right ship? What if our intel was wrong and we destroyed a floating hospital? From the looks on the faces wedged about the table, the others were having the same thoughts.

"It's nearly four in the morning. The sun will begin to rise in less than two hours, which means you will need to land on the western shore and hide until sunset, then resume your mission."

That caused another stir within the team, but still no one spoke.

"Once you have visual confirmation of a successful kill, you will cross the bay to the waypoint three miles north of Delfzijl. There's nothing for miles around but farmland. Make your way inland to the town of Bierum. It's less than a mile from your landing zone. The church is the tallest building in town. Go there and the priest will get you home."

The only sounds in the wardroom were the groans of the ship's hull and the breathing of a dozen shellshocked men.

"You will be crossing enemy-occupied territory wearing wet-suits. I don't have to remind you, but I'm going to anyway: do *not* let them see you."

Raines waited a moment to let his words sink in, then unfolded a page and read aloud: "To accommodate for this change in plans, each Mark-Two's equipment now includes eight limpet mines, three sets of paddles, a compass, a depth reel, a repair bag, a torch, a camo net, a watch, fishing line, two hand grenades, rations and water for six days, a spanner to activate your mines, and a magnet to hold your boat to the side of a target." He glanced up. "Oh, I almost forgot. Your rifles have been replaced by Colt .45s and a Fairbairn-Sykes."

The Fairbairn-Sykes fighting knife was an eleven-inch dagger with an acutely tapered, sharply pointed blade. It was the weapon of choice for the British commandos who needed stealth when making a kill.

"Questions?"

No one moved. It felt as if all of us held a collective breath.

"Men, what you do now will save more lives than you will ever know. You may very well save the war. That's not an over-statement, merely a fact. I am proud to serve with each one of you." Raines eyed each man, then checked his watch. "You have thirty-four minutes till deployment. See you topside."

Chapter Forty-Four

Will

Each pair stood in launch order beside our cockle: *Cachalot*, *Coalfish*, *Conger*, *Cuttlefish*, *Catfish*, and *Crayfish*. The plan was to launch each boat through the sub's hatch. Despite their hard bottom, the kayaks were semi-flexible, allowing us to navigate them along the sub's narrow passages and crawl spaces.

"*Cachalot*, go!" Raines commanded.

McLeod and O'Connor, already mounted into their boat, were shoved forward, as though launched through the torpedo hatch. Something caught, and the *Cachalot's* hull groaned, its fabric ripping and its bottom bending. The men managed to pull the damaged boat back into the sub before the ocean took her, but she was beyond repair. Our team leader and his partner were out of the mission before it began.

"*Coalfish*, go!" came the order once MacLeod cleared the tube.

Their cockle shot out without a hitch.

"*Conger*, go!"

Another successful launch.

Charlie's boat slid into place.

"*Cuttlefish*, go!"

They hit the surface and began paddling.

Ward and I were next. The crew shoved us forward, and my heart lurched into my throat. The angry sea slammed against the *Tuna*'s hull, as though Poseidon was angered by our presence.

"*Catfish*, go!"

We shot forward, and my only thought was to paddle with everything I had. The sea tossed our boat like a child's plaything, as wind whipped against my face. Sheets of rain pelted us, harder and far colder than we'd experienced back in England. The loch's rain was a warm embrace compared to the bitter bite of this storm.

I glanced back in time to see Thomas, aboard *Crayfish*, shoot from the *Tuna*'s maw. Seeing him stab his oar into the water, gaining distance from the sub, offered a moment filled with both relief and trepidation, but there was no time for thinking. The ocean's froth made it clear there was only one thought this night: survival.

We'd only paddled an hour when Ward's oar tapped into my back. I turned and followed where he pointed. Davies and Mitchell, aboard *Conger*, were turning back. Something had gone wrong.

In the darkness and confusion of the storm, that could mean only one thing: one of the other boats was in trouble.

Before I could consider our options, Ward gave a signal, swirling his hand in the air. He meant to turn back, to help with whatever emergency lay behind us. There was no yelling above the thunder, even if secrecy were not sacred. All I could do was signal a thumbs-up and follow my leader.

It only took ten minutes to reunite with *Conger*.

The sea had consumed *Coalfish*, but Smyth and Thompson had somehow managed to stay afloat long enough for the other boat to reach them. When we arrived, they clung to either side of *Conger*.

The kayak couldn't advance with two men clinging like that, so Ward signaled, and we pulled as close as the waves allowed, then Smyth let go and swam toward us. Waves crashed over him, sinking him below the surface.

His head popped up, then vanished again. Still, he swam.

When his hand gripped the rim of our kayak, the men of *Conger* signaled again, and we began paddling toward the western shore.

———◆◇◆———

We left our kayaks intact. The bulk of our gear inside made it impossible to collapse them without offloading the bulky packs, only to have to hide them as well. Hiding places were as scarce as trees, but we managed to find a decent row of brush in which to shelter, and the fields that lay beyond were dark. I couldn't see any buildings or lights. We pulled our cockles onto shore and hid them as best we could among rocky outcrops, then covered ourselves with camouflage netting.

The sun was already beginning to crest the horizon, and I doubted our flimsy cover would do much to protect us from roaming eyes who knew what to look for, but it would have to do.

The sun crossed the sky so slowly, I thought night might never come. Laying there on the hard ground beneath the netting, thoughts raging through my head louder than the storm the night before, sleep refused to come. By the blank stares on the men beside me, I knew they were wrestling their own frightening boredom.

All I could think about was Thomas. The last I'd seen, he and his partner were safely paddling toward our intended landing zone. They'd set out after us, but they hadn't followed when we turned back. Either they hadn't seen us returning for the capsized crew, or they'd run into troubles of their own. We were now separated, and the void of information left a gap large enough for speculation to fill the entire day.

I knew better, knew I shouldn't obsess over what *might* have happened. That energy was better spent planning our next steps. They were likely fine, sleeping on the shore a few miles further south, but not knowing gnawed at my gut every moment throughout the day.

When darkness finally descended, we put away the netting and gathered in a seated formation, sheltered on the sea side by a boulder and on the land side by shrubs.

Davies, the senior Marine present, took charge. "Smyth, you and Thompson are out. Make your way to the church and get home." He turned toward Ward and me. "The rest of us continue on-mission. *Cuttlefish* and *Crayfish* are likely miles ahead, so we should get started."

We watched Smyth and Thompson make their way across a field, keeping low, occasionally peering over crops to get their bearings and check for patrols. The Germans occupied the Netherlands, and there was no telling which locals sympathized with their German neighbors. Their escape was nearly as dangerous as our continuing mission.

"Let's get on with this," Davies said when the others were out of view.

We pulled our cockles out of hiding, rechecked our gear, and pushed off.

Chapter Forty-Five

Thomas

We lost sight of the others almost immediately upon leaving the *Tuna*. The seas were far rougher than I'd expected, even more harsh than the storms I'd experienced when training aboard ships in my early years with the navy. It was a wonder Roth and I managed to catch up with *Cuttlefish* and follow them to the waypoint.

We spent the day huddled under netting, cold, wet, and thoroughly cut off from our team. I tried to keep my mind occupied, but with nothing to do but sit and sleep, it was hard to stop thinking about all the things that could've gone wrong with Will and the others.

By the time the sun fled the sky, my muscles were stiff and my throat was hoarse. Charlie looked worse than I felt. His skin was pale, with a lime hue that spoke as much to the storm's fury as anything I'd seen. From the way he braced himself as he stood, I guessed the ground still moved beneath him, a mocking imitation of the waves from which we'd escaped only hours before.

"Listen up," Roth whispered. "The water in the bay is a lot calmer than what we went through last night. Those clouds are a lot lighter, so we probably won't see more than a light rain. If I have my math right, we're only a few miles from target. It should be just across there." He pointed across the massive expanse of water that was the Dollard bay. "We waited a couple extra hours to give the others time to catch up. Hopefully we'll see them in the clearer night and be able to coordinate our approach.

"The Americans promised a few bombs, just to keep the Germans on their toes, but they're supposed to keep those inland, well clear of our target zone. Stay alert, stay quiet, and don't fucking die."

Daniel Foster, the only other Royal Marine in our group, nodded and bumped forearms with Roth, yet another secret handshake we had yet to understand.

I looked toward Charlie. The combination of determination and glassy dullness in his eyes told me everything: he would execute his mission, even if he was miserable.

Without another word, we grabbed the ends of our cockles and put to sea.

Chapter Forty-Six

Will

The bay was calm, thank everything holy.

Ward and I paddled at a brisk pace, careful to keep the dipping of our oars quiet. Davies and Mitchell, aboard *Conger*, did the same, keeping within sight as we drifted quickly into the bay. Within a couple of hours, we reached our final landmark, where the land on the Netherlands side formed a sharp finger that pointed almost directly at Emden. It was our sign to turn toward our objective.

By some grace of the gods, it was also where we spotted the others about two hundred yards from the fingertip.

"*Coalfish?*" Roth asked when we pulled within whispering distance.

Ward shook his head. "Capsized. Smyth and Thompson are okay but are off the board. They're headed to the safe house."

"Alright," Roth said. "New plan. We stay in these two teams. *Conger* and *Catfish* approach from the west along the shore. *Cuttlefish* and *Crayfish* will come around and approach from the southeast. We have no idea where the target is docked, so we hit them from both sides. Eyes peeled for patrols. Stick the mines and run."

Everyone nodded.

Roth added, "No more talk. Hand signals until we're back on land."

Everyone raised a thumbs-up, then I dipped my oar in the water and watched as Thomas vanished from view.

Chapter Forty-Seven

Will

The distant hum of bombers in the sky briefly halted our progress as Ward and I both looked up. The moon was obscured behind a thick wall of clouds, but silhouettes of planes drifted against their puffy canvas.

The wail of a siren wrestled with the screams of dropping bombs, and the darkness of night was shattered by one explosion after the next. When the first dozen struck, then paused, I thought the quiet of the night might return. Then another round slammed into buildings and ships, and any hope residents of Emden might've had for a peaceful evening evaporated.

The American bombers were relentless.

While the inner harbor took the brunt of the beating, the outer line of ships remained unscathed. A casual observer might have wondered at this, but the Germans were likely too busy putting out fires and taking shelter to wonder at any particular ship's good fortune.

Nine ships spread before us. Our paddling slowed as we drifted. Two large patrol boats bobbed at the far end of the line. Next came freighters, then one last patrol.

We swung in a wide arc toward the shore, then aimed ourselves north at the westernmost ship.

Still the bombs roared.

Ward's paddle tapped my back, so I turned. He signaled toward the first vessel, the patrol boat, then pointed toward where the limpet mines were stowed. I nodded and reached down to untie the weapon.

Slowly, we crept toward the ship.

Dim lights from the interior told of crew inside. The sounds of the bombs and siren's wail drowned out anything we might've heard from aboard.

Ward steered us alongside, and I let the magnet snap into place, securing our kayak. I then hefted the limpet over the water and attached it by its own magnet to the hull, before turning back and giving Ward a thumbs-up.

We detached and paddled slowly around the stern until the next ship appeared. The white and red emblem of the world's most famous aid organization was painted across its hull. A flag bearing the same symbol snapped in the breeze below a Nazi banner.

The name *Gnade* was painted in Gothic lettering as tall as any man. This was our target.

Davies and Mitchell appeared in *Conger*. Ward signaled for them to take the next ship in line as we drifted alongside the *Gnade*.

Snap. We were secured.

Snap. The mine set in place.

Still, no sounds came from the craft.

Then a beam of light speared into the water from the next ship, and shouts in German echoed off the water.

Conger flew by as Davies and Mitchell paddled furiously, their kayak cutting through the calm waters.

More shouts rang out. More beams appeared.

Then a brilliant spear of light brightened the harbor, and bullets tore through the air.

We ducked against the hull of *Gnade* and watched in horror as a few shots became dozens.

Davies and Mitchell, no longer concerned for cover, fired back.

A German cried out, and a loud splash told of his fate.

Then *Conger* began to sink, and I knew this night would not end well.

Chapter Forty-Eight

Thomas

We paddled toward Pogum's shore, then turned to face our quarry. Two patrols rested at the end of the line. Freighters lay beyond.

Egret and Foster pulled *Cuttlefish* alongside the second patrol, while Roth and I took the one on the end. I could hear men on the deck above us scrambling, and assumed they fled the bombs.

I couldn't have been more wrong.

The moment our mine was attached to the hull, light poured down from one of the ships onto a faraway kayak. From this distance, I couldn't tell whose it was, but I prayed it wasn't Will's.

Then shots fired.

I started to disconnect us, but the sound of barking Germans echoed from the ships above, and new beams of light shone down on Charlie and Foster.

A man screamed, "*Lassen Sie Ihre Waffen fallen!*"

Drop your weapons!

A smaller boat appeared with four Germans whose rifles were pointed at our men. They snatched them out of the kayak and threw them down, where others quickly bound their hands. The last of the Germans reached down and removed the limpet then tied a rope to the cockle. A heartbeat later, they were headed back toward the shore.

We waited two minutes, then five, then ten. Finally, Roth signaled for us to move.

I dipped my oar into the water once, then again.

Then a massive light blazed in my eyes and we froze.

Chapter Forty-Nine

Will

We waited until the last of the lights died.

There was no saving our men.

Conger was lost.

We had, however, secured our mines to our target, and it was time to head home. The bombers could handle the rest.

Ward signaled for me to break us free, and we paddled slowly away, careful to avoid any noise.

We'd made it twenty yards when a brilliant light shone near the far end of the line of ships, illuminating one lone kayak.

Roth and Thomas sat on stage beneath that spotlight. Their paddles were frozen above the water and they stared without seeing into the beam. Then their hands raised above their heads, as a motorboat filled with rifle-bearing Nazis neared.

"We have to go back," I hissed.

Ward shook his head.

"Ward! They're going to—"

"Shaw, stop. There's nothing we can do."

I wanted to scream out, to paddle within range, to dive into the water and swim to them. I wanted to do something, *anything*, to save them.

Thomas's head turned toward us. I couldn't see his eyes, but I knew his heart was begging me to flee, to save myself. In the moments before he was thrown onto the Nazi boat, his mind was fixed only on me. I could feel it, and my heart shattered in his wake.

Like *Conger*, they were lost.

Ward drove us forward into the bay. Away from the ships.

Away from Roth and *Crayfish*.

Away from Thomas.

My heart exploded with each bomb that dropped behind us, and tears flooded my eyes.

"Detonate!" Ward hissed.

I could barely hear him.

"Shaw, press the button, damn it!"

My head snapped up.

"Don't let this be for nothing. Blow the ship!"

I looked down at the trigger in my shaking hand. I'd forgotten it was there. The only thing my mind knew was that Thomas had been captured.

I could barely think.

I couldn't move.

"Shaw, do it. Now!" Ward shouted loud enough for the world to hear.

And I pressed the button.

Chapter Fifty

Epilogue

Will

It took us weeks to make it back to London through a network of priest-run refugee routes.

Operation Falkirk was hailed a success.

Gnade was destroyed, and our assets within the Nazi hierarchy confirmed the elimination of the sarin research facility and records. We'd even managed to kill the project's leader, an SS-Sturmbannführer Jÿrgen Vogt, who reportedly spent time in France around the same period we were there.

To those of us who were there, it was a hard victory to celebrate.

Smyth and Thompson, the men of *Coalfish*, never made it to Bierum. They were picked up by a local policeman and handed over to the Nazis. Their execution was witnessed by local townspeople as an example for those who might consider aiding enemies of the Reich.

The fate of our four captured brothers remained unknown. The Nazis refused to give prisoner information, and our local assets had yet to turn up any leads.

Christopher Ward and I were the only ones to escape unscathed.

———◆◇◆———

The Brits had returned us to the safe house in Bedfordshire, where Bruce tended our wounds and made us welcome.

Sparrow left Holy Loch to join us. She was my greatest comfort.

The days were long, but the nights ... they were eternal.

I strode the house and grounds in a daze beneath the summer sun, barely seeing the natural beauty of Britain's heartland. I felt blank, like someone had erased all memory of words on my page, and nothing remained but dark smears where meaning once held sway.

When dusk came, demons roared to life. I tried to sleep, to enjoy the warm embrace of nothingness that might ease my grieving heart, but dreams were fickle, uncaring things, showing only what truly haunted the mind's eye. I lost track of the number of times I watched Thomas's hands raise in surrender. Each time the ships lit the inky night with brilliant flame, my body shook, and tears swelled.

After the first few hours of fitful screams, Sparrow would leave the sanctum of her room to curl beside me, wrapping herself tightly about my body to slow my tremors. Her presence eased my pain but failed to quell the terrors flooding my mind.

We might've fled capture, but no one escaped that night, least of all me.

On our third day back, I stood on the porch of the simple farmhouse, staring out at the fields but looking at nothing. The sun shone brightly, and the light breeze would've been pleasant had I not lost all interest in such things.

A dust plume in the distance marked a car's entry onto our drive, and I watched as a black sedan drove slowly toward the house. The squeal of the screen door preceded Sparrow's hand on my shoulder.

"Who's that?" she asked.

"No idea."

We watched as the car grew larger, then slowed and finally stopped a few yards away. A tall man in a dark suit climbed out and stepped toward us.

"Are you the birds?" he asked without preamble.

"Who are you?" I asked.

He eyed me, then Sparrow.

"Jamison Hurt, Office of the Prime Minister."

He waited for us to return the introduction. We didn't.

"Very well." His lips pursed as he reached into his coat and retrieved a sealed envelope. "Should one of the birds fly by, give them this, would you? The PM instructed I deliver it personally."

His smirk as he whirled around and slammed the car door behind him said he knew exactly who we were and didn't appreciate our obfuscation.

Screw him and his British sensibility.

"What do you think it is? New orders?" Sparrow asked long after the car and its dust plume had faded.

The last thing I wanted was another mission. They could shoot me for all I cared. Nothing mattered anymore.

"Want me to open it?" she asked gently.

"No," I said, tearing open the seal and removing a lone sheet of paper.

Shaw,

We found them.

Lt. Cdr. Drake Raines

TO BE CONTINUED . . .

Please enjoy the first three chapters of the next book in this series,
Hallum, on the pages that follow.

Did you know, your reviews do a lot more than provide feed-back. They also help other readers find our work and are an incredibly important part of an indie author's business. If you loved *Falkirk*, please take a moment to leave a review filled with stars.

HALLUM: Chapter 1

Bauke

> *"How wonderful it is that nobody need wait a single moment before starting to improve the world."*

ANNE FRANK, *ANNE FRANK'S TALES FROM THE SECRET ANNEX*

I hated early mornings in the autumn when the sun didn't bother getting up before me.

My sister loved them. She was weird like that.

The third morning in October was no different from any other. I crawled out from the warmth of my covers, stretched, stopped by the bathroom to pee, then headed toward the kitchen. My stomach gurgled as I whiffed the bacon frying down the hall.

Is that Sarr? I wondered.

Our *moeder* and *vader* told us never to name the animals, but we couldn't help it, and Lianne was worse than I was. She saw most of them before their own mother did, all gooey and gross. She practically wrestled them out of Papa's arms. Some of them wouldn't open their eyes for a while, but others, like Sarr, would blink up and make me want to squeeze them on the spot.

I hoped breakfast wasn't Sarr.

Sometimes, in war, we had to do things we hated, like eating the animals we'd named rather than selling them in the market or giving them to the Nazi collectors. I knew we had to do our part. The Hitler Youth at school taught us that. Still, it felt worse seeing them go to men with rifles than to other farmers or *Meener* Vermeer. He was the town's butcher—whatever that meant. He was always nice.

"Good morning, my *schat*," Mama sang as I stepped into the kitchen. She knew I hated when she called me "sweetie," but she did it anyway. "Hungry?"

I nodded and climbed into the wicker chair I always sat in when we ate. Lianne was already halfway through her breakfast. One of her long braids drooped in front of her chest and wiggled every time she used her fork. I giggled as it nearly fell into her plate when she reached for her juice. She glanced up and stuck her tongue out, a grin tugging at the corners of her mouth.

A plate of two strips of bacon, a boiled egg, and toast with grape jam landed before me.

"Eat up. No school today. Papa needs your help," Mama said, before brushing my mop of fiery hair back and kissing my forehead. As soon as her hand left my head, the curls flopped back into place.

I couldn't decide whether to be more excited or frustrated. Papa needing help meant work. School meant work. The Hitler Youth made us work. It didn't matter where we were or what *we* wanted, we had to work.

I glanced at Lianne, hoping for some hint of the day to come. She shrugged and focused on her plate.

Barks rang out.

Mama peered out the window above the sink then laughed and shook her head. Our pack of *patrijshonds* were as loyal as dogs came, but they were more goofy than helpful around the farm. Half the time, Papa had to scold them for terrorizing our poor chickens.

Their floppy ears were funny.

"Hurry up and finish," Mama said. "Papa should be in the barn with the cows."

At least we didn't have to work the fields. That was the one good thing about autumn and winter. The plants were asleep and the ground was solid, so the only things left to tend were the animals. Most of ours were cows. Sometimes, it seemed like we had too many to count, but Papa always knew exactly how many there should be. He was smart like that.

We had a few sheep and a bunch of pigs too.

The pigs were my favorite.

I swallowed the last bite of bacon and downed my juice, then scooted the chair back and made for the door. Lianne reluctantly followed.

When we started before the sun, the days felt like they lasted forever.

<hr />

By the time the sun reached her peak, we'd milked all the cows, fed the pigs, and shooed the sheep so they could eat whatever grass was still alive in the field. Papa had scattered hay along one fence row in case they were still hungry after the grass was gone.

As we stomped back toward the house, surrounded by our ever-present ring of pups who likely thought they were herding us home, Papa held his hand up to shield his eyes.

"Nazis are coming for their week's allotment," he said, more to himself than to us. "Go on, you two, get to the house. Tell Mama to get ready for Lieutenant Huber."

Lianne's eyes glazed over and her cheeks flushed. "What?" She shoved my shoulder. "He's handsome."

Papa rolled his eyes. "Go, run home. I want you inside before they get here."

The kitchen door swung shut behind us just as the German car ground to a halt, kicking up dust from our gravel drive in every direction. The truck that followed created an even larger cloud.

More than an hour later, the squeal of the kitchen door announced Papa's arrival.

"Isa," he called out to Mama. "Isa, they are gone. Where are you?"

"Coming." Mama's footfalls echoed against the wood of our hallway a second before her voice did the same. "Bauke is working his sums, and Lianne is reading another of her romance novels. I swear that girl will turn into a pool of syrup before she grows up."

Papa's rich laughter filled our home with warmth.

The moment they started whispering, Lianne and I tossed our books and headed closer. We hated when the grown-ups tried to keep secrets.

"... three pigs, two sheep, and they're coming back for a dozen cows," Papa said.

The groan of one of the kitchen chairs told me Mama had sat at the table. "So many?"

"Ever since the strikes ..."

Their voices were drowned out by the dogs braying at who-knew-what outside.

"The strikes?" I whispered to Lianne.

She cupped her hand to her mouth to hamper the sound. "Remember? In the spring, when miners and other workers walked off the job to protest how the *reichskommissariat* was forcing everybody to work for the Nazis."

Ah. *Those* strikes. The spring ones weren't the first, but they were the biggest. The papers—at least, the ones we could still get—said a lot of people had stopped working. So many farms in one region were set on fire that the sky turned red.

Reichskommissariat Seyss-Inquart[1] had a lot of people shot after that.

Papa stopped letting us read the papers from then on. I never understood why reading a newspaper was dangerous, but that's what he said. Most of the big Dutch ones quit printing when the Germans came anyway.

We could listen to the radio some, but most of it was in German now. We studied German in school, but I still wasn't very good with it. For some reason, all the Dutch shows we used to listen to stopped airing a while back, too.

We waited in silence for a long time before the sounds of Mama banging pots and pans told us their conversation had ended then scurried from our hiding spot as Papa rounded the corner, headed toward the living room and the comfort of his favorite chair. Most afternoons, after a long day outside, he would clean up, grab the same book he'd pretended to read for years, and fall asleep with it in his lap, only to wake when Mama poked him with the business end of a spatula or wooden spoon. The sudden hack of his interrupted snoring was our cue to get ready for dinner.

---

1. Reichskommissariat Arthur Seyss-Inquart served briefly as the Deputy Governor General in occupied Poland and, following the fall of the Low Countries in 1940, he was appointed reichskommissar of the occupied Netherlands.

That night brought the smoky scent of sausage mixed with the tang of turnips, as Mama laid a steaming bowl of *stamppot*[2] on the center of the table. Since the Germans took over, a lot of people talked about how meat was rare, but I never noticed that. I guessed that was one of the lucky things about living on a farm. We had to contribute to the troops, but if the Nazis wanted milk, they couldn't take all our cows. I didn't know why they let us keep the others, but I was glad for it. *Stamppot* was one of my favorites and it wasn't nearly as good without the sausage.

Lianna helped Mama clear the table and clean up, while Papa and I headed into the living room. We'd barely sat before his lids were closed and his breathing became low and steady. I sat on the couch opposite him, scanning the coffee table for anything to occupy myself. The corner of a newspaper peeked out from below a disheveled pile of old magazines. I reached down and pried it free.

I was surprised to find Dutch, rather than German, on the page. The title read *Trouw*[3] in bold block lettering. A hand-drawn image of Queen Wilhemina watching a rising sun underscored the forbidden nature of the page in Nazi-controlled Holland.

DE KONINGIN SPRAK (The Queen Speaks)
Countrymen in the Netherlands ...

"Son, what are you doing?" Papa snatched the paper out of my hands before I could sound out anything following the

---

2. Stamppot is a comfort food of the Netherlands made with mashed potatoes, smokey sausages, and a variety of vegetables such as carrot, onion, turnip, and spinach.

3. *Trouw*, translated as "Faithful" or "Loyal" in English, was one of many underground papers printed and distributed in occupied Netherlands. *Trouw* began printing in 1943 and continues to this day.

Queen's greeting. He folded it neatly, rose from his chair, and shoved it into a drawer in his rolltop desk. What he did next surprised me more than his snatch-and-grab had: he locked the drawer and pocketed the key.

When he returned to his chair, rather than lay back and drift off, he leaned forward and gripped my gaze with his own. "Listen to me, Bauke. I want you to forget you saw that, alright? It never existed. We are loyal to the Reich, and hold no love for the Queen. You hear me?"

My brows knitted together as I struggled with whatever bigger picture was at play here. All I could see was the Queen gazing at the sun. I knew Mama and Papa *loved* the Queen. None of this made any sense.

"Okay, Papa. But—"

"No buts. You do as I say. The only paper you've seen in this house for years is *Deutsche Zeitung*, and you don't read German well enough to know what it says."

"At least that part is the truth," I muttered.

His calloused hand gripped my shoulder. "Bauke, stop. This is important."

"Sorry, Papa. I promise."

He stared a moment, then released me and sat back. Still, he didn't relax. I could tell by how his forehead wrinkled and his eyes moved that he was thinking hard.

"Papa," I asked.

He looked toward me and grunted.

"Why don't we like the Queen anymore? You used to say she was like our *moeder* or something."

He stared, and his brow did that thing again. "The *moeder* of our nation, that's right." He nodded slowly. When he finally spoke again, it sounded like he was struggling to form his words. "Son, when you are older, you will find a wife of your own and leave our house. You will turn from your *moeder* to create your own family."

He gulped a time or two and looked down at his hands as he spoke. "Our nation has left our *moeder*. Now, we are married to the Germans."

His lips twisted like he had eaten something bitter, but he didn't go on.

I thought a moment. "Does that make Hitler our *vader* now?"

Something crossed his eyes and his whole body tensed, as if everything about him had seized up at the question.

"No, son, no. We have *no* parents now."

We didn't talk anymore that night. Papa stared into the bookcase until Mama and Lianne joined us some time later.

"Can we go outside now?" Lianne broke the interminable silence that had cloaked our living room in a feeling I didn't like.

"If you wrap up first," Mama answered. "And don't leave the farm. No further than the fence, alright?"

"Yes, Mama," Lianne said, hopping up and turning toward me. "Come on."

That's all it took.

I darted off the couch, determined to move faster than any protest our parents might issue. They'd given my older sister permission, but hadn't agreed to let me out of their sight. Fortunately, neither of them even watched me leave the room.

Moments later, Lianne and I were bundled in layers of sweaters and heavy coats. Winter had come early this year and the wind coming off the water was frigid.

We didn't care. Anything was better than the boredom of being cooped up in our house.

"You think they'll come again tonight?" I asked, smiling at the puffs that billowed from my mouth after each word.

She nodded. "I think so. They've come every night for almost a month."

As if hearing us from thousands of feet above, the distant hum of American bombers sang through the skies. I spun around and squinted up, seeing nothing but darkness and clouds. A second later, the distant wail of the air raid sirens in Emden sounded[4]. The bay was huge, and we were on the farthest point opposite the port, but sound carried over the water, sometimes making it feel like we were in the middle of the bombing runs rather than a country away.

"Here they come!" I hissed.

"Come on," she called, shifting from a steady walk into a jog.

My pride wouldn't let a girl beat me in a race, so I kicked it up another notch and ran past her, nearly slamming nose-first into our picket fence. One of our cows, chewing lazily nearby, glanced up with mild interest.

The anti-aircraft guns fired first, then falling bombs screeched, followed by blasts that had us ducking like they were dropping on us. The night that had been black only moments ago was now lit with hues of scarlet and ginger. The city of Emden blazed even brighter.

"Two dozen," Lianne muttered as the bombs continued to fall. "Twenty-eight, twenty-nine ..."

"Why are you counting?"

She shushed me. "Thirty-one, thirty-two, thirty-three ..."

One of the bombers was hit and hurtled toward the ground, exploding into a million pieces somewhere on the other side of the town.

"Whoa! That was bigger than any of the bombs," I said.

Lianne was quiet a moment—still counting, I assumed—before she said, "They probably had bombs on board before they crashed."

She crossed herself and closed her eyes briefly.

I stared up at her. She didn't know anyone in those planes. She didn't even know anyone in Emden. Why would she pray over—

---

4. The historical timing of the Allied bombing of Emden was altered to fit this story.

"Come on, let's get closer," she said. I watched, wide-eyed, as she climbed over the fence and hopped down onto the other side. "You need help?"

"Mama said—"

She cocked her head. "You coming or not? We'll be able to see better closer to the shore."

I started to argue, but the bombers were making their turn. They would likely go past us, then fly a wide arc until they were pointed back at Emden. They usually did two or three runs before the night stilled.

Fueled by a desire to better see the bombing, and aided by the thrill of doing something rebellious, I gripped the fence and climbed. Lianne had to grab my shoulder and help me over the top, but soon enough, I'd joined her on the other side and we were running toward the bay.

The bombers had made their circle and were nearly overhead. I could feel them as much as hear them.

I looked up to watch them pass and that's when I tripped, and the cold, hard ground reached up and smacked me in the nose.

Pain shot through my face and into my spine. When I reached up and touched my nose, my fingers came away wet and slick.

"Li!" I shouted, fruitlessly trying to raise my voice above the bombers. "Li!"

I will not cry. I will not cry. I will not cry.

It took a few seconds for her to realize I was no longer behind her, but then her hands were on my shoulders, lifting me into the light of Emden's embers as she examined my face. "Are you alright? Looks like you got your nose pretty good."

I nodded and bit my cheek, determined to be a man about my tumble, just like Papa taught me.

"I tripped over something big," I said.

We knew these fields like our own, and there were no boulders or logs, like there were near the forests further south.

Lianne's gaze moved from my nose to the ground behind me. She stared; her eyes narrowed, then they popped wide and her hand flew to her mouth.

She rocked back and rose to her feet, like someone had shoved her upward. "That's ... there's a body over there."

I leapt up and darted behind her, as though my sister could shield me from any danger the world had to offer. Sure enough, the long form of a prone body lay on its side a few meters away, the owner's face turned so we couldn't see it. The light of the bombs only offered a silhouette of whoever might lay there.

"What should we do?" I asked.

Slowly, she took a step forward, then another.

"Li, what are you doing?"

"Shh." She held a finger to her lips as she took several more steps toward the body.

I thought my heart might beat out of my chest. Plumes of heat exploded from my mouth as frightened breaths escaped.

When Lianne kneeled and reached toward the figure, I nearly bolted and ran for the safety of our house, but curiosity froze me in place.

"It's a man," she said, her hand pressing to his cheek. She carefully turned his shoulders so he lay on his back, then looked him up and down, hovering a hand over his mouth and nose.

"He's alive. But he's *freezing*," she said. "And his leg is bleeding."

"Is he a Nazi?" I asked, because I couldn't imagine who else would dare bleed on one of our farms in the middle of the night.

"No, I don't think so," she said. "It doesn't matter. He needs help. Go back to the house and fetch Papa."

"Li, I can't leave you—"

"Bauke, go. Run!"

HALLUM: Chapter 2

Bauke

"The only thing we have to fear is fear itself—and possibly the bogeyman."

PAT PAULSON

Years of working a farm will make a man strong.

At least, that's what Papa says. Even so, the man we'd found was unconscious, soaking wet, and heavier than all of us combined could lift. Papa had to race back to fetch his tractor so we could move him.

The moment we stepped through the door, Mama was a blur. She had Papa lay the man on my bed, then shooed us out so they could strip him down and tend his wounds. She would emerge every so often, snatch up more towels or hot water, then disappear behind the closed door once more.

Lianne and I sat at the kitchen table, curiosity gnawing as we watched the commotion.

"Who do you think he is?" I whispered.

"How should I know?" she hissed.

I didn't think she was angry. She sounded more worried than anything.

"What was that rubber suit he was wearing?"

Her eyes darted from the door to me. "I think it was a diving suit, something to keep him warm in the water."

"That didn't work so well," I said. "His face was almost blue."

She turned and started to respond, but the bedroom door opened and our parents stepped out. It was still an hour before our usual bedtime, but they both looked exhausted. Papa joined us at the table, while Mama washed her hands.

"Lianne, what were you doing beyond the fence?" Papa asked in a calm, even tone.

Her eyes fell to the table. "I'm sorry, Papa. We just wanted a better view across the bay."

He leaned forward, eyeing each of us for an eternal moment. "It is dangerous these days. You know this. I expect better of you, Lianne, especially when you are with your brother."

He never addressed me or the fact I was beyond the fence too. I thought that was odd but let my good fortune be.

"Will that man be okay?" Lianne asked, breaking the uncomfortable silence that had settled over the kitchen. Mama sat beside me and took my hand in hers.

"I don't know," Papa said. "I think so, but his skin was colder than ... I've never felt anyone that cold. And his leg needs a doctor. There's metal in it that will need to come out."

"Did he wake up?" Lianne asked.

Papa shook his head. "No. He groaned as we moved him but he never woke."

"Who is he, Papa?" she persisted.

Our parents exchanged a glance, and Mama's lips tightened as she shook her head once.

Papa blew out a ragged breath, then leaned back in his chair. "I'm not sure, but I think we should keep his presence here a secret for now. Until we know more. Don't tell anyone, not even your friends, okay?"

Lianne cocked her head and scrunched her brow. "Why not?"

Papa sat forward again. "Lianne, listen to me. This is important. The Nazis don't like strangers. They like us helping strangers even less. We have no idea who this man is or what he might mean to them. Until we do, we can't risk catching their attention. Do you understand what I am saying?"

Lianne held his gaze a moment, then nodded. "Yes, Papa. I understand."

"Good. Bauke, you will sleep with us until the man is gone. I do not want you going in there without me."

"Yes, Papa," I said.

"Do you think he's dangerous?" Lianne asked, her eyes wide.

Papa started to speak, then stopped. Mama squeezed Lianne's hand and said, "We need to be careful, that's all, until we know more."

Lianne relaxed, slumping back in her chair. Mama always knew how to make us feel better.

"Now," Mama said, turning toward me, "you have had enough excitement for one evening. Go get ready for bed."

I wanted to stay up, to wait for the man to wake up or for the doctor to come, but sleep tugged at my mind the moment Mama mentioned it.

⚫

The next morning, Papa roused us before the sun again. My eyes fought to stay closed until I remembered the stranger in my bed.

"What are you going to do with that man, Papa?" I asked as we sat at the table and waited for Mama to finish readying breakfast.

His mouth was set in a thin line, almost exactly like Mama's had been the night before. "I need you and Lianne to start the chores. I'm going to get some help for our ... guest."

"Aw, can I come with you?" I asked.

Papa shook his head firmly. "Absolutely not. You two start with the cows. I will help you as soon as I can. Remember, not a word to anyone about the man or what you saw last night."

I wasn't sure what else we had seen beyond an icicle in a rubber suit, but I nodded like I understood.

Papa was out of his chair and opening the door when a clatter sounded from my bedroom. Everyone froze.

"Stay here," Papa said. "I will check on him."

As he stepped from the kitchen, Mama reached out and touched his arm. They exchanged another of their looks, but he didn't stop walking. I watched as he turned the handle, opened the door, then closed it behind him.

Lianne started to rise, but Mama's glare locked her in place. "You two, eat," she said, dropping a plate of boiled eggs on the table. "Do not get up until I come back."

Without another word, she moved through the living room to stand outside my bedroom door, pressing her ear to the wood. A few minutes passed, then Papa called something and she vanished into the bedroom, leaving Lianne and me staring and unable to move.

That might've been the longest breakfast in the history of breakfasts.

When our parents finally emerged, their faces were unreadable.

Papa looked up, startled to see us still sitting at the table. "You two should go. Get started."

I could feel Lianne biting her lip. "Papa, what happened? Is he awake?"

Papa nodded. "He is in and out of consciousness."

"The poor man is in a lot of pain," Mama said. "He barely knew where he was."

"Did he tell you anything? Where he's from? Who he is?" Lianne asked, plucking the questions from my mind.

Mama gripped the back of one of the chairs. "He only said a few words. I am not even sure he knew what he was saying. I think he was himself for a moment ... before the pain took over. Barely long enough to give us his name. He called himself Wilhelm."

HALLUM: Chapter 3

Thomas

*"Touched bottom again. Decided to liberate myself
... We are never trapped unless we choose to be."*

ANAÏS NIN, *THE DIARY OF ANAÏS NIN*

E verything hurt.

I tried to blink the bleariness from my eyes, but even that sent jolts of pain through my lids and into my head. My hip pulsed, as though someone had jabbed an ice pick into it and was wiggling it around in circles. A part of me wanted to cry out, but my throat was raw, and I had no idea where I was.

The mattress beneath me was soft, and the muted pastels of the walls offered some comfort, but I couldn't figure out why there were tiny cars on a shelf just beyond my feet.

The doorknob rattled and someone stepped in. I tried to turn, but moving my head felt like a herculean task. A moment later, the unresolved shape of a man loomed overhead. All I could think as I flinched beneath his gaze was *please don't beat me.*

Why would I think that? Where had I been?

"*Kun je me horen*?" he asked, sounding distant, like he was calling from a faraway room. The words bounced around my head, unfamiliar yet almost recognizable. The knitting of my brows as I concentrated sent another stab through my aching temples.

"*Begrijpt u mij*?"

I blinked a few times, allowing the man's face to sharpen in my vision.

"*Deutsch*?" he asked, finally in a language I understood.

My mouth opened, but only a guttural croak escaped. "*Ja, Deutsch.*"

"Here, drink some water. You must be parched," the man said, switching fully into German. His accent was ... strange, like he was singing his German rather than speaking it. I couldn't place ...

He held a glass to my lips. It smelled clean, and I was in no position to argue, so I took a tentative sip. Relief washed down my throat, and I craned my head upward to gulp more of the liquid.

"Easy, a little at a time or you'll choke," the man said, his voice firm but not unkind.

I slowed to sips, then let my head fall back onto the pillow. The effort to lean forward had sapped the last of my strength.

The man set the glass on a side table, then sat beside me on the bed.

"What is your name?"

My mind spun. What was my name? I couldn't remember. I could barely think. The name Will popped into my head, but something in me knew that wasn't right. Maybe I knew a Will.

Did I have a brother? Flickers of a face flashed before me. I blinked them away.

An odd thought surfaced, more a memory than a thought: I was supposed to keep my name a secret. Maybe it was a good thing I couldn't remember it. Why was my name a secret? That seemed like an odd thing to hide.

Wilhelm. That was it. I mean, it wasn't my name, but it was what I was supposed to say. I didn't know why, but I was sure of that much.

"Wilhelm," I whispered, unwilling to test my voice further.

"I am Aart." The man blinked. "Where are you from, Wilhelm?"

"I ... I don't know. I can't ... remember."

A stab of pain nearly sent my stomach across the room and I moaned through gritted teeth. The man's hands pressed my shoulders down, holding me in place. The door opened and closed again, but I didn't dare open my eyes. Pain seared into me until ... everything went black.

Dreams replaced darkness, but they were even more jumbled than my waking thoughts, as if my subconscious couldn't order itself any better than the rest of me.

A blond-haired man in a white uniform with gold stripes on black epaulets ...

A young woman in a crimson gown ... no, a black gown with a crimson sash about her neck. Her hair trailed fire in curls down the back, and her smile ...

A guy with thick spectacles ...

A familiar face ... so familiar ... a man no more than twenty, perhaps a year or two older ... his features sharp, his body lithe, the set of his jaw and eyes serious ... his gaze into mine so warm and ... I knew him ... I know him ...

Screams ... so many screams ... water everywhere ...

I call out, "ADAM! Over here!"

I can't breathe ... explosions and heat sucking oxygen and darkness from the night ... the wail of rending metal ... the stench of charred flesh ... then bitter cold ...

Then nothing.

I woke again to find a different man bent over my hip. I would've bolted upright if Aart hadn't been holding my shoulders.

"Easy," Aart said. The other man barely looked up from whatever he was doing to my side. "He is a friend, here to patch you up."

I relaxed, and the pressure of his powerful hands eased.

"You have shards of metal in your hip that must be removed," the friend said, looking up from his work. "We do not have painkillers, so this will hurt ... very much."

I peered down to find several metal trays and a couple of buckets. The second man wielded silver instruments that reminded me of a dentist's office. I closed my eyes and blew out a breath. "Do what you need to."

Aart held a glass to my lips. Water. I sipped greedily.

Then he held a second glass forward. The scent bit into my senses and I reeled back.

Aart grimaced. "It tastes terrible, but it will help with the pain."

He held the vile stuff to my lips, and I immediately recognized whiskey as it warmed my throat and chest.

"Put this in your mouth and keep it there," the would-be dentist said, handing a thick strip of leather to Aart, who held it to my mouth. "I hope you do not need it, but it is better to be sure."

The moment the leather was in place, a volcanic eruption of pain burst from my side, raging over the whole of my body. I cried out through the leather, more moan than scream, and Aart added pressure to his grip.

Clink. Metal landed in a bucket.

Clink.

Clink.

Seven more times.

Seven more eruptions.

By the last, there were no more cries. I'd lost consciousness again.

Cast of Characters

C ## ast of Characters

Adal Köhler: German scientist

Adam P. Roth: RMBPD, Operation Falkirk, crewed the *Crayfish* with Thomas Jacobs

Anais: French host in Crécy-la-Chapelle

Andi: French Resistance fighter in Crécy-la-Chapelle

Arthur Doyle: Code name of British operative, also a guest in Scotland safe house

Arthur Wendel Ableman: Nickname Arty, code name Stork, Harvard student and best friend/roommate of Will, enlists and is recruited by Research & Analysis division of OSS

Baker Raymond: Navy mentor and best friend of Thomas

Baroness Isabella von Hohenberg: Prominent Swiss socialite and Red Cross patron

Bisch: The Baroness's butler at her Geneva home

Bruce: Caretaker at safe house in Bedfordshire, England

Charlie Booher: Code name Egret, OSS demolitions specialist, alias Heinz Wagner

Christopher Ward: RMBPD, Operation Falkirk, crewed the *Catfish* with Will Shaw

Claude Petit: Owner of Boulangerie Petit in Crécy-la-Chapelle, French Resistance

Commander Jeffers (US Navy): Military instructor of OSS trainee class at Harvard

Daniel Foster: RMBPD, Operation Falkirk, crewed the *Cuttlefish* with Charlie Booher

David Smyth: RMBPD, Operation Falkirk, crewed the *Coalfish*

Dieter Becker: Owner of Becker Chemical Company

Dr. Alexander Emile: Psychiatrist and member of Red Cross delegation

Elizabeth Clermont: Arty's fiancée

Father Lehmann: German priest at Ridermark Cathedral in Berlin

Felix Bauer: German scientist

George Creuset: French Resistance leader in Paris

George Eliot: Code name of OES host in Scotland

Hugo Bernard: French scientist

James MacLeod: RMBPD, Operation Falkirk, crewed the *Cachalot*

Janet Lynn Woodson: Nickname Janie, Radcliffe student and close friend of Will and Arty

John Milton: Code name of OES senior operative in Scotland

John Mitchell: RMBPD, Operation Falkirk, crewed the *Conger*

Liam Thompson: RMBPD, Operation Falkirk, crewed the *Coalfish*

Lieutenant Willard (US Navy): Military instructor of OSS trainee class at Harvard

Lieutenant-Commander Drake Raines: Commander of the *Tuna* (N94), Royal Navy submarine

Manakin: Poses as Major, OSS recruitment officer

Manfred Lang: German scientist

Marta: Seventeen-year old survivor of accidental poisoning on farm outside Berlin

Richard Davies: RMBPD, Operation Falkirk, crewed the *Conger*

Sarah Proctor: Code name Sparrow, OSS radio/communications specialist, alias Anny Bedeau

Sean O'Connor: RMBPD, Operation Falkirk, crewed the *Cachalot*

Sergeant Allen: Close quarter combat instructor at Camp X

Sergeant Major Stafford (US Army): Military instructor of OSS trainee class at Harvard

SS-Oberführer Bernard Fuchs (Nazi SS): Senior colonel at SS Headquarters in Berlin

SS-Sturmbannführer Jÿrgen Vogt (Nazi SS): SS officer

SS-Unteroffizier Uwe König (Nazi SS): Vogt's enlisted driver

Steven: Red Cross delegation attaché

Thomas Jacobs: Full name Thomas Arthur Jacobs du Pont, code name Condor, alias Wilhelm Müller

Victor von Steinbach: President of the Swiss Red Cross

Warrant Officer Landry: Enlisted chief at Holy Loch Royal Naval Base

William John Shaw: Nickname Will, code name Emu, alias Tobias Richter.

Reference (Warning: Contains Spoilers)

Operation Frankton, Beyond Heroism

There was no Operation Falkirk as described in this book.

I liberated the name in a very scientific manner: I stared at a map of the United Kingdom, Ireland, and Scotland until something spoke to me.

SARIN gas was indeed developed by the scientists who sought a solution to the weevil infestation that dogged many farms in and around Germany in the 1940s. Hitler refused to use the gas out of fears for the safety of his own troops. While his top generals argued for its use in England, he vetoed their plans because his scientists could not guarantee how quickly the substance would degrade, making a landing of troops impossible to plan.

There was no floating laboratory. I made that up to fit the final leg of the mission.

While I also made up the name of this mission, many of the elements were present in an actual operation carried out by the incredible men of the Royal Marines Boom Patrol Detachment. These events and actions are well documented and have even been featured in a Hollywood film. A monument to these brave souls was recently erected in their honor.

Operation Frankton was a commando raid on ships in the German-occupied French port of Bordeaux in southwest France. The raid was carried out by a small unit of Royal Marines known as the Royal Marines Boom Patrol Detachment (RMBPD), part of Combined Operations inserted by *HMS Tuna* captained by Lieutenant-Commander Dick Raikes. (The RMBPD would later form the Special Boat Service.)

The plan was for six folding kayaks to be taken to the area of the Gironde estuary by submarine. Twelve men would then paddle by night to Bordeaux. On arrival they would attack the docked cargo ships with limpet mines and then escape overland to Spain. Men from no.1 section were selected for the raid, including the commanding officer, Herbert 'Blondie' Hasler, and with reserve Marine Colley, the team numbered thirteen. One kayak was damaged while being deployed from the submarine, and it and its crew therefore could not take part in the mission. Only two of the ten men who launched from the submarine survived the raid: Hasler, and his number two in the kayak, Bill Sparks. Of the other eight, six were executed by the Germans and two died from hypothermia.

———————◆○◆————————

Theresienstadt concentration camp

The Theresienstadt concentration camp was real. The Red Cross mission to validate the quality of the "housing" for Jewish internment was real. This book places the timeline in 1943; however, the actual Red Cross missions occurred in 1944 and 1945.

The German Red Cross visited the ghetto in 1943 and filed the only accurate report on the ghetto, describing overcrowding and undernourishment.

In 1944, the ghetto was "beautified" in preparation for a delegation from the International Committee of the Red Cross (ICRC) and the Danish government. The delegation visited on June 23; ICRC delegate Maurice Rossel wrote a favorable report on the ghetto and claimed that no one was deported from Theresienstadt.

In April 1945, another ICRC delegation was allowed to visit; despite the contemporaneous liberation of other concentration camps, the ICRC continued to repeat Rossel's erroneous findings.

Also by Casey Morales

About your Author

Casey Morales is an LGBT storyteller and the author of multiple bestselling MM romance novels. Born in the Southern United States, Casey is an avid tennis player, aspiring chef, dog lover, and ravenous consumer of gummy bears.

Milton Keynes UK
Ingram Content Group UK Ltd.
UKHW020724211124
3009UKWH00032B/80

9 781960 165121